Clump, A Changeling's

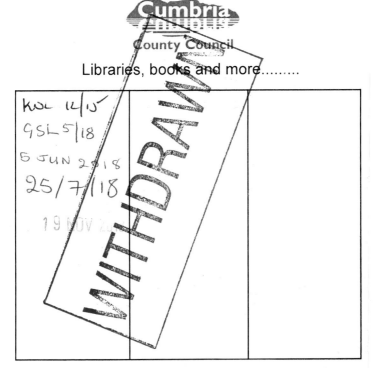

Cumbria
County Council

Libraries, books and more.........

KWL 12/1ᔆ
GSL 5/18
5 JUN 2018
25/7/18
19 NOV 20

WITHDRAWN

Please return/renew this item by the last date due.
Library items may also be renewed by phone on
030 33 33 1234 (24 hours) or via our website

www.cumbria.gov.uk/libraries

Cumbria Libraries
CLIC
Interactive Catalogue

Ask for a CLIC password

ALSO BY LYNETTE E. CRESWELL

The Magic Trilogy
Sinners of Magic
Betrayers of Magic
Defenders of Magic

Romance
The Witching Hour (Short Story)

For Sophie, Charlie, Rosie and Tyler, because grandchildren are our reward for having endured the perils of parenthood.

Published in 2015 by Feedaread.com Publishing – Arts Council funded

A CIP catalogue record for this title is available from the British Library.

Acknowledgements

Having written four novels, I'm finding writing the acknowledgements the most difficult part of the entire process. As you can imagine there is the chance that I may forget to mention someone important to me, so fingers crossed I don't!

It's been a marvellous year in general having hit the Amazon bestsellers list (twice) with *The Witching Hour* and *Sinners of Magic*, both reaching the number four slot. It's the most incredible feeling watching your books rise up the charts and I'm very proud to say I have my loyal readers to thank for such an honour.

Thank you also to my CEO, Wayne Miller, of Affilipede for working tirelessly on the web, creating wonderful links to my books, tantalising images and a following that has already reached over 90,000.

To my dear friend David Lane, for his constant support and great ideas. To Joy Wood, for her enthusiasm, loyalty and amazing friendship. To Sherry Foley for teaching me how to cull my gerunds. To all my family for their constant support even when it takes me away from them. To Luke Bailey for creating such a wonderful cover and to Sue Christelow who always brings my story to life.

Dear readers, for those of you who have read The Magic Trilogy you will find that this new story has some parts of *Betrayers of Magic* weaving through it. Although you may recognise some of this, the whole story is from Clump's perspective and therefore you will learn more about what happens with Crystal from his point of view. You do not have to have read *Betrayers of Magic* to enjoy this book but I hope you will be tempted to do so afterwards.

The Windigos live by day as a tribe; they have a village and reside in caves. By night, they transmute into timber wolves and hunt as a pack.

"Have pity on them all, for it is we who are the real monsters."

Dr Bernard Heuvelmans

From the Book: On the Track of Unknown Animals

Chapter 1

It was his eyes, round and frightened, that made Isis want to turn and run. They looked as wild as the forbidden mountains and she couldn't help notice how his lower lip trembled as she approached. Her fingers dipped into a silver bowl. Lifting a cloth, she squeezed out the water and gently wiped away the beads of sweat from his cold, damp forehead. She had no words of comfort to give him. All her attempts had caught in her throat and her eyes strayed to the mangled hand which hung like an unwelcome guest at his side. Drops of blood dripped towards the floor and she licked her lips, her stomach griping from being so empty. None of her kind had eaten anything other than bone bread for two whole days and the scent of his blood, mixed with the smell of raw flesh, made her hunger unbearable.

She glanced at the makeshift bandage covering his hand, unable to draw her eyes away from the dark, crimson stain. Isis shuddered, pushing the urge to gnaw at what was left of the damaged limb to the back of her mind. He was one of her own, a Windigo, therefore she felt ashamed, thinking such despicable thoughts, unable to stop herself. She noticed how the young male shivered, so she pulled an old woven blanket over his body, thankful for the distraction.

His name was Horith and he was one of the younger members of the tribe. Isis made him comfortable, doing her best to keep her gaze averted from the blood-soaked hand. Time ticked slowly by whilst she waited for their leader to arrive. Without doubt Manadeth would know what to do.

Isis gave a deep sigh. Manadeth was the chief and also the mother of her lifelong partner, Serpen. Isis cared for Manadeth deeply. She was not only wise but she was powerful and strong. Isis closed her eyes and allowed her mind to drift to a time long before she was born. For thousands of years her kind had been feared by those who called them monsters. Her ancestors once prowled the realms, taking whatever they wanted from the living, which was usually their lives. The tribes soon flourished until a time when they separated into new colonies, threatening each and every kingdom in the land.

The elves were the first to wager a war against them; wielding swords of magic, they culled her species to near extinction. Those that survived fled into the mountains and remained hidden for many, many centuries, living like scavengers off small animals and birds, barely able to keep themselves alive. Their insatiable hunger made them scream with despair and in time they became known as the demons of the mountains.

A sharp clatter brought her back to reality and she opened her eyes, surprised to see Manadeth staring at her. Her leader was well over seven feet tall with a body that was covered in fur from the tip of her head right down to the soles of her feet. Although there was nothing remotely human about Manadeth, she could, at times, be kind-hearted and compassionate to those whom she cared about.

The chief pointed a thick, hairy finger towards the fire that blazed in the centre of the cave.

"Bring me the axe," Manadeth urged, rushing over to Horith to inspect what was left of his injured hand. Isis understood, for it was plain to see that if he was left much longer he would most likely bleed to death. She turned towards the flames which danced before her eyes to see a long, smooth piece of iron protruding from the centre. She wavered momentarily before grabbing hold of a piece of thick cloth to wrap around the handle. A tongue of flame shot out from between the peats when she lifted the axe, the head glowing red like a dragon's eye as it was pulled from the amber flame.

Isis's mouth turned dry. With slow, meticulous steps she made her way to the chief's side and very carefully handed her the axe.

"Give Horith the ethereal vapours," her Elder commanded, taking the weapon from her grasp and Isis nodded once again, hurrying to Horith's side.

She looked down at the young Windigo, a wave of despair washing over her. This was Torolf's son, an advisor who had already lost his female mate just two winters past. It had been a terrible day such as this when a swarm of Red Dragons came down from the heavens and almost eradicated their entire village in one fell swoop. Now he was about to find that his son was to suffer a different kind of loss in his short lifetime.

Isis heard Manadeth take a deep breath and she instinctively covered Horith's nose and mouth with a cloth which had been soaked with a liquid that turned into vapour when inhaled. Horith didn't struggle, he simply whimpered, staring into her eyes until the light in them dimmed and he became semi-conscious.

Isis glanced up to watch her leader drag a tall, wooden block used for chopping meat to Horith's side. With an unexpected tenderness she placed the damaged limb carefully onto the curve of the block. Mesmerised, Isis was transfixed as the chief raised the axe high into the air.

In the small, sparsely lit room, Manadeth looked magnificent. Her strong limbs wielded the axe above her head and without hesitation brought the weapon down with a swoosh, slicing though skin and bone with one clean swipe. Isis heard the thud as the axe severed the hand just above the wrist and then the silence was shattered by a piercing scream. Horith jerked upwards, lifting the stump of his arm high into the air, screaming even louder when he realised his hand was no longer there. Manadeth dropped the axe to the floor with an almighty clatter. Her strong arms reached out to slam the young Windigo down onto the makeshift bed.

"Give him more vapours!" she shouted, "we need him calm so I can close up the wound."

Isis obeyed, soaking the rag to drag it over Horith's nose and mouth once again, only this time she held it there for considerably longer. His thrashing limbs finally slowed and when he lay still, Manadeth let go of his quivering body. Isis caught sight of the amputated hand which lay in a dish on the floor. She watched Manadeth bend down and pick up the bowl, prodding the limb with her finger before unwrapping the blood-soaked bandage from it. She threw the cloth onto the fire, the flames hissed and the smell of blood filled the room with a metallic aroma.

"You don't need to stay for I can deal with Horith from here on," she said, wiping her hands clean on a corner of the blanket. "Here, take this tasty morsel home and make good use of it. There's enough to make a stew or at least a good nourishing soup for Serpen."

Before Isis could protest, Manadeth pushed the bowl into her hands. "I know what you're thinking, but this limb is of no use to

9

Horith any longer. It would be a shame to waste it, so let's not."
Isis felt a lump grow in her throat but she didn't argue, instead she
accepted the bowl and gave a weak smile. The chief turned away,
and Isis watched her take hold of a bone needle and thread.

Her gaze swept back towards the severed hand and a wave of
despair washed over her. Although she was hungry, she felt it was
wrong to eat any part of Horith. However, she knew Serpen would
not see it that way. His temper was renowned throughout the
village and should he find out she had refused such a gift, his wrath
would no doubt become unbearable.

Isis dithered, but Manadeth was soon shooing her out the door
like an unwanted fly.

"Go home at once and make my son a hearty meal," she
ordered, pushing her outside.

As darkness fell, Isis fled. Breathing deeply, she cleansed the
lingering smell of blood and sinew from her nostrils whilst she
headed in the direction of home. The winding path which led to her
cave was lit by a rising moon. On her way she trod upon a few
desert flowers, the ground pale and dusty. Her thoughts were on
what she had just done and Manadeth's words rolled around inside
her head. It was true, food was extremely scarce yet the thought
that they were willing to eat their own kind out of desperation made
her feel that things were going too far.

The entrance to the cave was protected by animal hides and she
brushed them aside with one of her large hands. Like many of the
inhabitants of the mountains, the cave was sparse with the cooking
pot the main focal point. The battered cauldron hung over the dying
embers and Isis quickly made her way towards it. She stared down
at Horith's bloodied hand until her hunger became so intense that
she was unable to stop herself drawing the severed limb to her lips.
She licked the drying blood from each of the curled digits, the
sweet taste lingering inside her mouth. Her conscience pricked and
she recoiled, appalled at what she had just done, and so she dropped
the hand straight into the pot. It made a plopping sound as it hit the
surface and she bent over to stare down into the murky water,
watching the lump of flesh float to the top. Isis was frozen to the
spot. Transfixed, she couldn't move, fascinated by what she now
saw only as food, the meat turning from red to light brown until it

slowly peeled away from the bone. A delicious smell soon wafted from the pot, causing her stomach to rumble like thunder.

Isis felt a stir in the air and sensed Serpen was back from hunting. Like so many of her kind, his physique was powerful and strong. They were all seen by day as rather hairy creatures, sometimes the hair was so thick it looked like fur, making it difficult to differentiate between the males and females. Their bodies stood tall like humans, but their features were more like apes. They were indeed a strange concoction with their long ears and sharp teeth, each one of them born with great strength. When hunting, they would let out a terrifying scream so that their victims were paralysed with fear and therefore unable to run. There was no doubt, they were a formidable race yet surprisingly, to one another, they could be rather caring and considerate.

By night, the Windigo took the form of the giant timber wolf. This enabled them to eat small critters and keep hunger at bay when food was scarce until something far more appealing stumbled into their domain. Every living creature feared Windigos the most and no one ventured into the Red Canyon unless they were a fool.

Back in the village no one had eaten anything substantial for days and Serpen, like most, had returned once again empty-handed. When he entered the cave, his mood was dark and brooding. He threw his club against the wall and it fell to the floor with a dull thud. He did not try to retrieve it, instead he made a growling noise in the back of his throat and turned towards his mate, sniffing the air like a dog. The smell that filled his nostrils clearly grabbed his attention for he headed straight for the cooking pot. He almost managed a smile when he peered inside and spotted what appeared to be meat floating on the surface.

Without saying a word he grabbed a crudely shaped ladle which hung down from a spike and filled it to the brim with the hot, watery soup.

"Mmm, this tastes real good," he announced, nibbling at the flesh.

Isis was unable to look him in the eye.

"It's a gift from your mother."

"The chief?" he replied and flashed her a cold, hard smile.

Isis bit her lip, unable to meet his gaze.

11

"Yes, for I must tell you that Horith had a terrible accident today. He was chasing a hawk and wasn't looking where he was going and fell down a ravine."

"Within the Black Mountains?"

"No, the dark valley. He tried to stop himself by grabbing hold of a spindly root only his hand got snagged inside a crevice instead."

"Ouch," said Serpen, dipping the ladle back into the pot.

"Hmm, yes I know but thankfully he was not alone; some of his friends were with him when he fell. Between them they managed to free him and bring him home but his hand was all but severed."

"And they took him straight to my mother?"

"Yes, but there was no saving the limb, so Manadeth removed it."

"Alright, so let me guess. Not wishing to see fresh meat go to waste, she offered it to you for my supper?"

Isis nodded and Serpen dropped the ladle with a clang.

"I don't think we should tell Torolf what has happened to his son's hand," he declared, pursing his lips.

Isis nodded once again and knelt down to pick up the ladle, placing it back onto the spike. Serpen moved away from her and then she heard a familiar sound, a snarl. Isis spun around just in time to see a flash of black disappear between the animal skins. A howl, long and haunting, filled the night sky and before she could stop herself, she was kneeling on all fours. Her senses blurred and pain exploded inside her mind. She shook her head, trying to clear the kaleidoscope of inky colours which filtered behind her eyes. She went to rub her lids, but instead she saw her nails lengthening, becoming claws and she felt her heckles rise. Aware she was shifting, she simply lay back on the ground until the dull ache in her head eased and she was able to recognise the heightened senses brought on by turning into a wolf.

Within seconds the pain was gone. She waited until her mind cleared and then she licked her fur, cleaning herself. Her coat was as white as the snowy-capped mountains and her paws were tipped with spots of black. She bent her ears back and sniffed the air, the delicious aroma from the pot making her wet nose twitch. The steam from the pot attracted her attention and so she made her way over. She jumped up to glance inside, but the heat from the

12

cauldron scalded her paws. She whined in pain and then ran outside to join the rest of the tribe. The pack gathered, making themselves ready for hunting and Isis trotted, somewhat painfully to Serpen's side. When she reached him, she raised her head and bayed to a silvery moon.

*

There is an old custom of burning the dead instead of interring them in the Red Canyon. On a scorching summer's day, the dowager chief took her final breath after suffering an illness that could not be cured. Only Isis knew how long she had suffered but she never breathed a word to anyone, having been sworn to secrecy by her Elder. On her death, Manadeth left everything she owned to her only son. The funeral pyre glowed golden for two whole days but Serpen would seemingly not weep for his mother. Everyone was aware that he had been waiting for this moment for so long and that now his time had come, some worried he would rule with a fist of iron.

The villagers watched him with growing concern as Manadeth's body turned to ash. They believed her soul would be released to become part of the universe and all its glorious power. They consulted with the Gods, then made offerings to them of heavy gold and bright silver. The sky filled with thick black smoke and they danced the ghost dance, willing her spirit to break free and join the rest of her ancestors. When the flames died away, a mist like sparkling satin rose from the ashes and ascended into the sky. Tiny molecules of silver dispersed into the atmosphere and the tribespeople lifted their heads and wailed like banshees.

Isis was saddened by the fact that Manadeth would not be around to see her son's offspring come into the world. It had been something they had both wanted so badly yet in the end it had been a relief to watch her slip away. Isis returned to the cave and did not venture too far once the ceremony was all over. However, fed up of being alone, she wandered to the doorway and spotted Serpen talking with the Elders. She couldn't hear what they were saying but she guessed it would be about his role as chief. She saw how his strong shoulders were pushed back and when she accidentally caught his eye, she could see the glint was cold and hard. Isis

13

shuddered, bringing her hand protectively to her swollen belly and she gently stroked the dark hairs which covered her abdomen. Her confinement was due any day and she longed for the moment when she would hear the pitter-patter of tiny feet around the cave.

A sudden noise made her turn around and she saw a neighbouring Windigo draw near, carrying an old, battered wicker basket. It was always the custom for the closest to the bereaved to support the family as best they could until after three days of mourning. When he approached, Isis thanked Torolf for his kind offering before taking the basket from his huge, hairy hands. Out of the corner of her eye, she spotted Horith skulking in the shadows and felt a wave of guilt wash over her. Although he had made a full recovery, Horith was limited to what he could do and at night when he became a wolf he found running on three legs made him far slower than the rest of the pack. The wolves mocked him constantly, grabbing at his coat with their teeth and dragging him down into the dirt whilst they ran off to look for food without him. She caught his eye and judging by the cold glare he gave her, thought he must blame her for the loss of his hand and the respect of his peers.

Isis averted her eyes, not wishing to catch a glance at the stump which he waved around like a trophy, and so she stared at the contents of the basket instead. There wasn't much inside but she smiled broadly to show her thanks and appreciation.

"We are both grateful for your generosity," she mumbled, wishing only to get back inside.

Torolf shook his head.

"I know it isn't much, but it will keep your hunger at bay for a few days at least," he replied, looking a little crestfallen. He took a step away from her and before she could reassure him, he was heading straight back in the direction he just came from. Isis sighed, gazing towards the communal caves which ran alongside the Canyon. Several large families lived in these overcrowded dark holes but that had been the way for thousands of years. Her eyes drifted towards the Valley of the Green Witch. She had heard tales since her childhood of places where there were enough elves to keep them fed for a lifetime. However, as far as she was aware, not a single Windigo had ever dared to leave the Canyon for fear of persecution. Isis sighed again with growing discontent. She was not like the other Windigos for there was a strength about her that was sometimes seen as arrogance by her peers. She didn't care what they thought, from birth she had been betrothed to Serpen and this made her above reproach. Her heart yearned to see what lay on the other side of the Canyon but on hearing Serpen's heavy footsteps, she brought herself out of her daydream.

"Did Torolf bring us anything decent to eat?" he snapped, almost knocking the basket out of her hands as he walked on by. Isis knelt down on her knees and placed the woven basket onto the ground, searching the contents for anything that might pacify him.

"Yes, look, we have been given two rounds of bread, a selection of bones, a jar of blood and a package which contains torn slivers of some internal organs. There's also a lump of fat and a stomach of a small creature," she replied, tilting the basket so he could see what lay inside. Serpen's expression darkened. "A basket of dry, old bones and a few strips of meat," he spat. "Why, I'd like to see him manage off such meagre offerings at such a time!"

"Everyone knows that there have been no magic folk seen throughout the Canyon in months," Isis replied, rising to her feet. She walked over to him, offering him a round of bread and Serpen snatched it out of her hand, ripping out great chunks with his huge, sharp teeth. With wide eyes Isis watched him. Since Manadeth's passing he had become a beast in more ways than one and she worried where this would end. His temper, like his eyes, was growing darker day by day and she knew that once he became chief and leader of the pack she would be at his mercy forever. Isis shivered and looked away, taking the basket to a corner where a large table had been cut out of the rock. She laid the bones and the other gifts in a higgledy-piggledy line, slipping the basket inside a dug-out hole which she used to store all her utensils.

Serpen yawned, stretching his mouth until his jaw cracked. "I'm tired," he said with a sigh, "I'm going to my bed for a nap before I have to go out hunting again."

Isis remained silent, watching him move towards the back of the cave where a ladder rested against the wall which led to their sleeping chamber. She continued to stare long after he was out of sight, glad of the peace. Her attention moved to the contents on the table. Amongst other things, Torolf had given her a few dark green leaves of agave. The battered leaves would break up to reveal strands of strong fibre which she would store to make rope or weave for clothing at a later date. No matter what Serpen said, she was grateful for Torolf's offerings.

When the sun set, Isis lit the countless reed stalks which they used as torches. Under a warm, orange light she worked by grinding the bones to make flour for bread. Once finished, she prepared a meal ready for the morning. Using the blood, fat, and internal organs, she mixed them all together and put them inside the stomach, finally toasting it over the fire using agave string. The process was time-consuming and tiring, so when her waters broke a few hours later, it was an unexpected distraction. The first thing she did was look to the sky and saw that the moon would soon rise. Tonight would be the night her young would come into the world, but she was also alarmed because this meant she was about to give birth as a wolf. Isis leaned both hands on the table when the initial contraction gripped her belly and she shouted to Serpen to awaken. When he didn't come, her shouts became a little more desperate until he finally appeared, his face clouded.

He climbed down the ladder, rubbing the last of the sleep from his eyes.

"Why are you hollering?" he demanded grumpily, stomping towards her.

Isis turned to face him, her hands wrapped around her stomach.

"My time has come," she explained.

"Are you sure?" he asked, "I thought we still had a few more days."

"Clearly not," Isis replied, heaving a deep breath. "So, now would be a good time for you to go and fetch my closest female friend."

Serpen dithered, his brain clearly scrambled. Isis waited for a moment and then banged her hand on the table. "I need Lyra now!" she urged, "before I transmute."

Serpen immediately jumped into action and ran out of the cave shouting for Torolf to find his new mate. Isis could hear a growing commotion outside and hoped he would bring Lyra quickly.

16

Her friend soon made her way into the cave and came and stood beside her. She was a very large Windigo with unusually long ears for a female.

"You haven't much time, you must make your way to the birthing chamber," she urged, placing one of her calloused hands on Isis's arm.

Isis pulled away from her touch.

"I know but . . . the pain . . . it just keeps . . . h-o-o-o-w-l . . ." she gasped as the contraction took hold. It forced her to push harder against the wave of pain.

"We must hurry!" Lyra insisted, grabbing hold of Isis, almost dragging her towards the back of the cave. "Time is of the essence."

Isis looked up at her and tried to push her away.

"I don't want to give birth this way," she cried, petrified.

"It's only natural your body should wish to bring your cubs into the world the same way you were," Lyra soothed. "As you were born of a wolf mother then you will give birth the same way. Do not fear what is inevitable."

"No! I don't want to, it could be dangerous," Isis insisted, pulling away.

Lyra shook her head.

"Look, this is not the time to be stubborn. This has always been our way and you cannot defy nature."

Isis was close to tears. Despite her reluctance, she allowed Lyra to guide her to the place where she would soon see her cubs for the very first time. The room was cordoned off by a large piece of animal hide. Inside lay an area no bigger than ten feet by ten. It was very small but it was warm and cosy. A woven sheet of matting had been placed in one corner for her to give birth and in the other, thick layers of soft furs rested on a makeshift cot, built slightly off the ground. Isis knelt down onto her knees and sat quietly for a moment. High above her head a small hole, worn away by age and countless winds, enabled the first stars to shine down upon her. She turned towards Lyra and at that moment her terror was plain to see.

"Don't leave me," she begged.

"You know I cannot stay with you," Lyra replied, crouching down.

"But I need you!" Isis insisted.

Lyra shook her head and patted her friend gently on the shoulder with one of her huge hands.

"You know it would not be wise with me being hungry," she advised, rising up and moving closer to the doorway.

Isis looked up at her, her eyes wide, pleading.

"But I am afraid to be left alone. It is common for wolf mothers to kill their own cubs at birth and I fear that when I clean off the placenta, I will be unable to control my hunger and devour my own children."

"You are a pure-blood," Lyra soothed, "you won't make such mistakes."

"But how can you be so sure?" Isis insisted, her voice trembling. "You know it happens far more than we care to admit."

Lyra hesitated and let out a sigh. She returned to her side, dropping to her knees so she could sit beside her.

"I know I probably shouldn't give you this, but perhaps it might help," she said, fiddling inside her rather drab-coloured smock. After a moment she revealed what looked to be a black pearl.

Isis held her breath for she had never seen anything so beautiful.

"What is it and where did you get it?" she asked, reaching out to stroke the perfectly formed treasure with her fingertips.

Lyra glanced towards the doorway, her voice dropping an octave.

"It's a magic pearl that I once traded with a traveller," she explained, spotting a small cup and reaching over to collect it.

"A traveller?" asked Isis, looking a little perplexed, "did you not think to eat him?"

Lyra gave a chuckle before placing the cup down close to her feet. "No, little one, I did not think to eat the traveller because it was a grey mothman and everyone knows that no matter how hard you try, you cannot catch them."

Isis wasn't impressed and she pushed out her bottom lip. "So why would you be willing to give me such a treasure?" she asked, her brows furrowing.

Lyra grinned, showing a row of gapping teeth. "I actually traded it with you in mind," she confessed. "I have been watching Serpen and I don't like what I see. I understand it is his birthright to be our leader but I believe he needs something more in his life. I think these cubs will help give him a sense of purpose therefore I wish to help keep them safe this night."

Isis looked into her eyes and saw they were soft and meaningful.

"So you're just as worried as I am about losing the cubs?" Isis replied.

Lyra nodded.

"A little," she admitted, "and this pearl is said to be able to control your desires so it could stop you yearning to feed on them," she explained. "However, there could also be side effects so it's a risk you'll have to take if you decide to go ahead," she warned.

Isis studied the innocent-looking pearl.

"Hmm, I'm not so sure I want to," she said, biting her lower lip.

Lyra pressed the pearl into the palm of her hand.

"I understand and it will be your choice. However, if you do decide to go through with this you must first make a potion. To create it you must take the cup and fill it with a third of water, placing the pearl and a handful of dirt inside."

"Is that all I have to do?"

"No, you must wait. The pearl will rub against the grains of soil and disintegrate, turning it all into liquid. Once this happens, a small cloud of energy will rise above the cup before dispersing back into the water. Lift the cup to your mouth and at the same time think about something which you find so disgusting that the last thing on your mind would be eating your own children. Only then must you press the cup to your lips and drink every drop."

Isis simply stared at Lyra open-mouthed until a contraction bent her double. "You're starting to make me think I should just take my chances," she moaned, placing her arms around her abdomen.

Lyra lifted her hand and stroked the side of her face.

"No one's forcing you," she said, giving her a gape-mouthed grin. "However, you will not get a second chance," she added, rising to her feet. She made her way to the exit, lifted the animal skin and when Isis blinked, Lyra was gone.

As the contractions started to become more intense, Isis squeezed the pearl tight within her palm as though this gave her strength to cope. Unconsciously she glanced towards the hole in the roof which revealed a pale moon. She felt the first shudder as her body shifted. Her eyes blurred and at that moment she realised she could not go through all this pain and suffering to awaken in the morning only to find that she had, indeed, eaten her newborn cubs. It was then she made a conscious decision.

Whilst she still had the ability to think clearly, she reached for the empty vessel and quickly filled it with water from a large bowl which had been left on the floor in anticipation of her transformation. She then scooped up a small handful of soil and sprinkled it into the water, peeling back her fingers to reveal the black pearl.

Without a second thought, she dropped it into the cup, watching it melt away just as Lyra said it would. When the creative energies lifted above the rim like a light, fluffy cloud, she waited until it dissolved before she closed her eyes and tried to think of something that would repulse her. She found that because of the pain in her stomach, she couldn't concentrate, her mind unable to conjure any images that might sicken her to the core. Instead, Isis felt a pang of raw hunger and the image of a stack of newly carved Elvin ribs flashed inside her mind. She tried to push the thought aside, but she was running out of time and in less than a minute she would transmute and therefore not be able to remember why she was doing all this.

She screwed up her nose and downed the potion in one large gulp, the taste of earth distinctive on her tongue. The bland flavour made her think of the Canyon, of dry soil and burning heat and the image of the succulent ribs disintegrated in her mind's eye to be replaced by the thought of eating nothing but dry saplings instead. Revolted by the mere thought of living off vegetation, she crouched by the water bowl and drank thirstily, but no matter how much she swallowed, she couldn't wash away the gritty taste from her mouth or forget about the saplings.

Seconds later she morphed into her wolf form and the pain that wracked her body was like nothing she had ever before experienced. It was stabbing, cramping, violent. She crawled over to the coarse matting when the urge to push became unbearable and, lying down, let the first cub make its way into the world.

Her motherly instincts kicked in the moment the cub appeared and she licked the ball of fur clean until a cry of protest filled the chamber. Ignoring the pathetic whimpers, she nuzzled the cub, cleaning off the placenta with her long, pink tongue, before encouraging her newborn to crawl towards her underbelly. She let a deep moan escape her lips when yet another contraction forced her to push.

A wave of unbearable pain brought forth a second cub yet before she could recover, a third cub made its way out. She licked them all clean over and over, noticing how the last cub was much bigger than the first two and its lungs were clearly well developed, judging by the loud cry that passed from its muzzle.

Isis felt extremely weak and was panting from fatigue but she focused only on the well-being of her cubs. Once it was obvious there were no more on their way, Isis left the matting and carried her cubs one by one in her mouth, laying them gently on the specially prepared bed. She settled them down and curled her body around them whilst they suckled at her teats. Exhausted, she rested her head and closed her eyes, thankful her ordeal was finally over and her hunger satisfied by the three placentas she had eaten. She lay there with her new little family beside her and fell into a deep sleep.

She awoke abruptly when dawn broke to find she had changed back into the body of a Windigo, along with her cubs. A sigh of relief escaped her, her babies were alive and well, the potion had worked its magic. She looked down at her new brood, two females and a male. The male was much larger than the other two, his body a little round with a tuft of black spiky hair sitting between his ears, reminding her of a sod of earth, and so she named her son Clump and her daughters, Felan and Brid.

Chapter 2

Serpen waited just inside the main entrance to the Emerald Cave with Isis at his side. He had been called by the Protector of the cave to make himself ready for his initiation as chief. He was dressed in his ceremonial clothes. He was wearing a newly made tunic where the yoke had been decorated with vibrant colours such as yellow, white, black, blue and red. Over this he wore a jacket made of animal hide. The hem was decorated with dark blue ribbons, depicting a rattlesnake and every time Serpen moved, the snake appeared to slither over the dusty soil. Around his neck he wore a wide collar made from thin bone and polished crystals which were said to be the tears of his late ancestors. His ceremonial dress was finished off with a circle of feathers that sat between his ears. This was made with the sacred feathers of the hippogriff and they were woven with fossilised shells which shimmered with the colours of the rainbow whenever light struck them. Indeed, there was no denying that he looked magnificent in all his regalia.

The rest of the village did not attend as perhaps one would expect. Instead, Serpen would meet the Protector alone and therefore Isis would only stay with him until the drum rolled, signalling for him to make his way inside the cave. The Windigos believed such an honour was a personal affair, but there would be a hearty celebration once he returned.

Serpen looked about him and took great pleasure in all that he surveyed. Behind him sat the Black Mountains and the setting sun caught his eye and he half turned to see the dark cliffs shimmer the colour of pink damask. He felt his stomach turn over in excitement. This very evening, like his mother before him, he would become the chief of the Andark tribe.

"I think you will make a fine leader," Isis muttered, close to his ear.

Her compliment caught Serpen by surprise. Since his mother's death and the birth of their offspring, things had become rather strained between them. He had always been strong and proud and although he loved Isis with all his heart, he would never, in a million years, tell her such a thing. He believed that if he did, he would show himself as weak and therefore he kept his feelings well hidden. Of course he realised this would not help their relationship but he also knew Isis would never leave him.

He followed her gaze towards the cave.

"How long do you think you will be down there?" she asked.

This time Serpen shrugged his shoulders.

"I have no idea. All I do know is that I must wait for the signal," he replied, looking back at her.

"Do you know what the Protector looks like?" she asked, her face wearing a quizzical expression.

"What does it matter?" he replied, losing his patience.

"I was just wondering if perhaps he is not one of us, that's all."

Serpen smirked at her stupidity.

"Of course he's one of us," he scoffed, "but his whole life has been devoted to the Gods and he has sworn to never leave the cave. He is their servant and therefore lives a life of solitude."

Isis pulled a face. "I wouldn't call that much of a life," she muttered, screwing up her nose.

A solitary drum began beating from somewhere inside the cave and Serpen's eyes shot towards the darkness. This was the moment he had been waiting for and he stepped forward, Isis already forgotten.

He dashed down the dimly lit stairwell and was soon engulfed in a light green glow.

He stood mesmerised as the cave shimmered all around him. The walls gleamed like sheets of pale green ice and below a vast lake sparkled, the water the colour of freshly polished jade.

Serpen couldn't help but catch his breath. No one was allowed to venture so far unless invited and he was in awe at what he saw. He was surrounded by natural beauty and it was beyond anything he could have ever imagined.

He hurried along, his feet like feathers as they brushed the stone. When he reached the very bottom his eyes caught sight of a moving shadow, something which looked to be crouching in the darkness. Serpen checked that he had not been followed. Only the males were permitted to rest their gaze upon the Protector, Manadeth had been the only exception, and he was relieved to find he was, indeed, alone. A noise, like robes sliding along the floor, made him turn his head and he saw the Protector heading towards him, his long, black clothes swishing about his feet like silk.

The ancient Windigo approached him from the shadows. He held what appeared to be an empty challis in his old, gnarled hands and Serpen recognised it to be the sacred Cup of Anointment.

"So you're Manadeth's son?" asked the Protector, his face half-cocked and Serpen noticed his eyes were like onyx shot through with silver.

"Yes, I am," he replied, feeling a shiver of anticipation worm down his back.

"Hmm, you are not as old as I expected," stated the Protector, taking a lantern from off a dusty ledge. He busied himself lighting it and then he swung the cage up into the air to reveal an archway. It was covered with thick cobwebs and the Protector raised his hand, clawing at the darkness.

"Come, we must go through the Tunnel of Despair to reach the Enchanted Wheel of Andark," he explained, wiping a trail of black tendrils from off his robe.

Serpen took a deep breath. This was the moment he had been waiting for and he could feel his heart hammering in his chest.

The Protector headed off at a surprisingly quick pace, leading Serpen down a narrow corridor that twisted to the left and then to the right. It was dark even with the lantern but Serpen was not afraid. After travelling no more than a hundred feet, the Protector stopped dead in his tracks and turned towards him. A strange sound, soft yet menacing, was rising from within the darkness. Serpen grabbed the lantern from the Protector's hand and swung the light out towards the abyss. He took an unconscious step back, repelled by what he saw.

Just a few feet away the ground was alive with what looked to be a mass of poisonous snakes. Their long, green bodies recoiled when the light all but blinded them but their heads, like miniature dragons, rose in the air, their red tongues flicking as they hissed with contempt. Serpen recognised them to be dragon snakes and he watched them slither closer. On the top of their heads sat two small acorns and at first Serpen thought they were their ears. He lifted the light a little closer to get a better look and his eyes narrowed. They were not ears at all but talons and they looked sharp enough to cut his belly open with one swift slice. He stood there, trying to calculate how many snakes slithered about the floor but there were far too many so he soon lost count.

"Is this a test?" he asked calmly.

"Yes," replied the Protector. "You must slay them all and make it through the tunnel without being bitten," he explained, facing him.

"I see, very well, here, hold the lantern," Serpen ordered, thrusting it into the Protector's outstretched hand. He quickly dropped to his knees, slid forward and grabbed hold of two snakes. He caught them just underneath the throat, making it near impossible for them to sink their fangs into his flesh and inject a lethal dose of venom. They spat and hissed with fury, shaking their tails in an attempt to break free and Serpen opened his mouth and bit off their heads with his powerful jaws. He flung their decapitated bodies to the ground and grabbed another two. Within minutes he was wading through the bed of dragon snakes, spitting out heads like apple pips. The Protector walked closely behind, stopping to drain the limp bodies of every drop of blood, filling the challis to the brim.

Within the hour Serpen had killed every snake that blocked his path. He made his way to the end of the tunnel, his new clothes covered in blood and when the Protector acknowledged the fact that he had indeed passed the test, he gave a victorious roar.

His mighty voice echoed around him, bouncing off every wall, and the Protector took the lead, pointing to where an alcove glowed with a luminous ray of light. The roof was so low, Serpen had to go on all fours to make it through, but once he'd crawled inside, he found himself in a small, but brightly lit, cavern. In the centre of the floor sat an old, dilapidated spinning wheel and Serpen recognised it as the Eight-Folded Wheel of Andark. Carved by the Krylock Ogres who once lived in the enchanted wood of the silver-leafed oak, it was a gift from those who wished to remain at the bottom of the food chain.

The Protector placed the lantern onto the ground. He gestured for Serpen to come to him before offering him the Cup of Anointment.

"You have done well and gained your honour by killing the snakes that guard the wheel. Come, drink from the cup and rejoice in your victory."

Serpen nodded, reaching out for the challis. A delicious fragrance filled the air and he sniffed deeply, his upper lip curling. He looked past the rim of the cup to see it was made of gold and precious gems, and the outer casing depicted the Black Mountains with images of Windigos engorging on the blood of the dead.

"Can I drink all of it?" he asked, licking his lip in anticipation.

"Yes, enjoy, and drink your fill," the Protector replied with a chuckle.

Serpen grinned, lifting the cup slowly to his lips. His nostrils flared when he smelt the rich aroma of fresh blood and his tongue rejoiced when the first mouthful hit the back of his throat. He drank greedily until every drop was gone. When he finished, he wiped his mouth with the back of his hand and the Protector took back the challis, his gaze drifting towards the wheel.

"You have drunk from the cup of life and are therefore anointed by the Gods. Go; spin the wheel and find out at last what the Gods have in store for you."

Serpen felt a surge of power. It was true. Ever since he was small his only desire had been to be the leader of his tribe. He quickly glanced up and for the first time caught sight of the Protector's whole face. He had open sores on his cheeks and split, cracked lips. He tried not to blanch but the Protector caught his stare and attempted to smile but it looked more like a grimace, showing off green, mossy teeth. Serpen glanced away, a feeling of light-headedness washed over him as though he'd drank too much root wine. This sensation was followed by a red haze which seeped across his vision and he rubbed his eyelids with the balls of his fists.

"Is this normal?" he gasped, when he found he couldn't see properly. He glanced up as his vision cleared and he spotted the Protector moving closer to the shadows.

"Yes, it's nothing to worry about, it's simply your inner senses awakening," he soothed. "From now on you should see things very differently. Go to the Eight-Folded Wheel and prepare yourself for the next step of your journey."

For some reason which he couldn't explain, Serpen felt the hand of doom touch his very soul.

He turned his attention to the ancient Windigo.

"But what if the Gods show me something which I don't wish to see?"

The Protector clucked his tongue in the roof of his mouth.

"Like what, for instance? A lifetime without untold riches," he asked, sourly. "Sometimes there are simply no riches to be had," he added, shaking his head.

Serpen didn't quite understand what he was talking about and believed he should say something righteous in reply, but all his thoughts were flying out of his mind. The wheel pressed on his conscience and became his only concern. He drew closer, until he towered over the wooden frame which was emblazoned with eight golden dials. His fingers reached out, yet he hesitated, unable to touch the golden spike that was there for the sole purpose of spinning the wheel. He understood how turning this wheel would change his life forever and unexpectedly he found a part of him was afraid.

"Is everything alright?" asked the Protector, a thread of concern in his voice.

Serpen nodded and licked his lips. No matter what, he couldn't falter, not now. From within he drew his courage to the surface and, after taking a deep breath, he lifted his hand and struck the spike. The wheel burst into life and as it spun a projection of images filled every wall, surrounding him like a shroud of history. His eyes, now clear as crystal, tried to absorb every detail. The cave came alive with images of his ancestors who had once roamed this earth. He watched in awe as the wheel showed him a time when they battled with the elves. He saw the bloodshed and witnessed their tears. Then the pictures faded and Serpen's eyes widened with despair.

"Why are the Gods showing me such a terrible time?" he asked, aghast.

"Because you must understand how much your kind has suffered and now you must look for a solution to the troubles which haunt you every day."

"But I have no idea how to make peace with the elves."

27

"Then it will be your quest to find one," said the Protector, his voice rising.

Serpen went to say something but the dials on the wheel spun into life, turning in a clockwise sequence, grabbing his attention. He could see the wheel was made of eight quarters and as it spun, the segments folded on top of one another until only one quarter remained visible. When the wheel finally stopped spinning, the last remaining segment fell noisily to the floor.

"Pick it up and see what secrets the Gods have revealed to you," the Protector urged, and the moment Serpen bent down to touch it, a white light flared before his eyes and he could see a ghoulish apparition floating only inches away from his face.

"Manadeth?" he gasped, and he sucked in his breath, unable to hide the shock from his voice.

"Melt that ice around your heart, before it's too late," his mother whispered in his ear. "If you do not, then the path you choose will lead only to your destruction!"

Serpen took a step back. Although she was only an apparition, he could make out her once dark eyes and thick, puffy lips. She rose higher into the air, a finger pointing towards him. "Be forewarned, Serpen," she rasped, "because your future as chief depends on it."

For the first time in his life, Serpen was lost for words. He couldn't comprehend what his mother was trying to tell him and he rose to his feet, standing tall, refusing to be intimidated. Trying to stay calm, he bent down once again and picked up the piece of wood, staring at an image which was ingrained into the timber. When he finally glanced up, he saw Manadeth had vanished.

"I didn't expect to see the ghost of my mother down here," he announced, clearly ruffled.

The old Windigo sighed deeply and shook his head.

"One never knows what one will see in this chamber," he replied, his tone rather matter-of-fact.

Serpen let out a sigh of relief, glad Manadeth had gone, and then he gave his full attention to the crudely drawn image in front of him. It was a picture of one of his kind, a Windigo, with a cumbersome body and features that he thought resembled his son's. His eyes narrowed as his brain tried to unscramble the clues. He could see the Windigo, lying in a pool of his own blood, and a wolf was standing over him, powerful jaws clamped around his throat.

"What does all this mean?" Serpen gasped, his eyes searching for the Protector. "Why would the Gods show me death?" The Protector dragged himself from the shadows, his face never flinching as he took the segment from out of the new chief's clammy hands.

He studied the picture for quite some time, his fingers tracing over the lines before returning it to its rightful owner.

"It is an omen," he announced, his voice sombre. "I fear, in time, a member of your family will die."

"Who?"

"Can't you see?"

"Well, yes, there is a likeness, but ... surely this cannot be?"

"Don't sound so surprised," said the Protector, moving closer to the shadows, "you know very well you are ruthless enough to kill anyone who stands in your way."

"Yes, but not my own son."

"Really, now that is a revelation," mocked the Protector.

A noise like sand filtering over rocks filled the air and Serpen looked up to see the Protector vanish before his very eyes.

"I would never kill him unless he betrayed me!" Serpen roared out loud.

The voice of the Protector lingered in the air. "Then heed the warning from the Gods. In the end, it will all boil down to the decisions you make as to whether he will live or die by your hand."

Chapter 3

Over the next few months, as Clump grew, Serpen watched him like a hawk, aware of the prophecy from the Gods. Although it was not always possible, he did his best not to let him out of his sight and when he was forced to do so, it was only for the shortest of times.

As time passed, Serpen had to admit there was something rather peculiar about his son. He appeared secretive, keeping himself at a distance. Since he had been weaned off his mother's milk, no amount of coaxing would draw him closer to the fire to enjoy what precious meat they had together. On several occasions Serpen watched Isis try to entice him with titbits. Once she even offered him the whole breast of a grey hawk, but like always, Clump made some excuse. He was too tired, he'd already eaten, he had stomach ache or his tooth hurt.

Serpen was alarmed by his son's behaviour and at times he became angry, believing Clump to be merely attention seeking. However, whenever he wanted to chastise him, Isis would stand between them, using herself as a shield, and this would really irritate him. There was no denying there was a strong bond between mother and son, stronger than anything he had ever seen before, and deep inside his soul the first embers of jealously ignited.

As the days drifted into weeks, his role of chief started to take over his life and his time with his family grew less and less. Being the chief Windigo, he often travelled to see the other tribes hidden in the mountains. He would meet to trade what little food and wares they had, discussed their fears and concerns, and when he returned, the Elders would always demand his full attention. So by the time Clump was almost full-grown, his son's strange behaviour became the norm and the Protector's warning was pushed to the back of his mind.

One particular evening, not long after returning from the Black Mountains, Serpen was making his way back to his cave when he caught sight of something shifting about in the darkness.

As wolves the Windigos would often communicate to one another by using telepathy and he was quick to challenge one whom he thought to be an intruder.

Who's there? he growled, his ears straight, his teeth bared. The wolf pressed closer to the shadows and Serpen's hackles rose, his teeth flashing white in the moonlight. He snarled, his jaws gnashing, and a warning sound rose high into the air.

Show yourself! he demanded, and the wolf stopped dead in its tracks. Serpen sniffed the air, recognising the wolf's scent when a light breeze changed direction.

Clump, is that you?

The wolf drew away from the shadows to reveal himself. He trotted over, licking Serpen's muzzle the moment their mouths connected.

I'm sorry father, I didn't see you there.

Really, am I so hard to miss?

No, of course not, it's just my mind was elsewhere.

Serpen circled around him before sitting on his haunches. His red eyes bright, like rubies.

It's very late and you shouldn't be hanging around the camp at this hour, he admonished.

Clump threw himself on his back, thus exposing the vulnerable ventral side of his chest and abdomen.

I know father but I just couldn't sleep. He lifted his head playfully, his way of showing his submission. Serpen looked down at him, Clump's tail was wrapped around his hind leg, a sign he was aware he was in the wrong.

So why were you skulking in the shadows?

Clump jumped up and came to sit beside him. He then lay down on all fours so that his father was leaning over him.

I,- I,- I didn't want the scouts to spot me because I knew if they did, I would be in trouble.

So why did you not stop when I called you?

Clump's ears bent backwards and he gave a whine.

I'm sorry father but I simply did not hear you.

Serpen felt the first tremor of doubt. He had seen by the way Clump tried to hug the rock when he challenged him that he was lying. He was also aware that there was no reason for Clump to have been prowling around the camp at such an hour. Everyone was back from hunting, only the scouts were still out, busy checking the perimeter to ensure they were all safe from harm.

Serpen felt anger rise in his belly. He would not be lied to, especially by his own son, and it was then that Serpen pounced. Before Clump realised what was happening, Serpen pinned him down onto the ground, his jaws gripping his throat. He could hear Clump whimpering, the quiver of his cry vibrating through his fur.

Tell me, what you were doing out at this time of night, Serpen demanded, refusing to let go of him.

I just wanted some air, the night is stuffy and I simply couldn't sleep.

Still Serpen would not relax his grip.

You should never go out alone once we are all back from hunting, you know the rules.

Clump's whimpers merely deepened.

Father, I'm really sorry. I didn't realise it was such a big deal and it wasn't as though I intended going far.

Serpen finally relaxed his jaws from around his throat and took a step back, but his eyes were like pieces of burning coal.

Get yourself to your bed and I will speak to you again in the morning, he declared.

But, I ...

You heard me! Go! And I don't wish to catch you outside at such a late hour again, do I make myself clear?

Yes father, and Clump turned tail, heading back towards the cave, his ears low, his tail drooped. He ran several feet before turning back to look at him, lifting a paw.

Home, now! Serpen commanded, taking a step forward and Clump scampered towards the cave. Serpen continued to watch him, his red eyes still glowing with fury. He was confused as to why his son had been hiding in the shadows as though he was making his way out of the village. He stared after him for several minutes. He couldn't figure out the reason why Clump would be leaving camp. Was it really that he couldn't sleep or was it something else? Distracted by a lone scout who bayed for his attention, he trotted off to check the boundary. As he went, he wondered whether he was simply reading too much into this chance meeting with Clump or whether there was something more sinister going on instead. His mind tried to figure out what it could be. Perhaps it was the pull of the moon hadn't quite left his body yet and this was the reason for Clump's restlessness. After coming up with an answer to his quandary, Serpen decided that he may have been a little too harsh with Clump and that he had overreacted. He thought of a way to make it up to his son and decided that now was a good a time as any to teach his offspring the techniques of hunting.

Thus, the very next day Serpen announced he was taking his three cubs out to search for food and to practice their hunting skills. It was soon clear Isis was not happy about this. She asked for her son to stay behind but Serpen would not be swayed and so, under the cover of darkness, Felan, Brid, Clump and Serpen travelled beyond the ridge in search of food. As the alpha male, Serpen led the pack, his constant howl ensuring none of the cubs wandered off too far. He climbed another ridge, stopping just at the crest. He lifted his leg and urinated against the trunk of a single pine tree. A puddle of urine soon pooled along the hard, baked earth and Serpen trotted on through it, his scent now on his paws.

A low growl left his throat when he heard a rustle in the undergrowth. He turned to see three sets of eyes, two blue, one amber appear from out of the darkness. Serpen relaxed his guard. His cubs were all distinctively marked. Brid was the smallest; her pelage was the colour of the grey mist that came down from the mountains. Felan, her coat was a deep fawn mixed here and there with spiky tufts of white. Not surprisingly, being a male, Clump was the largest. His face was white, speckled with grey which was peppered over his forehead and down between his ears. Clump jumped out of his hiding place and Serpen saw his mane of black and fawn. He could also see by the size of his feet that his son would one day be powerful and strong.

As a pack they continued on their journey, perhaps travelling further than they should, hunger making them a little reckless. Serpen ran ahead with his daughters trying their best to keep up, but Clump stayed back, wishing to protect his family from anything which might attack them from the rear.

Serpen was the first to stumble upon the horse thief, just as the last flames of his camp fire were dying. He sniffed the air and then doubled back to tell the others.

I have found a very tasty meal just through those trees, he growled, excited.

Brid and Felan began jumping up onto one another's backs in excitement but Clump appeared less enthusiastic. Serpen snapped his jaws to keep his daughters in check but his eyes never left Clump.

No one does anything without my say so, he warned, circling his kin. *I don't want the first real food we've had in weeks getting away.*

Once Felan and Brid calmed themselves, Serpen led the pack towards the thief, their paws silent as they hit the ground. A twig snapped beneath Brid's paws and Serpen turned around and glared at her, his teeth bared. The thief must have heard the noise, sensed he had company, and spooked, he jumped to his feet, calling out into the darkness.

"Who's there?" he shouted, when the wind blew the clouds across the sky, causing eerie shadows to run like ghosts along the ground. Serpen left the pack to stalk his prey. Like a black ghost, he was invisible in the darkness and his feet never made a sound. He pushed his long nose between the thin branches of a bush and saw the elf wielded a mighty sword. He left his hiding place and trotted a little closer, his pink tongue lolling out of the side of his mouth. He sensed the elf was frightened for he rushed over to his horse and grabbed the reins. With one swift movement he was on the filly's back, the reins wrapped around one of his hands. A cry of panic left his lips when a menacing growl filled the air and he raised his sword, swinging it dangerously low, only narrowly missing his horse's ears.

"Don't come any closer or I'll chop you into little bits!" the elf proclaimed, but Serpen wasn't frightened. He was excited by the smell of fear which oozed from his pores. It was so powerful, it was like a tantalising seasoning and Serpen licked his lips in anticipation of the kill.

With one mighty leap he made his attack. Jumping high into the air, he used the elf's foot as a step where it stuck out from the stirrup. He landed onto the back of the saddle and in a flash was upon him. In desperation the elf tried to fight him off. He turned towards the wolf, his sword flashing like silver, but this merely sealed his fate. The minute Serpen saw the pink flesh of his neck, he thrust forward and his powerful jaws clamped down and ripped out his throat. The elf tried to scream, lifting his hands to where his throat had once been. Blood poured from the wound and down his chest, his hands covered with his own blood and within seconds he slumped forward and Serpen was able to drag him off his horse, down onto the ground. The horse bolted and Serpen let go of his victim in an attempt to grab one of the horse's hind legs, but the horse bucked, kicking its back legs, and Serpen had to dive out of the way.

It was clear the elf was dead so Brid and Felan came out of hiding and approached their father with highly exaggerated movements; Clump, however, was nowhere to be seen. His sisters curled their bodies and lowered their ears, pawing wildly in the air, almost grovelling at their father's feet. Serpen bared his teeth, blood dripping from his jowls, threatening them when they got too close to the kill. His daughters backed away. They waited a few moments but when Serpen snarled again they laid down and averted their eyes. Not completely intimidated, the juveniles crept closer whilst their father was feeding until he allowed them beside him without conflict.

Once they had fed and the sun had risen, Brid went to find Clump. She found him hiding inside a large bush, thorns stuck in his fur and bloodied scratches etched across his nose.

"What are you doing in there?" she hissed, pushing the leaves aside.

Clump could barely look at her, let alone speak, and it was only when she glared at him he attempted to reply.

"I- I- saw it all," he stuttered, "I witnessed father's atrocity."

Brid's face clouded.

"He's only catching food," she snapped. "Anyway, whatever's the matter with you?" she added, sounding cross. "Sometimes it's as though you're not one of us."

35

Clump opened his mouth to say something but Brid raised her hand to stop him. "Shush, father's making his way over so get out of that bush before he catches you."

He scrambled out of his hiding place and then, head low, scurried through the undergrowth to hide away for as long as possible.

*

Later, when Clump was forced to rejoin the group, he saw Serpen's eyes flash with annoyance and the muscles in his jaw tighten as he made his way towards him. Clump was aware he had not been at the forefront of the kill and this would mean his father would be simmering with rage.

"Where have you been all night?" Serpen demanded, his voice low, threatening.

Clump cast his gaze down at his feet, scratching his toe in the dirt, unable to look his father in the eye.

"I, err, thought we had company, so I went to check it out but it turned out to be nothing," he lied, looking at Brid in the hope she'd say something to help defuse the situation. He heard Serpen's fury rise in his throat.

"Why would you do that without my say so?" Serpen rasped, and Clump flicked his gaze towards him to see his hands ball into fists. He sensed he was in serious trouble and in desperation he licked his lips in anticipation of a fight. His eyes shot towards his two sisters, begging them to come to his aid.

"You were busy with the immortal," Clump declared, "I was concerned for our safety."

"Really? How noble of you," Serpen snapped in a sarcastic tone. "However, for all your gallantry I'm afraid to say that I don't believe a single word you've just said."

Clump felt himself tremble. It was as he feared, his father was about to punish him for hiding away.

"I believe him, Father," Brid suddenly burst, pointing behind him. "Back there, near the rocks, I thought I saw something moving in the shadows last night and I saw Clump double back to investigate."

Serpen's eyes were as hard as two flints when they rested on Clump. His voice held an edge when he said, "so what did you find so interesting, lurking behind those rocks?"

Clump gave an involuntary shiver.

"Err, I stumbled upon a group of tree people," he explained. "They had travelled from the upper ridge for water," he added, trying to sound convincing. "They told me this part of the Canyon belongs to them and the pool which is hidden between the rocks is where they come to drink each night." It was true, he had come across the tree people only they had simply carried on their way and he had not disturbed them.

Serpen opened his mouth, ready to challenge his excuse, but Felan coughed and caught her father's attention instead. "Can't you see we don't have time for all this, she declared, pointing to the rising sun. "We need to get out of here before we are seen."

Everyone turned towards her and Clump could see there was genuine concern shining in her eyes.

Serpen must have seen it too because his demeanour changed and he quickly nodded his agreement.

"Alright Clump; I'll let the matter drop this time. However, there will not be a next. I find it very strange that you did not join me in the kill and that you decided to stay out all night with a group of spindly twigs instead."

Clump lowered his head but he was still able to see Serpen walk over to what was left of the bloodied carcass.

"You must be ravenous," his father proclaimed, bending down and ripping off a forearm. He threw it towards him as though he was tossing a ball. He gave a loud chuckle. "Here, go on, gnaw on that," he ordered, flashing a devilish grin. "After all, I wouldn't wish for you to go hungry after you went out of your way to protect us."

Clump simply stared at the bloodied remains lying by his feet. He was repulsed by what he saw, ripped flesh and sinew covered in blood. He felt his stomach heave and he turned his head away.

"We haven't got time to let him feed now!" Felan announced, sounding exasperated. "He should have fed earlier, when he had the chance."

Clump saw his father contemplate her words and then he marched back towards him.

"Yes, that's a good point," he said, bending down to snatch the arm away as though it had been some kind of treat. "Let's get out of here and get this food back to those who truly deserve it," he announced, beckoning for Clump to help him carry what was left of the bloodied remains.

Inside, Clump's stomach knotted with despair. He didn't want to touch any part of the dead elf but he was wise enough not to voice his fears. For the rest of the day the group travelled in silence and when they arrived back at the village they were greeted by the tribe as heroes.

Chapter 4

Isis winced and drew a breath. "Clump, don't be such a baby," she complained, picking at the sliver in his hand with her needle. Clump's bottom lip trembled. "It's all Felan's fault," he groaned, "she asked me to pick the flowers and then she was naughty and pushed me into the cactus." He gritted his teeth when his mother continued to probe, digging the needle further into his skin. He looked across at his sister and saw she had both hands across her mouth, trying to stifle a giggle. Clump glared at her in return.

Isis gave a chuckle and finally pushed his hand away. "Where's Brid?" she asked, a row of creases appearing along her forehead. Clump thought about the whereabouts of his older sister until he was distracted by the fact his hand no longer resembled the underbelly of a porcupine.

He looked up, realising his mother was still waiting for an answer. "Oh, she's gone to the old plateau with Horith," he explained, playing with a tiny skin flap.

Isis didn't seem too pleased.

"What, again?" she snapped, sounding irritated. Clump nodded, oblivious to his mother's furrowed brow, too busy running over to Felan to show her how his hand was all better.

He heard a rustle and spun on his heels to see Isis heading towards the cave and then something clearly made her change her mind because she turned her attention back towards him.

"Clump, I would like you to go and find Brid and bring her home," she announced, with a wave of her hand.

Clump pulled a face.

"Aww, but I don't want to," he bleated, "can't you send Felan instead?"

Isis appeared to waver but then she lifted an eyebrow and shook her head.

"No, do as I say." Her eyes shot towards her daughter. "Felan, come and help me prepare our next meal."

His sister nodded and ran to her side, giving Clump a sarcastic grin as she passed.

Clump stuck out his tongue and Felan screwed up her nose in response.

Isis tugged at Felan's arm and made her stand by her side.

"Clump, be off with you and don't forget to keep your eyes open for any Elvin folk," she ordered, shooing him on his way. "The sooner you leave the sooner you'll be back so we can all eat supper together."

With a deep sigh, Clump waved goodbye. It wasn't that he was afraid of going out into the wilderness on his own; in fact it was quite the contrary. His only concern was that he didn't want to disturb Horith and Brid. Clump had seen the way they looked at one another; soon realising Brid only had eyes for the older Windigo. Clump liked Horith and had tried to make friends with him but Horith had never really given him the time of day. This lack of male companionship had turned Clump into a bit of a recluse. Windigos don't give birth very often so his only close companions were his two sisters. The other young males of the tribe were all far older than Clump and they always laughed at him when he tried to join in with their games. Even when they turned, all they did was make fun of him or try to bite him.

To make matters worse he was now too old to drink his mother's milk and since having to eat solid food things were turning disastrous. There had already been an incident just a few days previously. The village had rejoiced when they came across a group of wild horses which they said would feed the tribe for almost a month. Some ate the meat straight off the bone whilst others roasted the flesh over the fire. Clump waited excitedly for his first ever horse steak whilst most of the villagers were busy engorging themselves. The Elders sat in a large circle around the campfire, talking in deep undertones about the other realms, their leaders and their ways. Clump listened intently as he waited for his turn to eat, learning about such places as the Kingdom of Nine Winters which was ruled by the Elvin King Gamada and his arch enemy King Forusian who was the leader of the Nonhawks.

Isis interrupted his eavesdropping by coming over and offering Clump and his sisters a few large pieces of cooked meat. Clump grabbed his food with both hands, his nose sniffing the air, his mouth already watering. When the steak cooled, his tongue probed eagerly at the flesh and when he took his first bite, his taste buds waited for a tantalising experience to explode in his mouth. To his utter despair, he found the morsel tasted like ash and it was so bland and disgusting that he immediately spat it out, much to the surprise of Felan and Brid.

"What's wrong with you?" asked Brid, ripping into the steak with her bare teeth.

Clump pulled his lips into a tight line.

"Nothing," he replied.

"Did you get a stringy bit?" Felan asked, spitting out a piece of gristle.

Clump didn't know what to say, he hadn't expected to find the steak to taste so disgusting.

"It's just me, I'm not feeling too well," Clump lied and he had known, right then, that something was wrong, that he was somehow different from the rest of his kind. He glanced up at his mother and saw a dark shadow flit behind her eyes. Clump couldn't help wonder why she looked so guilty but Isis caught his stare and she turned her face away. Before he could say a word she jumped up from the fireside and headed off in the direction of the cave.

Confused, Clump decided to let the moment pass; his only concern was that his staple diet was flesh yet the mere thought of soft tissue ever passing his lips again made him want to literally throw up.

Clump stayed by the fire whilst those around him began transmuting into wolves and when he thought no one was looking, he dropped the horsemeat into the flames. He swore to himself that never again would he allow another morsel of flesh to pass his lips. He knew that none of the Windigos would ever understand his dilemma. Even if he was able to explain it, which he couldn't, he believed, in time, his dietary requirements would land him in serious hot water so he decided to keep his secret to himself. Meat was always scarce within the village so it wasn't much of an issue not to be seen eating it but he worried that his father was growing suspicious. He had already been caught leaving the village on his way to find something edible, although he would not be so careless again.

From that day on he ate alone, slipping out of the village in the dead of night whilst everyone slept, heading into the Canyon. There he would munch on a multitude of tasty flowers and shrubs and he would eat until his belly was fit to burst. He fed on the young shoots of amaranth which tasted like spinach and on desert raisins, nibbling their rusty yellowish green leaves which could be eaten fresh or dry.

Clump brought his attention back to finding Brid and bringing her home for her supper. On the way he snapped off a handful of orange hackberries growing on a bush, enjoying their delicious sweet flavour as he travelled. To everyone except Clump, the Canyon looked lean and wild, barbed and dry.

There was certainly a lot of red dust and brushwood blowing about so Clump wondered if it was his imagination playing tricks on him when he saw a strip of cloth waving at him in the breeze.

Clump blinked a couple of times then veered off course, heading for the piece of cloth that blew like a banner in the wind. His eyes narrowed when he caught sight of something familiar and his gut threw him an almighty punch. There, in the distance, he could see part of Brid's smock trapped on the sharp spikes of a yellow cactus.

He panicked and rushed forward, his fat legs pounding the earth beneath his feet. He brought his hand to his face and shielded his eyes but he couldn't see her anywhere and the hairs down his back stood on end. His eyes swept over the rough terrain in search of any clues to the whereabouts of his sister.

Then, something caught his eye ...

"Brid!" he roared, seeing her lying face down in the dirt. He bolted like a horse struck by a whip, his chest tight as though his breath had momentarily been squeezed from his lungs. On reaching her side he looked down, tears of despair already blurring his vision, but there was no mistaking his sister's body. He could see her simple dress was all torn up, practically in tatters, and her legs and arms were covered in a sea of blood and swollen welts.

"How did this happen?" he gasped, falling to his knees, and his arms circled her waist, turning her over so he could pull her upper body closer to his chest. Brid let out a low moan and Clump, thankful she was still alive, eased his grip, letting her slide back towards the ground so she could rest her head on the dry earth.

His eyes rolled over the rest of her body and he could see she had been whipped to almost an inch of her life. Tears fell as he digested her injuries. An eye was tightly closed, already swollen and bruised, and one of her cheekbones appeared to be crushed. He continued to assess the damage although he really couldn't bear it. She seemed to have been hit by some kind of blunt instrument such as a rock or even a very large fist. He traced his fingers across her skin and she cried out in pain when his fingertips touched where there had once been bone. Clump gasped and bit his lip so hard he drew blood and he gave a wail of despair. He started to sob whilst his mind whirled as to who would do such a terrible thing to his sister. He gazed down at what was left of her face, all smashed in and covered with blood. He couldn't comprehend why anyone would wish to do this to another living soul.

"Who did this to you?" he bleated, trying to keep control of a burning rage that was building up inside. Brid lifted one of her hands and brought it up to her face, shielding her good eye from the sun. She licked her dry lips, but no words came out of her mouth.

"Was it Horith?" Clump accused, "did he do this?"

Brid began to weep. At first it was just a whimper but suddenly it turned into a full blown cry.

"No, they took him," she sobbed uncontrollably.

"Who did?"

"A group of Nonhawk soldiers. I swear they came out of nowhere. They were on horseback and they headed straight for us. Horith tried to protect me, realising we were in danger. He told me to run for my life which I did, but I saw them tie him to a horse."

Clump just stared down at her, unable to believe his ears.

"But why would Nonhawk soldiers want to capture him?" he rasped, trying to stay calm. "They have never done anything like this before."

Brid shook her head and squeezed her good eye shut.

"I don't know. All I could hear was screaming, yet the riders must have conjured a spell in anticipation of this because none of them were affected by his wailing."

"What, none of them?"

Brid opened her good eye and stared up at him. Her voice was weak, almost a whisper.

"No, I realised I needed to get away as fast as I could but the warriors chased after me and I was outnumbered seven to one. I heard a whoosh and then felt pain in my lower leg and I fell to the ground. The next thing I knew the soldiers were upon me, beating me."

Clump lifted her up and pulled her closer to his chest, rocking her like a baby.

"In which direction did they go?"

Brid let out a howl of anguish, beating her fist against his chest.

"I have no idea," she wailed. "I soon became unconscious and when I awoke, I was lying in the dirt and the Nonhawks were gone having taken Horith with them."

Clump grabbed hold of her hand and held it tight. He studied her face and felt his heart break. He understood how much Horith meant to her and he secretly worried that he was probably already dead.

"Father will search for him," he reassured, trying his best to ease her heartache. "He'll organise a hunting party and none of us will rest until he's found."

Brid took a deep breath and Clump felt her whole body go rigid. "I truly hope so," she replied, reaching up to stroke one of his long dark ears. "I don't understand any of this. Most immortals think us demons and keep well away."

Clump made a scoffing sound in his throat.

"We've certainly got a bad reputation that's for sure."

Brid dropped her hand.

"Yes, and this means no one usually dares to cross us."

"Well, it looks as though the Nonhawks don't care about the consequences and father won't rest until they pay for what they've done," said Clump, with a shudder. The memory of his father ripping out the throat of the horse thief shot to the front of his mind. He shook away the savage thought and his eye caught sight of an arrow embedded in Brid's lower leg.

He pointed down to her calf.

"You know that needs to come out."

Before she could reply, Clump leaned forward, gently bending her knee. He patted the other affectionately and tried his best to look as though he knew what he was doing.

"Are you ready?" he asked, taking a deep breath.

Brid nodded, bringing her hand over her now closed eyes and he saw her body tense.

"Be ... be ... quick," she pleaded, refusing to look at him.

Clump braced himself and then one of his huge hands held the spine near the fletching feathers whilst the other, gripped the arrowhead.

He closed his eyes and took a deep breath.

Snap! The arrow broke in two.

His eyes flew open as Brid roared and bared her teeth, the veins in her neck protruding like rope and several birds rose high into the air, turning on their broad wings and wheeling away.

"I'm so sorry Brid," Clump whispered, patting her shoulder until she calmed, "but it isn't over yet." She licked her dry lips and turned her face away. Clump took another deep breath and gently, very gently, slid the rest of the arrow from out of the back of her calf. Clump stole a look at his sister and watched her beat the ground with her fist.

"It's done," Clump announced, throwing the arrow away and he ripped the bottom of his tunic so he could wrap it around the wound. He tied it in a knot and once the bandage was secure, helped her to her feet.

"We need to get you home to mother as quickly as possible," he said, wrapping her arm around his shoulders. "You've lost a lot a blood and your leg is open to infection." He noticed Brid didn't reply and her head lolled to one side. "Stay with me Brid," Clump urged, becoming frightened. "Talk to me and whatever you do, don't go to sleep." Brid murmured something incoherent and Clump set off at a fast pace, almost dragging his sister along the dusty plain.

Sweat soon poured down his face. She was no lightweight and the heat from her body made him all the more uncomfortable. The sweat dripped into his eyes almost blinding him but he wouldn't stop, not until he got Brid home safely. The journey took twice as long and Clump was exhausted by the time he spotted the black hole which led to his home, which was easy to miss amongst the dark shadows and rocks.

Near the entrance to the caves a crowd of Windigos clustered together. It appeared to be almost the entire tribe. He called out, his voice almost a rasp, begging for someone to come and help him and when the village scouts finally ran towards him, he saw their eyes were wide in fear and a cacophony of bleating arose from their throats. The fittest males reached him first and the moment they took Brid from out of his arms, Clump collapsed, face down into the dirt.

Chapter 5

It was an angry crowd that forced its way inside Serpen's cave. From a darkened corner where he was recovering from his ordeal, Clump saw Torolf push his way in. He could see his jaw was tense and his steely features made it plain that he was trying to hold himself together. He had always been proud yet serious. He moved to Serpen's side, crouching down to sit on the floor beside his leader. Clump couldn't help but pity him, aware of his family's tragic history, and sensed by the distant look in his eyes that he was inwardly praying to the Gods for his son's safe return.

Already there were many in the cave, mainly the Elders but a few of the younger males had crept inside, excited by all the commotion. The smell of cooking wafted in the air, but Clump had long since lost his appetite. Crudely carved wooden bowls were handed out to the chosen few and Isis and Lyra were busy filling them with some kind of homemade concoction. Clump spotted Felan out of the corner of his eye and he was not surprised when she came to sit beside him.

"How's Brid doing?" Clump asked, watching her cross her legs and give him a sad smile.

"As well as can be expected," she replied, pulling two small furs over her knees. "Brid lost a considerable amount of blood but thankfully you found her in the nick of time. Most of her wounds are to the bone but the Protector has been kind enough to give us a special healing paste which should help her recover."

Clump's face took on a look of intense concentration.

"Why do you think the Nonhawks did such a terrible thing to her?" he asked.

Felan shrugged her shoulders.

"I have no idea. They have never done anything like this before but I overheard mother talking to Lyra and she thinks they have done this for sport."

"For sport?" Clump repeated, his face aghast.

"Shhh, lower your voice," Felan hissed, her eyes wide. "You mustn't let anyone hear you or you could start a riot."

Clump nodded, but he gave her a look of confusion.

Felan sighed. "I heard mother say that the king of the Nonhawks is known throughout the land to be a very cruel and sadistic leader. He persecutes his own people and if he can, takes others to imprison so he can torture them in his murder holes."

Clump turned pale.

"That's terrible," he gasped, unable to believe his ears.

Felan nodded, pulling the furs a little closer.

"Yes, that's why father must leave the Canyon and find Horith before it's too late."

"But to venture into Nonhawk territory would be far too dangerous," Clump cried, alarmed.

A dark shadow swept across his sister's face.

"So, would you have father leave Horith to rot?"

"No, never," Clump blurted, "but no one has travelled so far in centuries."

"Then perhaps it's time," Felan replied, with a shrug of her shoulders. "We have the ability to kill many Nonhawks with one scream even if those who rode out today were bewitched. Not all of them can be protected and they must pay for what they have done today."

"So you think they did this on purpose?"

"Yes," said Felan, clearly vexed. "Deep inside my bones I think they did, knowing how we would react."

"Then why should we go after Horith, it could be a trap?"

Felan gave a sour expression.

"Because, dear brother, we have no choice."

*

Zebulon, the most ancient of the Elders, gave a loud roar, grabbing everyone's attention, and Serpen rose from the floor. The chief turned to face an overly excited crowd, he waved his hand in the air and the last of the stragglers fell silent.

Serpen pursed his lips. "Alright, enough's enough. I'm sure you have all heard by now what atrocity happened today at the plateau with Brid and Horith. Let me start by saying that we cannot allow the Nonhawks to take our kind without retaliation. We owe it to Brid to avenge her suffering and, of course, to bring Horith back to us."

48

Zebulon lifted his hand and Serpen stopped abruptly, staring him straight in the eye.

"Yes, what is it?" he asked, sounding annoyed at being interrupted so soon.

Zebulon cleared his throat.

"Great leader, none of us have ever travelled further than the Canyon. Do you think this a wise move?"

"Wise? No, perhaps not, but do you have a better idea?" Serpen snapped, his tone curt. "Maybe you would have me whimper at the Nonhawks' feet and beg them to come and take more of us?"

Zebulon, who flaunted a long mane of white, shook his head.

"No, of course not, that was not what I meant," he replied, his hand brushing the soft hair around his own throat.

Serpen's eyes flashed red.

"Then what exactly are you implying? As far as I am concerned we must ensure the Nonhawks receive a clear, distinct warning."

Zebulon didn't waver beneath his leader's hostile gaze. Instead, he turned to his peers and they spoke together in low voices for several minutes. When they had finished, the Elder turned his attention back to Serpen.

"Yes, you're right," he agreed. "We cannot allow today's brutal actions to go unpunished. We have survived this long without incident but we must ensure that the Nonhawks never do this again. However, this could, if we are not careful, escalate into a war which we could not possibly win. The Nonhawks would undoubtedly have the support of the magic folk so we must tread carefully."

Serpen didn't appear the least bit pacified.

"I never said it would be easy, yet it's time for the Nonhawks to feel our wrath," he bellowed, raising his fist to the heavens and the cave erupted with a thunderous wailing made by the entire assembly. A few eager males almost started a fight and it was Zebulon who intervened.

"It's no use taking your frustrations out on one another; indeed, this will get you nowhere," he proclaimed. "The elves are itching for an excuse to finish us off therefore we must not appear to be the aggressors here."

"Are you asking for us to sit on our laurels and do nothing?" someone shouted, and Zebulon turned quickly, his shrewd eyes unable to single out the troublemaker. His attention returned to the chief.

"By all means, go and seek out the Nonhawk King and deliver him a message that he cannot ignore. Tell him he must release Horith unharmed and in return we will spare him his life. However, should he decline our offer, we will not rest until we have eaten every vile Nonhawk in the entire land."

A tremendous roar of excitement exploded throughout the cave. The younger Windigos unleashed their fury by wailing at one another, slapping each other's arms and upper torsos.

"Enough!" Zebulon cried, snarling at his neighbour when his elbow accidentally jabbed him in the eye. "Let our great leader explain what he plans to do next and tell us who will join him in the hunt."

At his command, the crowd quietened and all eyes returned to Serpen once more.

The chief made his way over to where there were a few dried old bones lying on a shelf. He reached out and grabbed hold of a large thigh bone. Snapping it clean in half, he lifted the two ends to his lips, sucking noisily, stripping each shaft clean of the juicy marrow held inside. Once finished, he threw them to the floor with a clatter.

"That is what I will do to King Forusian if he doesn't agree to my terms," he declared. "I will suck him dry and then I will do the same to every sour-breathed Nonhawk I meet. Tonight, we will head straight for his castle. When I gain entry I will ensure the Nonhawk leader learns of his grave mistake."

"How many of us will you take with you?" Zebulon interrupted.

"No more than five and we will leave before the moon is at its highest."

"Have you decided who will go?"

"Yes, and I think I have chosen wisely. Firstly, it is only fitting that I call upon Torolf to join me in the search for his son."

A trill of noise rose high in the air and Torolf stood tall with something that could have been perceived as a painful expression displayed upon his face. He was a very large Windigo, his long hair black and tan, and he glanced around the cave, placing his fist against his heart.

"I'm honoured to travel with the chief," he said gruffly, and he bowed his head. Serpen acknowledged him and the Elders nodded their approval. Torolf sat back down and the rest of the villagers waited to hear who would be running with the chief.

Serpen was quick to divulge such information.

"Although you may think it strange, I have made the decision to take Clump with me," and he pointed a finger towards his son.

A huge gasp filled the chamber but Serpen merely gave a smug grin. "I understand how some of you may be surprised by my choice but I feel that although he is young and inexperienced, he is also very strong. One day he will take my place as leader so he needs to learn quickly how to conquer our enemies."

Clump was shocked that his father had chosen him when there were far more experienced Windigos to choose from. The sound of someone catching their breath made him turn, and he witnessed Isis bringing her hand to her mouth. However, before she dared speak Clump saw Serpen give her a cold, hard glare that clearly made her words die in her throat. With a shudder, Isis appeared to pull herself together and continued to fill the bowls with food, but Clump could see she was upset. He couldn't go to her. This would only antagonise his father and if he showed any affection towards her in public, he would be dually punished. He watched Serpen's attention return once again to the Elders and Clump felt his heart break for his mother. She would not want him to go, as he was so young, but Serpen's word was final.

"Who else will you take?" shouted one of the younger males, becoming bold, and many took a step back, afraid Serpen would be angry with the sudden outburst.

To everyone's surprise this was not the case because Serpen didn't appear the least bit aggravated. Instead, he gave a broad grin, pointing towards the one who had spoken out.

"I understand that some of you are older and far more experienced than my son. So I look upon you to do what is right. Whoever I choose, you must understand that when we leave tonight it is highly likely that you may not make it back alive so I have decided that I will take two volunteers. I want wolves at my side that are willing to die for the cause."

A bellowing noise exploded inside the cave as many young Windigos, anxious for the chance of adventure, screamed for his attention. Serpen sat down and his face was hard to match his eyes. "Do not think this is a mere game," he warned. "Your life will undoubtedly be in great danger and the likelihood of returning to your family is very slim." The noise inside the cave merely intensified and Serpen pointed indiscriminately to two large Windigos.

"You, what is your name?" he demanded. His nostrils flared at the one whose chest stuck out boldly.

"Crowle, great leader."

"And you?" he asked, his eyes now fixed on the dark-haired male who stood at his side.

"Ettin, master."

"Very well, you both look strong and eager to run by my side so I will have you two as my chosen companions. I insist that you enjoy a small meal before you leave, but I want you light on your feet." His voice was as clear as a starry night and his intentions were even clearer.

"We must make an offering to the Gods to help keep us safe," he declared. He jumped up and pushed through the crowd and the rest of the Windigos rose up to follow their leader out of the doorway.

Chapter 6

I wonder if I am to be killed immediately or whether I am to be tortured first, Horith thought as the darkness from sleeping lifted from his eyes. In the faint light he could see the grey walls of his prison which surrounded him, causing him to give an involuntary shudder.

His thoughts returned to the plateau. The moment he had spotted the warriors riding along the plain he had wailed like a banshee. He screamed until his voice was hoarse, but the Nonhawks with their crated skin and lifeless eyes only appeared to dig their heels into their horses' bellies even further. Their hooves sounded dull on the ground, grinding the dust and soil under their feet to create a haze of cloud behind them and it was at that moment when he realised they were both in serious danger.

At first he was filled with confusion. No living creature could ignore the wailings of a Windigo and he thought perhaps they were simply too far away to hear him and so he gave yet another earth-shattering scream. The vibrations from his throat made his own ears ring but to his dismay he soon realised what should be stopping them in their tracks was having no effect.

In a blind panic he searched for help but the plateau was deserted, there was no one else around. He needed to get Brid to safety and so he pushed her in the opposite direction, begging her to run for her life. He was surprised when she faltered, her small eyes filling with tears and he could see fear fought against her loyalty to stay with him. In sheer desperation he became angry, shoving her away until she broke into a run. He held his breath, watching her head back towards the village, but her heavy frame made her slow and in less than a minute she was surrounded.

In his cage, he screwed up his eyes and pushed back the tears, refusing to relive the moment she was attacked. To his despair, he felt his stomach heave and he vomited all over the floor. He was bent double for several minutes until the pain in his gut eased and he lay against the bars of his prison, taking a few deep breaths to calm his nerves.

Horith had been taken captive the moment the Nonhawks reached him. Showing no mercy, they dragged him like an animal to Forusian's castle. He had never met such vile creatures before. They mocked him, whipped him and tied him to a horse that was not a horse at all. He had tried to bite the animal to stop it from taking him away, but his mouth bit only fresh air. He was stunned, realising the horse wasn't real, just a mirage, yet his arms were bound to the saddle. He tried to break free, but his bonds were so strong they merely cut into his flesh. He roared out in pain, his wrists dripping with blood, but no matter how much he struggled, he could not free himself. He had never witnessed such magic before and he was afraid. Even though he only had one hand, his bonds were so tight he couldn't even move his stump.

As the sun began to set, they had taken him through the gates of the castle whilst the soldiers on guard jeered at him and threw whatever was at hand towards his head. He was hit by flying rocks and small stones, his forehead suffered a deep gash and his fur was covered in blood and rotting vegetable matter.

The Nonhawks dragged him into the courtyard and within seconds he was surrounded by terrifying monstrosities, creatures that he had never seen before. His mind flew to the nights when the Elders talked of unspeakable monsters which roamed the other realms. Around the campfires they would tell the young Windigos horrifying stories which made them quake and all the while Horith smiled to himself, never truly believing such tall tales; that is, until now.

He peered around to see he was encircled by two-headed beasts, goats with arms instead of feet, large human-sized owls with red glowing eyes and huge hairless creatures that couldn't possibly be elves. Never in his wildest nightmares had he ever seen such a terrifying menagerie of beasties. He thought they must all be captives, his ignorance of life outside the Canyon making him appear stupid.

The spectators sniggered and snarled at him, some tried to reach out and rip his skin with their vicious claws and he tried to scream, to make them stay away, but he found not a sound came out of his mouth.

The soldiers merely laughed at him when he recoiled from their touch. He stared into their faces, their black, lifeless eyes shining like jet. He had never met anything so outwardly repulsive and he watched as one of the soldiers turned on the crowd, forcing the audience to disperse. He was untied from the horse and taken inside one of two tall stone towers and placed in a cage that was barely large enough to hold him. He was angry and he was scared. He wasn't strong enough to break out of the cage with having only one hand but he shook the cage fiercely, out of desperation. One of the guards heard the commotion and came running. He shoved a spear through the bars, trying to pierce his side but Horith was quick and moved out of the way.

"Keep quiet if you want to live," the soldier yelled, cursing under his breath. "Either that or die right now, your choice." Horith fell back, lifting his huge hand over his face until the soldier turned and walked away. Horith closed his eyes, grateful he had been spared but once again his mind drifted back to Brid. He could still see her lying on the ground, the soldiers beating her with their heavy weapons and horse whips until her fearful cries fell silent. He had been unable to save her and he simply didn't know if she was alive or dead. He couldn't fathom out why the Nonhawks would attack them so brutally, but since his capture he had managed to overhear a couple of the soldiers talking. It appeared the soldiers had been lying in wait after the king, whilst out hunting, caught sight of Brid on a previous occasion.

Horith opened his eyes and let out a deep sigh. To think the king had travelled so far in search of something new to torture made Horith want to rip out his heart. He sat on his haunches overlooking a stone wall that was filled from floor to ceiling with instruments that were used for torturing poor souls. Most of the contraptions he'd never clapped eyes on before but already he had witnessed one of them being used upon another prisoner. Since being brought to the castle he had seen only one other being that, like himself, was incarcerated.

It had been in a place where a fire burned day and night and where the constant stench of urine, blood and sweat made the air foul smelling and repugnant. Within the confines of a small room a prisoner, his hair matted with blood, was taken from his makeshift bed. Horith thought he was an elf but he wasn't sure. His hair hid his ears and it hung in thin wisps over his face, his features unrecognisable after suffering what appeared to be several earlier beatings.

"Get off me, you vile creatures," the male cried, trying to get away, but the guards merely laughed at him, one of them hitting him on the back of the head with the butt of his sword. The prisoner fell like a sack of potatoes onto his knees. One of the Nonhawks pulled at his shackles and he fell forwards, his face in the dirt.

Horith gagged with fear when he saw another soldier use a spiked, wooden club to hit him. There were five Nonhawks in all who were beating what appeared to be an Elvin warrior, shouting out that he was a spy and demanding an immediate confession.

The prisoner merely gasped out loud as each blow connected. He tried to stand but the guards used their boots to push him back towards the floor.

"Tell us why you're here," one of the Nonhawks hissed. "We already know you're one of King Gamada's men!" The elf shook his head, blood pouring from his mouth.

"Start talking!" another of the soldiers shouted, "or we will make you."

Horith hoped the warrior would say something that would save him but when it was clear the prisoner refused to talk, the soldiers were quick to resort to torture.

Horith watched as they dragged the bleeding warrior along the floor. Then one of the Nonhawks placed a device between the elf's breast bone and throat, just under his chin. The contraption was secured with a leather strap around his neck and then they used chains to hang him from the ceiling. Suspended in the air, there was no way the warrior could lie down. The soldiers left him hanging there and Horith could see the elf was doing his best to stay awake but as the hours ticked by his head dropped with fatigue and the prongs underneath his chin pierced his throat and chest. He cried out in agony, seemingly in great pain and the soldier on duty simply laughed, clearly enjoying watching the blood turn his captive's tunic deep crimson.

Horith huddled in a corner of his cage and prayed to the Gods for someone to come and save him. He could see now that there was only one end to his capture if no one arrived soon. Brid filled his mind once again. He pushed the thought that it was most likely that she was dead to the back of his mind but if it was true, a part of him would always be grateful that she would not have to endure such a terrible fate as was waiting for him. At the very end, he would try to be brave, in memory of her.

Horith looked up to see three Nonhawks enter the room. It was clear the elf was weak from loss of blood and that he would probably not live for much longer. A circle of crimson pooled around the prisoner's feet and the soldiers cursed loudly when their boots slipped.

"He will confess before he takes his last breath," spat one of the Nonhawks, but Horith knew they had left it too late. Although he wouldn't admit it even to himself, deep inside Horith was terrified. His cage was so small he couldn't even pace the floor, and he knew it was only a matter of time before it was his turn to suffer at the hands of these vile creatures. He felt a knot of fear twist inside his gut. A soldier came over and hit the bars of his cage with his sword.

"Not long now before you swing," he hissed, showing a row of small, pointed teeth. "I've heard, you're next," he jeered, and threaded an iron link through a ring at the top of the cage.

Horith gulped. Was it really his turn to die so soon?

All he could think about was the warrior with blood running down his chest from the terrible injuries sustained by the spikes. He prayed to the Gods that if he could not be saved then to make sure he suffered a quick death. He closed his eyes and thought about how much he had hoped to achieve before he died. His deepest wish had been to have Brid for himself but now he realised his desires had only been a foolish daydream. He would never have been able to persuade Serpen to allow such a joining but he'd always believed where there was a will, there was most certainly a way. Brid had been betrothed to another from one of the mountain tribes yet even though Horith had always known this, there was something deep inside him that would not allow him to accept their fate. He was not a fool, he knew if Serpen found out he would kill him and so they had been forced to keep their feelings secret, yet he loved her more than life itself, and she him.

He was shaken from his thoughts when another Nonhawk brought a low cart. He drew it alongside him and then between them, the soldiers lifted the cage as though it was made of nothing more than paper.

"Only a matter of time before the fun begins," snorted one of the soldiers, leaning over to release the brake. The wheels rolled into life and Horith was jolted by the sudden movement. He didn't know where they were taking him and his fear rose a notch.

From within the cage, Horith saw the confines of the castle. Wherever they were taking him, he noticed there were no windows, or natural daylight. He passed by a place where several Nonhawks sat around a campfire. It was noisy and smelly and he could see axes propped against the walls and highly polished swords swinging from their belts.

The cart drew to a halt outside a set of chambers.

"Get him inside the murder hole," shouted one of the guards, "King Forusian has given me strict instructions that he wants the prisoner ready for when he arrives."

Horith once heard that such holes were usually situated at the main gates of castles, however, this one was actually inside the soldiers' living area. One of the soldiers must have read his mind because he said, "Haven't you heard? The King delights in dropping dead bodies into the living quarters of his men."

The two soldiers laughed heartily; taking the cage off the cart they pushed it with ease into the first of the chambers. There wasn't much inside but in the centre of the floor lay a gaping black hole.

"Let's get him set up," said one of the guards, who Horith had decided to name Spiky due to the club he carried. There was nothing he could do but watch as the cage was connected to a pulley that lifted him clean off the floor.

"That should do it," said Spiky, "King Forusian will most likely use him for target practice until he becomes bored and decides to play, dropsy."

His comrade chuckled, his voice sounding as though he was being strangled.

"Yes, and I can see a few of his favourite toys in the corner," he said, pointing to a table covered with all kinds of bloodied weapons. "Why, I'm sure he'll have a lot of fun occupying his mind with those." Horith looked over and spotted a quiver filled with arrows lying beside a long bow which was sandwiched between what looked to be a meat cleaver and a silver sword. He felt his chest tighten and to his dismay, the two soldiers headed off, taking the cart with them. The door closed with a clang and Horith had no choice but to sit and wait for the King to arrive, already playing out in his mind how this was all going to end.

Chapter 7

Serpen peered through the trees and looked along the trail. It was far too dark for any elves or magical folk to see, but as a wolf the bright moonlight was like daylight, the silver rays glowing like sunshine between the trees.

Serpen laid down in the dirt, aware his pack was close by. He remained unnaturally quiet, the soft leaves covering the ground cooling his underbelly. It had taken them days to reach King Forusian's kingdom and now they were here all they could smell was death. As they walked they found the land to be littered with artefacts of the dead. Swords and shields lay rotting in the earth and as they travelled closer to the castle, they came across many small hovels and cottages that had once belonged to Forusian's tenants. Those whose crops had failed or who had simply suffered hard times found the sharp edge of a sword in their gullet when they could no longer pay the rent. Their bodies lay where they fell and not even the wolves would pick their bones clean.

The pack found that the forest led out to Forusian's castle, which sat on a hill by the sea. There looked to be only one way inside and Serpen knew this was going to be a challenge. They watched the comings and goings of the castle for two whole days, hidden amongst the thick foliage and bracken. Every night they noticed that a group of the King's guards left the castle in darkness to places unknown and he soon realised this was their only chance.

An owl screeched, cutting through the silence and Serpen cocked his head. A twig snapped and he rose on all fours, a soft growl leaving his throat. Torolf trotted up and nudged his flank; Serpen sniffed the air aware something had spooked him and a repugnant scent that smelt like rotten cheese clung to his nostrils.

The drum of horses' hooves shook the ground under his paws and then five black horses carrying Nonhawk soldiers cantered towards the ambush, the soldiers' heads covered with metal helmets and their bodies dressed all in black. Big and brutish, the Nonhawks themselves were known to be vile murderers. Their skin was the colour of the swamp, their features marred with large holes but not everyone who lived in the castle was a Nonhawk. The King himself was once a powerful magician but he chose the dark side of magic and was banished by his own band of mages. Many races lived within the castle walls such as river trolls with three heads and trows, a type of goblin that had rows of razor-sharp teeth, bent backs and were so ugly even their mothers couldn't love them.

Serpen let out a howl, a signal, and the rest of the pack jumped to their feet. The horses caught a whiff of their scent, tossing their heads in alarm and the Nonhawks reached down for their swords. From within the darkness, Serpen sprang from his hiding place with Torolf at his side. They ran straight towards the Nonhawks, teeth bared.

The front runners saw two huge beasts heading towards them and they raised their swords with a sharp cry. The first Nonhawk soldier pushed his horse forward but the stallion refused to move, throwing its rider and bolting back towards the castle. Serpen was upon the warrior the second he hit the ground and agonising screams filled the air. They fell on deaf ears. Torolf had already dragged a second Nonhawk from his horse and Crowle and Ettin had attacked two more. The other riders tried in vain to push their horses on, divots of earth flying from their hooves, their swords hacking aimlessly into the air. Desperate cries left the Nonhawks' mouths as they tried to escape, but they were no match for the huge beasts with teeth that ripped their flesh apart.

Just off the trail, Clump huddled behind a bush, terrified, but he knew that if he didn't join in the hunt the pack would turn on him and kill him. A horse and rider rushed past and he lunged forward, chasing after them. His four powerful limbs ran alongside the frightened mare and he nipped at the flesh at the top of her hooves until she finally tripped. The Nonhawk soldier swung his sword and nicked Clump's ear as he fell, but Clump was too involved with the hunt and never felt a thing. The warrior rolled in the dirt and then he jumped to his feet, his dark cloak blowing menacingly in the wind.

"Come and get what you deserve," the soldier hissed, his sword flashing like silver, and Clump's hackles rose.

From the darkness came a low growl, and then a dark shadow sprang from the undergrowth and hit the Nonhawk from the side, knocking him straight to the ground with a thud. A cry of agony filled the night air and Clump saw Serpen lift his head, blood dripping from his muzzle. He growled fiercely, his anger at Clump for almost letting the warrior escape, shining in his vile red eyes.

Clump lowered his ears and backed away, watching the other wolves join the pack leader. They all howled at the moon, their tune long and haunting. Clump turned tail and hid in the undergrowth. He watched the pack from the safety of his hiding place, the wolves feeding on only one carcass, attacking the meat ravenously and then dragging the rest of the bodies into the undergrowth. Clump knew what Serpen intended to do. The plan was to strip the dead of their clothing and in the morning, dress themselves in their clothes to gain access into the castle. The problem was they now had no horses to take them there and everyone knew this would look rather suspicious. He glanced around and spotted some plump raisin berries growing on a bush and so he snapped off a few with his teeth before finding somewhere to hide away for the rest of the night.

He never moved again until dawn, when Serpen came looking for him. He could see the anger still simmering in his father's eyes and so he took great pains to keep out of his way. In silence he stripped the Nonhawks' of their clothes. Last night the pack had gone to great lengths not to rip the soldiers' clothing apart but blood was splattered everywhere and a multitude of dark crimson stains had already dried into the cloth. There was nothing they could do so the Windigos dressed in the Nonhawks' uniforms, each placing a black cloak around their shoulders to try and hide the blood. Clump was grateful that the Nonhawks were such a large race and that the garments they wore hid them all well. It felt strange having to wear restricting trousers and a tight tunic, not to mention that the helmet rubbed his nose making it sore, but he had the sense not to moan.

Clump watched his father put on a pair of black leather gloves and then pick up a sword, placing it into the sheath that now fell from his hip. No Windigo had ever been taught to fight with a sword, it was not their way, and Clump lowered his gaze when he saw his father walking toward him.

"Time to head on out," Serpen declared, and Clump looked up and saw his father's lip curl. He nodded, moving closer to the others and his father turned to face them all. "We must stay close together and no matter what happens, don't get separated from one another. We will try and gain entrance to the castle via the main gate. Should anyone ask the whereabouts of your horse, you are to say that we were attacked last night and that we must speak with the King."

Torolf simply nodded, whilst Crowle and Ettin let out an excited yelp.

"We are not through those gates yet," Serpen snapped, giving them both a warning glare, "so I suggest that you save your juvenility for when we have the King at our mercy."

Both Crowle and Ettin fell quiet, hanging their heads like chastised children, turning to stand long-faced at Torolf's side. Serpen flicked his head, a gesture for his son to come to him and Clump obeyed. They travelled on foot, leaving the forest behind them and followed a path that would lead them straight to the castle.

It was a good thing that the Windigos had already eaten because there were a fair few travellers on the road that day. They passed a farmer with a broken-down cart, his wheel snapped in half, and a group of Nonhawk women laden with tall baskets filled to the brim with vegetables fresh from the fields. Clump's eyes rounded when he saw the huge green marrows carried on their shoulders and his mouth began to water. He averted his eyes when his father, thinking he was staring at the women, pulled sharply at his cloak. Clump turned his attention towards his companions. Their strides were strong and powerful and they overtook several slow-moving travellers in their haste to get to the castle.

A beggar woman, her body bent over with old age, was walking in the centre of the path, making it difficult for them to pass.

"Get out of the way," Serpen snapped, and in his haste he pushed her aside. She gave a pitiful cry as she fell to the ground. Without thinking Clump jumped to her rescue. His strong hands wrapped around her small frame and he gently brought her back onto her feet.

"My father didn't mean to hurt you," he said, checking to make sure she was alright, and a gasp left his lips when he caught a glimpse of her grotesque features. Apart from the Nonhawks they had killed, and those who travelled on the road, the only other human creature Clump had ever seen was the horse thief his father had slaughtered. He sucked in his breath when she caught his eye for there was something rather disturbing in the way she stared at him, as though she could see deep into his soul. He shuddered and recoiled, but before he could say another word his father was once again dragging him away by his cloak.

His attention was soon drawn to the soldiers guarding the castle's entrance. The Windigos walked towards the main gatehouse where two armed guards barred their access, each pushing out their chests as they approached.

"Halt, where do you think you're going?" asked one of the guards who blocked their path. He raised his sword, suspiciously. Clump felt his knees start to shake but Serpen stood tall, his dark cloak blowing gently in the breeze.

"Let us pass," he commanded sharply. "Last night we were attacked by a group of changelings and although we were fortunate enough to have killed them, we lost our horses." He pushed his way forward but the guard refused to let him enter, pointing the sword at his chest.

"What type of changelings?" he persisted, tilting his head to one side, his eyes filled with distrust.

"Windigos," spat Serpen with contempt. "They were in their wolf form when they attacked. It was a bloody battle but we slaughtered every one of them."

The guard's shoulders relaxed. "Yes, we heard they were seen entering the realm a few nights ago," he remarked, lowering his sword. "I'm guessing they've shown up due to the young male we captured several days ago."

Serpen was seen to tense at his words and Torolf moved a little closer to his companion.

"Then the King will be pleased to learn that we have rid him of these troublesome creatures," he declared, and he took a step forward. The guard hesitated, and then moved aside to allow them all to pass.

"You'd better inform the commander of what's occurred. You'll find him in the main tower," he said, pointing them in the right direction. "Just keep going straight and then head on through the courtyard."

Serpen nodded and the group hurried through the gates.

Torolf's shoulders appeared to relax a little. "That was too close for comfort," he whispered out of the side of his mouth.

"Yes, but we made it through the gates, so all we need do now is find the King," said Serpen, striding ahead. "The guard said to head to the main tower but perhaps it will lead us to more than just the commander?" They made their way to the courtyard but unexpectedly Torolf stopped dead in his tracks. The stones and grit underneath his ill-fitting boot crushed dryly as he turned. "Something isn't right," he said, pointing to the empty streets.

Serpen nodded. "Hmm, you're right. "It looks to me to be market day yet this place is deserted." A thin piece of yellow silk skimmed across the ground and caught on the heel of his boot. He bent down and picked it up and Clump watched him sniff the material before throwing it back to the wind.

Clump waited for his father to say something, but instead Serpen stared up at the soldiers on the battlements. Suddenly, he let out a deep-throated growl and Crowle and Torolf responded by doing the same.

"I think we've walked into a trap," Serpen hissed, and the moment the words were out of his mouth Clump heard 'swish' 'swish' 'swish' and he looked up to see arrows flying through the air, landing close to his feet.

Serpen let loose a piercing scream and Torolf and Crowle followed suit, opening their mouths and creating an earth-shattering noise that should have been powerful enough to make their enemies' eardrums burst. Ettin sprang into action when two armed soldiers ran towards them, ripping off his gloves and helmet as he went. He grabbed the nearest guard by the scruff of the neck and held him up into the air, feet dangling. His huge fingers tightened around his throat, crushing his enemy's windpipe as though he was nothing more than sand. His companion raised his sword and charged. Ettin threw the dead body to the ground and turned, forcing the sword out of the soldier's hand by snapping his wrist. The soldier let out an agonising scream and the blade fell to the ground with a clatter. Ettin lunged forward and seized the soldier's head, jolting his spine and breaking his neck with one swift crack.

"Take them!" cried one of the guards and a scuffle of noise made Clump spin on his heels to see several Nonhawks approach with gleaming swords held tightly in their fists.

He stared blindly when one of them shouted out, "your wailing won't kill us, we're all protected." Another set of arrows sailed through the air and Clump ducked down on his haunches, his bottom resting on the back of his heels. Both Serpen and Torolf grabbed hold of a couple of lids from a set of water barrels and used them as shields. Crowle continued to wail, as he dived this way and then that, to try and stay clear of the arrows.

All too soon it became clear that no amount of screaming would be enough to save them.

"I think the soldier speaks the truth and they're bewitched," Clump cried out in despair. Just then a Nonhawk warrior ran over to him and lifted his sword, swinging it backwards and forwards, trying to slice off his head. Clump threw himself onto his side and rolled out of the way and the Nonhawk's sword hit the ground. With a flick of his wrist, the warrior turned, saw Crowle, and lunged.

"Look out!" Clump yelled, but he was too late, the sword sliced like butter across Crowle's gullet. Blood spewed like wine from his throat and Crowle lifted his hands to his neck in shocked surprise. Clump watched in horror as his eyes glazed, blood pouring down his arms and then he dropped to the ground, dead. Clump had never witnessed one of his own kind being murdered before. To see him lying there in the dirt, a pool of red blood slowly seeping over the small stones, terrified him and he ran and hid behind a wooden cart. He brought his shaking hands to his mouth. Crowle's death had been so quick, so final.

The roar of those who battled on was loud in his ears and he peered out from behind a wheel to find his father and Torolf still fighting a group of Nonhawks. Clump realised he was far too inexperienced at combat and he could see how they were all terribly outnumbered. He watched his father fight, killing several of the soldiers with his bare hands, but the more he killed, the more they came. Clump saw their weapons, mainly swords, fall to the ground but, like his father, he didn't know how to use them. Swords were of no use to the people in the Canyon and they only ever took spears and clubs from those they killed.

A pitiful cry rose in the air, like a bear that was mortally wounded and Clump braced himself. To his utter despair, both Torolf and Ettin were now lying dead on the ground, slain by those they thought could not hurt them. Clump saw their lifeless bodies lying side by side in the dirt and hot tears pushed their way to the surface when he realised only his father was left alive. His stomach knotted into a cold lump and he felt paralysis worm its way down both legs. He didn't know what to do, but one thing was certain, he couldn't let his father die out there, alone, not without trying to save him first. Grief at seeing his dead comrades lying in the dirt made him rise to his feet. He could no longer hide like a coward behind the cart and he took a step forward, ready to die at his father's side.

When he took his first step, a dazzling array of bright colours exploded in the darkening sky and Clump looked up, transfixed with the silvery stars that shot across the skyline. He found it difficult to draw his eyes back to the courtyard and when he did he espied the old beggar woman from off the road standing no more than six feet away from him.

"You!" he said, his eyes widening in surprise, what are you doing here?"

The old woman threw back her head and gave a loud cackle.

"No time for questions," she said, raising a piece of whittled wood and circling it towards the heavens.

A spiral of light came down from the sky and spears of lightning encircled the castle.

Clump looked back towards his father and it took him only seconds to realise that everyone was frozen in time.

"What have you done?" Clump roared, becoming afraid.

"I have given you the chance to escape and to take your father with you, but only if you agree to help me."

"Help you?" Clump asked, sounding incredulous, "how could I possibly help you?"

The witch gave another cackle, edging closer, the hem of her ragged cloak dragging behind her in the dirt.

"I have seen into the future and there are events that will happen which I cannot, for the moment, explain. Sometime soon I will need to call upon you and I want you to do it without question," she replied.

Clump hung his head and the witch reached out and grabbed his wrist. Clump, taken by complete surprise, threw his arm out to make her let go and the witch stumbled backwards causing the large black hood to fall from her face. Clump blanched when he caught sight of her face for a second time that day. Her features were wrinkled beyond recognition and her skin smelt of rotten decay. The witch hissed her displeasure and swiftly replaced the hood.

Clump took a deep breath, filling his lungs.

"It's not that simple. My father would never forgive me if I left here without finding Horith."

"Horith?" said the witch, cocking her head to one side, "who the hell is he?"

"He is one of my kind who was taken prisoner by the Nonhawk king a few days ago," Clump explained, with a sigh.

"And the reason why you're here today," said the witch, giving him a knowing smile.

Clump nodded as the lightning cracked above his head, startling him.

The witch lifted her stick up towards the heavens.

"If you accept my terms I can hold the spell for a little longer," she said, temptingly. "But if not, you and your father will die where you stand."

"Then I accept your terms if it means I have a chance to save both my father and Horith."

"So we have a deal?"

"Yes," said Clump, "we do."

"And you will tell no one?"

"Not a soul."

"You promise?"

"I give you my word."

"Very well, then I suggest you head to the murder holes which are located inside the second turret instead of the main gate for I'm guessing you will find Horith there. If you do track him down, you will need to physically touch his skin to awaken him. However, be aware that the same rule applies to the Nonhawks so whatever you do, keep your distance. I will try to keep your father safe until you return, so hurry for I cannot hold the spell forever."

The witch pointed a long bony finger towards the turret.

"What are you waiting for?" she snapped, rolling her eyes, "you're running out of time!"

Clump glanced at his father standing there like a stone statue and then he was running, running as though the hounds of hell were snapping at his heels.

On reaching the lower door to the tower, Clump forced it open and fled up the spiral staircase. At the top he was faced with another door through which he could see a row of cells. He quickly opened it and saw several Nonhawks suspended in time standing guard. He manoeuvred around them, careful not to touch them before reaching the first door. He found it to be locked and so he quickly looked about and spotted a bunch of keys dangling from the waist of a Nonhawk soldier. Still careful not to touch, he lifted the keys from off his belt and grabbed a metal bar lying abandoned on the ground. Wasting no time, he unlocked the first door, pushing it wide. He gasped in horror when he saw something covered in blood lying face down on the floor. It was so badly hurt he couldn't tell for sure whether it was Horith or not and so he dashed forward, grabbing hold of the body and gently turning it over. He felt instant relief when he realised it wasn't Horith but at the same time a wave of despair washed over him. He became angry at seeing this poor creature left to die in such squalid conditions.

Clump stood up and gave a mighty roar which almost shook the walls. He grabbed the chain which was bolted to the wall, and snapped the links in two with his bare hands. He couldn't understand how anyone could be so barbaric. His kind may be known to be cruel but it was only because they needed flesh from the living to stay alive. He already understood that this was a crime against humanity but there was nothing to be done. The Nonhawks did despicable things to others just because they were powerful and he decided at that moment that they were the true monsters. He left the prisoner, heading back into the corridor and raced to the next cell, only this time he didn't waste any time fumbling with keys, he simply ripped the door clean off its hinges.

His eyes widened in disbelief; there was Horith in a cage suspended in the air above a murder hole. A ledge no more than a foot wide encircled the hole. Clump felt the blood drain from his face but he quickly spotted a pulley system which was holding the cage above the hole. He ran over and within seconds he began lowering Horith closer to freedom but no sooner had he started than one of the links jammed on a cog. The cage jarred, swinging dangerously about fifteen feet in the air. Clump's eyes quickly scanned the room for something to use that could free the cage, as the iron bar was useless. He spotted a large hook embedded deep into the wall. In a flash he leapt into the air and grabbed the underside of the cage. He pushed the metal bar inside and then forced his fingers through the gap until he felt the soft underside of Horith's foot. He ticked the pink flesh with his fingertips until Horith stirred into life and Clump, using his great bulk and weight, began swinging the cage towards the wall. Gaining momentum, he managed to grab the hook with his spare hand whilst at the same time holding onto the cage.

"Get out of there," Clump bellowed and Horith sprang into action, grabbing the metal rod to prise open the bars. Using his good hand and both his feet he was able to make a hole just big enough to squeeze his mighty frame through. He jumped down from the cage and onto the ledge, just as Clump let go.

The cage smashed against the wall and the chain broke, the cage falling through the murder hole. Clump dived out of the way and then they were both racing along the corridor and down the stone steps, three at a time. They ran so fast everything became a blur, but then Clump caught sight of a flash of colour from out of the corner of his eye. It was like nothing he'd ever seen before and he stopped dead in his tracks, his eyes unable to comprehend what they saw.

There, just to the left of him in the doorway of the second tower was a flame of fire. The blaze was the colours of orangey-red and a multitude of burning tongues licked viciously at the wood. Clump continued to stare. Something wasn't right; the flames didn't look real as though they were simply an illusion. An object moved inside the doorway and that was when he saw it ... a huge golden wolf surrounded by burning flame, yet seemingly unharmed. Clump was stunned for he had never seen anything so beautiful yet equally terrifying. He caught the wolf's attention unable to break its gaze. He was transfixed and then, to add to his confusion, the wolf bowed its head and lowered its front paws. Clump understood this to be a sign of respect and, intrigued, he took a hesitant step forward but then Horith grabbed his tunic and pulled him behind a stack of broken barrels.

"What do you think you're doing?" he hissed, grabbing his arm to make him turn to face him. "Are you trying to get us both killed?"

"Didn't you see it?" Clump whispered in reply, pointing to the doorway, his eyes wide with disbelief.

"See what?" Horith snapped, pushing Clump's head down, closer to the ground.

"The wolf?"

"No, was it your father?"

"No, of course not."

"Then it must have been a common wolf, there's lots of them around these parts."

"No, there was certainly nothing common about it."

"What do you mean?"

"It was gold and on fire."

Horith's eyes fixed on his.

"Are you serious?"

"Yes, totally, and the really weird thing is that it was as though the fire was emanating from the actual wolf."

Horith licked his lips. "I've never heard of such a wolf," he declared, and, after checking the coast was clear, dragged Clump away from the tower.

They headed straight to the courtyard but to their dismay they saw the Nonhawks were coming back to life and neither the witch nor Serpen were anywhere to be seen.

"It looks as though the spell has broken and my father's got away," Clump said, both relieved and dismayed at the same time. His eyes continued to scan the area, until he saw Torolf, Crowle and Ettin were still lying where they fell.

He turned to Horith and placed his hand on his shoulder.

"Horith, There's something I must tell you."

Horith went to shake his hand away.

"Not more about the wolf," he said, sounding slightly irritated.

Clump held him firmly, until he looked him in the eye.

"Come on, what is it?" Horith urged, "we need to get out of here!"

Clump found it hard to swallow.

"It's your father, I'm afraid he didn't make it."

Didn't make it? What are you talking about?"

"He was part of the hunting party that came to save you but he was taken down by the Nonhawks when we first entered the courtyard."

Clump watched the blood drain from his companion's face.

"What? But how?"

"It was a trap, as soon as we entered the Nonhawks attacked."

"So where is he now?" asked Horith, his eyes shining with unshed tears.

"He's lying over there."

Clump pointed to the centre of the courtyard and Horith peered over.

Within seconds he fell back and pushed his good hand into his mouth, trying his best not to let out the wail of anguish that bubbled up into his throat. Clump pulled him to his chest and held him tight.

"I'm so, so, sorry," he whispered, holding his friend even tighter when the tears began to fall.

"We need to leave, I'm afraid there's nothing more we can do," Clump said, his voice raw with emotion and Horith pulled away, his eyes all red and puffy. He nodded, wiping his runny nose with the fur from his forearms.

"Yes, you're right, let's go," he croaked, and he checked it was safe to leave. Clump watched him with a heavy heart. He felt sad at having to leave Torolf and the others behind but he knew there was nothing they could do. Horith signalled the coast was clear and they both shot out, heading for the main gate. Clump was surprised to see the Nonhawks appeared dazed, some staggering around whilst others seemed to be asleep on the floor. Clump clung closely to the outer wall, careful not to be seen. He spotted the two soldiers who guarded the main entrance, busy checking the dead for anything valuable and he realised this was their one and only chance to escape.

To his surprise, a fanfare blew out from one of the turrets and all the Nonhawks who were awake staggered forward to form a line in the centre of the courtyard. Clump and Horith seized the moment and bolted for the gate. With the Nonhawks attention elsewhere, they slid past the portcullis and made it through without being seen. Once free, they ran as fast as their legs would carry them towards the trees and when they reached the woods, they lay low, hidden within the tall grasses until the moon rose high in the sky and they were able to run back to their village as wolves.

Chapter 8

Clump returned home but now he was standing inside his father's cave, surrounded by a lot of angry faces. Almost the entire tribe had turned out to meet him when he returned with Horith but, surprisingly, he did not receive a hero's welcome as he'd expected. Instead, he found himself in a serious predicament. His father had fled the castle believing his son to have simply run off like a common yellow belly, leaving Serpen to defend himself. Of course, he could not have been further from the truth yet it appeared that no one, except his mother and sisters, believed Clump's side of the story.

Serpen circled him, his eyes never leaving his face.

"You abandoned me!" he declared, pointing an accusing finger. "You left King Forusian's castle without knowing whether I was dead or alive."

Clump didn't know what to say, he'd never expected to be treated in such a cold manner by his own father.

"No, wait, you know I would never do that. I just assumed you'd already escaped the castle."

"Liar."

"No, I'm not! I managed to save Horith and when I made my way into the courtyard you were nowhere to be seen so I thought you had made it out safely."

"You're lying, I can see it in your eyes," Serpen persisted, his mouth turning down with distaste. "You left me there to rot, your own father!"

"No! Why would I?" Clump insisted. "You know I would never do anything like that to you and anyway, you're here safe and well aren't you?"

Serpen continued to glare at him, refusing to answer his question.

"So, tell me, how *did* you manage to save Horith when everywhere in the castle was chaotic?" he hissed, his nostrils flaring. "The last time I saw you I was completely surrounded by Nonhawks and Torolf, Crowle and Ettin were lying dead on the ground. Do you think me a fool and expect me to believe that you

74

managed to sneak past the guards, make it inside the murder holes and free Horith without my knowledge?"

Clump felt the blood drain from his face. Hearing it said like that, out loud and in the open, did make him sound rather guilty. Clump thought his version of events did seem a little sketchy in places, but he was also aware he couldn't tell anyone about the pact he'd made with the witch. His lips were well and truly sealed and, even if he did tell Serpen what actually happened, would he really believe him? His mind was scrambled and his thoughts kept returning to that fateful day inside Forusian's castle. He knew if he hadn't met the witch they would surely all be dead and if he didn't wish to endure her wrath he had no choice but to keep his mouth shut.

His refusal to tell them all what really happened sealed his fate.

"It's just as I suspected," Serpen bellowed. "Horith escaped during all the confusion and now he is merely protecting you."

"No, that's not true!" Horith shouted, jumping to his feet, "Clump entered the murder hole and saved my life."

"Silence," Serpen snapped, his eyes glowing dangerously. "We have always known you blamed my mother for the loss of your hand and I guess this was the perfect revenge."

Clump watched the colour drain from Horith's face.

"What do you mean?" he gasped. "I have never blamed anyone but myself for the loss of my limb."

Serpen shook his head and pointed an accusing finger towards him.

"I am not an idiot. I can see perfectly well how your mind works. You simply met up with Clump on your way back to the Canyon and you both tried to save his skin by hatching out this poor excuse of a plan."

"No, that's not what happened," said Horith, his eyes pleading, "why won't you believe me?"

"Because I can always tell a conspiracy when I see one."

"There is no conspiracy, we simply thought you had gotten away!"

"Enough I say, I will not stand here and listen to any more of your lies."

Zebulon, the Elder with the mane of white, rose to his feet. His face was without emotion and his cold eyes stared vacantly at Horith. In his hand he held a ceremonial spear and he raised it in the air and pointed it towards his chest.

"Horith, son of Torolf. Because your father fought bravely and laid down his life to save our leader, we are willing to show you leniency in his memory. However, be aware that should you ever try to betray one of us again then let it be known that you will be banished from the Canyon and never allowed to return."

Lyra, who had been seated next to Isis, gave a pitiful roar. An outcry from a few of the females was quickly silenced when Serpen turned and glared at them. "Do not interfere with things that do not concern you," he spat, staring each one down. "I warn you all, do not protest too loudly or next time you could find yourself helping him to pack." No one made a murmur and all eyes turned back to the tribal Elder. Zebulon nodded to the chief before pointing the spear towards Clump.

"Clump, you are the chief's only son and therefore the crimes against you are far greater. I have spoken to your father at great length. I believe what he says to be true and the sheer fact that you left the castle without first finding the chief has shown you to be a great coward. You were born to be a leader yet you shy away from responsibility. You have shown immense weakness and we cannot have you tainting the younger males with your cowardice. We have come to a decision, and the penalty for your crime against your own flesh and blood will be ... death!"

A gasp left the crowd and Clump stared in disbelief at his father. Surely there had to be a mistake? No matter what happened, Serpen would not wish to see him dead.

Isis sprung on her feet like a cat on hot bricks.

"No! Please, he's innocent," she screamed and in a flash, Serpen's hand shot out like a viper. He grabbed her by the throat. "Get out of here before I decide to let you join him," he hissed, pushing her closer to the door. Isis's hands flew to her neck and she grappled at his fingers which pressed down on her airway.

He pushed her between the hides and threw her onto the ground outside. Isis gasped for breath when he let go of her and she recoiled when Serpen continued to tower above her.

76

"From this moment on you are no longer my lifelong mate," he declared. "You gave me a son that was weak and pathetic yet I need an heir who is fit to be chief. I will go and find myself a new mate, one that is fit for purpose. Our home is no longer yours so you had better hope someone is willing to take you in or you will soon be rich pickings for the mountain trolls."

"But Serpen ... I don't ..."

"Shut up. I don't wish to hear your whining voice ever again. You have done me a great wrong by giving me a son such as Clump."

"But he is a good son," Isis argued, and she lifted her head, her eyes connecting with his.

Serpen's nostrils flared in anger. "He's no son of mine. I was foretold by the Gods that his destiny would rest in my hands and I choose to see him punished for his crimes against me."

"No! You mustn't do this," she begged and she flung herself at his feet. "Think what you are saying. Clump would never betray you."

Serpen kicked dirt in her face. "You are a fool if you believe that," he mocked, turning away.

By now almost everyone had left the cave and Clump was brought out with two young males standing either side of him. Surprisingly, he wasn't tied up and Isis suddenly jumped to her feet, screaming at the top of her voice, "Run! Clump, run!"

Clump stared at his mother and saw raw terror had turned her skin deathly pale. He dithered, realising she was trying to save him, but he didn't want to leave, not like this. He came to his senses and before anyone managed to grab him, bolted, Isis still screaming for him to run for his life. He ran like a hunted animal, zigzagging across the ground, trying to lose the two scouts that chased after him. He instinctively headed for a thin line of trees, refusing to stop running even when he reached them and strong branches whipped at his bare legs.

Blind with fear he kept on going, only glancing over his shoulder once. To his dismay, Serpen had overtaken the scouts and was now close on his heels, his powerful legs closing the gap between them.

Clump felt his own terror rise in his throat. The scouts would most probably fall back now his father was on his tail and he knew if Serpen caught him, he would kill him right there where he stood. In desperation he scanned the horizon for a place in which to escape, spotting a small overhanging rock face. He raced towards it, his feet climbing the lower slabs of stone until his hands could grasp the rock. His fingers searched for finger pockets or small edges and, almost apelike, his strong arms pulled him further out of harm's way. A high scream almost split his ears and Clump closed his eyes, aware it was his father's frustration breaking free. He unconsciously bit his lip but this time he didn't look back. Instead he focused on getting away, his eyes lifting towards the sky where he hoped he could find a way to escape. The sun was fierce, beating down on his back, but Clump didn't waver when the sweat poured down his face. The fear of being caught by his father was enough to make him stay focused, wiping the beads of sweat away with the back of his hand. He climbed steadily, his agility and balance almost perfect for one who was seen to be blighted by such a cumbersome body.

Exhausted, Clump reached the summit and was able to drag himself over the ledge. He lay face down in the dirt, the pain in his lungs almost unbearable. He waited until his heart had finished pounding and then he struggled to his feet. He was bone weary but alert enough to still be on his guard. His legs were like dead weights but he dragged his feet to the very edge of the rock to peer over in search of Serpen. His eyes scanned in-between the cracks and crevices for any sign of him. He studied the terrain for a glimpse of his father but he could see nothing. He continued to stare for several minutes, convinced he would spot him soon enough. He then gave a huge sigh of relief when there was clearly no sign of him and he almost managed a smile. He half turned, the adrenalin beginning to wear off when a dark shadow crossed his face.

Clump looked up and his features froze. Serpen stood right in front of him.

He had never seen him look so angry, saliva frothing at his mouth and his father snarled, baring his teeth, his lips thick and fleshy.

Clump felt his legs buckle.

"How ... how... did you ...," he gasped, but before he could finish his sentence, Serpen lashed out with one of his mighty fists. His knuckles connected with Clump's jaw and blood spurted from his lips. Before he could recover, Clump felt a second strike knock him off his feet. In a flash Serpen was upon him, his gigantic hands tightened around his throat, throttling him.

Already winded, Clump gasped for air, whilst a constellation of shooting stars formed in front of his eyes. He tried in desperation to pull his father's hands away from his throat but he was far too strong. Darkness crept into his mind, unaware his eyes were rolling to the back of head. His body turned limp and his mind ran towards unconsciousness but then, the tightness around his throat eased and he was suddenly gasping for air.

Someone turned the lights back on, causing a stream of tears to run down his cheeks. He thought he saw his father slump forward and he felt a dead weight drop across his chest.

Coughing and spluttering, Clump managed to sit up. He glanced downwards to see his father's somewhat unresponsive body lying across him. Clump caught a sudden movement and he let out a yelp, realising there was someone else there on the ledge with him. Confused, Clump's fear return and he looked around for one of the scouts.

He tried to shield his eyes, shocked to find a thin old man standing in front of him instead. He was dressed in simple white robes and, like many mountain folk, wore a cloth bag over his shoulder. In his hand he held a smooth rod that looked to be made of acacia. Clump thought the man to be very old, aged perhaps a few hundred years or more. His hair was surprisingly dark for his age, black skin and eyes as white as milk. On his chin sat a small tuft of bristles that really couldn't be called a beard. The hairs were as grey as the morning mist and looked rather odd against the dark colour of his skin. Clump had never seen anyone with so many wrinkles before, not even the ancient females had such lines across their faces and this made it hard for him to get to grips with the fact that this old man had somehow saved him from the clutches of his father.

"Do not fear me for I will not harm you," said the stranger, clearly able to read the young Windigo's thoughts.

His words had the adverse effect.

"Who ... who ... are you?" Clump stammered, finally wriggling free of the dead weight that pinned him down on the ground. A barrage of stones and pebbles fell over the cliff behind him with a clatter.

"The ledge is struggling to bear such immense weight so I suggest you stay very still if you value your life," commanded the old man, changing the subject.

Clump turned his head and saw the stranger spoke the truth. Hairline fractures had appeared on the surface of the upper rock face.

In a flash, the stranger grabbed Clump's ankles and dragged him to safety. Leaving Serpen slumped in the dirt.

"Don't worry, we'll get him to safety too," said the old man, his face grim. "My name is Bruis and if you wish to live past this day then you had better come with me."

Clump simply stared at Bruis, realising he didn't really have a choice. He was well aware what awaited him should his father regain consciousness and so he nodded his compliance. Bruis stood over him and offered his hand and although he was filled with despondency, Clump allowed the stranger to help him to his feet.

"I know a place far from here where you will be safe," Bruis announced, pointing west. "It's a long way over yonder and through the forbidden mountain pass and it will take us many days."

"Are we going as far as the Black Mountains?" Clump asked, aghast.

Bruis tried to smile, showing shrinking gums and a few yellowing teeth.

"Much further afield than that I'm afraid," he replied.

Clump nodded, and then he helped Bruis drag his father to safety before he took one last look at him. He felt a pang of desolation, aware he would probably never see any of his family again. He loved them with all his heart yet he was aware of the consequences should he try to return to his village. It was obvious that after today he was seen as an outcast. He took a deep breath;

he'd never really fitted in anyway. Now the tribe wanted him dead there was no turning back. With a heavy heart, Clump followed Bruis away from his father and the only life he'd ever known.

Chapter 9

The mountain pass was like a long, twisted snake. In the distance, more mountains lay ahead, with their white peaks shining against a sky of pale blue.

The path they followed was thin and dangerous. Clump could see how, over many centuries, the wind and rain had eroded away a huge part of the trail, making it extremely perilous to use.

Bruis explained to Clump that going through the pass was the only way to keep Serpen at bay and Clump agreed. By the end of the first day they had travelled a considerable distance and by twilight they were thankful to find a cave in which they could camp for the night.

"We need shelter and this is perfect," said Bruis, when he spotted a large crevice which led inside the mountain. He was of slim build and slipped through easily, but Clump, being considerably larger, struggled. His rounded belly got stuck between a sliver of rock and he endured a lot of huffing and puffing until he managed to wriggle inside. Within the cave the roof was low and both Clump and Bruis had to stoop their heads but it was warm and dry inside.

"This will do nicely," said Bruis with a smile.

Clump decided he liked Bruis. There was a kindness in his manner and he appeared gentle and understanding. He sensed he was powerful and thought he was most probably a magician. He was a little terrified at this thought though; aware, after listening to the tales of the Elders, that to upset a magician could prove to be very unwise.

Bruis set about lighting a fire. There wasn't much in the cave except a few twigs blown in through time, yet this seemed enough for Bruis. He had no tools to light a fire but when Clump came to sit beside him he was surprised to see small flames leaping into life by his feet.

"How did you do that?" asked Clump, rather impressed, and his eyes shone with delight.

"I know a few tricks." Bruis chuckled and Clump relaxed, feeling safe.

"Why did you help me, earlier on the ridge?" he suddenly blurted.

Bruis stared into the flames.

"What else was I supposed to do?" he replied with a shrug. "I was heading back towards the mountains when I came across you. I knew it was dangerous to try and split up the fight, but seeing as your father was practically throttling you, I felt I had no choice but to knock him unconscious and save you."

"But how did you stop him? I mean, all I remember is his great weight pinning me to the ground."

Bruis looked away from the fire, but the flames still danced in his eyes.

"Why, I hit him with my rod of course. 'Clunk' right at the back of the head." He gave another chuckle. "My rod is enchanted and although I am not a magician, I know how to use its power."

"Really?" said Clump, lifting an eyebrow. "So if you're not a magician, then what are you?"

"Oh, don't you know? I'm a Plainwalker. I tend the lands and gardens of all the realms."

"How is that even possible?" asked Clump, scratching his head in puzzlement.

Bruis sighed. "It isn't easy I can assure you. My job is to look after the crops and flowers of all the lands and as long as I do so they will prosper. If I fail and the crops die, then there will be famine throughout the kingdoms."

"Wow, that sounds very important."

"Yes, I guess it is," nodded Bruis with a grin. "However, I'm all but one of the brothers belonging to Mother Nature."

"What? Do you mean there are more like you?"

"Why, yes, of course, who do you think looks after the sea and turns day into night?"

Clump raised both of his hairy eyebrows at once. "Well, I guess I've never really given it much thought," he admitted, staring towards the crevice and out at the looming darkness to catch a glimpse of the sky.

Silence blanketed them both until Bruis cleared his throat.

"So now you know who I am, perhaps it would be better for me to know a little more about you."

Clump pulled a face and for the thousandth time that day, wished he could just go home.

"There isn't much to tell," he said, drawing his knees to his chest. It was obvious he didn't really want to talk about his life, but he knew it would appear rude not to.

As if the Plainwalker had read his thoughts he said, "I do understand it is very painful for you to speak of your past but if we are to become friends I need to learn everything there is about you."

Clump couldn't help but think about the family he'd been forced to leave behind. A stream of tears trickled down his face the moment he thought about his mother and his two dear sisters. He tried to pull himself together, wiping his eyes dry with the short sleeve of his tunic. He sniffed loudly, finding it hard not to cry, the pain in his heart unbearable.

"I can see you love your family very much," said Bruis gently, "and I'm sorry that I have asked you to reveal such things that are clearly painful to you; however, if we are to travel together I do not wish to learn of any nasty surprises on the way."

Clump understood Bruis's dilemma and tried to smile, exposing his sharp, white teeth.

"I understand what you're saying," he said with a nod, "and I will tell you as much as I can about myself."

Bruis appeared satisfied and remained silent whilst Clump talked of his life in the Canyon. The Windigo left not a stone unturned in his life story, telling the Plainwalker about his inability to eat meat and how he did not like to hurt people, unlike the rest of his kind. His words spilled from his mouth like wine, however, when he came to the part about the castle, he didn't break his promise to the witch and so he did not mention the deal he made with her. He could not bring himself to speak of her at all, but he did explain the consequences of leaving his father in the courtyard and why he had ended up in such a predicament.

Clump was relieved when Bruis did not press him for any further information. It was late and the moon was rising.

"I will have to leave you soon," Clump declared, pulling a solemn expression.

Bruis caught his eye. "I'm not afraid, therefore you can stay here by the fire tonight if you so wish."

Clump almost choked in surprise. "Are you mad?" he gasped. "Why, I might kill you in your sleep or tear you limb from limb."

Bruis let out a chortle. "I feel that would be highly unlikely," he said, opening his bag to reveal two shiny apples.

"Here," he said, throwing one to Clump. "It isn't much, but it will keep hunger at bay until morning."

Clump stared at the luscious red apple. He had never seen one before and he brought it to his nose and sniffed. A sweet aroma filled his nostrils, causing his mouth to water, and so he bit into the outer skin. The juice of the apple shot from his lips, running down his chin and Clump giggled like a child, wiping the trail away before taking another bite.

"Mmm, tastes real good," he mumbled.

Bruis's shoulders shook up and down as he laughed. "Yes, so I see," he acknowledged, and he threw a second apple towards him. Clump caught it with his free hand and gave him a confused look.

"You can have it," Bruis insisted, digging deeper inside the bag, "I have plenty more where that came from."

Later, they both settled down for the night and it appeared that once Bruis fell asleep there was no waking him. As the hours ticked by Clump became fidgety, fretting over his transformation. He was scared he might attack Bruis in his sleep, not sure how he would feel once the change had taken place. He'd never been within a mile of any magical folk before except for his experience at the castle and when hunting with his father.

He decided to leave the cave and venture outside. On his tiptoes he quietly left Bruis's side and pushed his way out of the cave. It was raining and he cursed the weather but he knew that once he turned he would not mind the rain so much. His thick fur would shield him from the cold and so he stood a while and watched the moon turn into a bright silver disc. He felt the first tingle of his transformation as soon as the clouds gathered across the moon's surface. He gave a heavy sigh, aware it was time. His change started with a sudden tic above his right eye and then saliva filled his mouth and he had to concentrate hard not to vomit. He then saw bright, silver stars behind his eyes and his vision blurred. Pain snaked down his face and he felt his neck contract. His oesophagus constricted and he automatically brought his hands to his throat, unable to breathe.

He sank down onto the path; the dirt cool beneath his feet. He wished with all his heart he did not have to go through this terrible ordeal each and every night. An agonising sensation shot down his back and, wracked with pain, he bent over on all fours. Unconsciously he let out a howl as his vertebrae crushed together to reshape his backbone. When his ribs broke, he was convinced he was about to die. His mouth felt as though it was filled with sand and his mind could only think of washing it all away. Fire travelled down each of his limbs, and he stared towards the ground and saw black claws tearing through his bloodied hands.

It took less than thirty seconds for Clump to turn into a timber wolf, yet to him it felt like an eternity. The pain that wracked his body finally eased and, like the tide, slowly ebbed away. Clump lifted his head and let out a long, pitiful howl which echoed across the mountains. With the transformation complete, he was soon able to grasp his bearings and he trotted away from the cave, his paws moving silently in the dirt. He didn't intend to go far but he wanted to keep a safe distance between himself and the Plainwalker. Although he didn't want to believe he could hurt him, he found he couldn't trust himself – not completely.

He understood his mind wasn't quite his own as a wolf and sometimes he woke up to find himself in a different place to where he remembered. He once found a few feathers lying close to his feet, a broken wing discarded on the ground. Its tiny bones were protruding where it had once been attached to a body and he had been sickened by it. He had licked his lips to check if he could taste blood in his mouth but he couldn't taste a thing. He was scared that he had eaten the bird without knowing it. His father had been with him at the time and he had laughed when he saw him checking for feathers in his mouth.

"Who cares who has eaten the bird," he roared, "it's not as though it was big enough to have touched the sides of your stomach!"

Clump had remained silent and didn't speak about the matter again but the doubt had always remained. He trotted on, the rain having ceased, and with his exceptional eyesight Clump could see in the distance what looked to be a puddle of water. He licked his lips in anticipation of quenching his thirst.

He slinked over and bent his head, his tongue already lapping up the icy droplets. Then he heard a noise that sounded like something breaking away from the side of the mountain. He lifted his head and shook the last drops of water from his muzzle. Another sound caught his attention and his ears pricked up as a large boulder tumbled from high above. It fell down the mountain with terrific speed. Clump jumped out of the way, broken trees and debris following right behind and the boulder cracked on impact. It fell no more than twenty feet from where Clump stood and he took a cautious step closer and sniffed the air.

Something wasn't right, the boulder didn't smell like stone. In a flash the giant piece of rock reached out and tried to grab him and it was then that Clump saw that it wasn't a boulder at all but a mountain troll. The rock lifted from the ground and a set of thick, hairy legs appeared. Startled, Clump turned tail and ran back towards the cave. He was fast on his feet and he fled but the troll, although heavy and cumbersome, didn't give up and chased Clump back up the mountain pass.

Clump shot into the cave, his feet skidding in the dirt. He opened his mouth and gave a loud howl of distress.

*

Bruis awoke with a start. He sat up poker straight to stare into the amber eyes of a timber wolf. Surprised to see a wolf standing before him, he quickly grabbed his wits and reached for his bag and acacia rod. He jumped to his feet. "What's the matter, Clump?" he asked, "has your father stumbled upon our hideout?"

Clump turned his head towards the opening to the cave just as the earth beneath their feet shook. Bruis instantly understood what the earthquake meant. "It's a mountain troll," he gasped, aware that should it reach them, it would swallow them whole as though they were little more than titbits.

"Okay, I've got this," said Bruis, trying to keep calm whilst looking around for a means of escape. A noise of rock being torn away reached his ears and he saw the troll pulling at the crevice, breaking off huge chunks of rock with his gigantic hands.

"Oh no, that's not good," Bruis wailed, and then a hand was thrust inside and troll fingers searched blindly. Clump raised his hackles, snarled and snapped his jaws.

"Like that's going to do any good against a troll," Bruis proclaimed, rolling his eyes. "Look, even if you managed to sink your teeth into one of those solid fingers of his, it would be as though you'd simply jabbed him with a fork. No, I know what we must do. My rod has the power to create a hole in the wall, however, the only problem with that is we won't know where it will lead."

Clump turned back towards him, cocking his head to one side.

"Alright, don't look at me like that! I can see for myself it's our only way out of here."

Clump suddenly yelped causing Bruis to glance across to see the troll had caught hold of the tip of the wolf's tail. Without a second thought, he dashed forward, hitting the troll's fingers with his rod causing a sound like a hammer hitting stone to ricochet around the cave. The troll let go, roaring in pain but then he gave a cry of fury and started to use both fists to smash the stone until the entranceway crumbled. Another mighty blow saw a hole appear, big enough for his shoulder to squeeze through.

Bruis gulped, dashing to the back of the cave he used his rod to scratch out the shape of an archway onto the surface of the rock. As though it was charcoal, he brushed the tip along the stone, colouring in the hole as though he was an artist creating his first ever masterpiece.

The moment the drawing was complete Bruis called out to Clump to come to him and the Plainwalker stepped inside the black hole. Within seconds Clump was at his side and so Bruis used the palm of his hand to rub away the entrance. The hole disappeared and they were soon cocooned in darkness.

"Phew, that was close," Bruis said, noticing they were in a tunnel. He glanced at Clump to see his two amber eyes shining in the darkness. The Plainwalker stared ahead and to his surprise, saw a luminous glow radiating in the distance. Like a blind man, he used his fingertips to help guide him along the passageway, heading towards the rather eerie, green light. He felt earth beneath his fingers and realised they were in some kind of burrow. Deeper they travelled until the path widened and the source of the glow became clear. To his dismay, he found the walls crawling with thousands of minute glow worms, each emanating a pale light the colour of topaz. The worms throbbed and thrashed about, some in bunches whilst others, in their solitude, left only a trail of slime behind.

Although he was grateful for the light, Bruis hated being so close to such writhing creatures. He felt as though their grub-like bodies were reaching out to try and touch him. He saw, to his horror, that a mass of worms had fallen to the floor and he cringed inside when he felt the squelch of their bodies beneath his feet.

He peered ahead for a way out when the light from a swinging lantern caught his eye.

"Oh no, I thought it was too good to be true, he said, patting Clump lightly on his back. "It appears we've jumped out of the frying pan and into the fire," he whispered, and there, heading towards them, were three rather furious Dwarfits.

Chapter 10

Serpen was seething. He awoke with a terrible headache when a light rain began to fall and darkness was descending upon the Canyon. He couldn't remember everything that had happened, but a lump, as big as a Basilisk's egg, protruded from the back of his skull. He was confused as to who had hit him, aware it couldn't have been Clump because his hands were busy around his throat when everything around him went black. As the rain washed his face and refreshed his skin, his mind cleared, analysing the last encounter with his son. It was obvious someone had crept up from behind and hit him over the head with a blunt instrument. His mind eliminated the scouts. They wouldn't dare touch a single hair on his head let alone interfere between a father and his son. No, it had to have been Horith or perhaps even Isis. His eyes narrowed. Who else would be foolish enough to dare lay a finger on him?

Inside his darkened heart, a vile bitterness grew at what he saw as treachery. He would find out who had betrayed him and when he did ... they would pay dearly. He wiped the drizzle away from his lids and began his descent down from the ridge, heading back to the village. He didn't bother to look for Clump. He wasn't stupid. He knew he'd be long gone by now. As he jumped from rock to rock, he pondered over how he would explain him getting away. He didn't want to admit that he had been knocked unconscious; he felt this would make him look inadequate. In the eyes of the Elders, if he couldn't kill his own son, he would appear weak and this would lead to discontent within the tribe. He decided he would say nothing, letting everyone assume Clump was dead and he would only reveal the truth once he had found the culprit who had allowed him to escape. This thought cheered his frozen heart a little. Yes, he would let them all believe Clump was dead, including Isis.

He returned to his village just as the moon peered through an array of thickening cloud. When he arrived home, he was met by lots of curious faces but none dared ask him whether Clump was dead or alive.

He headed towards his cave. He was aware he would soon face questioning by the Elders and sure enough, Zebulon came towards him from out of the darkness. After years of living in dim caves, his vision had weakened but he was known to have a keen sense of smell which had grown more acute with age. Zebulon lifted his head and began sniffing the air. He took a step closer, opened his mouth and bellowed like a banshee, the sound shattering the peaceful silence. Serpen froze, his muscles tensing like the rocky ridge he'd just left. He found he couldn't move, taken by complete surprise at the Elder's unexpected outburst. He'd never seen Zebulon behave so fiercely towards another tribe member, not in all the years he'd known him, and the muscles in his jaw twitched when he unconsciously clenched his teeth together.

For one so old, Zebulon appeared to lunge towards him, his long face twisted with utter despair.

"What have you done?" he almost screamed in his face.

Still shocked, Serpen took a step back; no one had ever dared speak to him this way before and he could see Zebulon's eyes burning with what looked to be a combination of fear mixed with anguish.

The village must have heard the commotion because when he glanced over his shoulder, he saw several males heading towards them. His mouth twisted into a bitter line. He didn't wish to explain himself to anyone, not now, not until he knew for sure who had allowed Clump to go free. Misreading the look in Zebulon's eyes, he thought the Elder was angry because he had not brought back Clump's body. Without saying a word he turned on his heels and, with his head held high, headed back to his cave.

He pushed aside the hides and entered, surprised to see the reed stalks were not lit and the fire out. He cursed under his breath when he remembered what he'd said to Isis and his belief of her being a traitor intensified.

He stomped over to the stalks and used the flints stored inside a leather pouch to light them one by one. He heard a commotion and turned to find Zebulon standing behind him.

"What has upset you so much that you would dare to scream at your leader," Serpen demanded angrily.

Zebulon only stared at him, his body heaved and his mouth was turned down in a grim line.

91

"You have gone too far this time," the Elder declared. "Your mother would turn in her grave."

"My mother has no grave!" Serpen retaliated, spitting his words out like a viper, "and what's more, I have only done my duty as your leader."

Zebulon raised his arms into the air and brought them to his chest like a charging ape, his fury seemingly no longer contained and he roared so loudly that Serpen's ears rang.

He lifted his hands to block out the noise that tried to penetrate his skull. The piercing sound appeared to last forever until others came and tried to calm the distraught Elder.

Serpen finally lowered his hands when Zebulon was coaxed into silence. He couldn't understand what had gotten into him. He was always so calm, so composed, yet he was acting like he was crazy. He watched as two more Elders entered and tried to pacify him.

"What's wrong with you, have you completely lost your mind?" Serpen spat, once Zebulon appeared to gain some self-control. "Why, in all the years I have known you I have never seen you act this way!"

Zebulon looked back at him with his small, lifeless eyes. "It's him, I can smell *him* all over you."

"What are you talking about?" Serpen asked in dismay. "Surely you can't mean Clump?"

"No, not Clump. I'm talking about the Plainwalker," Zebulon rasped. "You have angered the God of the Feast and no doubt we will pay dearly for what you have done."

Serpen made to scoff at his remark but a shiver ran down his spine instead and he unconsciously reached up and probed the bump at the back of his head.

"No, that's impossible," he said, almost under his breath. "I would know if a God came anywhere near me."

"Not necessarily, a Plainwalker can move so quickly he's practically invisible to the naked eye. However, one thing is for sure, he always leaves a scent behind."

"What kind of scent?"

"That of rich earth."

"But how can you be so sure?"

"Because the aroma which emanated from your fur when I first approached you was so powerful, it took my breath away. One of the reasons why I was chosen to be an Elder was because of my ability to smell the Gods when they are amongst us."

Serpen's mind shot back to the ridge.

He had been sure that it was just him and Clump out there on the rocks. Usually he could smell anyone coming for miles but now he had to admit that he had been totally unaware they had company. His mind whirled, his brain trying to figure out if he had missed some kind of clue. Either way, surely the God of the Feast would not help Clump escape?

"Tell us, what happened out there?" Zebulon pressed, and Serpen stared back at him, feeling a sense of unease. A shiver wormed down his back but he remained tight lipped. Instead, he crossed the living area, pushing his way past Zebulon and avoiding his burning glare. He went back outside and to his astonishment, saw Isis waiting for him. For a moment he was relieved to see her and he opened his mouth to tell her the fire was already lit but before he could speak, Isis raised her hand and the words died in his throat.

"Where's my son?" she demanded, her voice a harsh whisper.

Serpen glared at her. If she had been the one to hit him over the head at the ridge she would know Clump was still alive. She had never been a good liar and now was a perfect opportunity to see if she was merely playing games with him.

"Your son?" Serpen mocked. "Why, he's lying dead in the Canyon."

Before she could react he reached out and grabbed her arm but she jerked back to force him to let go. He heard her catch her breath, her eyes filling with tears.

"You are nothing more than a vile monster," she cried, holding her stomach as though she was about to be sick. "How could you do such a terrible thing to your own flesh and blood?" He watched her raise her hand to her mouth and realised her fingers were trembling.

For a second he felt regret, sorry he had lied to her, but it was only a fleeting moment of weakness which soon passed.

"I never want to see you again and both myself and your daughters are now staying with Lyra," she hissed, tears spilling down her cheeks.

Serpen frowned but he knew he only had himself to blame. "Why are you telling me this? It's not as if I care," he snapped and he rushed forward, pushing her aside.

Without looking back he headed towards the communal caves. He would show her that he was willing to find himself a worthy mate and have another son. He entered, not too sure where he was going. He'd only ever ventured along this particular chamber once before – during his naming ceremony when he was just two winters old. His own offspring had yet to reach that age and a pang of something he couldn't quite name shot through his heart. His only son would now become nameless, struck from history and in time would become nothing more than a distant memory.

He cleared his mind of such thoughts and entered the chamber. The roof stretched way beyond the reach of the many scattered cooking fires which littered the ground. Stalactites hung from the ceiling in long, thick horns, many lying broken on the floor after being used to stir the cooking pots. A few females stood hunched by the fires, wide eyes reflecting back the twitching flames of their hearths. He walked past the smaller entrances which jutted off and which were used as private warrens for each family. On hearing his footsteps some of the males poked their heads out as he passed, probably fearful someone wanted to steal one of their females.

Serpen gave a smug grin. They were right to be worried.

He continued into the deepest and blackest part of the cavern. A gentle light was shining from a long jagged opening which zigzagged from the ceiling all the way to the floor. Something glowed inside, filtering through the slender crevice. It shimmered, as though the light was bouncing off water and Serpen turned sideways and squeezed his way through.

He entered another cave, the walls slightly narrower and he travelled down a well-worn path, covered in earth and small stones. His eyes soon grew accustomed to the dim light and he carried on until the path widened and a blue glow lit the way. He could hear the flow of water somewhere ahead and a flutter of excitement made the insides of his stomach tremble.

From out of the semi-darkness, echoes of laughter bounced from the walls and velvety whispers soon filled his ears.

"Come and join us," they murmured, "we are more than happy to give you what your heart desires."

Serpen stumbled mid-step. These were the voices of celibate females, those whose fathers kept them hidden inside the cave until they were betrothed.

Their soft laughter teased him from within the darkness.

Serpen hesitated. As leader he could choose as many females as he wanted. However, up until this moment Isis had been more than enough for him. She had been betrothed to him from the day of her birth. She was born a pure blood; therefore she had been a prize worth taking. Unlike the females he was about to meet, Isis would never have to wait long for a mate.

With careful steps Serpen moved around the bend to face a pool with a large black rock in the middle. Sitting in the centre were a handful of young females, quietly washing and grooming one another. His eyes devoured their youth, their innocence and when they saw him a volley of feminine sounds, like laughing hyenas, rose in the air.

He smiled, his eyes widening with pleasure. He had never seen such beauty and was pleased.

A gentle splash made him turn his head and there, swimming towards him was an exceptionally stunning female. She waded out of the water, naked, her thick fur covering her modesty. Serpen caught his breath; he had never seen anything so ravishing. He watched, transfixed as she shook her fur dry. She didn't come to him as he'd expected, instead her fingers reached out for a brush made of porcupine bristles. She sat down on a smooth rock and brushed her coat until it was sleek and smooth. Serpen couldn't take his eyes off her. Her fur reminded him of satin and he thought her beauty alone would be enough to make Isis green with envy. His eyes were drawn to her mouth and he imagined biting her pink flesh. He licked his lips in anticipation, but then a vision of Isis danced before his eyes. He quickly shook his head, determined to disperse her from his thoughts.

The other females swam back to shore, their laughter echoing around them.

"Have you come to find a mate?" one of them asked on reaching the shore. "Only don't be shy," she teased, "that's what we're here for."

"Do tell us your name," called out another with fur the colour of flax.

"You can call me Serpen," he replied, a little sharper than he'd intended.

"What? Does that mean you're our great leader?" she asked, daring to take a step closer.

Serpen nodded and she bowed her head.

"It's an honour to meet you and please, look around and choose your heart's desire."

Serpen glanced over to the young female sitting on the rock.

"I choose you," he said throatily, "what's your name?"

"Greer," she replied, putting down the brush.

He decided her name was like a magic talisman, a soothing balm to his tormented mind. His eyes followed her as she made her way over to where a common smock lay upon a few protruding stones. He watched her dress in the rough, beaded tunic. He gestured with his index finger for her to come to him and she quickly obeyed.

"You belong to me now," he said, offering her his hand and Greer placed her large hand inside his palm. He watched her smile at the others, helpless envy in their stare.

"I will make you very happy," she promised, and she brushed his lower lip with her finger. A faint smile curved his mouth and he shuddered with intense desire. Her scent was driving him wild and he knew how much it would hurt Isis to see them together.

"I have waited for this moment for what seems like a lifetime," Greer said, pulling him close and Serpen grinned, drawing her even closer. She lifted her head so that their chins were touching and then she bit him roughly on the mouth. He turned his head away to hide his smirk, she would do nicely. He would simply play with her until he grew tired of her or until Isis begged him to take her back. Then, when he'd had enough, he would take Greer into the Canyon and kill her. He chuckled to himself, he liked his plan – a lot. So, with his arm wrapped around his new mate, he guided her towards the light and out of the chamber.

Chapter 11

Clump had never actually seen Dwarfits before, although he knew them by a different name, he called them Thumpers. They were strange magical folk who lived deep inside the mountains and always out of sight. They looked like dwarves, with small, short limbs and long scraggy beards but they also had the largest, hairiest feet ever seen. When in danger, they thumped the ground like rabbits, warning others they were in trouble and this was how they kept each another safe from harm.

Bruis was doing his best, trying to keep everyone calm, talking to the Dwarfits in a quiet, controlled manner, but it didn't appear to be working.

"Now let's not get upset," he said in a smooth tone. "I understand we must have given you a bit of a fright turning up unannounced, but we had found ourselves in a bit of a predicament."

One of the Dwarfits shuffled closer and Clump growled, showing off a perfect set of white fangs.

"Oh, let's not be upsetting our new friends," Bruis scolded, tapping Clump lightly on the nose. Clump wasn't too pleased about him doing that. Since transmuting into a wolf he was actually quite proud of the fact that he hadn't tried to hurt anyone and didn't appreciate being told off for protect them both.

The Plainwalker turned his attention back to one of the Thumpers who had a head of white hair and whose foot was raised off the floor.

"No! Please don't be so hasty! We truly don't mean you any harm, we were just running away from a mighty troll," he explained, trying to make the Dwarfit see sense.

The white-haired man glared at them with suspicious eyes.

"So how did you get in 'ere then?" he demanded, folding his arms across his chest, his foot poised in the air.

"I'm afraid to say that I was forced to use magic," Bruis confessed. "I know none of us are supposed to create spells outside of our own realms but well – sometimes needs must."

The Dwarfit appeared pacified with his answer and lowered his foot.

"So where're you from?" he asked with a grunt.

Bruis appeared to ponder over his question and then he said, "I'm a Plainwalker, so I'm pretty much from ... everywhere."

Another Thumper, dressed in a green smock and with a head of thick, dark locks, decided to intervene.

"Do you have a name?" he interjected, his eyes bright with interest.

"Yes, of course, it's Bruis and this is my companion ... Clump."

All three Thumpers turned towards the wolf and Clump saw them give a shudder.

It was clear Bruis had seen their reaction because he said, "I can assure you he looks far more dangerous than he really is." He gave a wiry smile.

"Well, he doesn't look very friendly to me," announced the last of the Dwarfits. He was dressed in a large red tunic, a thick leather belt fastened around his waist. He had no hair at all on the top of his head yet it was touching his shoulders everywhere else.

"No, he's just like the rest of us, relatively harmless as long as he's not hungry," Bruis insisted, letting out a slight chuckle.

The Thumper wearing red finally smiled.

"I'm Bodwin," he said at last. "This 'ere's Todwin and next to him is my other brother, Rodwin," he explained, pointing to both of his siblings.

"Ah, so you're triplets," said Bruis, rather jovially. "How wonderful, however, I must say, is there any chance we can get away from these damned glow worms, this sickly green is starting to make me want to vomit."

Bodwin, Todwin and Rodwin gave a loud chortle and turned to face the opposite end of the tunnel. "Step this way, but no funny business mind," said Rodwin, setting off at a fast pace. As he moved he waddled from side to side a bit like a duck, clearly doing his best not to trip over his own two feet. Bodwin dressed in red and Todwin in blue followed close behind.

Bruis bent slightly and tickled Clump's ear.

"We don't want to frighten them again, so no more growling," he said, in whispered tones. "It's a miracle we've made it this far without them thumping for backup."

Clump stared back at him with his two amber eyes, letting out a low whine.

"Good, that's settled then," said Bruis, patting him between the ears, "let's get moving, we don't want to get left behind."

The three mountain Dwarfits were moving fairly rapidly considering their cumbersome feet. Heading down from the tunnel they didn't stop until the glow worms could no longer be used as light. Instead, they reached a place where yet another lantern hung on the wall, the soft glow highlighting several large barrels filled to the brim with wriggling glow worms.

"We trade these throughout the mountain," Todwin explained, sticking his hand inside one of the caskets and grabbing a handful. Clump heard some of the little critters squelch between his fingers and he watched the Dwarfit thrust a writhing mass into his mouth.

Under all that fur Clump blanched.

Todwin was oblivious to his discomfort as he sucked in a squirming body from between his lips. "Mmm, this batch is very juicy and will bring a pretty penny," he said, munching noisily. Clump glanced up at Bruis, thinking he looked a tad green around the gills.

Clump couldn't imagine eating anything so gross, deciding that no matter how hungry he ever became, he would never lower himself to digest any type of worm.

The Dwarfits didn't linger, travelling down yet another tunnel until the mountain spread before them like a vast open plain. Below lay a connection of underground tunnels and burrows, above them long winding paths cut out of the rock with strong wooden bridges and thick ropes hanging by invisible bonds. A spiral staircase, hundreds of feet in the air, loomed in the very centre. Clump stopped in his tracks, lifting a paw as he stood transfixed.

To him it was like a magnificent wonderland, and he could see the mountain was a hive of activity. There were hundreds, no thousands, of magical folk going about their daily tasks. Most were Dwarfits but he could see mountain dwellers such as mining trolls and Gremlins, all busily going about their business. Clump suddenly gave a whine. He felt a little uneasy, especially when he caught sight of the Gremlins with their stick green arms and bent-over backs running over the ground as quickly as mice. He glanced away, looking for something a little less ghastly and was pleased to see lanterns illuminating every nook and cranny. Their golden bodies glowed like large, fat honey bees, setting the mountain ablaze with warm, yellow light.

Bruis saw Clump staring at the Gremlins and moved closer to his side.

"Don't worry about them," he said, "I'm sure they have far more important matters on their minds than to think about the likes of you and me."

To his relief they left the Gremlins far behind, heading down one of the long dirt tracks which hugged the inside of the mountain. They turned a sharp corner and Clump saw Rodwin almost bump into two elderly Thumpers. Bodwin and Todwin hurried forward, chatting to the newcomers and one of the wizened Dwarfits glanced up and pointed in his direction. The old man shot Clump a couple of odd looks and in return, Clump stared back. He tried to strain his ears, to hear what was being said but their voices were muffled and he wasn't able to catch one damn word. The five Dwarfits continued chatting for a few minutes and then the two elderly Dwarfits went on their way without causing any trouble.

Bruis caught Clump's eye.

"I'm guessing they were relatives," he stated with a shrug, "they're probably a little wary of us and who could blame them?" he added, arching one of his bushy eyebrows.

They crossed over a wooden bridge and Clump could hear his claws scratching against the grain. They entered a long corridor which seemed to be never ending. It twisted this way then that, snaking through the mountain until they came to a small, rounded door. The door was carved in oak panels and held a shiny knocker.

Clump watched Todwin push at the handle and the door flew open. The Dwarfit stepped inside, followed closely by his brothers. Bodwin turned, beckoning them both inside.

"Welcome to our warren hole," he said pleasantly. "It isn't much to look at but it's ours."

Clump's paws stepped over the threshold and he had to admit he was pretty impressed. The floor was covered with bright, red matting, the walls, smooth and clean. Coats and hats hung on several wooden pegs and drawings of ancient Dwarfits littered the corridor.

"I say, this is rather nice," said Bruis, with a smile. "In fact, I'd go as far as to say your home is very much like a hobbit hole."

Bodwin, Todwin and Rodwin looked very pleased at this remark and both Todwin and Rodwin proceeded to show Bruis the rest of the warren.

Bodwin hung back and although he was a little timid, gestured for Clump to go and sit by the hearth.

"Why don't you lie down over there for a while," he said, pointing to an inglenook fireplace. Clump had only ever seen open fires before but he could see the flames flickering behind the glass and the smell of burning wood reminded him of home.

He hesitated before trotting over and lying down on a rug made of the softest wool. It yielded gently beneath his feet, so he curled up and laid his head down, but he refused to close his eyes. He thought the room was very cosy. There were polished chairs and long dark tables stacked high with piles and piles of books. There were also wooden racks with lots of food on them, eggs and bread and other essential items. It was a home and Clump was grateful the Dwarfits had decided to accept them as guests. A few minutes later Rodwin and Todwin walked in to the room with Bruis.

"Please make yourself comfortable," said Bodwin, offering the Plainwalker a chair.

"You're very kind," said Bruis, sitting down. "I have to admit I thought we had gotten ourselves into hot water when we bumped into you earlier."

Bodwin chuckled, bringing with him a plate, knife and fork in one hand and a mug of something white and frothy in the other.

"Yes, it could have been a different story but thankfully we realised who you were before we embarrassed ourselves." said Bodwin, placing the kitchenware down on the table next to his guest.

"I am very grateful," Bruis said, with sincerity in his voice, "and I thank you for being good enough to accept Clump also."

"We would never harm a Plainwalker but I'm sure you can understand we had our doubts about the wolf."

Bruis smiled. "Yes, I can understand your dilemma and I am thankful you have given him the benefit of the doubt." Rodwin, who had just recently left the room, came back carrying a large white bowl. He laid it at Clump's feet.

"Apparently you're not keen on meat," he said, his face clearly doubtful. He walked over to the rack and began to prepare a meal for everyone else. Clump stared at the fresh winter berries and chopped pumpkin. He licked his lips, his nose soon in the dish.

He gulped down every morsel and when he finished, he licked his lips, his eyes searching for more. "I never thought I'd see the day when a wolf enjoyed a bowl of fruit but I'm afraid that's all we have," said Rodwin, sounding a little apologetic. "That is, unless, of course, you care to feast upon a barrel of glow worms?"

Clump's lips curled inwards and both Bruis and the Dwarfits burst out laughing, crow's feet appearing around the Plainwalker's eyes.

"I think Clump will be just fine," said Bruis, cheerily.

Once the Thumper had prepared a light snack, he came and sat at the table. The Plainwalker was offered a large chunk of bread, some rather smelly cheese and a cluster of red grapes.

"Oh I love cheese and the smellier the better," said Bruis in delight, holding the thick wedge to his nose, breathing deeply. "Why it smells simply delicious," he added, taking a mouthful and then he was closing his eyes and nodding his approval. "Yes, very tasty," he acknowledged, smacking his lips before taking yet another bite.

Bodwin gave him a warm smile.

"So, where were you both heading before you were attacked by the troll?" he asked, unfastening his leather belt and placing it on the chair beside him. He scratched his belly and let out a deep belch.

Todwin and Rodwin broke out into peals of laughter.

"We do apologise for our brother's rather disgusting table manners," said Todwin, trying to keep a straight face, but failing miserably.

Bruis lifted his hand in the air. "Let him enjoy his meal," he said, his own shoulders rising with amusement. "I'm sure he deserves far more after working such long hours in semi-darkness."

Bodwin chuckled in agreement.

"I'm with you one hundred percent," he said, saluting the Plainwalker with his mug. "However, you still haven't told us where you're going."

Bruis leaned closer, his face turning serious.

"We're heading through the pass," he explained. "I'm planning on taking Clump to the other side of the mountain, to a place where I feel he will be much safer."

Bodwin let out a long, exaggerated sigh.

"Is there really such a place?" he asked, taking a gulp of his ale. He placed his tankard down on the table with a thud. "I mean, the mountain can be a deadly place but the surrounding realms can be just as dangerous."

Bruis shuddered.

"I hear what you're saying and I know it can often be treacherous out there but I'm heading for Gobb Loch. At least Clump will be safe there until he is a little older."

"Isn't that the place closest to the Kingdom of Nine Winters?" Bodwin asked.

"Yes, that right," Rodwin interrupted, "and doesn't the land belong to the King of the Elves?"

"That's a total misconception." said Bruis, shoving the last of his cheese into his mouth before taking a gulp of his ale. "The loch once belonged to the Dwarves but over time has become no man's land, an oasis between the two realms which I hear is now a rather beautiful wilderness."

"I heard it was a little like Fortune's End, the place owned by the Oakwood wizards," said Todwin, reaching for a second slice of bread.

"No, Fortune's End is just a traveller's rest belonging to the realm of Raven's Rainbow." Bodwin argued. "I believe the rest is actually owned by a powerful magician who allows weary travellers to stay there for the night as long as they lay down their weapons."

It was Bruis who now gave a long, exaggerated sigh.

"Fortune's End isn't the kind of place I'm interested in. I need somewhere where Clump can actually live his life without fear of persecution and I certainly don't wish him to suffer the wrath of a powerful wizard for trespassing."

"Why can't he go back to his own pack?" asked Bodwin.

Bruis waited a moment before he replied.

"He's been ostracised."

"By whom?" asked Todwin.

Bruis glanced over to Clump before letting out a low groan.

"By his father," he said and his voice held a note of despair.

"Oh, some kind of family dispute?" said Rodwin, nodding his head wisely. "I've seen that happen many times, family members biting the hand that feeds them."

"Yes, something like that," Bruis acknowledged, "only I'm sorry to say his father was the one doing all the biting."

Clump placed his head in his paws and found he couldn't hold back the whimper that rose in his throat.

"Well, you're more than welcome to stay here with us for a day or two more," said Rodwin, grabbing a knife and buttering a slice of bread, "there's plenty of room."

Bruis shook his head and sighed.

"Thank you for your kind offer but I'm sorry to say we cannot stay. We have a long journey ahead of us and I'm afraid we must leave before dawn breaks."

"But you've had no sleep," cried Bodwin, aghast. "At least stay until we've seen you rested."

"No can do," said Bruis, shaking his head. "We need to leave long before the sun rises."

"Very well," said Rodwin, rising to his feet. "If that's the case, you'd better leave now."

Chapter 12

If it was at all possible, Isis was beginning to despise Serpen that little bit more. After what happened with Clump, she could barely set eyes on him but now she found she couldn't believe her ears either. Only this morning Lyra told her that Serpen had chosen to take a new mate. Isis was secretly stunned. She had been his partner for most of her lifetime, yet due to no fault of her own, he had spurned her for another as quickly as rain fell from the sky.

In Lyra's cave the mood was low. Isis was busy trying to take her mind off Serpen by focusing on Brid's welfare. Although her daughter was recovering well, it had been a very slow process and both Lyra and Isis were thankful for Horith's help. Since returning from his imprisonment, he had barely left Brid's side. Having been given a special healing salve by the Protector, he stayed with her night and day, tending to her wounds and persuading her to eat and drink as often as he could.

Isis knew they were in love and that it would not end well. If Serpen found out there would be serious trouble because Brid was already betrothed to another. From birth, both Felan and Brid had been chosen to be part of the Polak tribe, Windigos who lived on the west side of the mountain. The tribe offered Serpen untold riches for both his daughters and as leader he would earn great respect from the alliance. Serpen had liked this idea and secured the deal before Felan and Brid were a day old. The sad fact was that the Polak elders would not care that Brid was now disfigured. Their only concern would be for the healthy continuation of their bloodline and to ensure that Brid would bear cubs that would grow big and strong.

Isis was deeply troubled over what the future would hold for her daughter. She was already aware how she would never enjoy the close bond of a true male companion, forced only to do her duty and keep the honour of her tribe. Her life would be one of hardship but at least she would have Felan close by to help her endure it, and this thought made Isis believe she would sleep a little easier at night. A deep sigh left her lips and her thoughts drifted to her son. Echoes of pain swam inside her moist eyes. Since that fateful day

105

when Serpen chased after Clump, something in his demeanour had changed. He had told her their son was dead and yet, she felt he had been lying to her. Isis worried over this. If Clump was dead surely she would feel it in her heart, but she felt nothing but growing terror.

Her mind drifted back to Serpen. Although she no longer cared for him, she was anxious over what would happen now he had chosen Greer to be his new partner. She had already seen for herself how young she was and her eyes appeared bright with life. Isis knew it would not be long before she was pregnant with Serpen's offspring. Aware that if Greer were to give him a son, her daughters would no longer be of interest to him.

Horith came to her side and placed his hand gently upon her shoulder and she almost jumped out of her skin. She smiled at him sheepishly, having to admit to herself how he'd grown into a fine male. His coat was long and dark, the hair on his face no longer fluffy like baby down. The bitterness she once thought simmered behind those dark eyes was now only a distant memory. She frowned; if Brid's circumstances had been different, she would have welcomed Horith as a son with open arms.

"She's asking for you," Horith said, wearing a faint smile. "I'm afraid I must leave. It's getting late and I have to get ready for hunting."

Isis nodded and rose to her feet. "Thank you for looking after Brid so well," she said, glancing over to where her daughter was lying on a makeshift bed.

Horith's smile slipped from his face. "It's the least I can do after what happened to her at the plateau," he said, with a shrug.

"It wasn't your fault," Isis insisted, and she reached out and placed her hand on his lower arm. Horith reacted by placing his hand on top of her fingers.

"I hear what you're saying, but I can't help myself. If only I hadn't encouraged her to come with me that fateful day."

"You mustn't blame yourself, however, this can't go on," Isis warned, her voice firm. "I have eyes and I see how you look at her. End it now, before you break her heart."

Horith froze.

"I ... I ... can't ...," he stammered, staring at her as though she had gone quite mad. "Don't you see, I love her."

"Your love won't make her yours," Isis interrupted, wearing a frown. "You know full well she is betrothed to another."

"But she loves me, and she's all I have," Horith blurted, his eyes pained. "Surely that's enough."

Isis felt a stab of sorrow.

"No, Horith, although your love for Brid is honourable, it will not pacify her father. Only the promise of gold and the luxury of high status will keep him satisfied."

Horith hung his head.

"I will try and make him see sense," he persisted, snatching his hand away. "Just give me a little more time to prove myself."

Before Isis could reply a horn blew out and Horith stepped away from her.

"I have to go, that's the signal," he stated, pushing the hides out of the way. He stepped outside and the darkness cloaked him all in black.

Isis heaved a deep sigh. It was just as she feared. She scolded herself for not saying something sooner. Cursing herself for pretending not to see what was happening right before her eyes. She walked over to the fire and spied Felan crouched by her sister. The orange and gold flames made her features appear soft and she crept closer, not wishing to break the tranquillity of the moment.

"It will soon be time for us to join the others," she said at last, bending over to lift back the blankets. "I think it's best if we get Brid inside one of the higher chambers tonight where she will be safe until morning."

Felan scurried to her mother's side but Brid waved her hand in the air to make her stay away. "No, please, there's no need to help me. I can manage just fine by myself," she insisted, getting to her feet and heading for one of the agave ladders which was propped against a wall.

"Alright, if you insist," Isis replied, unable to stop the light smile that touched her lips, amused at her daughter's wilful streak. "However, we need you to be quick and get your backside up into that chamber before we leave for the night."

Brid giggled and climbed the ladder.

"Come on, hurry up slow coach," Felan urged her sister, sounding impatient.

"I'm going as fast as I can," Brid mumbled, doing her best to hurry. She turned to smile at her sister and somehow missed a rung and almost fell.

"Hey! Watch what you're doing!" Isis cried out, dashing towards her. "The last thing I want is for you to fall and break your neck!"

Brid half turned and gave a sheepish grin.

"Sorry," she mouthed, flopping down inside the chamber and Isis grabbed hold of the ladder, dropping it to the floor.

She slapped the dust from her fingers.

"I feel better now that no hungry wolves can reach you whilst I'm gone," she said, looking up at her daughter and feeling a moment of contentment. Brid sat down with her feet over the edge of the chamber. She glanced towards her mother, placed her large hands onto her hip bones and pulled a face.

"I don't believe anyone would ever dare do such a terrible thing," she said, sounding exasperated. "And besides, we're not supposed to eat one another."

Isis wouldn't be swayed. "Yes, that's the general idea, however, that rule doesn't apply if you are from another tribe. I have known many who would hurt those who were supposed to be friends. I'm taking no chances and I'm making sure no harm will come to you whilst I'm gone."

Brid gave a pout. "Mother, do you always have to look on the dark side of life?"

"Yes, indeed I do," Isis insisted, putting her arms around Felan and heading back towards the fire. "You see, one thing I have learned over the years is that you should *never* trust a Windigo."

*

During the night the females stayed close to the village boundaries, prowling the surrounding area, checking for any unwanted visitors that might stray into the village.

Later, when everyone had left, Brid transmuted and then curled herself into a ball, her tail tucked close to her body and she slept with her head on her paws. When dawn broke she changed back

108

into a Windigo and waited for her mother and sister to return to the cave and prepare breakfast.

She heard a noise when someone entered and then the ladder was propped up against the wall. She pushed her nose out expecting to see Isis lighting the fire or Felan waiting for her to climb down but to her surprise, she saw Horith standing there instead. He pressed his finger to his lips, his eyes pleading for her to stay quiet and then he gestured for her to climb down. Brid was confused. What on earth was Horith doing back before the females? She noticed a bag she once made him with leftover fibres of agave slung over one of his great shoulders and that he was keeping an eye firmly on the doorway.

"What's wrong? Brid whispered when she climbed down the ladder and reached his side. "Why aren't you with the others?"

Horith took both her hands in his good one and gently nibbled her top lip, a sign of endearment.

Brid smiled, but she noticed his eyes looked troubled.

"What is it?" she asked, tilting her chin.

Horith's face darkened.

"We need to leave," he said, drawing her closer to the doorway.

"What?" Brid gasped, snatching her hands away. "No, don't be silly, we can't just up and go, that's just plain crazy."

"Listen to me," Horith begged, grabbing her arm. "If you want us to be together then we must leave right now."

"But my mother, Felan?"

"Your mother has already put two and two together which means others will have probably done the same."

"But how? I thought we were careful?"

"Obviously not enough and the fact remains that if your mother knows about us, then it's just a matter of time before your father does too."

"Oh, no, he'll be so angry," Brid whined, bringing her fingers up to her face and she unconsciously touched her crushed cheekbone.

Horith sighed, "I know and the moment he's aware, he'll send you away to be with ... him."

Brid caught her breath. The thought of being with anyone else except Horith filled her with utter dread.

"No, he can't, I love you."

"Your father doesn't care about love," Horith hissed, pulling her even closer to the door.

"This is the only chance we have to get away," he coaxed, peering out towards the campfires. "Serpen has been lucky enough to bring back a dead griffon. Most of the females are busy plucking the feathers from its wings whilst he gathers the other males, boasting about how he came across the beast."

Brid felt the cold hand of dread creep down her spine. If she left with Horith and they were caught, well, she didn't want to think about the consequences. She stared at him for what felt like a lifetime. She saw her terror mirrored in his eyes and her love for him rose inside her like a gigantic wave. The surge was so intense that it almost took her breath away. She could see how much he loved her, more than life itself and if they were to ever taste a moment of true happiness, she would have to be prepared to make many sacrifices.

Horith peeped out between the hides one last time and then he looked back at her and she nodded her consent. She placed her hand inside his huge palm and he pulled her sharply out of the cave.

It was the first time Brid had been outside in the fresh air since that fateful day at the plateau and she found the sun was so bright it almost blinded her. They both quickened their pace although Brid's leg dragged a little in the dirt but once they were out of sight, they followed the curve of the rock which led them deeper into the Canyon.

"Where are we headed?" Brid whispered, once she realised no one had seen them leave. Horith didn't reply, instead he tugged at her tunic and they broke into a run.

Brid did her best to keep up as they followed the river until it forked. Horith edged closer to an overhang of rock where a small alcove had been dug deep into the bank, possibly made by some kind of large animal.

He stopped and turned to her, his eyes wide with anxiety.

"What's wrong?" Brid asked, taking a nervous step towards him.

"I have something to show you which I think will help us escape."

"Really? Like what?"

Horith hesitated but then he grabbed at a ton of brushwood and broken branches, pulling leaves and twigs out of the way. Brid glanced inside the hole but she couldn't make out anything of interest. She watched as Horith disappeared into the darkness, her eyes wide with curiosity. To her surprise he came back carrying a strange contraption. It was at least twelve feet long, made of wood and covered with soft brown leather or some other kind of material.

Brid inched closer. She had never seen anything like it before although it reminded her of a dragon she had once seen in the sky, its long red wings outstretched.

"What is it?" she asked, touching the soft leather with her fingertips.

"I don't think it has a name, but it's enchanted, and it flies," Horith replied with a grin.

"Yes, I've already spotted the wings, but where did you get it?"

"I traded it."

"With whom?"

"A mining troll. I came across him one day at the bottom of the mountain. He wasn't much of a catch, barely little more than a mouthful really and I was just about to bite his head off when he begged me to spare his life. He said that if I let him live, he would show me a hidden artefact he'd recently stolen and that he was willing to give me the spell which would enable it to fly."

"And you believed him?"

"Yes, of course, he was pretty terrified."

Brid pulled a face that told him she thought him a fool.

"So, do you actually know how this thing works?"

Horith shrugged his shoulders.

"No, but how hard could it be?"

"Are you serious?" she almost choked. "You're not trying to tell me that you've never used it before?"

"Well ... err ... no. The troll told me the magic spell would only work the once, so I wasn't going to waste the spell by testing it out."

Brid rolled her eyes in disbelief.

"You are such an idiot!" she proclaimed. "Haven't you thought he was probably just trying to save his own skin?"

Horith let out a deep sigh and dragged the wooden frame out onto the Canyon floor.

"Yes, he was scared out of his wits, but then, for the first time, I realised we might have a chance to escape. I decided it was well worth the risk, so I let him go once he revealed the contraption and the spell. I dragged the frame closer to home and then waited for the right moment to use it."

His face turned serious. "Brid, at the end of the day this is our only way out of here. I hate to say it but you know as well as I that once your father realises that we've run off together, we're both as good as dead."

Brid pursed her lips and looked into his eyes, knowing he spoke the truth.

"Alright, so what are we waiting for?" she mumbled, helping him find an area where they wouldn't snag the wings on any overhanging trees. Once they found a decent spot, Horith pointed to a pair of leather reins which hung from the centre of the frame.

"The troll said we have to strap ourselves into the harness and then jump into the air from a high point," he explained, wiping his brow with the back of his stump.

"What! You're not serious!"

"Yes, I'm afraid I am."

"But if we jump from the ridge we may as well commit suicide!"

"No, it's not such a drop that we would die. Look, we just have to be in the air when this thing takes off, otherwise the magic won't work."

Brid wasn't convinced.

"This is beyond crazy. How can you be sure the spell will work?"

Horith looked back at her and she saw a moment of doubt pass behind his eyes.

"Because it has to," he replied, his mouth firm.

Brid shook her head in exasperation.

"Do you realise, if this doesn't go to plan we're doomed?"

"It will, I promise," Horith insisted.

Brid let out a heavy sigh.

"Okay, well, I guess there's only one way to find out. Let's do it, before I change my mind!"

With a nod, Horith gave her a warm smile and gestured for her to climb inside the flying contraption.

Chapter 13

Bruis and Clump were led out of the mountain by the Dwarfit brothers long before the sun peered over the horizon. They were taken down through the many secret passageways known only to the mountain folk until they came across a large boulder which blocked their path. Todwin and Bodwin rushed forward, using their shoulders to push the giant stone out of the way; it looked to be heavy and they were soon both red faced. As the stone rolled away, a gentle breeze forced its way inside the tunnel, ruffling Clump's fur. He looked across at a dark sky, and was pleased to see the sun had not yet risen from its bed.

Bodwin cleared his throat, grabbing his attention.

"I have to admit pushing that boulder gets harder each time, but I always enjoy feeling the mountain air brush against my skin." His brothers came to stand beside him and Clump thought they all looked a little sad.

"I guess you'll need to be on your way," said Todwin, and his brothers nodded in agreement.

Clump felt a lump rise in his throat. The Dwarfits had shown him great kindness and he was very reluctant to leave. He heard Bruis say goodbye and in return, the Dwarfits offered him a firm handshake.

"It's been a pleasure to meet you all," the Plainwalker said, adding, "and I'm eternally grateful for your help and hospitality." Clump noticed he didn't wait for the Dwarfits to reply, instead he headed straight out of the mountain. Without hesitation, Clump followed.

"I'll be seeing you," shouted Todwin, and Clump turned to see the stone roll over the entranceway. He gave a whimper and Bruis came over and patted him gently on the head.

"Yes, I know, they were very endearing fellows but I hope you understand that we had no choice but to leave. I'm fairly positive that they would not have been quite so friendly once they realised you are a Windigo." He gave Clump a knowing smile.

Inside his head, Clump was forced to agree, so he trotted after Bruis who had set off down a dirt track at a rather brisk pace.

"Why, this is simply marvellous," Bruis proclaimed, getting his bearings and Clump lifted his nose and sniffed the air. "Don't you see where we are?" he asked, pointing over to the horizon. "Why, those wonderful chaps have done an excellent job of leading us to the very edge of the mountain pass, saving us days of arduous travelling."

Clump's ears pricked up as he searched for landmarks. He soon realised he couldn't see anything familiar but he could hear the solitary cry of a black eagle. He watched a dark silhouette circle overhead, the bird clearly searching for food. He looked back at the ground, the bird of prey already forgotten. A shudder wormed down his back. He didn't recognise this place and it was obvious he was a long way from home. Behind him sat several snowy-capped mountains and ahead, large rolling hills rose towards the sky.

"I'm pleased to say it shouldn't take us too long to reach Gobb Loch," Bruis said, pointing east, and in reply, Clump lifted his head and howled.

*

Together, they carried on their journey until it was plain to see that a new day had dawned. When the sun broke through the early morning mist, Bruis waited for Clump to change back into a Windigo. They had reached a small copse of trees and, once inside, they soon heard the sound of running water. Bruis was the first to discover the silvery stream and he didn't bat an eyelid when Clump shot off in the opposite direction to hide behind a thick bush. He understood only too well that changelings did not like to be watched when they made their transition. Who could blame them? Bruis once had the misfortune of seeing a Leshy turn back from a bear. These spirits were lords of the forest and had bonds with such creatures. He had stumbled upon the changeling by accident one day whilst collecting seedlings in the forest. He had seen the bear between the trees and then, unexpectedly, a strange little man had torn himself from inside the bear like a chick hatching from its shell. Bruis was aghast when the bear split in two, blood and guts exploding everywhere. He was shocked to the core, standing there, frozen to the spot, yet unable to turn his eyes away.

The spirit stepped into the light and Bruis saw he bore horns and a tail. The strange little man wriggled his fingers and a golden light formed around what was left of the bear's carcass. Like stardust, the bloodied remains disintegrated into a shimmering mass of bright light. The light rose into the air, and the golden particles clung together like a swarm of honey bees. The Plainwalker watched in awe as the spirit opened its mouth and made what he could only describe as a strange sucking sound with his lips. The bright glow shot towards him, entering his mouth and the Leshy's body shook spasmodically as the particles shot down his throat. A blinding flash saw the spirit's body glow with golden light. Bruis was fascinated. He had never witnessed anything like it before and as he continued to stare, the Leshy simply vanished into thin air.

Shuddering at the memory, Bruis bent down, cupped his hands and drank from the stream. The water was cool on his lips and he enjoyed listening to the stream spill over the stones. The water gurgled as it travelled and he closed his eyes, enjoying the pleasant tinkering sound it made. A second later he heard a splash and he opened his eyes to see Clump grinning at him. Bruis smiled back, noticing how the Windigo was only ankle deep in water.

"Don't you like getting your thick hair wet?" he asked.

Clump pulled a face. "I'm not keen," he admitted, "and I've never been much of a bather."

Bruis chuckled.

"All the same, I think we should take this opportunity to give ourselves a good wash," he said, and reached inside his bag. He took out a smooth object, holding it in the palm of his hand. He threw the bag onto the bank and his clothes swiftly followed. Soon he stood as naked as the day he was born.

This time it was Clump who chuckled.

"What's so funny?" Bruis asked, lifting an eyebrow.

Clump put his fingers to his mouth. "You remind me of a skinned rabbit," he replied, with a chortle. "Why, there's hardly any meat on your bones and your arms are as thin as branches."

"I'm sure I don't look that bad," said Bruis, flexing one of his muscles to prove a point.

Clump merely broke out into peals of laughter.

116

"Call that a muscle," he roared, presenting a powerful bicep of his own.

Bruis gave a sniff of discontent.

"I'll have you know I've got muscles in places you've never even heard of."

"Yes, and it's too bad none of them are in your arms," Clump replied with a titter.

"Ha-ha you're very witty for a monster," said Bruis dryly, bending down to flick water over his back.

"Well, I'm only speaking the truth. You are a bit on the lean side and if my father ever tried to eat you, he would probably spit you out."

"Good job he's not going to get the chance then," said Bruis, in a sarcastic tone.

Clump suddenly caught sight of what he thought to be a small stone in his friend's hand.

"What's that?" he asked, pointing. "Only we never use stones to wash, oh no, back home we use pieces of wood that are rough to the touch that scrub our bodies."

Bruis showed him the white object and then he placed it under the water. To Clump's amazement, a cluster of kaleidoscopic bubbles floated to the top of the surface and then rushed away downstream. The colours were like those seen in the rainbow and Clump stared after them.

"That's not a stone," Clump said, dropping into the water and bum-shuffling through the ripples to get a closer look. "Is it magical?"

"What, this?" asked Bruis, lifting up the lump of white so the Windigo could see it more clearly.

Clump nodded, his nose all wrinkled as he sniffed the air.

"Hmm, yes, and I notice it smells of apples," he added, bending forward to try and take a bite, much to the Plainwalker's amusement.

"Oh, it's not for eating!" Bruis declared, and he quickly snatched his hand away.

Clump's face fell. "Oh, that's a shame," he said, pushing out his lower lip. "So what's it for then?"

117

"It's for washing," Bruis explained, his eyes bright. "It's called soap and if you wet it, it goes into a lather which helps to get rid of all the dirt and sweat from your body."

Clump lifted his arms and sniffed his armpits, screwing up his nose when an overpowering odour hit his nostrils.

"Can monsters use it too?" he asked.

"Yes, of course," Bruis said, offering it to him.

Clump went to take it from his palm, but the moment his fingers curled, the soap slipped out of his grasp and dropped under the water. Surprised, his hand dived beneath the surface as he tried, in vain, to catch it. He spotted a blob of white sitting between two grey pebbles by his feet, but as soon as his fingers touched the slippery object, it shot off downstream.

Clump looked up, clearly perplexed.

"Bruis are you playing tricks on me?" he asked, but before the Plainwalker could reply, Clump lunged forward, slipped on a mossy stone and lost his balance. Splash! He fell, head first into the stream, a spiral of water shoot up into the air and drenched poor Bruis. He gasped out loud, resembling a drowned rat, but after the initial shock, he could only see the funny side and broke out into fits of laughter.

Clump wasn't so amused.

"There's something wrong with your soap, it must be bewitched because it's turned into a squishy lump of lard," he announced, standing up, his fur soaking wet and bedraggled.

Bruis had to purse his lips to stifle yet another giggle that bubbled in his throat. It was obvious he thought the whole incident was highly hilarious and he was struggling to keep a lid on his composure.

"Maybe you should just use plain water and a stick next time," he suggested, making his way back to the bank. Bruis climbed out of the stream and sat in the sun to dry off.

Clump decided to join him.

Bruis gave a welcoming smile as he sat down. "I have to say that was fun, especially when you got soaked from head to foot."

Clump smiled to himself. So Bruis thought it was funny when he got drenched. He quickly rose to his feet and with all his might, started to shake himself like a wet dog. Water flew from his fur and

118

into the air and Bruis was once again soaked to the skin. The Plainwalker squealed like a little pig, jumping to his feet, his arms outstretched, and Clump laughed so hard he was soon bent over double. He quickly recovered and, like a naughty child, chased Bruis through the long grass, shouting that when he caught him he would throw him back into the stream. Bruis cried out and fled, which caused Clump to laugh even harder.

*

Later that same day they finally entered Gobb Loch. A storm struck as soon as they reached the outer rim of the lowlands. Bright spears of lightning crashed in jagged bolts across the sky, illuminating the dark forest ahead in sharp bursts of blinding radiance, causing Clump to shiver.

In one of those bursts, Bruis appeared to find what he was looking for and guided Clump closer to the water's edge. Clump was busy dreaming of a warm bed and a decent meal when Bruis stopped abruptly. They were at the side of the loch and the rain was so heavy it was like a dark curtain drifting over the water.

"You need to remember this very spot," said Bruis against the wind and he pointed to a tree which had been hit by lightning years earlier. Its black, charred trunk stood out against the rest, rather like a dark phantom.

Bruis walked with a brisk pace towards the water and only stopped when the tide reached his toes. He picked up a small piece of driftwood and held it tightly in his hands. Closing his eyes he mumbled what Clump thought to be a spell, and then the Plainwalker returned to his side. He opened his palm and offered him the piece of driftwood.

"I need you to take this," he said.

"What is it?" asked Clump, turning the wood over.

"It's the key to your new home."

"I'm sorry, I don't understand," said Clump, in reply.

Bruis smiled, his milky-white eyes crinkling at the corners.

"This isn't just any ordinary stick, it's magical, and it will keep you safe," he explained, taking back the driftwood. "You see, whenever you need shelter, draw an image of a cave, shack or tunnel into the sand and a place will appear right before your eyes."

Clump pointed down towards his feet. "What, right here?"

Bruis nodded.

"Yes, that's right and the moment you step away from the drawing, it will come alive. Once you enter, the dwelling will vanish from sight and no one will be able to see you or find you from the outside world."

"Wow, that's incredible," Clump gasped, taking back the stick and he flicked it over as though he would find something interesting underneath.

Bruis put a warning hand on his arm.

"Clump, you must keep it safe at all times because if you lose it, you will never be able to find shelter in this place again and you will become vulnerable to those who would wish to harm you."

Clump felt his heart beat a little faster.

"I understand," he said, looking into the Plainwalker's eyes, "so can I try it out now?"

"I thought you'd never ask," said Bruis, pointing to the sky and the never-ending rain clouds.

Clump knelt down on one knee and drew a basic picture of a rounded cave in the sand. He stood up and Bruis pulled him back. The ground shook beneath their feet and dark rocks protruded through the sand.

Clump stared at the ground as the sand was pressed away and a cave pushed its way to the surface.

He simply couldn't believe his eyes and he jumped up and down with excitement. "This is unbelievable!" he cried, dashing towards the cave. Bruis was right behind him and the moment they both stepped inside, the entrance sealed itself with what looked to be a curtain of rippling water. Clump was amazed that he could still see outside.

"You can see out but no one can see in," Bruis explained. "You are no longer visible to the outside world so you can rest easy knowing you are completely safe in here."

"But what about when I'm a wolf?" Clump asked.

Bruis shrugged his shoulders. "You will have to stay hidden in the undergrowth and surrounding hills until you can return to your cave to sleep. It shouldn't be too difficult as long as you keep your head down."

Clump sighed deeply. "I can do that," he said, relaxing a little.

"Good," said Bruis, patting him on the back. "Then I guess it's time for me to grab a few hours' sleep before I go on my way."

"What! Do you have to leave so soon?"

"Yes, I'm afraid I must. The gardens won't be able to tend themselves for much longer."

Clump's good mood evaporated as quickly as early morning dew.

Sensing his displeasure, Bruis placed a caring hand on his arm. His eyes appeared to glow, like that of a dragon when hit by sunlight.

"Come now don't be so glum," he said, giving it a squeeze. "Seize the chance to go out and about, gather essential items whilst you still have plenty of daylight. You are going to need fresh water and you must find yourself some decent food to store."

"I don't want to stay here by myself," said Clump, turning stubborn.

"But you must," said Bruis firmly.

Clump shook his head.

"No, I don't want to be left all alone," he sniffed, "I'm a little scared, if I'm honest."

Bruis let out a deep sigh.

"You'll be fine and you know I would take you with me if I could, but I can't."

"But why not?"

"Because where I'm going no changeling must tread."

"But I promise I won't get in the way, you won't even know I'm there."

Bruis's face took on a stern expression.

"No matter how much I care about your welfare, I cannot break the sacred laws," he said, clearly trying to explain that his hands were tied. "Not even for you."

"So I have to stay here and rot ...," Clump snapped, jutting out his chin like a spoilt child.

Bruis appeared to droop a little.

"It's not forever," he insisted, dropping his hand. "Trust me, you won't always be so vulnerable. Just give yourself time to mature, then wait and see what life has in store for you."

Clump's lower lip trembled. He understood that he must stay here until he was full-grown but he was frightened to live alone nonetheless. With a heavy heart he accepted his fate and whilst the rain continued to fall, he wandered out into the wilderness in search of food.

Chapter 14

The witch awoke with a sudden start. She blinked, unable to fathom what had jolted her from her slumber, so she pushed back the pile of old woollen blankets and slid out of bed. After placing a cloak around her shoulders, she shoved her toes into a pair of worn-out slippers and hobbled across the cold, damp floor. She shuffled towards a low table made from a bunch of tree roots and a flicker from her hand saw a tall candle flare into life. A golden glow bounced against the dark walls and she turned, her back stooped from old age.

Without a sound, she headed towards the hearth. The fire was low but still alight and small amber flames teased the air. The witch bent down and grabbed a handful of cinders, throwing them swiftly onto the dying embers. The fire hissed and crackled and a tendril of smoke billowed up in retaliation. The witch closed her eyes and waved her hand towards the wisp of black and mumbled a spell. When she opened her eyes, the smoke had been manipulated to create an image. It was of a beautiful young girl, perhaps no more than sixteen or seventeen earth years old. Her face was one of beauty and her bright smile was dazzling.

The witch cackled softly to herself.

"So, Crystal, I see you couldn't stay away," she mused. Her thoughts drifted to a time many years earlier when this child had been brought to her door only hours after her birth.

Amella must be relieved to see her daughter returned to her bosom ... she thought, her mind drifting to the newly crowned Queen of the Elves. She clicked her tongue in the roof of her mouth, aware her father, King Gamada, had been killed by the vicious Nonhawk King. She waved her fingers to disperse the illusion of the princess. Black tendrils curled and twisted, floating in long, dark wisps until they disappeared into thin air. The witch left the fireside feeling a little more contented now she understood the reason why she had awoken so abruptly. Her hand shot out, snatching the candle and she made her way into yet another chamber.

The room was wrapped in black; only the light from the small, flickering flame stopped the darkness from enfolding her. Her fingertips brushed against a dusty shelf. Her eyes caught sight of something shiny and blue and her fingers curled around it. She smiled to herself as she shook the vial to check the contents and, satisfied, moved to yet another dusty shelf. It was filled with strange objects, collected over many years and covered in a layer of thick cobwebs. She clawed at the webs with her bony fingers, wiping the sticky threads down the front of her night clothes, oblivious to the black and silver spiders which scurried away in haste. Her old, rheumy eyes soon adjusted to the gloom as she busied herself and selected ingredients to make what she thought to be, a very powerful spell. She raised her arm above her head, clawing at a bunch of dried herbs which dangled from the ceiling. The room immediately smelt of rosemary and thyme, and a rich aroma of the forest filled the air, causing her nostrils to flare.

"Ah-choo! Ah-choo!" sneezed the witch, feeling her eyes stream and she wiped the tears away with the side of her hand. She rubbed at her burning lids, annoyed that even after several centuries she still suffered from something as common as hay fever.

Through a red haze, the witch's eyes wandered to a ledge where she could see rows of precious stones and polished crystals. She made her way over to browse the assortment, inspecting the stones one by one, until finally choosing a particular piece, a rock filled with slivers of amethyst.

By her side sat an old battered basket with a dozen or so feathers inside. Some were plucked from ravens and crows, others stolen from the wings of owls or other wild birds. A bony hand delved inside, the softness of the plumes lost to her touch. She pushed the feathers aside until she found the one she needed. A crooked smile stretched across her thin, pale lips as her fingers curled around a feather that stood out from all the rest. The plume was large, the colour of sulphur.

The witch grinned, showing a row of rotten teeth and then she carried all of the ingredients over to a long wooden table which was used for the specific task of creating spells. She placed the candle on a ledge, the light revealing bright splashes of colour which were ingrained into the wood. The table bore years of neglect and

124

suffered multiple scorch marks from countless spillages and misfired spells. The witch reached for her spell book and quickly flicked through the well-thumbed pages. Her eyes widened with excitement when she spotted what she had been looking for and after checking she had all the right ingredients, she began the arduous task of creating the spell. Much to her frustration, the spell was complicated and she made countless mistakes. Getting the balance perfect took a lot of time and patience, (which the witch did not have) and the magic was so complex that it took her eight moons to get it just right.

Exhausted, yet feeling triumphant, the witch pushed a cork down into a bottle which now held a very powerful enchantment. Placing the vial onto a small table, the witch reached for her crystal orb. Her long, bony fingers wiped away a thin layer of dust and then she spoke out loud, her breath forming condensation upon the glass.

"Where will I find the Windigo, Clump?" she hissed.

A small light glimmered inside the orb.

"Show him to me," the witch demanded, peering closer.

A display of colour exploded inside the glass. Dancing and swirling, the vivid colours of red, gold, brown and blue curled around one another until they blended together to form an image of lush countryside.

The witch cackled from sheer delight, clapping her hands with glee.

"Ha! Ha! Why, he's at Gobb Loch!" she screeched, her eyes wide. "Why who'd have thought he'd have travelled so far from home, yet he's close enough to be in my clutches by the time the next moon rises."

Without further ado, the witch prepared herself for the journey. She grabbed the newly made potion and shoved it into her coat pocket along with a thin-bladed knife. Hitching up her skirts she grabbed her broomstick, opened the door to a sky full of stars and without looking back, rose high into the sky.

*

Clump didn't want to admit it but he was missing Bruis dreadfully. The Plainwalker had left several days previously, having to return to the Canyon to tend his many gardens. Clump tried very hard to settle as best he could into his new life. Bruis had been gracious enough to leave Clump his bag with all its wonderful contents. At the time, Clump had tried to decline but Bruis was adamant he should take it, and already Clump had eaten the apples, found a very nice blanket, a few tools and a bag full of seed. Bruis had also left two bottles of scrumptious Buttermead, which Clump decided to save for a special occasion.

He found his life soon fell into a routine. In the mornings he foraged for food, collected ample supplies to bring back to his cave before heading off to bed. Water wasn't a problem because the loch was actually a freshwater lake and Clump soon felt contentment for the first time in his life. Of course he still missed his family *terribly*, but he tried not to think about them too much. It was hard though. His mind was constantly flying back to the village in his sleep and he would dream of his mother, Felan and Brid. Whilst asleep he would wonder what they were doing, conjuring images of them cooking, washing clothes or simply playing games. In his dreams he would be there, joining in with all their daily activities, hugging his mother whilst he ran wild with his sisters.

Clump shook his head, trying to focus on the long night ahead and not his family. He had decided to take a walk by the shore. Most of the nocturnal wanderers were awake but the birds were now asleep in their nests, their songs having died away many hours ago. He liked this time of night. It was peaceful and only the gentle lapping of the tide could be heard against the cool breeze. Clump glanced up at the moon. He still had a few hours yet before the silver disc would be at its highest and then he would run into the bushes and wait for the inevitable to happen.

He raised a hairy eyebrow when something black shot across the surface of the moon. Clump felt a sudden stab of foreboding when a dark shadow appeared to head straight for the shore. Something inside his brain told him to hide. He quickly dashed towards a bush and hid behind it. His two amber eyes peered out between the thick green leaves, his attention never leaving the dark silhouette which loomed ever closer by the second.

Clump was soon able to make out the outline of an actual person flying in the sky. The figure was wearing a hooded cloak and the dark material flapped wildly in the breeze. He lowered his head and closed his eyes, hoping that whoever drew near would simply fly away.

Seconds crept into minutes and just when he thought it was safe to open his eyes, he heard someone call out his name. He gasped, unable to stop the shudder of dismay which ripped through his body.

"Come out, come out, wherever you are. I know you're in there," said a voice he recognised.

Clump closed his eyes once again and felt his heart drop like a stone.

It's the witch I met at Forusian's castle, he thought in alarm. *She's come back for me.*

He didn't move a muscle, watching her slowly climb off her broomstick. His eyes followed her as she dragged the broom over to the trees and then leaned it against the trunk of the burnt oak tree.

"Don't make me come and get you," she grumbled, sounding irritated. "I haven't the time or the inclination to play your silly games."

Clump held his breath and, with some reluctance, rose to his feet.

"Ah, there you are," said the witch, sounding pleased. She beckoned for him to come closer and Clump found himself walking towards her, his feet having found a life of their own. He pushed through the undergrowth and then he could feel soft sand between his toes. All too soon he stood right in front of his unexpected visitor.

"What do you want?" he asked, his voice shaking a little.

The witch glared at him with her shrewd eyes.

"What! Have you forgotten already?" she spat, shooting a menacing glare.

Clump glanced down at his feet and shook his head.

"Hmm, I thought as much," said the witch, and Clump heard the rustle of her cloak.

Clump worried about the reason she was here. He was secretly terrified of the witch, wondering what her sudden appearance would mean. He had heard many frightening stories of how witches turned those who annoyed them into poisonous frogs or warty toads. He didn't like the thought of being poisonous or suffering ghastly warts for that matter so he forced himself to look her straight in the eye.

"Why have you come?" he asked.

The witch gave a hiss, her eyes glowing red like burning coals, and, taken by surprise, Clump jumped back in alarm.

"Because we have unfinished business," the witch declared, and although reluctant, Clump nodded. The witch fumbled inside her cloak. She pulled out the vial with her most treasured spell hidden inside and a small knife wrapped in a yellow sheath.

"Do you remember your promise?" she asked, lifting both the vial and knife closer to his face.

Clump gulped, suddenly afraid.

"Yes," he mumbled, his voice little more than a whine.

"Good, then now is the time to repay your debt," the witch urged, grabbing his hand to shove the bottle and knife into the centre of his palm.

Clump stared down at the two items. "What do you want me to do with these?" he asked, wishing the earth would open up and swallow him whole. He was afraid of what she was about to ask of him, especially after seeing the knife, and he felt his knees shake.

The witch turned abruptly.

"Walk with me," she commanded, following a path which had been left by the tide. Clump obeyed and like a puppy, kept to her heels.

"There's a lot I need to explain to you in such a short time," said the witch, looking out across the water. She pointed in the direction she had just flown. "In the Kingdom of Nine Winters there is much unrest and you are perhaps not aware of this but King Forusian, King of the Nonhawks, is dead."

Clump couldn't believe his ears but inside he was pleased as punch, especially after what had happened at the castle.

Clump simply stared after her.

"I can't say I'm upset to hear that," he said, trying hard not to sound relieved.

The witch continued to gaze towards the horizon.

"That may be so, but unfortunately his death will not bring peace to our lands as one might have expected. Instead there are those who will use his death to seek power and revenge, making the rest of us extremely vulnerable."

"What do you mean?" asked Clump, and his eyes searched the distance to see what fascinated the witch so much.

The witch spun around to face him, which caught him off guard.

"Let me start at the beginning," she said, pushing away the hood of her cloak. Clump was repulsed at seeing her face again and as the witch talked, he tried his best not to look at her hideous features.

The witch cleared her throat, seemingly oblivious.

"Many moons ago, Queen Amella gave birth out of wedlock to a daughter. The Elders found out that the father was a magician and this went against their laws so they banished the child."

"Banished her, to where?"

"To the ordinary world, of course, where Crystal would be raised by a woman, a mere mortal."

"Raised by a mortal," Clump repeated, "that's bizarre."

The witch stepped closer and Clump caught a whiff of her body odour and he thought she smelled sour, like milk left out in the sun. He stepped out of her way and she shuffled along the shore, the tide lapping about her feet and the bottom of her cloak was soon soiled.

Clump didn't leave her side. He was curious and wanted to learn more about the princess.

"How come the mortal didn't grow suspicious of her new daughter?" he asked.

The witch turned towards him, her mouth pulled down into an unflattering line.

"The late King of the Elves, Amella's father, paid me well to switch the newborn child with another which had died. He then told me to lay an enchantment so no one would ever learn the terrible truth of what he'd done."

"That's awful," Clump declared, his face aghast. "So, did they send the child away forever?"

The witch nodded.

"Yes, that was the plan, but now the child has returned and there are those who wish to see both her and her family dead. If this became a reality, the realms would start a great war and in time those who are deemed magical would be sold into slavery."

"Isn't there something that can be done to stop all this?" cried Clump, in despair.

"Yes, there is a way, and that is why I need your help. Queen Amella's life is in great danger and only her daughter can save her."

"So, do you have a plan?"

The witch appeared to chuckle and pointed to the vial which he still held in one of his gigantic hands.

"Inside that bottle there is a spell which will create a firebird. The creature will take you back to the Canyon before heading off and retrieving the princess. Once the bird has kidnapped her, it will return to the Canyon and place Crystal in your care."

"What! Me! ... are you out of your mind? and anyhow, I've only just escaped from there myself," Clump burbled, a tad upset.

The witch remained seemingly cold-hearted.

"Yes, I understand your dilemma, but I'm afraid you'll have to go back."

"No, that's just it, you don't understand, I can't."

"I'm afraid you don't have a choice. You must do what I ask so that we can throw a false trail ensuring those who wish to harm the princess will be unable to track her down."

"What do you mean?" Clump queried, bringing his finger to his mouth and biting his nails. "You're not making sense."

The witch gave an exasperated cry and lashed out to grab his arm. She pulled him close, holding him tight and he was shocked by the strength of her grip.

"What's to understand?" she hissed, menacingly. "To repay your debt I need you to take the princess to the Stannary Mines of the Lost Trinity. There you will find the Book of Souls and awaken the fourth mage."

"But ... but ... the Book of Souls is guarded by demons!" Clump stammered, trying to force her to let go.

"Yes, so I've heard," said the witch, relaxing her hold, "however, she's going to need the book and it's your job to find it."

Clump rubbed his arm, his round eyes wide with fear.

"So ... so ... the blade ... it's for Crystal to use?"

"Yes, that's right. It's a ceremonial knife used by wizards. The Book of Souls will only open when blood is dripped upon it. Thankfully Crystal's father is a magician so when she uses the knife, her own blood should be powerful enough to make the book open its pages to her. Of course, there are no guarantees."

Clump was beginning to realise he was in way over his head.

"I really want to keep my end of the bargain, honest I do, but I don't think I'm the right person for such an important task. I mean, how can I take care of a princess?"

"You will do fine," snapped the witch in response. "The elves would never suspect a Windigo to have taken Crystal plus a firebird isn't real so they will be unable to track it down. Your cover is perfect. All you have to do is get her to the mine, find the book and help her to unlock the fourth mage."

Clump had to admit, said like that, it didn't sound quite so bad.

"So, you're telling me that if I do this I will be released from my obligation to you?"

"Yes, then we call it quits."

"And you'll not bother me anymore?"

The witch lifted an eyebrow and her lips twitched ever so slightly at the corners.

"I may be a witch, but I always keep my promises, good or bad," she replied, her tone curt.

"Very well, I accept."

"A wise decision," said the witch with a sudden cackle, "because I wasn't going to leave here until you did!"

Chapter 15

Horith and Brid flew as the crow flies across the Valley of the Green Witch and for them, into unknown territory. Back in the Canyon when Horith spoke the words of the spell which the mining troll had revealed, the flying contraption had soared high into the air and taken them many miles away from home. Horith steered the wings, his stump resting in a loop he'd made which was attached to the frame. Brid was situated behind him, strapped in a separate harness although she clung to him for dear life, her hands clasped around his broad chest.

Brid was in awe of flying. She had never experienced anything like it in her short lifetime and she now wished she had been born a bird so she could enjoy the freedom of the open skies over and over again.

She watched her old world disappear, to be replaced with green trees and woodland. All her life she had only experienced the red dust of the Canyon and to see such a carpet of beauty, filled her mind with wonder. She sensed Horith felt the same. He was busy laughing and whooping at everything he could see from the long dark river that ran through the Canyon to the ice-peaked mountains that towered before them in the distance.

Brid also found that the further they flew away from the village, the more peace she felt inside her soul. She loved Horith with all her heart and she couldn't wait until they started their new life together. She was still aware of the tough decision she had made to leave her family behind, but her love for him would make everything they had to endure, bearable.

As the sun rose high in the sky, they flew past a vast set of black caves and Brid shuddered when she saw smoke billowing out from several dark holes. She instinctively recognised the homes of dragons and was unable to stop the shiver that shot down her spine.

"How much further?" she shouted in Horith's ear, just as the wind tried to whip her voice away.

"I'm not sure. I guess we'll be going wherever the spell takes us," Horith yelled back and Brid looked down to see a copse of trees lying below them.

A strong wind rose up, and they shot forward and Horith shouted for her to hold on tight. A back draught of air tickled Brid's neck and she automatically glanced over her shoulder. Her eyes caught sight of something that glistened like shards of glass in the distance and her heart skipped a beat.

"Look out! I think we've got an Ice Dragon on our tail," she almost screamed at Horith and she wriggled to break free of the harness.

"Keep still," Horith warned, steering the wings as best he could but Brid panicked, watching the huge dragon as it pounded its wings, cutting through the air at breakneck speed. A deep-throated rattle filled her ears and a sound which reminded her of a furnace door being opened roared through the air. A burning sensation touched the back of her neck and Brid didn't need to turn around to know the dragon wasn't far behind them.

Another great roar filled the air and a powerful flame must have shot from the dragon's mouth, the very tip reaching Brid, scorching the back of her tunic. She felt as though her body was on fire; the thick hairs on both her arms and legs curled up and withered away, like paper touched by a candle.

"We're going to die!" she cried, and a blaze of heat soaked her body in sweat.

"Just hold on as long as you can!" Horith begged, trying to manipulate the wings so that they dropped closer to land.

"Can't you get this thing to go any faster, before it's too late?" Brid pleaded, still trying to get out of the harness.

"I'm doing my best!" Horith gasped, "but all that wriggling isn't making things any easier."

Brid stopped what she was doing to look back once again but this time she could only open and close her mouth like a goldfish.

To her horror, she saw the dragon was upon them and it would be just a matter of seconds before they were both fried.

"Do something!" she yelled, pulling at the neck of Horith's tunic and almost strangled him in the process. Horith yanked the cord which made them bear right. As they turned, he grappled inside his bag and pulled out a sharp-bladed knife. He reached up and hacked away at the rope which held the leather wings to the wooden frame. He sliced through the twisted fibre, his hand

133

moving back and forth until the strands withered and snapped. The rope fell away and the wing flapped wildly in the wind, causing the contraption to lose momentum. Like a bird suffering a broken wing they fell from the sky. Brid's eyes widened with fear when the dragon locked its wings and prepared to dive, its furious cry filled the sky.

"Try and land by those trees!" Brid begged, tightening her grip around Horith's neck.

"That's what I'm trying to do, but I can't seem to steer it in the right direction," he bellowed in reply.

"Look out!" Brid cried in dismay, "we're heading straight for the river!"

Sure enough, they crashed to the ground, rolled and ... Splash! They plunged straight under its icy depths and sank like a stone below the cold surface. The water was deep and Brid panicked when she found she was trapped. In desperation, she pulled at the harness, her fingers unable to find the fastening which held her body prisoner. The instinct to survive forced her to grab the leather strap and yank it as hard as she could. From using sheer brute strength, the piece of leather snapped and bubbles of oxygen left her mouth as she gasped in shocked surprise. With her bonds broken, she swam towards the surface but sensed Horith hadn't managed to break free. She half turned and to her dismay, saw he was being dragged closer to the riverbed.

Brid continued to swim back towards daylight and after breaking the surface, she took a huge breath, filled her lungs with sweet air and then diving back under the water. She made her way back towards the riverbed, her strong arms cutting through the water, and in seconds she spotted Horith still trapped inside the harness. To her horror, she realised he wasn't moving.

Fear stabbed at her heart and her pulse quickened. The thought of him drowning after everything they'd gone through made her use her powerful arms to swim quickly to his side. As soon as she reached him she lifted his head, saw his eyes were closed and in a panic, shook him, trying to get him to awaken. When there was no response, she lifted his face, placing her thick lips over his. She held his nose and blew oxygen into his mouth and felt a moment of exhilaration when Horith's eyes flew open.

Overhead, the river ignited with an ice-blue glow. Flames of indigo mixed with azure shimmered upon the surface. Brid pulled away, seeing only the beauty of the Ice Dragon's flames which were rolling over the surface of the river. Horith grabbed her arm, causing her attention to switch back to him. Her fingers ripped at the harness until he was free and then she gripped his wrist, lifting him towards the surface. He was a dead weight, her injured leg making their progress slow, but she willed herself to drag him closer to the shore. They both coughed and spluttered the moment they broke the surface and it appeared to Brid that it took them ages to haul their weary bodies onto dry land.

Brid laid Horith onto his side before collapsing, exhausted, onto the bank. Her breathing was laboured after her ordeal not to mention her injured calf throbbed like hell, yet all she could think about was the fact that they had survived the Ice Dragon's attack. She looked down and spotted a vast array of grey stones beneath her feet. Picking up a smooth pebble, she held it in the palm of her hand, grateful she was alive, enjoying being able to hold onto something solid.

Once she got her breath back, she walked down to the water's edge and stared at the calm surface. No one would ever know just how close they had both come to drowning, the flying contraption now hidden forever in a watery grave. She looked about, getting her bearings, moving several stones to reveal the wet earth underneath. She pressed her toes deep into the mud before walking further along the shore, making sure her tracks were seen to be going upstream. After doubling back, she sat waiting for Horith to get over his ordeal. After a few minutes she watched him roll onto his side, so she urged him to get to his feet.

"We can't stay here in case we're seen, it's too dangerous," she reasoned.

To her despair, Horith didn't move a muscle.

"Come on, get up!" she snapped, pulling roughly at his good hand. "We're too exposed out here."

Horith moaned and flayed his arms by his side, coughing and spluttering in reply.

Brid felt frustration rise inside her gut.

"Listen to me! We need to get out of sight," she urged, and bent down to shake him. She could see he was suffering after his terrible ordeal but she also knew they were still in great danger.

A dark shadow appeared in the sky and Brid looked down and saw the silhouette of a giant beast travelling along the surface of the water.

"Oh no, it's the Ice Dragon!" she shrieked, grabbing hold of his forearms, "it's returned to kill us!"

She roared with frustration, determined they would make it out of here alive. She pulled at her mate with all of her might and saw him dig his heels in-between the stones and push himself up. He finally rose and they staggered towards the trees. Brid glanced back to see the dragon flying low, smoke trailing from its nostrils. They hid behind the pine trees for what seemed like hours, both terrified of being seen or, worse, burned into nonexistence.

As darkness fell, they moved further inland and were surprised when they came across an abandoned shelter. They had never seen a stone dwelling before but they could see the place had been empty for years.

They entered with caution; afraid of what might be hiding inside, waiting to pounce. Now that Horith was feeling a lot better, he took the lead and made Brid hide behind him. Very slowly he pushed the door open, his one and only knife held securely in his hand. When the door only budged a fraction, he pushed harder and a broken hinge creaked eerily. Horith raised the blade and a flash of colour saw something fly at his face. He staggered back in surprise and Brid let out a cry.

A distressed squawk filled the air and a flurry of feathers saw a speckled mousebird fall to the floor and then run from the shack. Its four pink feet scurried across the ground, its stunted wings flapped yet it was unable to fly. Horith lunged forward and brought the knife down just behind its head. He pinned the rodent to the ground, it squealed, collapsed and died at his feet. Horith pulled out the knife, wiped the blood from the blade against the door frame and then placed it back inside the bag. He bent down and seized hold of the large rodent.

"At least we have dinner," he said, and a huge grin split his mouth from ear to ear. He turned and entered the dwelling, his feet

136

silent against the ancient floorboards. Brid followed, looking about her and saw only tumbled down walls and blackened timber. To her right sat a broken oil lamp on a table that was covered in a thick layer of dust. She fiddled with the lamp, not sure how to get it to work but soon realised it was of no use, there was no oil left inside.

She found the whole place consisted of only one room. It was rather sparse but it held a fireplace and a hearth which was covered in black soot. Horith moved the oil lamp and plonked the rodent onto the table with a thud, white feathers flying up into the air.

"At least we should be able to eat here without being disturbed," he said, patting the dead carcass.

Brid nodded, pleased they were able to fill their empty bellies at least. She glanced around her new abode and then looked up to notice there wasn't much holding the roof together.

"This will do for now," she said, seeing the first stars peer through thickened cloud. "At least we have plenty of cover in the woods tonight and tomorrow we can sleep here and then move on in a day or two when you have fully recovered.

Horith walked towards her and Brid flung her arms around his thick, hairy neck, hugging him tight.

"For a moment out there I thought I'd lost you," she breathed in his ear and Horith reacted by pulling her even closer.

"It will take more than a river and a hungry dragon to finish me off," he said gruffly, and Brid relaxed her arms so she could look deep into his eyes. She would be eternally grateful for his unconditional love. Even after everything she had gone through and the scars she would bear for the rest of her life he still, and always would, love her. She unconsciously brushed her cheek with her fingers and felt pain fill her face from the shattered cheekbone. Her thoughts ran to when she had been brought home by Clump and how she'd been unable to eat a thing for days, unable to open her mouth even an inch. She had watched how her mother had been beside herself with worry. Isis had made some watery soup and her sister used a flat paddle to spoon as much as she could past her un-cooperative lips. It had been a slow process, but it was enough to keep her alive. When Horith escaped from Forusian's castle he had barely left her side, coaxing her to eat and drink until she was strong enough to rise from her sickbed.

"What's the matter?" Horith asked, letting her go.

Brid merely sighed.

"Oh, I'm just missing everyone," she said, looking for something to busy herself with. She found a dirty old mat stuck between the table and a broken chair and she grabbed one of the corners to pull it out of the way. Dust rose in the air and she coughed and spluttered, wiping her nose when particles of dirt tickled her nostrils, unaware she was spreading a thick black line across her face.

"We had to do what was right for us," said Horith, as she turned to see the hurt look in his eyes. "Oh, I don't regret our decision for one minute," she insisted, dropping the mat to rush to his side. "I just wish mother and Felan could have come with us, that's all."

Horith nodded but his shoulders sagged and he placed his bag next to the dead mousebird.

"Yeah, me too," he admitted, clutching her hand so he could give it a squeeze. He then lifted his hand to wipe away the dirt from her face.

Brid caught his hand and kissed his fingers.

"Let's eat and then hide the bag somewhere so we can head on out into the woods later without worrying about losing it."

Horith's grin broadened and she could see she had lifted his spirits.

"Yes, that's a good idea as we need to explore and find our way around," he agreed, grabbing hold of the bag to head towards the fireplace. His hand shot up the chimney and he gave a loud chuckle. "Great, just as I'd thought. There's a hole inside the cavity, I can leave the bag in there and hopefully no one will stumble across it whilst we're gone."

Without saying another word he rolled up the agave bag and stuffed it inside the fireplace.

"I'm sure it will be safe in there until morning," he said, moving to her side. He took her hand in his, guiding her out of the shack and towards the trees.

"How did you know there would be somewhere to hide your bag inside those stones?" Brid asked.

"I didn't, I just guessed."

138

"Really? Well, I have to say I think you're a very clever Windigo," Brid declared, impressed.

"I know," said Horith, putting his arm around her neck. "That's why you love me."

Chapter 16

Since the incident with Clump, a sense of foreboding had swept throughout the entire village and there appeared nothing Serpen could do to stop it. Zebulon was behind it all, insisting their misfortune was because he had angered the Gods and as time passed by, Serpen began to believe he could be right. It appeared the whole village now suffered great hardship. Food was scarce and tempers flared and on more than one occasion, Serpen had seen an accusing finger point in his direction.

One night Serpen went out hunting alone. He was determined to find enough food to keep the village from starving and he felt a moment of euphoria when he came across the body of a dead griffon. He sniffed the carcass suspiciously but when he checked, there wasn't a mark on the body. Its eagle wings were both intact and its lion's mane and thick ropy tail had not been touched. Serpen pawed at its mouth until its gums were visible and saw several teeth missing. He looked at the head and saw flashes of grey and he soon came to the conclusion that the beast had died from old age. He gave a loud howl of contentment, his breath rising like white smoke. He felt the worry in his shoulders ease; finding the creature intact would be seen by the Elders as a good omen. He ran back to the campfires and assembled several hunters who dragged the stiffened carcass back to the village. When they returned, the entire pack gathered around the dead body, and their excited howls only melted away when dawn broke.

The morning sun rose and the tribe's butcher was quick to gather his tools. Unlike the rest, he was skilled at carving flesh and he worked tirelessly, ensuring every edible part of the great beast was cut away from the bone. Nothing was wasted and the best cuts were given to the chief. Serpen accepted his share, his shoulders back, proud of his recent achievement. He knew bringing back such a prize would win him favour amongst the Elders who would believe their troubles would now be a thing of the past.

Unfortunately for Serpen, Horith and Brid chose that very morning to disappear. At first, when he heard they were gone, he wasn't too alarmed, thinking they were probably lolling in the sun somewhere after eating their fill, but when Isis became agitated with worry, he sent out the scouts to find them. Hours later he was surprised when they returned empty-handed, their mouths fixed in a grim line. He questioned them both, convinced the youngsters had been merely overlooked, but the scouts shook their heads, refusing to accept such a notion. Serpen's puzzlement deepened when the scouts swore that their tracks ended close to the river. They explained how they stopped abruptly at the water's edge and Serpen shook his head, refusing to believe that the two could have simply vanished into thin air. The troubled scouts pointed to the horizon, adding how they had searched the Canyon floor and along the mountain ridges but found no trace of the two young Windigos anywhere.

Isis tried to convince him they had been taken by another tribe and Serpen was persuaded that this could very well be true. He headed straight to the Polak tribe to see if they had either seen or heard of the whereabouts of his missing daughter. He visited the chief, but did not get the warm welcome he expected. Instead the long-coated Windigo met him with a cold, hard stare, stating that should his wayward daughter return, she would not be accepted into the Polak tribe and that she was no longer betrothed to his eldest son. The Andark was outraged at this turn of events and swore revenge. He could not believe they dared to question his daughter's honour and a fight broke out. Serpen was restrained and forced to leave before things got ugly but he swore he would never forgive the chief at what he saw as betrayal.

He therefore returned to the village without answers, aware the tribe was once again beginning to lose faith in him as a leader. To make matters worse, his new partner was proving to be a complete disaster. Greer was the worst homemaker he'd ever met and she was too shy to mingle with the other tribe members. She didn't know how to cook or clean, to wash the clothes or mend the holes in his tunic. Her only thoughts were to make herself beautiful. For hours she would sit by herself, grooming her coat and combing her long, silken ears. Serpen decided she was simply a pleasant distraction and nothing more. He found himself staying out of her way and when they ate together he was not a good companion.

141

At night if he didn't go hunting he pretended he was sleepy or not feeling well. He soon realised he did not want to be around her, in fact, he had to admit to himself that he did not care for her at all. He had been drawn only to her pretty face and youthful nature, but now he realised he did not find her character so appealing. In the end, he decided he had made a terrible mistake and no longer wished to be with her, his only thoughts were of Isis and how much he wanted her back. He was aware that she was living happily in Lyra's cave. Having forced her to believe Clump was dead, he knew she would never forgive him, or allow him back into her life.

Of course, Serpen was far too proud to ask for forgiveness or to admit he had not taken Greer to his chamber and mated with her like he'd intended. The truth was that on the day he brought her back to the cave, he had seen Isis walk by; she'd caught his eye and the passion he'd felt for the young female evaporated away like rainwater. He tried to win her favour by bringing her small gifts such as the griffon's claws and teeth, which could be used to make necklaces, but Isis rebuffed him time and time again, until he grew angry and his love turned to hate. Unable to bear being around her any longer, he used Horith and Brid's disappearance as an excuse to get away from the village, to spend some much needed time alone.

Serpen was sick of hearing idle gossip, the low whispers from the Elders which said they had run away together. He cursed them all, thinking them stupid, aware that Brid would never dare do such a terrible thing against her family. It was now obvious they had been taken, he just needed to prove by whom.

He set out early the next morning whilst the sun was low in the sky. He took his bone-handled hunting knife, a gift from his mother, a few bits of meat and an animal skin filled with water, placing them all inside an agave bag. He snuck out of the cave, whilst Greer was still asleep, hoping he would not disturb her and save himself from having to listen to her perpetual whining. He headed away from the campfires. The village was peaceful at this time of day with most of the villagers sleeping. He often found that only those with young ones would not yet have gone to their beds. He carried on at a swift pace until he heard footsteps coming up from behind, he swung around to see Isis hurrying after him.

"Where are you going?" she gasped, reaching his side.

Serpen felt his shoulders tense.

"What do you care?" he snapped.

He saw her eyes narrow.

"Look, whatever you're thinking, you shouldn't go out there alone," she replied, glancing down towards the knife.

Serpen lifted the blade closer to his chest.

"Why? What's it to you? I would have thought you would be pleased to see the back of me," he retorted.

Isis threw her hands into the air. "Why do you always have to act like a stubborn pig!" she exclaimed, stamping her foot in the dirt. "Tell me, why can't we have a decent conversation just once in a while?"

Serpen felt his temper rise.

"I haven't time for all this, what is it that you want?" he demanded, his upper lip curling.

Isis folded her arms across her chest and let out a deep sigh.

"Are you going in search of Brid and Horith?" she asked.

"Yes," Serpen replied with a scowl, "although it isn't actually any of your business what I do."

Isis cleared her throat, her stance making her look a little uneasy.

"So, what will you do should you find them?" she asked in a low voice.

"Well, that all depends," Serpen growled and the knife flashed in his hand.

Isis licked her lips, a sign she was anxious.

"I need to know what your plans are, I mean, if you find they haven't been taken."

At her words, Serpen lifted both brows. He was surprised by her question. Surely she didn't now think Brid would be foolish enough to run away with the likes of Horith? He resisted the urge to laugh in her face; instead, he flicked his tongue across his mouth and pulled his lips tight.

"Do you mean if they have run away together?"

Isis nodded, refusing to look him in the eye.

"Then I'll kill them both where they stand and place their heads on a spike."

143

He thrust the knife towards her, stopping only inches from her ribcage. Isis never moved, her eyes fixed upon the blade. It was clear from the look on her face that she understood what he was capable of. He lowered his hand, opened his mouth to speak, but before he had chance to utter a word, Isis turned her back on him and head towards the caves.

Serpen watched her leave with growing contempt. In the pit of his stomach a fire of fury burst into life. How could she think, for just one second, that their daughter would dare to dishonour him? In anger, he thrust the knife inside the bag and turned on his heels. Setting off at a brisk pace he headed deeper into the Canyon, determined to prove Isis's notion to be completely unfounded.

He advanced past the rocks and soon reached the river where Brid and Horith's tracks had ended. Serpen looked up at the ridge and pondered in which direction he should go. He decided to head north, travelling towards the Valley of the Green Witch. His gut feeling was that whoever had taken the youngsters would have most likely come from the other side of the mountain. He didn't believe for one minute it was the elves, it was simply not their way.

When darkness descended, he found a dry hollow and filled it with pine needles and small branches, making himself a bed for the night. Because he was in unfamiliar territory, he decided that later, when he shifted, he would not roam far. Instead he ate a little meat and hid himself away.

Serpen had been curled up in his wolf form for some time when he was jolted from his slumber, his breathing somewhat ragged. His heart raced, having suffered a terrible premonition. This was the first he'd ever experienced since his initiation from the Gods. His body felt as though it was on fire and dark images swirled like ghosts in the forefront of his mind. A powerful vision revealed to him that Clump was still alive. His dream showed his son to be flying on the back of gigantic bird. It was like nothing he'd ever seen before, and he could see the creature clearly with its magnificent sulphur-coloured wings and crown of golden feathers. He couldn't unravel the clues which the Gods were trying to tell him, sensing instead that the forewarning was a bad omen. In the vision Clump had not been alone; there was a young girl with him, whose face rippled like the surface of a pond, making it impossible to glimpse her facial features. When he could bear seeing the images no longer, he left the safety of the hollow and wandered into the embrace of a cold night's kiss. He trotted off to a nearby stream and washed the dust from his throat. When his nerves calmed, he went back to his bed and fell into a deep slumber.

It was still early morning when he awoke, yet he had been so traumatised by his experience he had slept right through his transformation. Serpen was deeply troubled by what he'd seen and couldn't make head nor tail of his newfound knowledge. There were many things he still needed to learn and understand and whilst he mulled over these thoughts, he cleared out the hollow. He did not want anyone finding out he had travelled in this direction, ensuring there was no trace of a wolf having rested here for the night.

After eating a meagre breakfast, he collected his belonging and headed towards unfamiliar mountains. Although he was quite a large Windigo, reaching over nine feet tall, he was surprisingly light on his feet. He set off on his journey and soon broke into a run. His powerful legs crossed the rugged terrain with ease as he focused on reaching the valley ahead by nightfall.

Serpen carried on running until he entered a place known as the Dragon's Plateau. Over the horizon he could see the north valley and to the south, a deep ravine. This was not the same place where Horith and Brid had suffered their ordeal at the hands of the Nonhawks. Here, an eerie silence followed him with each hastened step. The ground was covered in a multitude of ancient rock formations, a vast area where magma had once spewed over the terrain. Serpen could also see obvious signs that dragons still roamed these parts. Unidentifiable charred remains littered the ground alongside decomposing bodies of large animals. Serpen watched his step and trod with care. The crunch of small bones under his feet sounded loud in his ears, and he could see an array of charred skulls strewn along the ground. Like trophies, some were perched on high ledges whilst others sat lost and abandoned between the igneous rocks. Serpen was no fool and didn't linger.

At midday he came across a raging river. Jumping from one large slab of stone to another, he was taken by complete surprise when a rock crumbled like flour beneath his feet. He lost his balance, tumbled between several jagged rocks, and landed on a hard bed of stone. He winced, let out a cry, pain shooting down his neck and spine. Cursing, he glanced over the rocks to see the contents of his bag strewn across the ground. He spotted the knife, lying just a few inches away. He gritted his teeth when the pain in his neck lingered yet he managed to roll onto his side. A noise, a light hiss close to his ear made him freeze on the spot. A menacing sound, a warning, convinced him he had landed in a nest of vipers.

With slow, meticulous movements, Serpen tilted his head so he could see exactly what he was up against. He turned only a fraction to see the face of a cobra. The snake flicked its long black tongue towards him and Serpen's eyes widened in disbelief. He counted not just one snake, but nine. He glanced down and unconsciously sucked in his breath because all nine heads were connected to just one body. He had never seen such a snake before, and although he was quite astounded, he realised he was also in serious trouble. He stared at each head in turn, whilst nine long tongues flickered and hissed in his direction. His eyes searched for the blade. It wasn't far away, lying just a few inches from his hand, and he stared at the handle, almost willing it to jump into his palm.

As quick as a flash, he thrust himself forward and grabbed the knife, turning swiftly to slice the edge of the blade across all nine necks. The snake didn't have time to react before each head fell to the ground, one by one, like dominoes. The body, now limp and lifeless, dropped to the floor, lying in the dirt in a coil of bloodied flesh. Serpen found he was breathing heavily. He fell back, his head resting on a stone, unable to believe his luck at killing the nine headed cobra before it had time to strike.

He tried to calm his beating heart, adrenalin still pumping through his veins. After taking several deep breaths, he stood up, his legs a little shaky and he twisted his neck from side to side, rounding his shoulders to check neither was broken. Relieved to find his bones intact, he gave a huge sigh of relief. Bending down, Serpen swept all of the severed heads into the palm of his hand. Flicking one into his mouth he bit down on the flesh and, finding he liked the flavour, devoured all nine at once. When he'd finished, he licked his fingers clean, then cut up the snake's body into bite-size pieces. He threw away the tip of the tail, a yellow and green streak flashing against a pale sun. He gathered the food and his belongings, before searching for a bridge or someplace where he could cross the river.

He set off at a fast pace, heading upstream for about a quarter of a mile but to his dismay he found nothing that would help him reach the other side. Serpen grew impatient but the water was a little calmer now, and so he decided it would be far quicker if he simply swam across. Although the current was fast moving, in his opinion, it didn't look too deep and time was of the essence. Eager to cross, he waded in, startled when the water rose right up to his waist and it was so cold it took his breath away.

He placed his bag on the top of his head so that the contents wouldn't get wet and pushed through the icy waters. With the noise of the river loud in his ears, he reached its centre to find the current was far stronger than he first anticipated. To make matters worse, the stones under his feet were covered with algae and water moss, making them very slippery indeed. Aware of this fact, Serpen took slow, calculated steps. He looked down and saw a flash of silver and then pain shot through his foot when something bit his big toe.

The shock caused him to lose his balance and before he knew it, he was under the surface. His legs struggled to find firm ground, his arms flailing in the water and he soon became disoriented. He fought his way to the surface; his hand still clasped around his bag. He struggled to stay afloat, he was not used to swimming for long periods of time and he cursed his misfortune. Exhausted, he tried to swim back to shore but his strength was all but gone and, to his dismay, he was washed further downstream. His attempts at reaching the bank were futile as the current dragged him away, but through sheer determination and a bit of luck, he was finally able to grab hold of a low hanging branch and pull himself to safety. He heaved himself from the river and then staggered onto the shore. He sat in the dirt, thankful to still be alive. He found his lungs ached and his big toe throbbed as though a hammer had smashed down on it. For the very first time since he'd started out on his journey, Serpen wished he'd stayed at home.

Chapter 17

The morning after the witch visited, Clump went fishing. He waded out into the water with just his bag at his side and waited. Clump was a very patient Windigo and had become quite good at tickling fish. Bruis had shown him this technique, and although he still preferred wild berries and tasty shoots, he found he was rather partial to the odd fish supper.

As the morning sun glowed above his head, Clump caught himself three shiny fishes before making his way back to shore. He was preparing himself for his new adventure and although he was scared about what he was about to do, he was also a little excited.

After the witch explained everything he needed to know about Crystal and his quest, he realised he was going to be involved in something which could change his life forever. He hoped that when he met the princess, she would not be too mad at being kidnapped and, more importantly, he prayed she did not think him frightful or terribly ugly. He understood only too well that the elves thought very little of Windigos and that they feared them above all other creatures.

He therefore decided that once he reached the Canyon, he would show the firebird the whereabouts of a cave, hidden in the side of the mountain. It was high up, almost out of sight, and would make the perfect place for the bird to deposit its royal passenger. He'd used it once before, to escape the wrath of his father, however, the rock was known to crumble, making it treacherous to climb. He decided he'd take his chances and use the cave so that Crystal would be unable to run away. Also, if she screamed when she saw him, no one would be able to hear her cries. He was happy with this idea and once he made up his mind that he was ready, he filled his bag with what he thought to be essential items, gifts which Bruis had left behind. He grabbed the small bag of seed, the two bottles of Buttermead and the ceremonial knife given to him by the witch. Once he had collected his few belongings, Clump took the piece of driftwood which the Plainwalker had given him and buried it deep in the earth, just at the base of the burnt oak tree. He believed it would be safe there until he returned and he certainly didn't want to risk losing such a special gift on his travels.

He then made his way to the shore. The water lapped in-between his toes as he braced himself and uncorked the tiny glass vial. He was nervous but excited at the same time. He wondered what his mother would think of him helping a witch and a cold shudder ran down his spine. He already knew the answer, aware she would not be pleased. He shook these thoughts from his mind and tipped the bottle to one side. When nothing happened, he tipped it a little further and a stream of golden particles slipped from the bottle neck. They glowed like the morning sun, lifting high into the air and Clump watched, mesmerised.

A shimmer of light spread across the sky, and soon he could make out the shape of the firebird's wings, tail feathers and crown. In just seconds, colour flooded the apparition and the firebird flapped its great wings, flexing its smooth, curved talons. Clump stared in awe as the gigantic bird flew down onto the sand and gave him a sweet trill of acknowledgement. The firebird was so vibrant in colour it almost hurt his eyes to look at it. He had to admit he had never seen anything so beautiful or exotic, but the witch's warning jangled inside his head. She had made it crystal clear that he must be on his way as soon as possible, and that the spell would only last for a day, perhaps two at most.

He stared at the magnificent creature standing before him and decided because the bird was so beautiful, it had to be female. He understood she wasn't real, just a magic spell, but watching her preen herself made him feel she really existed.

With cautious steps he made his way to her side and the firebird lowered her head in greeting. "You must take me to the Red Canyon," Clump said with a gulp, and he reached up to stroke her breast feathers. The firebird squawked her compliance and dropped down onto the sand so that Clump could climb onto her back.

Clump hesitated but then he swung his huge legs over the widest part of her back and once he was settled, grabbed hold of the feathers around her neck.

"Let's go," he cried, closing his eyes and the firebird let out another squawk and vibrations shook his body as she ran along the shore. Clump felt the wind in his hair and his long ears blew wildly in the breeze. He heard the rustle of feathers as the bird outstretched her wings and his stomach did a double somersault. He opened his eyes and clung on tight as they flew over the loch. He had never experienced anything so exhilarating and he laughed out loud, enjoying every second.

If only Brid and Felan could see me now, he thought, *what a hoot.*

They flew between the mountains and over rivers that resembled twisted snakes. Clump had never witnessed such delights. Glancing down he saw huge pine trees, their brown trunks like tiny sticks pushed into the ground and he grinned with utter pleasure. He felt alive as though he was really seeing everything for the first time and he drank in his surroundings as if dying of thirst.

The firebird flew on and on until it reached the Red Canyon, the warm scent of the desert wafting high in the air. He continued to enjoy the ride until everything around him became familiar and when they flew over his village, Clump tried to hide within her thick plumes. He saw black rocks and campfires, and small little pinheads that were his tribe running about like ants on the ground. Clump felt a sudden burst of homesickness. He tried to see if he could spot either his mother or two sisters. Within seconds the village was out of sight and Clump guided the firebird closer to the cave which lay hidden inside the mountain.

The bird swooped low and flapped its wings in firm, even strokes. "Leave me at the foot of the mountain," Clump cried. "There's no point me waiting inside the cave until you get back as you'll be gone for hours and I'll go stir-crazy in there." The firebird did as she was asked, her wings dropped back, and she dived closer to land. Her feathers dipped and her talons scraped along the earth before she came to a standstill.

The sun was still an orange ball when Clump slid off the firebird's back. His feet touched solid ground and he enjoyed feeling sand and grit between his toes once again.

He turned to face the firebird, his eyes solemn. "That was fun but you know what you must do now," he said, and the firebird gave a sharp cry and flapped her wings fiercely. She once again rose into the air and Clump watched until she disappeared over the horizon.

With the firebird gone, Clump made his ascent up the side of the mountain. Although it would have been far easier for the firebird to drop him inside the cave, Clump thought that this way his mind would be kept preoccupied. He knew the climb could be dangerous. If the mountain folk spotted him he would be in serious trouble, but he understood the way of the mountain well enough to know that the risk he was taking was minimal.

It took him several hours to make the climb and by the time he entered the cave, he wished he'd not been such an idiot and, instead, allowed the firebird to drop him inside. He was exhausted, but at least he hadn't died of boredom which had been his only other option.

He looked about for something he could use to start a fire. The evening had turned cool and it wouldn't be long before night fell. Once he'd found a few twigs and enough wisps of brushwood to light a fire, he felt a foreboding shiver creep along his spine. He had no idea what Crystal was like or whether the witch's magic was stronger than the princess's. The witch had told him that the royal visitor would not be a problem but he didn't quite understand what she meant. He wanted to question the witch further but didn't feel confident enough to ask her to go into more detail. He truly hoped the princess would not turn him into one of those warty toads he'd heard so much about and he brought his fingers to his lips, afraid of being transformed into something small and helpless.

He gazed out from the mouth of the cave and saw the silhouette of a large bird cross the surface of the moon. The firebird gave a cry as she descended into the cave and Clump flung himself against the wall, trying his best to hide in the shadows. He wished now that he hadn't agreed to help the witch and he gripped his stomach when he thought his bowels were about to open from fear.

He heard the firebird settle her wings and then tiny footsteps belonging to the princess, crept closer. The cave curved to the right so he was hidden from sight, only the flames from the flickering fire were visible. Clump knew it was no good, he was going to have to face the princess one way or another and eventually, he found his courage and lunged forward. The moment he came around the bend he saw a vision of beauty, a young girl with hair the colour of fire. Their eyes locked and to his dismay she let out an earth shattering scream. She took a step back, almost stumbled, and then she turned and ran in the opposite direction.

"Don't be afraid," he cried, chasing after her. "I promise you, I'm not here to hurt you." His words clearly fell on deaf ears because the princess tried to climb onto the firebird's back. He finally reached her, his two strong arms enfolding her waist as he tried to stop her from getting away. She screamed again, sounding hysterical and almost perforated his eardrum. The princess was like a wildcat, struggling to break free but Clump merely tightened his grip until he felt her body go limp. Concerned, he relaxed his hold, frightened in case he'd accidentally hurt her. He was relieved when she raised her head to stare up at him once again and he tried to give her a reassuring grin. He saw her eyes widen and then she let out yet another blood-curdling scream.

"Shhh, be quiet," he pleaded, peering down at her. "I'm only here to help you."

"Who are you?" the princess rasped, clearly afraid.

"My name is Clump, I'm a Windigo."

"Sorry, a what?"

"A changeling."

"Oh, I've heard about your kind from one of the magician's back at Nine Winters. I was told you eat immortals, especially elves."

Clump bit his lip. "Yes, most do, but not me."

Crystal continued to gaze at him, her eyes filled with uncertainty. "So what makes you so different?"

Clump shrugged his shoulders.

"I don't know, I just am."

"That's not much of an answer, but I suppose it'll have to do. After all, you're the first Windigo I've ever met."

"Well, I am one of a kind," said Clump, doing a rather bad impression of a twirl.

He was pleased to see that Crystal appeared a little less frightened. With her consent, he once again placed his arms around her, only this time he did it very gently and carried her over to the fire. He placed her feet down on the floor, afraid she would break if he wasn't too careful. She was so petite, so fragile and he was scared he could harm her by accident. He watched her huddle

152

closer to the flames, her skin pink within the soft glow, flawless like porcelain. He saw her push a stray curl behind her ear and thought it odd that she didn't have pointed ears. His mind drifted back to the witch, remembering she had said Crystal's father was a magician and guessed this was the reason why. He waited until she appeared a little more settled and then he came and sat beside her.

"I'm really sorry for scaring you," he said, apologetically. "I just thought it best for us to meet up here where no one could hear your cries," he explained, and he saw Crystal's eyes round with fright.

"Oh, I didn't mean it like that," he added, raising his hand in defence. "It's just, well, I knew you would think me a monster and become frightened the moment you saw me."

He watched Crystal peer down at her feet. He noticed she was wearing animal pelts and her trousers were made of leather. He thought it strange that a princess would be wearing such un-princess like clothes.

"Why have I been kidnapped?" she suddenly asked, glancing up at him and her mouth was fixed in a tight line. Clump felt his own mouth go dry.

"There's a lot I need to explain, but let's eat first," he said, his eyes pleading. He grabbed his bag and busied himself, hunting for something inside. He soon found what he was looking for and he pulled out the three fishes he'd caught earlier in the day, lifting them up by their slippery tails.

"See what I've brought us," he said, giving each fish a shake and he gave her a wide grin that showed a long row of rather large teeth.

Crystal heaved a sigh. "You're changing the subject although I must admit I am rather hungry after my ordeal and your fish do appear quite plump."

Clump was pleased to see she was eager to share a meal with him. Apart from being with Bruis, he had always eaten in secret so this was a real treat for him indeed. He jumped up, searching for something he could use as a skewer.

"I shall cook us a hearty supper and then I will tell you everything I know," he promised, stepping towards the firebird to throw her the biggest fish.

153

The firebird swallowed the offering in two large gulps before trilling its thanks.

"It's a pleasure," said Clump, stroking her soft, feathery down. "I think you've worked very hard today and you deserve it." The firebird trilled a little deeper as though she understood his compliment.

"You really care for her, don't you?" Crystal observed, turning towards him.

Clump nodded. "Yes, I do. You see, there hasn't been much colour in my life and you have to admit she is a bit of a beauty." He chuckled, but it came out more like a choked sob instead. Crystal came to his side to stroke the firebird's soft chest feathers. The bird made a noise of contentment in the back of her throat.

"Oh, I think she likes you," said Clump, pleased. He watched the bird preen herself and dislodge one of her beautiful tail feathers. It floated to the floor.

Clump bent down to retrieve it.

"I think this is for you," he said, holding out the plume.

Crystal stared at the feather and Clump pushed into her hand. "The tail feather of a firebird is exceptionally rare."

"It's also rather striking," said Crystal, clearly in awe of such a gift.

"There's something else about the feather that you should know," said Clump with a grin. "If you rub it between your thumb and forefinger, it will light up like the moon in the sky and show you the way through the darkness."

"Wow! That's incredible," Crystal gasped, staring down at the colourful plume.

"I recommend you keep it somewhere safe," he urged, closing her fingers around it.

"How about your bag, will it be safe there?" Crystal asked, her eyes shining. Clump nodded and they both turned back towards the fire. Once the feather was tucked safely inside his bag, he got to work preparing the fish. He had already gutted them that morning so they were soon roasting over the fire. Whilst they ate, Clump explained about her mother being in serious danger. He spoke about the Stannary Mines and how they needed to find the Book of Souls and awaken the fourth mage.

Crystal listened intently, until he'd finished his story.

"I really don't understand any of this," she said with a sigh, "and why the fourth mage and not the first, second or third?"

Clump told her the story he'd heard long ago about four magicians who once ruled the entire land. They were each born with special gifts to help them rule the realms but only one of them was pure of heart and wished to save his people. He explained how the trusted fourth mage then gave his soul to Merguld, the wizard of the mountain, in exchange for the right to be brought back to life should he ever be needed in the future.

Crystal seemed more and more confused.

"But what does all that have to do with me?" she asked.

Clump tried to keep his mind on the current situation, but he had to admit Crystal was a bit of a distraction. Her features were exquisite and her eyes were shining back at him like sparkling sapphires. He was drawn to her mouth every time she uttered a word. Her lips were red, like the luscious apples Bruis had given to him many moons ago, and he closed his eyes as he tried not to think about nibbling on them. Instead he focused on helping Crystal to piece together the puzzle which would lead her to the fourth mage.

"Clump, are you alright?" she asked, sounding a little concerned.

Clump jolted upright, opened his eyes to stare at her as though he'd been alone with only his thoughts as company.

"Err, what? Oh yes, I'm fine, thank you," he said, and spluttered an apology.

"I was just asking about the fourth mage," Crystal pressed, leaning a little closer.

"Well, according to legend, the fourth mage has the power to save your kingdom and, more importantly, your mother's life."

"But how?" asked Crystal, in an exasperated tone. "I mean if he's so powerful then why hasn't anyone else released him?"

Clump shook his head, clearly bewildered. "I have no idea," he said honestly. "I'm not the one with all the answers. There are those who are far greater who wish only for you to release the mage and I'm sure in time everything will become clear. You must simply trust those who seek only to serve you."

Crystal nodded but looked a little sceptical. "I guess I'm willing to take my chances," she said, sounding thoughtful. "If it's true and my mother is in great danger and the only way to save her is by going to the Stannary Mines, then I'll do whatever it takes."

Clump leaned over and patted her hand.

"That's good to hear and I'm sure you've made the right decision. However, the moon is rising therefore I must leave you now 'til dawn."

Chapter 18

When dawn broke, Brid opened her eyes and the memory of her mother and sister crashed down on her like a gigantic wave. She was lying outside in the forest having found a hole in which to rest, and for some reason had nodded off. It felt good just to lie there, hidden from the world but at the same time she felt a piece of herself was truly missing.

A twig snapped and she lifted her head, her eyes alert. The shack was only a few feet away and she saw Horith making his way towards her. She relaxed, lowering her guard.

"I see you're still tired," he noted, twisting a long blade of grass in his mouth. Brid watched him chew the tip with the edge of his teeth.

"We need to find something to eat," she said, rising to her feet, and she rubbed her empty tummy.

"Breakfast's ready," Horith announced, throwing the blade of grass to the ground and Brid cocked her head, raising one of her thick eyebrows.

"But we've already eaten the mousebird and we didn't find anything else last night," she said, a little disheartened.

Horith gave a chuckle and his teeth gleamed white in the semblance of a smile.

"Oh, I've caught us something much bigger and far tastier than that little morsel we swallowed last night."

Brid was intrigued.

"Really? Like what?"

"I've got us a goblin. He was sneaking around the shack this morning, probably up to no good."

Brid reached out and touched his good hand.

"How on earth did you manage that?"

"Well, it was quite by accident if I'm honest. I was heading back to the shack after you fell asleep and I didn't know he was in there. Anyway, I threw open the door and the little blighter was hiding behind it. I heard a thud and the door bounced back and when I looked behind it, he was lying unconscious."

Brid licked her lips. "I've never eaten goblin before."

157

Horith chuckled. "No, me neither, but Lyra once told me that they're very tender and that their bones make great bread."

Brid almost squealed with glee.

"Let's eat him now!" she declared, refusing to wait any longer. In a flash they both raced back to the shack.

Brid shot ahead, her belly rumbling and her limp almost forgotten at the thought of having such a delightful breakfast. She rushed through the door, a bright smile on her lips and she looked around but couldn't see any sign of a goblin anywhere.

Horith rushed in right behind her and she turned to see a frown drag across his lips.

"Where is he?" Brid asked, looking around an empty room.

Horith just stood there, slightly bewildered. "I ... err ... don't understand ... I left him right here," pointing to the table. Brid's smile slipped from her face. "Oh no, he's escaped, but didn't you tie him up?"

Horith shook his head. "No, I didn't expect him to come round so soon. He'd taken quite a whack."

Brid rolled her eyes. "What! You didn't think to restrain him?" she gasped, incredulous.

Horith's head drooped and he stared down at his feet.

Brid let out a disappointed sigh. "Never mind, let's go and look for him, he can't have gone far."

Horith raised his head and his eyes were keen and bright.

"Yes, you're right, let's search the woods." They both dashed outside, their eyes and ears alert.

"I'll look behind those thick bushes," Brid said, pointing ahead.

"Yes, alright," agreed Horith. "I'll head on over to the river, but don't go too far afield and keep within calling distance."

Brid nodded and shot off, desperate to find her breakfast.

She ran over to the bushes to sweep away the dark green leaves in the hope of finding the little escapee – nothing.

Her eyes shot between the branches of the trees and then they narrowed when a bush shook not thirty feet away from her. She bolted straight for it, her heart pounding at the thought of catching the goblin so quickly.

Rushing forward she almost jumped on top of the bush only to find the little fellow had vanished. She glanced up to spot one of his bare feet sticking out from behind a thinning tree. With an anxious roar she hurried to where the goblin was hiding, her large feet taking only five strides to reach him but – too late! The goblin was on the run.

A splash of bright green from the goblin's tunic flashed between the trees and she leapt after him, the lush bracken whipping her legs as she dashed by. The undergrowth was thick, dense in places but she didn't care, she was gaining on the little fellow and she wasn't about to give up the chase now. He appeared to zigzag through the trees but her eyes remained focused on the back of his scrawny neck. He jumped over a broken log and she was right behind him. The goblin turned towards her as he ran, a light smile teasing the corner of his mouth and she cursed out loud as he mocked her.

An old woodworm-infested log, lying vertical, came into view and the little creature dropped on all fours and scurried inside. The log was just wide enough for Brid to get inside and so she squeezed her large frame through the tight hole. The moment she entered, she realised this was probably where the goblin lived.

On her hands and knees she crawled through the dirt. She carried on until she came to a fork and saw tiny golden lanterns dangling on the left-hand side of the tunnel. She also noticed the tunnel was much wider so she turned and headed that way. Her knees rubbed against the soil as earwigs and woodworm tried to scurry past. She continued on, turned a sharp bend and ... 'twang' – she rebounded on something that wasn't there. Brid felt a soft sticky goo cover her face. She tried to lift her hand to wipe it away but it was stuck, covered in the same sticky substance. She attempted to shuffle back, her legs still free, but she found she couldn't move and then the goblin reappeared. She tried to spring forward, to catch the little blighter, but a mass of silken threads were holding her fast. The goblin crept closer, a smile across his face.

"Ha! Ha! Serves you right!" he declared, jumping up and down on the spot. Then he gave a loud whistle and several other goblins hurried along the tunnel. They were all what were commonly known as Knocker Goblins. They lived closely with the mining trolls and specialised in ensuring the mines they worked never suffered a cave-in. They would knock on the walls with a tiny hammer and would know if it was safe to continue working there. Dressed all in green with their skinny little bodies and pointed ears, they possessed long noses and sharp chins. Although they were usually friendly, if anyone should try to hurt one of them, they could turn rather menacing.

The thread vibrated and Brid shuddered, spotting a web-spinner scuttle into view. She gasped, staring at its long cylindrical body and black ant head. Its two feelers flicked through the air and its jaws moved backwards and forwards, heading straight for her.

"Bind her up!" the goblin ordered, pointing a thin bony finger and the web-spinner scurried towards her, its front legs crossed over like carving knives.

Brid opened her mouth to let out a petrifying scream but before she could find her voice, the spinner shot thread straight into the back of her throat. She gagged, trying to spit out the strands, but it was stuck like gum to the hairs on her face. She heard a noise behind her and she tried to kick out when she felt her legs pinned up against her back. Her eyes widened in fear as the huge insect inched forward and Brid tried to snap her bonds by wriggling free, but it was no good, the web-spinner was able to cocoon her like a fly. Brid was terrified, trapped within the silk, perhaps entombed inside forever. The ant-like insect spun its web around her, faster and faster, yet all she could hear was the goblins' continual laughter. Within less than a minute Brid was sealed within the silken threads like a corpse waiting for burial.

"Let's take her to one of the lower tunnels and leave her there," someone shouted as she was lifted into the air. She heard the sound of shoes scuffling along the floor and a multitude of small hands ran along her back. Her mind was frozen with fear. What was going to happen to her now?

Although she was relieved that she wasn't going to be eaten by the web-spinner, at the same time she was petrified that she was going to be left to die. She sobbed aloud, tears running down her cheeks as she wished she'd never followed the goblin inside the hole. It was too late, she was going to be punished and it was all her own doing.

It was dark within the cocoon and Brid found she couldn't move a muscle. She felt herself travel through the air for what seemed like forever, but eventually she was dropped onto the floor.

"Right, this place will do," said a stern voice and she began to whimper in fear.

"Yes, that'll teach her to chase goblins," said another and she heard a barrel of laughter. The sound of voices soon died away and she strained her ears in the hope of hearing someone else pass by. Only silence echoed around her and she realised she was all alone. She was very afraid, but already she found that the web inside her mouth was beginning to disintegrate, melted by her own saliva.

Although she still couldn't move a muscle, she was able to shout for help.

"Is anybody out there?" she cried, wriggling and pulling at her bonds to no avail. "Will somebody please be kind enough to release me?"

She waited, her ears straining, yet there was no movement around her and the air was quiet and still. Brid started to tremble; realising she had been left to die and she closed her eyes and wept. She cried until she had no tears left and then she simply lay there in the hope that some help would come. The darkness terrified her and she couldn't even see a wisp of a shadow. She had been abandoned in the bowels of a very dark place and so she prayed to the Gods that if she was about to die, that she would not suffer a long, lingering death.

Chapter 19

When Clump reappeared the next morning, he brought with him enough food to feed both himself and the princess. He entered the cave bone weary. He'd had a busy night sneaking through the Canyon and even though he knew it was dangerous, he had returned to his village. The truth was he just couldn't stay away. Desperate to see his mother and his sisters one last time, under the cover of darkness he waited for them to check the perimeter of their boundary line. He was overjoyed when Isis trotted into view. She was such a beautiful wolf and Clump almost wept with joy at seeing her again. He was hiding between two large boulders and he was just about to reveal himself when one of the larger males, whom he did not know well enough to trust, scampered by. Clump was surprised to see a village scout working with the females and he wondered why. The scout sniffed the air and Clump was sensible enough to stay well hidden.

His mother was clearly not impressed to have a male interfere with her role within the pack. When he came towards her she growled and her top lip curled, showing her white fangs. The male snarled, his ears pinned back and Isis crept forward, making a threatening stance. The scout hesitated and then he turned tail and ran off in the opposite direction. Clump thought this was his chance to catch her alone, but to his dismay, Isis chased after the scout and disappeared into the wilderness.

Clump hung his head low, aware he would just have to be satisfied in the knowledge that his mother was safe and well. He'd not caught sight of Felan or Brid and this made him a little miserable. He couldn't believe how he'd managed to get himself into such a mess. He never wanted anyone to get hurt, yet whenever he was involved, that was always the case. He longed to be with his family and friends but he knew that his life within the village was gone forever. He spun around, his powerful paws silent in the dirt and without a backwards glance, left the outskirts of the village with his tail firmly between his legs.

*

162

Later, when he entered the cave, he saw the fire was still alight and that Crystal was waiting for him. He was relieved to find that she hadn't tried to escape and was pleased the firebird was still asleep in the corner.

He found Crystal to be rather chirpy considering she looked as though she hadn't slept a wink all night and Clump found he enjoyed her company.

He busied himself making her something to eat which mainly consisted of fruit from a flowery cactus. It wasn't much, but it was enough to keep hunger at bay for a little while longer at least.

Crystal sat and ate her meagre breakfast whilst Clump nudged the firebird awake and fed her the seed.

"So, what's the plan for today?" Crystal asked.

Clump pointed out towards the Canyon.

"We need to head on out to the Valley of the Green Witch."

"Is it far?"

"No, not when you're riding on the back of a great firebird."

Crystal grinned up at him.

"I'm ready when you are," she declared, helping him gather up all his knick-knacks.

Once they had collected his belongings and put out the fire, Clump helped the princess onto the firebird's back before climbing on himself. He made sure they were both comfortable and then he put his arms protectively around her waist. He could smell her scent, which smelt good. This was not in an, 'I want to eat you kind of way' but in a 'flower of the desert' kind of way. He tried not to sniff, desperately wishing he could fling his nose into the centre of all that luscious red hair. The firebird flapped her wings and gave a loud cry which echoed around the cave for several seconds and Clump forgot all about her wonderful-smelling hair. The bird moved to the edge of the cave and Clump held on tightly to the princess, afraid she might fall from such a height and be killed.

A strong gust of wind filled the blue sky and the firebird plummeted head first from the cave's mouth. Clump couldn't help let out a cry of fear and Crystal's voice echoed his own, both terrified they were about to die. The bird outstretched her huge wings moments before hitting the Canyon floor and then swooped back up into the air and Clump almost applauded with relief. The firebird's wings beat with powerful, even strokes causing a gentle breeze to blow through her fine, golden feathers.

Clump tried to enjoy the view. He'd never been to the Valley of the Green Witch before although he'd heard many tales from the Elders. It was said to be simply lush and his eyes stared at the dark green hills on the horizon. Unexpectedly the firebird gave a rather distressed shriek and her whole body shuddered with a violent spasm.

"What's wrong with her?" Crystal cried out and Clump's mind was quick to recall the witch's warning.

One day, two at most, he heard the witch say inside his head, *and then she will disappear forever ...*

Before he could explain, a chunk of the firebird's thigh broke away and fell towards hard ground. Clump paled, they were nowhere near the Valley of the Green Witch and already the firebird was disintegrating.

"The spell is broken!" Clump declared, not quite sure how to tell the princess that they were in serious peril. His mind whirled with despair; they had come so far yet now they would probably not survive the fall from such a great height.

Crystal shouted for him to do something and seconds later the firebird nosedived towards the Canyon floor at breakneck speed.

"Hold on as tight as you can!" Clump yelled, pulling the princess closer and bracing himself. A loud noise filled his ears and then there was an almighty crash as the firebird hit the deck and Crystal was thrown from his arms.

Clump suffered a stab of sharp pain when his head connected with something solid. He felt his body slide along the ground and for several seconds, he forgot all about the princess and their quest. Inside his mind's eye, he could see and hear his mother calling his name and he was so pleased to see her that he wanted to stay within the confines of his hallucination. His eyelids fluttered as he continued to hear someone shouting out his name and he forced his eyes open, allowing reality to flood his mind like sea water. He winced. His head hurt like hell, his lower back too, but he didn't care about himself – when he looked out towards the horizon, he saw the firebird was nowhere to be seen.

Clump was devastated to lose her so soon. She had been the first thing of real beauty he'd ever seen and now it was clear she was gone forever. Broken remains, like shards of glass were lying by his feet and he picked them up, trying to fit them back together. She had been magnificent, her powerful wings soaring through the sky and he felt hot tears roll down his face when he realised the pieces could never be fixed.

He mourned the loss of such a beautiful creature and then, unexpectedly, he felt Crystal put her arms around his shoulders, hugging him tight. He had never been cuddled since he was a little cub and he adored her touch, her warm embrace. For the first time since leaving home, he felt wanted and yet he couldn't believe that this young girl, a mere stranger, could be so kind. This made him cry all the more and so Crystal let go of him. He could feel a river of snot running down his chin but he didn't care, he was affected by today's upsetting events.

"Are you hurt?" Crystal asked, checking for any signs of broken bones and Clump shook his head, pushing himself up onto his feet.

"No, I'm fine," he whimpered, "I'm just upset about the firebird, that's all." Crystal looked back at him with her wide, blue eyes and nodded. Her face turned serious and then she glanced away and ran to where his bag was lying in the dirt. She hurried back to his side with it in her hands and Clump managed a smile of gratitude when she pressed it to his chest.

"We should make haste and get out of sight," Clump said, pulling himself together and he threw the bag over his shoulder. "We didn't make it to the Valley but we're close. If you look over by those mountains you can see we haven't too far to go. However, be warned, the Canyon can be a dangerous place so we shouldn't linger in plain sight."

Crystal nodded once again and they both headed for a cluster of tall, spindly trees. They walked in silence, inhaling fresh, clean pine scent. Suddenly Clump sniffed the air, smelling something completely different and he signalled for Crystal to stay put. He left her by the trunk of a tree, a few thin bushes at either side. He was worried. He could smell something oddly familiar and that could mean his father was on their trail. He wasn't quite sure, but he thought it likely that Serpen was still looking for him. He shuddered, remembering the last time they had been together. With considerable caution, he crept between the pine trees, his footsteps silent in the dirt. A twig snapped and he shot around half expecting Serpen to be standing there with a gigantic rock in his hands to bash in his skull. He sucked in his breath, both shocked and surprise to find Bruis standing there instead.

"For goodness' sake why do you always feel the need to sneak up on people?" Clump snapped, his brow furrowed but he was secretly relieved nonetheless to see the Plainwalker instead of his father.

Bruis chuckled. "Because I find it fun and I also like being irritating," he replied, a smile playing at the corners of mouth.

Clump's shoulders relaxed and he reached out and patted Bruis affectionately on the back. "One of these days you're going to get yourself hurt. I mean, just appearing like that, it's enough to give anyone a heart attack," he admonished, unable to stop a grin splitting his lips. He pointed to where he'd left Crystal just minutes earlier.

"Come on, there's someone I'd like you to meet."

"Who? That girl you're with?"

Clump stared back at him in disbelief. "What, you've seen her already?"

"Yes, of course, I've been watching you since you both landed."

Clump shouldn't have been the least bit surprised. "I should have known," he admitted, setting off at a quick march to where he'd left the princess only a few minutes earlier.

Bruis hurried after him, his acacia rod gripped firmly in his hand.

"You know she shouldn't be out here without protection. If Serpen should get a whiff of her scent, she's as good as dinner!"

"That's why we're trying to reach the Valley of the Green Witch," Clump explained.

"So why are you heading that way? I mean, I thought you were all settled at Gobb Loch?"

"I was, I mean, I am ... Bruis, I haven't time to explain everything right now," said Clump, trying his best not to divulge

166

too much information. He trusted Bruis with his life, however, he couldn't let slip about the arrangement with the witch.

"Are you going to tell me what's actually going on here?" Bruis pressed, refusing to let the matter drop.

Clump stopped and turned sharply.

"The princess and her family are in serious danger and Crystal needs to find the Book of Souls so she can release the fourth mage."

"And what does that have to do with you?"

"Nothing. I just said I'd help."

Bruis reached out and grabbed his arm. "There's something you're not telling me," he said, refusing to let go. Clump looked down sheepishly at his feet.

"The princess was sent to me because she needs my help and unless I take her to the Stannary Mines, the Kingdom of Nine Winters will fall."

"Sent to you? By whom?" Bruis demanded suspiciously.

Clump felt a worm of uncertainty wriggle inside his belly. He couldn't tell him about the witch no matter how much he wanted to.

"I can't tell you, so please don't ask," Clump replied, snatching his arm away.

Bruis fell quiet and then he said, "as you wish, but I'm not so sure you always put your faith in the right people." Clump had to admit what he said made sense but he believed the witch would not have gone to all this trouble if she simply wanted to kill Crystal and the Royal family.

"Perhaps you're right," he mused, heading over to the princess, "however, my gut's telling me I'm doing the right thing."

"Very well," said Bruis, giving him a tight smile. "I will help you all I can. It will be dark soon; do you have the piece of driftwood I gave you so you can draw a cave for the princess to stay in for the night?"

Clump looked back at him and then down at his feet again.

"I left it back at Gobb Loch," he mumbled, smacking his own leg out of irritation. "I, err, thought it would be safe there until I got back."

Bruis heaved a sigh.

"Oh well, the princess had better stay with me for the night, although we must hurry if we are to make it there before nightfall."

Clump nodded, still refusing to look him in the eye. He felt such a fool. Why hadn't he thought to bring the driftwood with him? He cursed his own stupidity and argued with his conscience that perhaps Bruis was right and that he was not the right person for such an important quest.

His negative thoughts were soon broken when he introduced Bruis to Crystal. The Plainwalker appeared to be a little solemn but polite, and he was quick to explain the situation of staying out in the Canyon, asking the princess to follow him to his hideout.

Clump could see she was a little fearful of Bruis but he was quick to disperse any worries she might have concerning the Plainwalker. Soon they headed towards the very edge of the Canyon. Clump made sure Crystal didn't lag behind. Her legs were not as long as his and he could tell she was struggling to keep up.

"We're nearly there," said Bruis, when they came to a place where it was not so barren and pretty wild flowers grew. Clump bent down and picked a stem of bright yellow petals with heads the shape of stars and offered the small cluster to Crystal. The centre stalks were a vibrant orange and the princess gave him a wide smile, placing the flowers in her lapel. Clump smiled back, thinking the flowers looked beautiful, just like her.

They travelled on until they came across a large grey boulder. Bruis made his way over to it and hit it hard several times with his rod. To Clump's amazement, the ground began to shudder and then Crystal's hand shot out and she grabbed hold of his hand. Clump felt electricity shoot up his arm from her touch but he held onto her fingers and didn't let go. He could sense her fear, yet all he wanted was to keep her safe.

He turned his attention back to the boulder to see it was now a light grey matter, like a cloud filled with rain.

He watched Bruis turn towards the princess. "You will be safe here until morning," he reassured, beckoning her to follow.

Crystal hesitated. "I'm not sure I want to go in there," she whined, tugging her new friend a little closer and Clump turned to her, his eyes soft.

"It's just until tomorrow," he mouthed. "I will change into a wolf very soon and it isn't safe for me to be around you when I do." He let go of her hand and gave her a gentle push until she shuffled, rather reluctantly to where Bruis waited. He saw she was dragging her feet, but he let out a sigh of relief, thankful she was seeing sense at last. Without waiting to make sure she was safely inside, he rushed off, scared she would change her mind and try to sleep out under the stars beside him. He couldn't take the risk, especially not here in the Canyon. Bruis was different, he could handle himself but the thought that Clump might accidentally hurt Crystal made the hairs on the back of his neck stand on end. Without looking back he headed straight for cover.

Chapter 20

The sun gave up its feeble light and the day darkened, clouds thickening over a once blue sky. Serpen watched the gentle rain beat down upon the ground whilst the wind lifted, blowing though the trees and causing the branches to dance to its tune. He raised his head, feeling refreshed when the raindrops washed away the dirt from his face. It was a pleasant distraction, an uplifting moment and when the rain finally eased, he simply wiped the last of the droplets away from his eyes. His belly rumbled like thunder and he rubbed his stomach, aware he was ravenous. There was not a scrap of food left in his bag, not even a piece of snake, and he'd not come across anything remotely edible during his travels. Most animals sensed his presence and immortals were few and far between. He continued on his journey, still heading north, until he came across yet another river. This one was much wider than the last, but the clouds lifted to reveal gentle ripples moving across its surface. He gave a heavy sigh, relieved to find the river calm, especially after his earlier ordeal.

A fin flicked on the surface of the water, causing a light splash. Serpen turned, then hurried closer to the riverbank.

"Dinner," he whispered, licking his lips and his stomach growled in reply. His mind couldn't help but wander to the time when his mother had taught him to fish. Manadeth had shown him that by lifting the fish by their bellies and flinging them onto the bank, they could eat a hearty meal. He'd learned this trick the first time they had visited Isis's family. They had travelled together through the forbidden mountains for three whole days. The jagged pink and white peaks had reflected snow from the remains of the setting sun. It had been breathtaking and it was there where they came across a silver lake. It was unusual for mother and son, but they had shared a whole day of fun together, their huge hands catching many fish and their loud roars of laughter echoing throughout the mountains. His nostrils flared at the memory and, for a brief second, he felt the pain of her loss. He pulled himself together, his thoughts moving to Isis and a heavy sigh escaped him when the image of her parents came to the forefront of his mind.

They had accepted him like a son, welcomed him with open arms, proud to let their only daughter go back with him to his tribe. Tragically, it had only been a few short months later when, with the rest of the village, they had been killed by a colony of hungry Red Dragons.

A feeling of melancholia washed over him, but Serpen shook the painful memories away like dust from a rag. Once again he turned his attention to finding Horith and Brid.

If I find they have betrayed me ... he growled to himself then shuddered, picturing in his mind what he would do to them both should he find they really had run away together. He gave another growl, louder this time, his eyes scanning the earth, unable to comprehend why he hadn't been able to pick up any tracks. He sat on his haunches and swept his fingers through the dirt. He would give it one more day and if he still hadn't tracked them down by then, he would return home to the Canyon.

He watched another flicker of life stir the still surface and he threw his bag onto the ground, wading straight into the freezing water. He pushed his way further out to where he'd just seen a circle of gentle ripples, made by a passing fish. The water soon reached above his knees and he stopped, made himself comfortable and waited for his supper to come to him. He stood deathly still for what seemed like hours, the icy waters numbing both his hands and feet. The cold wormed its way into his bones, making him shiver, but Serpen refused to move. He had seen several fish swim by, but it was as though they sensed his presence because they all kept at a safe distance.

He glanced ahead and a shimmer of colour glistened; Serpen held his breath when a large flat-headed hammer fish swam towards him. Serpen's spirits roared. His large hands were still under the surface and he tried his best to keep still, the fish swimming ever closer. Its twelve long fins, which floated like silk, appeared to glide through the water until they were almost touching him. Serpen realised he was holding his breath when the fish swam in-between his fingers. Gently he moved his hands closer together, trying not to touch the sharp, armoured scales which covered the back of the fish. He bit his lip through sheer determination, but just when he thought he had it, the fish jumped back, flicked its long tail and leapt out of the water.

Determined not to let the fish escape, Serpen lunged forward. Thrusting his hands together, he tried to grab hold of its body, but the fish was far too slippery and it fell back into the water with a splash. In frustration, Serpen slapped the surface with the palm of his hand, furious at the loss. Anger filled his mind and he turned back towards the bank. He felt something shift between his toes and, without warning, the shelf of stones beneath his feet broke away and Serpen plunged straight under the surface. He panicked at being unable to feel anything solid beneath his feet and water and filth filled his mouth. Dirt spread through the water like ink, clouding part of the river, making it impossible for Serpen to see even his hand in front of his face. He was disoriented, the water now so deep Serpen felt himself sinking. In a blind panic, his eyes searched for the surface but he caught sight of something else instead, a glimpse of what he thought to be a familiar shape lying on the bottom of the riverbed.

The particles of dirt drifted away long enough for him to see a glimmer of light and his powerful arms pushed up towards it. He broke through the surface, gasping for air. His thoughts filled with the strange image he'd seen below and, intrigued by this, he took a deep breath and dived back under the surface. He swam to the bottom when his eyes glimpsed a pair of wings. He was thrilled, believing he had spotted a recently deceased dragon. He was so hungry his stomach hurt and a few mouthfuls of dragon flesh would soon ease the pain. His hands reached out to touch raw flesh, but to his dismay, his fingers brushed against something leathery and rather wooden instead.

Bitter disappointment surged through his veins like fire. This was clearly nothing edible and he half turned to swim away when once again something caught his eye. He turned back, peering through the murky depth, as grit and sand filtered closer to the riverbed. His fingers brushed against a tuft of fur trapped within the wooden frame. A few bubbles left his nose in surprise as it wafted in his hand like a sea anemone. His air was running out so he swam back towards the failing light. He broke the surface with a roar and made his way back to shore.

He staggered onto the bank, exhausted, still clutching his newfound treasure. He made his way over to a broken log and sat down to study his findings. With care he opened his palm, afraid the wind would blow the small cluster of hair from his grasp. He pinched the tuft between his thumb and forefinger and raised it just a touch. The fur was the colour of charcoal and he gave it a hard sniff, his mouth soon turning down into a grim line. He rubbed the hair between his fingers, watching it begin to dry, the colour gradually transforming to a soft grey, like the early morning mist seen covering the mountains.

Serpen growled with discontent.

So, you were here after all, he thought, sniffing the fur once again. His eyes narrowed, he could still detect a slight odour, it was faint but he recognised the scent to belong to Brid. Confused, his mind ran through different scenarios as to how her fur had ended up stuck to a wooden pole that was now lying at the bottom of a river.

So what's the connection? he pondered, unable to figure out why Brid would have been heading towards the Valley of the Green Witch.

Where was she now?

Perhaps she had drowned?

Serpen rose to his feet and went back to the river.

If this was true, then where indeed was her body?

He stared along the riverbank, his eyes searching for anything which might resemble a dead Windigo and when he saw nothing which would confirm his suspicions, he began to probe along the shore, searching for clues.

Moving further upstream, he stumbled upon a set of large footprints. He sat on his haunches and his fingers touched the smooth, embedded imprint of a foot. One of the feet appeared to drag slightly and his instincts told him it belonged to Brid. He bit the inside of his lip. Something wasn't right. Why would Brid head along the river when she and Horith would undoubtedly need shelter? He stood up and stared back towards the trees. Perhaps she was sick, even injured and had simply wandered off, but, then again, where was Horith? He glanced over at a copse of trees, wondering if they had taken refuge there but after much deliberation Serpen decided to head upstream and follow the tracks instead.

*

Horith soon realised the goblin was long gone. He had headed straight for a stream that had broken away from the river and by the time he'd reached the bank something told him to turn back. He tried to ignore his sixth sense at first; Brid wasn't that far away but to reassure himself he called out to her. His words echoed throughout the trees and when she didn't reply he called to her yet again. Anxiety suddenly gripped him, causing the hairs on the back of his neck to rise like marble columns. He rushed back to the dwelling, jumping over thick shrubs and small rounded bushes. The path seemed long and winding and he was filled with a sudden sense of foreboding. He felt a shiver run down his spine and he broke into a run. He pushed through the last of the bracken and headed straight for the shack.

"Brid, are you there?" he shouted, throwing open the door to charge inside. He was greeted by silence, the room was empty, nothing stirred and so he rushed back outside and called to her once again.

"Brid!" he bellowed, his voice desperate, "Brid, stop messing about and get back here," he demanded.

Still she didn't materialise and a flock of wild birds rose from their nests instead. Horith lifted his hand to shield his eyes to watch them fly south. He let his hand fall and then his eyes narrowed as they searched the surrounding woodland for any signs of life. Inside, he tried to convince himself that she would not have gone far. He jumped off the wooden step and headed in the same direction Brid had taken only a few minutes previous.

He rushed along the track, finding the woods to be eerily silent. He couldn't hear a sound, not even the birds foraging for food and a knot of apprehension twisted in his gut. He had warned her not to wander off yet she had clearly disobeyed. Through fear he became angry, all he ever wanted was to keep her safe from harm, but now he was worried because he couldn't find her anywhere.

He bent down on all fours and sniffed the dry earth, his sharp eyes searching for her tracks. He spotted the outline of a large footprint and glanced up, a branch had been snapped in half and he rushed over. His fingers touched the splintered wood and his eyes darted between the trees, it was clear she had passed through here. Relieved, he dashed forward when he saw four further prints. He headed to where the tree trunks were thicker and close knit, and he cursed Brid for travelling so far afield. His mind whirled with possibilities as to where she could be, unable to comprehend why he wasn't able to pick up her scent. His nerves jangled when her tracks stopped abruptly.

He was standing beside a large, broken log which, unbeknown to him, was the one Brid had chased the goblin down just a few minutes earlier only now it was sealed, just a tree felled in the forest. He stood rooted to the spot, staring blindly down at the bark whilst his brain tried to figure out how her tracks could suddenly disappear without trace. As his mind whirled, it dawned on him that she could have been captured by any one of the magical creatures who lived within the forest. Yet another shiver ran down his spine, yes, it was all beginning to make sense because how else could she simply vanish into thin air? He made the decision to go and search for her and so he ran back to the shack for his few belongings. He grabbed his bag and his hunting knife and headed straight back into the wood.

He was determined that he wouldn't leave a blade of grass unturned until he'd found her, and his mind spun with notions of who had the courage to take her from right under his nose. He was no fool, and guessed it was most likely the goblin who had somehow tricked her into a trap. Horith felt his gut tighten, this was all his fault.

He'd heard stories all about these malicious creatures and knew they were very clever and, more worryingly, menacing if made angry. When he was much younger, many times around the campfire, Torolf told tales of nasty goblins that lived and worked inside the Stannary Mines. His father said there was no such thing as a pleasant goblin and to always be wary of them. Horith now wished he'd heeded his warning, cursing himself for ever setting eyes on the spiteful creature. He'd thought his luck was in when he'd knocked the goblin unconscious and now chastised himself for not finishing him off when he had the chance. He understood only too well what it would mean should the goblin escape; he had been far too confident and now look where that had gotten him. He unconsciously bit his lip, deciding the goblin may well have led Brid straight towards the Stannary Mines. He knew what he must do, there was no choice; if he wanted to get her back alive he must first find the mines.

He had no idea how to get there, but he was aware the mines were somewhere inside the Valley of the Green Witch. His sense of direction wasn't up to much, but yesterday, when they'd flown closer to the mountains, he was sure they had been heading in the right direction. He didn't know how long it was going to take him to reach the valley or to find Brid, but one thing was for certain, he'd die trying.

He hurried on his journey, praying his hunch was right and that he was on the right track to finding Brid. He'd only travelled a couple of miles when a deep rumble underneath his feet forewarned him that something big and threatening was heading his way. A horrific smell wafted through the air and he sniffed, recognising the stench, and he bolted into the surrounding woodland for cover. He ran over to where the roots of a tree had forced themselves above ground, creating a slight overhang where the forest floor dipped. It was covered with dark green moss and bunches of pretty wild flowers and he ran over and scurried inside an arch-shaped hole. He pulled his bag close to his chest and pressed his back into the hard baked soil. He felt tree roots dig sharply into his flesh but he didn't dare move a muscle.

The earth began to shake more vigorously and a river of broken twigs and dying leaves were pushed over the edge, spilling down over his body. Horith closed his eyes and prayed the ogre would simply walk on by. In his mind he could visualise its huge feet stomping closer to his head and then the vibrations stopped and he opened his eyes, cringing inside, thinking the ogre had found him.

He waited for the fatal blow to crush him like an ant but a piercing cry which did not sound like a noise made by an ogre filled the heavens instead. It was followed by a fierce roar and then he thought he heard the ogre move away.

Very slowly, Horith turned his head, finding a tiny hole within the upturned tree roots to peer through. At first he could only see the ogre's bare feet complete with broken toenails pointing in his direction, but then the giant turned just enough to enable Horith to see he carried a gigantic club.

A piercing cry filled the sky, the sound made by a flock of carrion which flew through the trees, their wings beating in a state of sheer panic. The noise was deafening and Horith realised they were being chased by a predator. The ogre grunted and proceeded to swing his club high in the air. As he swung the huge weapon above his head, it connected with the rush of birds and like flies, many dropped down dead, their little black bodies making a soft thudding sound as they hit the forest floor. The ogre continued to flail his club in the air and then, to Horith's surprise, a magnificent Wyvern flew into view, its talons splayed and its high-pitched squawk, screeched even louder in fury. The ogre swung the club, and a powerful blow connected with one of the Wyvern's huge wings. Horith watched in horror as the flying serpent fell to the ground and he slid to the edge of his hiding place to peer a little closer. His eyes rounded when he saw the ogre corner the grey and purple chested Wyvern, ensuring it couldn't escape. A cousin to the dragon, the huge beast was rarely ever seen and was renowned to be a far more deadly opponent in the air.

Although concerned for the Wyvern, Horith really didn't want to get into the middle of a fight, not when both challengers were extremely dangerous. Then of course there was the slight issue that both of them would eat him given half the chance.

He watched the ogre lunge forward, still swinging his club. He aimed at the creature's head but the Wyvern jumped back and the club whistled through the air, missing its target by inches. In retaliation, the Wyvern gouged the earth with its sharp claws and as quick as a flash, flicked its arrow-shaped barb tail, right at the ogre's legs. The giant leapt into the air, the barb only narrowly missing his thighs.

Horith weighed up the odds and decided it was most likely that the ogre would be taking home the Wyvern for his supper. In fact, he would go as far as to say he would wager ten roasted hippogriffs that the serpent would not win the fight. He knew it was selfish, but he wished they would hurry up and finish their business so he could be on his way.

177

As though he'd read his mind, the ogre swung his club once again. The Wyvern couldn't escape due to its broken wing, but it was obvious it refused to back down. Standing tall on its two hind legs, the Wyvern hissed like a viper and threw back its neck, teeth sharp like razors.

To his amazement, Horith heard a female voice invade his mind.

Help me, I will not survive if you just stand there gawping from your hiding place ...

Stunned, Horith spun on his heels. His eyes searched in-between the trees to see who it was who had spoken to him.

My name is Serephine, please, can't you hurry for I cannot keep this irritating monster at bay for much longer.

Horith stared in disbelief; he didn't know Wyverns could communicate with other species. He shook his head and gave a sigh. He couldn't turn the other cheek, not now, not when the creature begged for his help. With some reluctance, he sized up the ogre. He was of solid build, with a rather round head and a mouthful of prominent teeth. He was probably five times taller than Horith, his brawn obvious by the size of his huge biceps. The giant was indeed strong and powerful and there was no doubt that one smash from that club and Horith would be pulverised.

Horith heard desperation in the Wyvern's voice so he took a deep breath and dived from his hiding place, waving both arms up in the air.

"Hey, I'm over here, come and get me!" he shouted loudly and the ogre, who was rather stupid, stopped what he was doing to stare back at him with his wide, gormless eyes.

"Come on, I know you're hungry, so let's play chase. If you win you get to eat a Windigo," he cajoled. He started yelping and yelling, pretty much acting like a crazy imbecile. The ogre didn't waste much time and lunged, Horith meanwhile, had the sense to run. He didn't quite know what he was doing but he headed out to where he thought he'd seen a cliff. He remembered flying over it with Brid and he hoped his memory wasn't about to fail him. He glanced over his shoulder, the ground shaking underfoot, and several times Horith felt his own feet rise from the floor.

178

He broke through a set of trees and was relieved to find his calculations were right. He skidded to a halt and then turned to face the giant. The ogre roared in fury, spittle leaving its mouth, and he charged, head down like a raging bull. Horith stood his ground, until the ogre was almost upon him and then he dived straight over the side of the cliff. The ogre snatched at nothing but air, his arms splayed as he lost his balance and tumbled after him. He gave another loud roar as he sailed through the air and seconds later, the earth shook as he hit the ground - dead.

Horith jumped onto his feet and his head and shoulders appeared from behind a sliver of rock. He glanced over the edge to check the ogre had indeed, fallen to his death. He was relieved to see his body was still, and that he had not miscalculated the drop. He was standing on a small ledge that jutted out from the side of the cliff. It was no more than six feet wide but it had been enough to save him. He climbed back onto solid ground and then made his way back to the Wyvern. The creature hadn't moved from the spot, its broken wing hanging limp at its side. The serpent hissed as Horith approached but he wasn't afraid, however, he did have the sense to keep well clear of its poisonous tail.

"How is it I am hearing your voice inside my head?" he asked, bewildered.

The Wyvern simply stared at him, whilst making a strange clicking noise in the back of her throat.

Some of us have the ability to use interpersonal communication through unspoken mutual understanding.

"Interper- what?" was all Horith could say in reply, confused.

It means I use telepathy.

"Oh, yes, right, well, we use that too," Horith snapped, feeling foolish, "I mean, when we're wolves."

Oh, I see, but unlike your kind, we can only communicate with those who are actually on our wavelength.

I'm surprised I'm on anyone's wavelength," Horith muttered under his breath and a light smile touched the corners of his mouth.

Yes, it's very rare for us to be able to communicate with others species, but I thought I'd give it a try considering the circumstances.

179

Horith nodded and edged a little closer. "Yes, you were lucky, however, I think that wing of yours is going to need a splint on it," he coaxed, trying to point to the damaged limb without losing his good hand. The Wyvern gave a loud screech of protest.

"Look, you asked for my help and that's what I'm trying to give you," Horith said, exasperated. The Wyvern lowered her head, a sign of submission, and then she shifted slightly so he could reach the broken wing.

Horith let out a heavy sigh.

"I'm glad you're starting to see things from my perspective," he replied, leaving the Wyvern's side so he could thrust a few broken branches under his arm. He delved inside his bag and brought out his knife. He saw the Wyvern flick its tail.

What do you think you're going to do with that blade?

"I'm going to use it to smooth out these branches so I can make you a splint." Horith explained, stripping away the bark. The serpent fell quiet and Horith busied himself looking for something he could use to wrap the wood around the wing. He found a bunch of tall grasses that were strong yet flexible. He used his teeth and his good hand to plait them together and made them into thick bands to tie around the wing. It took him much longer than he'd anticipated and he began to curse himself for losing so much time.

By early evening Horith had finished making the splint and as he approached the Wyvern, its sharp blue eyes watched his every move. He reached out to touch the damaged wing and to his surprise Serephine lay down in the dirt to make it easier for him. Horith struggled with only having one hand but again, by using his teeth, he was able to fix the homemade splint to the broken wing.

Serephine nudged him with the tip of her nose.

Thank you, I am eternally grateful for all your help.

Horith smiled down at her. "You're welcome, but I hope you realise you're going to have to keep out of sight until your wing heals."

Why? Can't I come with you? I promise I won't get in the way.

"What, are you serious? Of course you can't. Why, I'm positive the moment you feel better you'll wrap that nasty tail around my neck long enough to bite off my head.

No, you saved my life, I owe you.

180

"That's not the point. You will have to fend for yourself. You're not my responsibility."

Then I will die and my death will be on your conscience.

Horith gasped in disbelief.

"I can't believe you're trying to make me feel guilty," he cried. "You know I have already done more for you than I should."

I know, I'm sorry, but if you leave me here then I will simply become rich pickings for any hungry ogres which pass on by.

"And if I decide to let you come with me you will simply slow me down."

No, there's nothing wrong with my feet, just my wing is broken.

Horith let out an exasperated sigh. For a Windigo he had more heart than he cared to admit.

"Oh, very well, but I'm warning you, one false move and I will chop you up into little pieces and eat you bit by bit."

Serephine, made a low growl in the back of her throat.

And to think, you said you were worried about me eating you!

Horith gaped at her. "Look, we both need to know where we stand, that's all."

Serephine lowered her head onto the ground and for a moment he was almost tempted to stroke her.

"Are there any others like you around here?" he asked, placing the blade back inside his bag.

Serephine's eyelids flickered.

Yes, I am one of six.

"So, where are they?" Horith asked, glancing towards the sky.

Hunting, no doubt.

"Will they not come looking for you?"

Perhaps, but I will not be missed for several days.

"Nevertheless, I think it's time we left."

Horith hoisted his bag over his shoulder and Serephine immediately jumped onto her feet. He wandered off and the Wyvern rushed to his side.

Tell me, where are we heading?

"I - am on my way to the Stannary Mines."

Really, so I'm guessing you haven't been there before?

"No, why?"

Because you're heading in the wrong direction.

"How do you know that?"

Because you need to cross the river.

Horith's heart sank. He really didn't wish to go near any water ever again especially after his recent ordeal and he felt his shoulders droop. He turned to face the Wyvern.

"Alright, if you insist, but perhaps it would be better if you simply lead the way because I really can't afford to waste any more time."

Serephine pushed him out of the way with her good wing, her strong legs gripping the earth.

Do you know, that's the first thing you've said that's actually made any sense, she acknowledged, blinking her beady eyes at him and without further ado, she hurried off in the exact same direction Horith had just come from.

Chapter 21

The next morning Clump waited outside Bruis's secret hideaway for Crystal to materialise. He had been there for quite some time, long before the boulder turned once again into a white fluffy cloud. He was excited to be seeing the princess again although he wasn't looking forward to the journey ahead.

When the princess emerged, he felt a pang of bitter disappointment when she appeared to stare right through him. He moved a little closer, his eyes never leaving her face and he sensed all was not well and that something had shifted between them. He thought she acted a little edgy and wondered why she was keeping her distance.

He glanced over to Bruis who was making his way towards him and he could see his face was creased with what he interpreted to be lines of worry.

"What's wrong with Crystal this morning?" Clump asked, as soon as the Plainwalker was in earshot.

Bruis wiped his brow as if he was erasing a memory.

"We had quite the discussion last night."

"You did, about what exactly?"

"You."

"Me?"

"Yes, during supper. She asked why you lived alone, so I did my best to explain your sorry situation without giving too much away."

"What else did she want to know?"

"Pretty much everything – and… why you hadn't tried to eat her."

Clump glanced down at his feet, unable to look his friend in the eye and a wave of despair crept over him.

"What did you tell her?"

"The truth. She's a sensible girl and I can see she already cares for you. I thought it wise that she understood about your family and, of course, your rather bizarre diet for a Windigo."

Clump was mortified. He didn't want Crystal to know that he couldn't live with his own kind because he was so different – in fact, it was hard to bear. He was embarrassed and, worse still, ashamed that he'd never been able to provide for his mother and his sisters. His inability to kill another living soul had simply ruined his life.

He didn't notice the princess edge closer and when she came to his side he almost jumped out of his skin. He felt his lower lip tremble when he saw how sad she looked. He went to say something which he hoped might make her smile, but she stopped him by placing a gentle finger over his mouth.

"Clump, we have more in common than you realise," she said, giving him that smile he so desperately needed. "I too was banished from my home because I was different, and for many years I never saw my real mother or father. I realise that we've only just met, and it's hardly been through the right circumstances, but I need you to know that I believe in you, enough to trust you with my life." She lifted her finger away from his lips and began to stroke his long ears with obvious affection.

Clump thought he'd simply died and gone to heaven. Her touch sent shivers down his spine and he couldn't hold back the sharp sob that filled his throat. "I promise I will never hurt you intentionally," he rasped, unable to resist the temptation to lick her hand.

Crystal gave a sigh and beamed up at him. "Don't you think I know that already? I have an arduous and dangerous task ahead of me if I am to succeed in my quest, yet I feel far more confident because I know that I have you at my side." Clump thought his heart was about to burst with pride. He couldn't believe how much the princess trusted him and he was deeply touched by her sincerity.

Bruis let out an exaggerated cough which grabbed his attention. "Now listen here you two. What matters most is that there are no more secrets between you. From now on you must focus your minds on reaching the Stannary Mines safely."

"So, do you know the quickest route we should take?" Crystal interrupted with a shy smile.

Bruis nodded and placed his hand on her shoulder. "Yes, the mines aren't too difficult to find but the road ahead may be treacherous. Beware any dark shadows that cross you from the air and whatever you do, keep hidden within the trees as much as you can." He turned away to scratch in the dirt with his rod, creating the basic outline of a map.

"Once you're through the Valley of the Green Witch, continue north."

"How long will it take us to get there?" Crystal asked the Plainwalker. Her hand moved to Clump's jaw and she tickled him underneath the chin. In return, Clump purred softly with delight.

"That's a tricky question. It could take days if you travelled on foot and then you'd have the added worry of bumping into a few nasty predators along the way. However, what really bothers me is your lack of magical ability because this makes you extremely vulnerable."

"I'm not a complete novice, I know a few spells," Crystal insisted, jutting out her chin. "It's just that they don't appear to work out here for some strange reason and, apart from that, I haven't been living in this world for very long so I have a lot of catching up to do."

Bruis chuckled out loud.

"I'm not disputing your capability, it's just that your knowledge isn't enough to keep you safe from harm. I, on the other hand, might have just the answer." He grabbed hold of a little bag which was held on a belt around his waist and began to untie it. Clump watched as he threw what looked to be fine dust upon the ground. His eyes widened in fascination as Bruis mumbled a spell. Clump took a step back when the tiny particles rose up into the air and within seconds an outline of what looked to be a horse materialised. Right in front of his eyes, the animal's skeleton formed and then blood cells ran around inside the frame, connecting to a powerful heart which was beating in perfect rhythm. Clump brought his fingers to his lips in awe. He heard the princess gasp when a white shroud of fur wrapped itself around the skeletal body. Clump shivered from head to toe as the horse shuddered into life.

A white stallion stood before them and lifted its head, its lashes protecting two large bluish-purple eyes. The horse swished its long tail and the princess was the first to take a step towards the magical creature. To his dismay Clump was horrified to see the horse kick out its front legs, forcing Crystal to jump back in alarm.

"Hey! That's no way to behave in front of a princess," Bruis admonished, sounding quite stern. He reached out and stroked the beast's quivering neck. The stallion whinnied and threw its head, its soft mane of fine, grey hair blew gently in the breeze. Bruis continued to caress the horse until he quietened and then he gestured for Crystal to come closer.

"He's much calmer now," he soothed. "He's always a bit out of sorts when he's first created. I don't think he likes the sensation."

Crystal shook her head, clearly afraid. "I don't think he likes me," she declared, "and I cannot ride without a saddle." Bruis almost laughed in her face.

"Are you serious?" he said, turning his attention back to the horse. "This animal is unique, you don't need a saddle and I promise you he'll not harm you in any way. I can't deny that he can be a little temperamental and needs a firm hand, but he is strong and loyal and will take you to the Stannary Mines without delay."

"What's his name?" Crystal asked, still a little wary.

"Kyte, and it's time you came and said hello."

It was clear to Clump that Crystal still felt unsure, but it wasn't long before she was sitting on Kyte's back. Bruis came over to him and his face was serious. "I hope you're aware just how perilous a journey you're about to embark upon," he said, with a firm handshake, his way of saying goodbye.

Clump nodded. "At times we must all be seen to do things which others may think are insane."

"This isn't your fight," Bruis interrupted, and his eyes flashed.

Clump refused to listen. "I understand what you're saying, truly I do. Within these lands I'm known only as a monster yet this could be my one chance to help save humanity. There are beasts out there that pretend to care for their own kind when really all they want to do is harm those they claim to protect."

"But it is not your responsibility to keep the elves safe."

"Do you think I don't know that? However, in protecting the princess and the Elvin Queen, I am proving that we are not all callous creatures. My kind only ever kill to survive and never for pleasure or sport unlike the immortals such as King Forusian. Tell me, Bruis, did you think to turn the other cheek when you saw I needed help? Did you walk away and leave me to die?"

Bruis sighed deeply and shook his head.

"Then you of all people should understand what I'm trying to do. I want to prove to the world that not everything which is deemed terrifying is actually a monster."

Bruis looked back at him, his expression less solemn.

"Just be careful," he muttered, "and, most importantly, beware of those damn demons."

*

By early afternoon, Kyte, Crystal and Clump entered the Valley of the Green Witch. The journey had not been plagued with any misfortune and Clump was secretly relieved. To pass the time away Crystal taught him a few games which she said she had learned as a child. Clump thought they were all great fun but he particularly enjoyed 'eye spy'. He had never had the pleasure of playing such games before. In his village, to idle away the hours he'd played 'tig' with his sisters and he was very good at 'catch your tail' too. The Elders had never encouraged him to use his brain so he enjoyed interacting with the princess. She was such fun to be around and not only that, she had a wicked sense of humour.

Kyte carried them both on his back whilst they continued with their games until they came across a gigantic rock formation. Clump felt a shiver worm down his back. It was not quite a mountain, but it was huge, and it was a mass of black chambers and dark holes.

"Where are we?" Crystal asked, trying to turn on her rump to search his face for clues.

"We're near a place called the Dragons Plateau, home of the Ice Dragons," Clump explained. He didn't really want to go into too much detail. Secretly, he felt afraid. The caves were filled with the deadliest dragons that ever roamed the lands. Although they were frightening and unpredictable, they were also the most beautiful. Their sculptured bodies were flawless. Like ice, their torsos were transparent; their bright golden eyes shining like polished stars. Their nature was to be cruel, killing everything they came across in the sky and Clump just didn't wish to dawdle, not here of all places.

A gigantic puff of black smoke blew out from one of the darkened caves and spooked Kyte who immediately broke into a trot, his ears pinned back. Clump held on tight to Crystal. He could feel she was trembling and so he put his arms around her waist. She cried out for Kyte to go faster and the horse obeyed. He lifted his head, quickened his pace and set off at a canter. Frequent snorts of anguish shot from his nostrils, leaving a light trail of white in the air and Kyte didn't slow down until the caves were far behind him.

Chapter 22

Serephine guided Horith several miles upstream where the rocks were so closely knitted together it made it relatively easy for them to cross. The Wyvern leapt from one stone to the next, her powerful claws gripping onto their slippery surface, her one good wing flapping in the air to help keep her balanced.

Horith, however, wasn't quite so sure-footed and almost fell in a couple of times. He pushed on and only through sheer determination did he finally make it to the other side, without getting wet.

He didn't know it yet, but he had entered the Valley of the Green Witch. He looked up and saw the land was indeed green and very pleasant. Yellow flowers carpeted the rich dark soil and a winding path led deeper into the valley.

They both carried on until they came across a gully. It was only small and overrun with thick brambles so they kept moving and headed further upstream. The pretty sound of the water flowing gently over the small stones was calming to Horith and he watched Serephine stop several times to drink. He heard a noise and smiled to himself. Was it possible that the Wyvern was actually humming to itself?

Serephine made her way back to his side, shaking the last of the droplets from her mouth. Horith explained to her that he would soon be leaving for the night.

"I really don't want us to split up but it'll be dark soon and I need to be far away from you before the inevitable happens." He pointed towards the sky, just as the first glimmer of a star broke through dark clouds.

There are plenty of hiding places within the hills and there's a small outcrop of rock about a quarter of a mile away which you might like to use.

Horith nodded his thanks. "What about you, where will you go?"

I will stay close to the gully although I will not tell you my exact location for obvious reasons.

Horith understood perfectly. He glanced to where the path disappeared between two hills. "We'll meet in the morning by the foot of the largest hill." he said, pointing west. "Until then, stay hidden, and if you see a large black wolf with red eyes wander past, keep low and downwind of him.

I will, but who is this you speak of?

Horith hesitated. "His name is Serpen and he's the father of my mate. He is a dangerous predator and if he's half as hungry as I am, he will attack you and have you devoured before the sun rises from its bed."

I am not afraid, but I will heed your warning.

"Heed it well," Horith insisted. "Like me, Serpen will only be focused on finding something to eat. When we are wolves we cannot differentiate between those we see as friends and those we see as food. The instinct to survive is far stronger than any other impulses and inclinations we might have. Serpen is a natural-born killer and he will not think twice at sinking his fangs deep into your throat."

The Wyvern lowered its head. *Huh, I'd like to see him try.*

"What did you say?"

Nothing, I was just saying I would probably try and fly! The creature folded its good wing, staring at him with her intelligent eyes.

Horith stared back. "Alright then, I will see you at first light." He turned away from her and without uttering another word, headed straight for the hills.

*

Serpen was very pleased because he had found an egg hidden in a nest in the ground. It was quite a large egg, at least several inches in diameter, and he didn't waste much time cracking open the light-blue shell and gulping down the contents. He guzzled the rich yolk, enjoying the sensation as it slid down the back of his throat. When he'd finished, he wiped his mouth clean with his hand, before disposing of what was left of the shell.

The trail for Brid had gone cold and now he didn't know which direction he should go. He sat contemplating his next move when a distinct aroma overpowered his senses. He didn't recognise the odour, perhaps it was Elvin, but whatever the smell, it was most certainly left by an immortal. The fragrance filled the air in its entirety; it was so powerful Serpen licked his lips, wanting only to devour the flesh of such a supreme being. He sniffed the air and realised the invisible trail wafted from the other side of the river. He immediately forgot all about Brid. Finding the immortal was far more important, indeed his daughter could wait. He ran upstream, whilst his eyes shot ahead, desperate to find somewhere to cross. He spotted a small black speck bobbing about on the water and he almost jumped for joy, unable to believe his luck. He could see a small boat tied to the bank. He dashed over, scanning the area for any sign of its owner, ready to rip them limb from limb should the need arise. When none materialised, he bit through the rope with his bare teeth and then stepped inside the small hull. He had never been inside a boat before and he almost tipped it over when he tried to move. He immediately sat down, the boat rocking from side to side. He noticed there was just one paddle but he thought it enough to get him across the river. The current was strong, but Serpen's arms were powerful and his slow, meticulous strokes broke through the water like a knife cuts through butter. In no time at all, the boat was marooned on a sandy bank, just inches from the shore. Serpen jumped into the water and the tide lapped around his feet. He pulled the boat onto dry land before heading towards the lush, green hills in the distance.

It wasn't long before he transmuted. In his wolf form the aroma he'd smelt earlier intensified, the pheromones he could smell were intoxicating and all he could think about was his claws ripping flesh. He ran on past a gully, not even stopping for a much-needed drink such was the desire. The aroma was so powerful it was making him giddy yet he could think of nothing else.

After travelling several miles, he spotted black smoke rising in the distance and his instincts told him it was the smoke of dragons. He felt a shiver of unease worm down his back but he carried on throughout the night, refusing to sleep.

Over hill and dale he crept stealthily within the shadows and when he approached many dark caves, he watched in awe as the sky above became alive with blazing trails of fire. He hurried on, head low and through the dead of night travelled further inland. He moved like a ghost, his black fur blending into the never ending darkness.

His nose twitched as the scent he craved, drove him wild. He was so hungry he thought he would soon go insane if he didn't taste flesh soon. He carried on until he came to a place that had several large holes held up with timber and large stones. He edged closer and his red eyes pierced through the darkness. He could see a young girl standing at the mouth of a cave. He sniffed the air, overwhelmed by the tantalising aroma that filled both his nostrils. Without doubt she was the one he'd been hunting. She appeared to be without any weapons or companions and he licked his lips in anticipation of the kill. He truly couldn't believe his good fortune. He would devour her flesh without interruption and then spit her bones into the dry earth. He stared at her for several minutes, his mouth watering. He thought her to be Elvin. How he despised the elves and he would take great pleasure in ensuring this young creature would die a painful death and never see the light of day again.

Chapter 23

Clump had arrived with Crystal at the Stannary Mines just as the sun was setting. They both climbed down from Kyte and the horse shook its head and then ran off, back in the same direction from which they came.

"Where's he going?" Crystal asked, looking alarmed.

"Oh, he'll be back, he's just left to have a little fun and relaxation."

"Really? Well, it's alright for some," she said, with a sniff and Clump let out a chuckle.

"I think he's suffering some slight trauma after travelling past those dragons. He probably thought he was going to get that beautiful tail singed."

Crystal grinned and Clump noticed how her whole face lit up.

"Yes, he did appear a little freaked out by it all," she agreed, giving him a broad smile.

Clump drew closer, "I don't think the art of being brave will ever be one of Kyte's strong points."

Crystal nodded, heading closer to the entrance of the mine.

"So, we've finally made it," she said, turning back towards him.

Clump looked past her, staring at the dark mouth of the mine instead. "Yes, thankfully, but its growing dark so we should hurry and make camp."

"Where's a good spot?"

"Just by the mouth so we can hear anything that's down there."

Crystal's face clouded and Clump saw her shiver.

"What do you mean, what's down there?"

"I don't know, but we must remain vigilant," replied Clump, refusing to look her in the eye. In silence they made camp whilst Clump tried to help Crystal settle. He went out and brought back a rabbit, skinned it and then placed it on a spit over the fire to roast. Although he was a vegetarian, he understood Crystal's needs and when the food was cooked, they sat together whilst the princess ate his meagre offering.

Clump turned to the princess and watched her pick at her food.

"So, why don't you tell me a little bit about the Kingdom of Nine Winters."

The princess turned and smiled at him.

"Sure, what would you like to know?"

"Hmm, I don't know, how about telling me a little about your family?"

Crystal's eyes turned misty.

"Okay, well, as you know my mother is Amella, the Queen. She is very beautiful and is also very kind."

"And what about your father?"

"Oh, Bridgemear, he's as stubborn as a mule," she laughed lightly, "a lot like me."

Clump laughed too. "Clearly this is where you get being so headstrong?"

Crystal nodded. "Yes, I guess you could say that."

"Do you think he'll be searching for you?"

Crystal wiped the grease from her lips, using the cuff of her sleeve.

"Hmm, oh yes definitely, everyone will, and that includes my father's blood brothers, the other magicians of Oakwood. They won't stop until they find me and then of course there's Niculmus." She stopped abruptly, her cheeks flushed.

"Is he your mate?" asked Clump, feeling a teeny-weeny bit envious.

"No, not exactly, but I do like him, a lot," Crystal confessed. "However, he's very good at getting under my skin a little too much for my liking," she added, with a shy grin.

"I sense he means a lot to you," Clump said, throwing a few twigs onto the fire.

"Yes, he does, but I haven't told him yet. I don't know, there's something very special about him. He's just so different to all the other boys I've ever met."

"Will you tell him how you feel when you return home?"

"I might," she replied with a shrug. "We'll just have to wait and see how the mood takes me."

Clump smiled at her, watching her eat the last of her food. He was hungry himself, but he would find something more enjoyable

194

later. The moon was rising so it wouldn't be long before he was forced to enter the forest for the night.

Sure enough, Clump soon sensed it was time to leave.

"I hope you're not going to worry about me whilst you're gone," Crystal stated, when he appeared a little reluctant to go. "You see, my father taught me this really cool spell that will cover me in a protective shield. It's like a force field which so far no one has been able to break through."

"That's only if your magic works out here," Clump said, doubtful.

"Well, I'm willing to give it a try," Crystal replied, wiping her hands down her pelts and standing on her feet.

Clump saw her grab the amulet she wore around her neck and then she mumbled a spell. The centre stone glowed amber and a magical aura, like a colourful haze, began to wrap itself around her. Clump sat poker straight, he was delighted to see that her magic appeared to be working.

He clapped his hands with glee when she'd finished and Crystal turned towards him and gave a low bow, her eyes shining. Clump reached out and tried to prod her arm. His finger immediately bounced back without touching her. He chuckled, his eyes rounding with delight. He tried to push his fingers through the protective shield without success, and Crystal laughed at his wasted efforts.

"I told you it would work," she teased.

Clump felt relieved.

"I have to say I feel a whole lot better about leaving you on your own," he acknowledged.

Crystal pulled a face.

"But, there's no reason for you to go now that I have protection," she declared.

Clump shook his head.

"I'm afraid I must. I still need to feed and anyway, what would happen should your protective shield fail?"

Crystal gave a miserable sigh. "Why are you always so negative – about everything!"

"I'm not, I'm just practical," said Clump, scratching his head and wondering why she sounded annoyed with him.

He was really pleased that her magic worked out here. Watching her create the protective spell made him thankful that she'd been unable to cast any spells whilst in the Canyon. There was no doubt the witch was behind her lack of power and he guessed she had probably laid a powerful enchantment that lasted until they entered the valley.

*

When it was time to leave, Clump headed off into the dark forest surrounding the mine. He travelled for no more than a mile before his transformation took place. Once he became a wolf he trotted through the thick vegetation in search of food. There were plenty of bushes dotted about and it didn't take him long to find a few bursting with ample, sweet berries.

An owl hooted somewhere in-between the branches of the trees and Clump looked up to see the feathery predator swoop down and grab a small rodent. He watched the powerful wings beat in a slow rhythm, two golden eyes shining back at him from within the darkness. The breeze blew through his thick fur, and then he heard it ... a noise which made his blood run cold.

It was the solitary cry of a wolf.

No, it can't be ... he thought in dismay, and in a panic, ran back towards the mine.

Although his wolf mind didn't think the same way as when he was a Windigo, his instincts told him to hurry. He vaguely remembered meeting a human creature and the need to protect her was strong even though he couldn't remember why. He soon arrived back at the mine and circled the perimeter. He found nothing suspicious but he could see a girl whose face flashed before his eyes every time he went to sleep. She was standing there, alone, just a few feet away from him.

"Hello!" she called out, stepping away from the mine's entrance. "Is anybody there?"

Clump pushed his nose through a group of leaves, parting a bush in two. Although he was wary, Clump wasn't afraid, there was something about the girl that made him feel safe and so he dropped his head and trotted closer.

He caught the scent of another wolf and he stopped, lifted a paw and sniffed the air. A powerful odour rose from the ground, making it clear that he had stepped into another's territory. He clenched his jowls and gave a low-throated growl, his amber eyes alert.

A rustle in the bushes made him turn his head and a warning cry pierced through the darkness. A flash of black shot before his eyes and then Serpen was standing there, right before him. His father bared his teeth, his eyes dark with hatred. Clump raised his hackles and made an unyielding display, standing firm.

The black wolf snarled, his long white fangs dripping with saliva and Clump felt his heart almost leap from his chest. He was thankful the girl had the sense to jump out of the way enabling him to remain focused on the intruder.

In a flash, Serpen pounced and hit Clump full force in the chest. It was so hard a blow that Serpen almost bounced off his body. Before Clump realised what was happening, Serpen bit down, ripping at his fur. He felt sharp fangs sink into his neck and, although in pain, he quickly turned his head, trying to do the same, but Serpen was much stronger, his teeth now tearing at his throat. Clump realised he was no match for his father and in seconds, Serpen had dragged him to the ground and pinned him down. Clump had never been so scared in all his life. He let out a whimper, trying to send a pleading message to his father, his tongue licking away his own blood from his jowls. His whine fell on deaf ears and when Serpen refused to back off, Clump knew this was the end. There was no doubt that his father was about to kill him. It was clear now he would never be strong enough to beat him. Did he lack courage? No, he didn't think so, only aggression. In desperation he tried to think of a way to stay alive and then an idea rushed to the forefront of his mind.

He quickly relaxed his neck muscles so that Serpen would need to get a better grip of him. The second he let go, Clump thrust himself forward, sinking his own teeth into Serpen's neck. The black wolf was taken by surprise and no amount of snarling or throwing his head could shake him off. Clump jumped to his feet and this time he was able to knock his father to the ground. He bit deep into his throat, blood oozing from the four puncture wounds he'd made, but he wouldn't let go. He stood over his father, realising he now had the upper hand, Serpen couldn't move.

Panting, he held his father in a vice like grip, refusing to let him go and then he heard it ... the unexpected howl of surrender.

Chapter 24

Brid was filled with terror. She'd been thrust up inside the cocoon for hours and hours and now she really needed to pee. It wasn't that she was shy or anything like that, oh no, she was an animal and used to going outside but just because she was an animal didn't mean she wanted to get her fur all wet and end up sore and smelly. It was very dark inside the cocoon but she could still make out shadows drifting past whilst she had been lying there, alone. Many times she tried to call out, to communicate with whoever shuffled by, but no one stopped to help her and she soon became weary and afraid.

Suddenly she heard a noise, voices.

"Hello, is anyone out there?" she cried, trying to wriggle and grab their attention, "I'm stuck inside here, please help!"

"Oh heck! What's that? It looks like a gigantic chrysalis," she heard someone say.

"No I don't think so. It could be a spider's thread or a web-spinner so best not to get too close, you never know what's inside."

Brid heard a unison of voices agree.

"Best be on our way then."

"Aye, let's get going."

In desperation Brid wriggled all the more.

"Wait, please don't leave me down here."

"Hang on, did someone say something?"

"No, I don' think so, well, if they did, it wasn't me."

"Wasn't me neither."

"Well, someone said something!"

"Perhaps it's coming from the cocoon?"

"Yes, you could be right. Do you think there's something alive in there?"

"If there is, it could be twice the size of us, I mean, look how huge that thing is."

"Best leave it then,"

"Aye, best leave it."

Brid's heart sank. It was no good she was going to be left down here to die. She felt hot tears slip down her hairy cheeks. She

199

thought of Horith and the life they would never have together, all because she was stupid enough to go and chase after a goblin. She gave a deep sigh and allowed more tears to flow.

"I can hear someone crying," said a voice.

"Crying? Who would be sissy enough to do that down here?"

"It must be the cocoon."

"Cocoons don't cry, silly."

"Well, it can't be a spider because spiders don't cry."

"Shall we be brave and have a look what's inside then?"

"Are you serious, what if it bites?"

"I didn't mean set if free. What I meant was we can unravel just a part of the thread and if we don't like what we see then we can run a mile."

"That sounds like a good idea."

"Alright then, let's do it!"

Brid felt a fleeting chance of hope and immediately stopped crying. She closed her eyes and prayed to the Gods that whoever it was standing outside her prison wouldn't be frightened and run away when they saw her.

Brid heard scuffling and then the shadows grew large.

"This 'ere thread's as tough as old rope."

"Ah, stop your moaning and get on with the job."

"No, you get on with the job."

"I am, look, can't you see, I've already made a hole."

"Oh, can you see anything?"

"No, the hole's too small."

"Well, make it bigger."

"No, you make it bigger."

"Now that's enough you two and for goodness' sake will you both stop arguing!"

Brid shook her head in exasperation. Whoever was out there, they were certainly trying each other's patience. A noise like a little mouse chewing through wood caught her attention and then she looked across and saw a small hole break through the wall of her prison.

She blinked in surprise. A beady eye blinked back.

"Can you see anything?"

"Yes, but it's not like anything I've seen before."

200

"What is it?"

"It's some kind of monster."

"No way! Let me see?"

Sure enough another beady eye stared at Brid. She tried to smile.

"Look, now its baring its teeth."

"Please," said Brid, trying not to burst into tears yet again. "I promise I won't hurt you."

"Oh, I think it wants to be friends," said a voice that was clearly taken by surprise. "What do you think we should do with it?"

"Well, we can't just let it go, we're miles below the surface and it'll never find its way out."

"Then perhaps we should just leave it for someone else to find?"

"Aye, maybe we should."

"No! Please, don't do that," Brid begged, trying to break free.

"Oh, she's a bit feisty."

"How do you know it's a girl?"

"I can tell by her voice. Can't you?"

"Hmm, well now you come to mention it ..."

"Will you two shut up for one minute and help me get her out of there."

Brid let out a huge sigh of relief and within minutes her bonds were being torn apart.

Her arms were still fastened to her side when she saw her rescuers for the first time. She was staring into the faces of three Thumpers who were wearing bright-coloured clothes. Two were holding pickaxes whilst the other held a small oil lamp.

A white-haired Thumper lifted the light a little closer.

"If we let you go, do you promise not to eat us?" he asked.

"I promise I won't harm a single hair on your head," Brid replied, her eyes hurting from the bright light.

The one dressed in green nudged the one in red.

"Could be a bit of a problem for you then," he remarked, rubbing his companion's bald head.

The one in red pushed his hand away and gave him a fifthly look.

"Rodwin, that's quite enough!" snapped the one holding the lamp. "Right monster, we'll soon have you out of there."

"If you don't mind, I have a name, and it's Brid."

"Oh, right, well in that case, I'm Todwin, this 'ere's Bodwin and him in green is Rodwin."

Bodwin gave her a little wave and she smiled in return.

Todwin shook his head and rolled his eyes.

"Okay, now we have been formally introduced, let's get you out of here."

Sure enough, after a lot of huffing and puffing and much help, Brid was able to break free from her bonds. The thick thread that had bound her so tightly finally gave way. She roared with happiness, grateful to be free at last.

The three Dwarfits chuckled to themselves. "Well, that's our good deed done for the day, however, what we're going to do with you now is another matter."

"Can't you take me home?" Brid asked.

Bodwin and Todwin looked directly at Rodwin.

"No-can-do, I'm afraid. You're a monster and monsters don't belong underground. We'll try and find a way of getting you out of here although we have a real problem. Most of the tunnels are too small to get you through."

"But I got in here through a tunnel."

"That maybe so and I bet it was through a goblin's trap you made your way in here."

Brid nodded.

"That's just as I suspected. You see, they are very clever and they used magic to lure you inside. Now they have captured you, the spell has broken and you're trapped in here indefinitely."

"But can't you do something?" Brid begged, frightened. "You all know I can't stay down here forever." Bodwin came to her side and pattered one of her large hands. "There are no tunnels large enough to help you escape. Only the ones on the surface are wide enough for someone your size."

"So I'm well and truly trapped?"

Bodwin nodded. "Yes, I'm afraid so."

"But what about when I turn into a wolf, what then?"

Bodwin's eyes narrowed.

"Are you saying you're a changeling?"

"Why, yes!"

"So, when do you shift?"

"Every night at midnight."

Bodwin turned to look straight at Rodwin, his face wore a worried frown.

"Tell us the truth Brid, are you dangerous as a wolf?"

Brid looked down at her feet. She didn't want to look them in the eye. She wouldn't know how she would react once she'd turned.

"I might be," she mumbled, trying her best to look meek and mild, "I don't honestly know."

"We'll have to think of something before nightfall," said Rodwin clearly the motivator of the group. "At least when you're a wolf we have a better chance of getting you through the tunnels."

"That would be wonderful," cried Brid, feeling a little better about the whole situation.

Rodwin nodded thoughtfully. "Well, it will be, that is, if you don't eat us first," he replied, tartly.

Chapter 25

The morning air was chilly when Horith headed back to the Wyvern. He ran as fast as he could, refusing to stop even when his breath came in great gasps. As he pounded towards two hills, his thoughts were interrupted when Serephine's voice rose inside his head.

Hurry up, what's taking you so long ... Horith puffed out his cheeks, he was doing the best he could. He had travelled further than he'd expected in his wolf form. He could feel the Wyvern worming her way into his thoughts and he did his best to shake his mind free. He thought she had a nerve invading his mind like that.

By the time he found her at the foot of the hill he was exhausted and so he lay down on the ground to get his breath back, his powerful leg muscles aching.

Serephine, her head larger than his torso, came to rest by his side. Horith stared at her large, sapphire eyes. She yawned, flashing rows of sharp, white teeth.

Are you alright?

"I'm just tired. It's been a long night."

I saw him ...

"Saw who?"

The black wolf.

Horith immediately sat up. "Are you sure?"

Yes, I'm sure.

"What, he came through here?"

Yes ,just a few hours after you left. He appeared to be in a hurry.

"That's not good, he's very dangerous and he could still be around. You must take me to the mines as quickly as you can. "

Then take off the splint.

"But you've only worn it a day."

I'm a quick healer, the wing will be fine.

Horith jumped to his feet and Serephine rose up beside him. With his good hand, Horith untied the splint.

"Are you sure about this?" he asked, letting the bandage fall to the ground. The Wyvern nodded her head, her large eyes wide with excitement. The minute the splint was off, Serephine jumped into the air, flapping both wings before settling back onto the ground.

That feels so good, I can fly again!

Horith smiled up at her, "I'm glad I could help."

You did more than that, you saved my life. Now, quick, get onto my back and I will take you to the Stannary Mines of the Lost Trinity.

Keeping away from her tail, Horith used her lower leg as a step before jumping onto her scaly back, checking his bag was secure before throwing his good arm around her neck.

Whatever you do, hold on tight and don't let go! Serephine warned.

He closed his eyes and calmed his mind. He didn't care admitting to himself that he was scared. He could hear the beat of her long, bat-like wings; feel the power pulsating through her body. The air whipped around him and it was so cold he couldn't stop the shiver that snaked down his spine. He opened his eyes just as Serephine rose up from the ground and she hung there for an instant before flinging herself forward and flying up into the sky. He tightened his grip around her neck, suddenly afraid of being thrown from her. Underneath he glimpsed the river as she rounded in the air. They flew on as the crow flies, over hill and dale, and in no time at all Serephine drifted closer to the treetops. Her wings flapped slowly, meticulously, as she lowered herself into a clearing, her two legs running along the ground and when she landed she did several small hops before she finally settled.

Horith glanced around to see several openings to the mine.

"Are you sure this is the right place?" he asked, sliding down from her back.

Yes, there are many entrances to the Stannary Mines but these are used the most by the mountain folk.

"Are we talking mining trolls and goblins?" he asked.

Yes, usually, although there are other creatures living below the surface of the mine. Just remember, you need to be vigilant once you enter. All I can tell you is that the folk who work down there are known to be rather devious.

He moved closer to her face. Gently he stroked her cheek. He was surprised to find it smooth, not rough and scaly as he first imagined.

His eyes turned soft.

"Thank you for bringing me here so swiftly," he said, with a light smile.

I said I would didn't I? Although I'm afraid I must now say goodbye.

"What, so soon?"

Yes, my family aren't far away and I must go. If they sense I am close by they will come looking for me and could hurt you if they see us together.

Horith didn't want to admit it but he would miss the Wyvern. She had been a good friend to him and he enjoyed her company, very much.

"Oh yes, that's right, I remember and I certainly don't wish to end up as their supper."

The Wyvern screeched in reply, he guessed she thought his comment amusing.

Keep yourself safe and I hope you find your mate soon enough.

Horith nodded. He understood she had kept her promise to him, but he couldn't help feel a little sad.

"It's been a pleasure," was all he said, and Serephine threw back her head and trilled. She flapped her long wings and a strong gust of wind blew in his face.

Farewell my friend and stay clear of the black wolf ...

She made her ascent, the trees bowing with the force, but Horith simply turned away, deciding he wasn't going to watch her fly away. That would make him feel abandoned, even a little lost, so he headed towards the entrance of the mine without looking back.

With Serephine gone, he focused on finding Brid and within minutes he was stood just inside the hollow doorframe. The entrance to the mine was rather cold and it was most certainly very draughty. He couldn't resist it and took a sneaky peek, glancing over to the horizon, and spotted Serephine in the distance, making her way back to her family. Although he was a little miserable to see her go he was also pleased she had made a full recovery. He hoped she would not be unlucky and meet any ogres on her travels.

Horith turned away from the horizon to step further into the mine. He was grateful that his eyes were used to bad light because he was suddenly surrounded by darkness. His eyes soon got used to the gloom and he was able to notice a few knick-knacks, mainly tools, lying about in the dirt. He wandered over and spotted a lantern, left behind by someone who would perhaps return for it at another time. In his bag he searched for the flints he'd had the sense to bring, and after setting a few twigs alight he was able to use them to bring the lamp to life. He lifted the light above his head, watching eerie shadows dance along the walls. The glow from the lantern was dim but it was enough to show him in which direction to go. Horith continued deeper into the mine, all the time praying to the Gods that he would find Brid alive and well.

Chapter 26

Clump sobbed like a baby. His whole body hurt, one of his eyes was closed and his leg throbbed like hell. Crystal was beside him, doing her best to bathe his wounds. She had boiled some water in an old, battered bowl she'd found slung into the undergrowth and was busy wiping away blood and dirt.

Will you keep still," she scolded, when he wouldn't stop fidgeting. Clump looked back at her and scowled. "It hurts," he blubbered, trying not to swallow when he found his throat was swollen. He dodged her attempts to clean his wounds and then, unexpectedly, she threw down the cloth and stared at her hands.

"What's wrong?" asked Clump, peering closer. "Have you been stung or something?"

"No, it's my fingers, they're burning," Crystal replied, turning them over and Clump immediately stopped crying.

"What do you mean?" he asked, intrigued, "did you make the water too hot and you scalded yourself?"

Crystal looked back at him and he saw her eyes were shining with excitement.

"No, it's not that. I mean, they're hot as though they're filled with magic," she cried, trying her best to explain. Clump shook his head and pulled a face. He didn't actually have a clue what she was talking about. He went to stand, but Crystal pushed him back. She stroked his fur as her delicate fingers travelled over the contours of his face. Her fingertips were so light, so gentle, that it was as though butterfly wings were touching him. Her hand moved to his neck and he felt a strange tingling sensation, like a tiny zap of lightning, zigzag through the outer layer of his skin. The pressure in his throat eased and the throbbing around both his eye and down his injured leg faded.

Crystal took a step back and laughed out loud. "My hands have healed you," she exclaimed, her eyes wide with wonder. "I never knew I would be blessed with such a precious gift."

Confused, Clump felt for his injuries only now he couldn't find them. His vision was once again perfect and the holes in his throat had vanished. He threw out his arms to grab Crystal's hand, spinning her around on the spot, overwhelmed at witnessing such a miracle. Clump was a little dizzy so he let her go, stumbled, and almost fell into the fire. Crystal tried to stifle a giggle and hid her mouth behind her hand. Clump chortled happily in response.

"We should really be on our way," he said, once they both calmed themselves. "We need to head on into the mine so that we can spend as much time as possible searching for the book before nightfall."

Crystal, who was walking as though she'd drunk something intoxicating, staggered towards him.

"Yes, that's fine with me although I really want to ask you something, but ..."

Clump turned toward her, a bright smile covered his face.

"But what?"

"Well, I was wondering what actually happened out there, last night. That wolf, it tried to kill you, yet you let it live?"

Clump's smile was instantly swept away. His hairy brows furrowed and sadness filled his eyes. He remembered everything. The stench of his father, the fact he attacked him and also tried to kill him. He lowered his eyes, his mind clouding with sorrow.

"We don't have to talk about it if you don't want to," Crystal reassured, coming over and gently squeezing his hand. He lifted his head to gaze back at her, a gentle creature who could only see the good in everyone. He didn't really want to talk about Serpen, but the princess deserved to know the truth.

Clump cleared his throat.

"I don't kill anything unless I have to, and besides, I think the wolf came here for you." He saw her startled expression and the doubt that filtered behind her eyes.

"What are you talking about? Of course the wolf didn't come here for me."

"Yes, I think he did," Clump insisted. "Although his sole purpose was probably to hunt me down, it was your scent that brought him here. Most likely he would have been able to smell your immortality the moment you entered the Valley of the Green Witch."

"What, you know who attacked you?"

"Yes, the wolf was my father."

Crystal gasped out loud and Clump reached out and grabbed her arm, pulling her close.

"Look, you don't have to worry, he won't be back."

He saw she was dumbstruck.

"How do you know for sure?" she asked, pulling away.

"Because last night he lost his honour to me. He should have killed me back in the Canyon when he had the chance, but thankfully, Bruis saved me. He thought he could have his cake and eat it, devour you and then enjoy a moment of sweet revenge."

"So does that mean you are able to go back to your village now?"

"No, I can never go back, not whilst Serpen lives."

"Serpen, is that his name?"

Clump nodded. "Let's forget about him and concentrate on finding the Book of Souls," he said, picking up his bag and delving inside. He brought out the beautiful tail feather of the firebird. He offered it to the princess. "Rub it between your fingers and see what happens," he urged. She did as she was told and the whole area lit up with a stadium of light.

*

When they entered the mine it was very dark and creepy. Clump found a piece of old rope which he tied around Crystal's waist and then his own to stop them getting separated. After several hours and a lot of climbing down rickety ladders, Clump felt it time to tell the whole truth about the exact location of the Book of Souls. He'd always known about the demons which were said to protect the spell book but he didn't know for sure if they truly existed. He'd been told by the witch that they did indeed exist and that the book was buried underneath the Demon's Altar. Now that he felt they were possibly drawing near he couldn't keep this information from the princess any longer. As he expected, she didn't take it too well.

"What do you mean the book is buried under a demon's altar?" Crystal gasped, clearly horrified. Clump felt a pang of guilt. He'd never really meant to lie to her, he just didn't want to tell her the truth until the right moment, and that moment had never really presented itself.

"I can't believe you failed to tell me something so vital," she hissed, becoming infuriated. "I trusted you! I thought you were my friend."

"I am your friend," Clump bleated, looking rather dejected. "I just didn't want you to be frightened."

"Frightened, are you serious? You've led me into a dark mine that's apparently home to demons and you expect me not to be frightened?" She paced the floor like a caged animal.

Clump could see he may have made a fatal error. Her fury had exploded like wildfire and to his dismay, she headed back towards the entrance, dragging him along with her.

"We can't go back, we've come too far," he whined, trying to make her see sense.

"You should have thought of that before you lied to me."

"I have never meant to; I just wasn't forthcoming with the truth, that's all."

"Is that how you're going to justify what you've done?"

Clump reached out to grab hold of her arm to force her to stop. Crystal turned towards him and he could see tears swimming in her eyes.

"I was only trying to protect you," he insisted, feeling his heart break at the pain he'd caused her.

Crystal wouldn't look at him and he could see her top lip quivered.

"You let me down," she whispered, wiping a rogue tear away, "you should have told me right from the start so that I could prepare myself." Clump looked down at his feet and he moved the dirt around with his big toe. She was right, he shouldn't have held out on her.

"I'm so sorry," he sniffed, looking up at her with what he hoped were doleful eyes. This appeared to work because her shoulders sagged and she let out a deep sigh.

"Oh, alright," she snapped, "come on, which way do we go?"

Clump was elated. He was overjoyed at the fact that she had forgiven him so easily and like a puppy he bounded towards yet another ladder.

"Over here," he said, pointing down a black hole. He waited for the tight rope around his waist to slacken and then he descended into the never-ending darkness.

*

Clump decided there was something rather chilling about this place. There were eerie noises echoing down the tunnel and he felt very ill at ease. It wasn't anything he could put his finger on, but his senses told him to stay alert at all times. Crystal was still carrying the feather so they could see where they were going but the light cast gigantic shadows across the walls, creating huge giants which made him shiver inside.

They soon came across an old mining wagon, abandoned long ago, and Crystal crept over and took a peek inside.

"Clump, come over here," she beckoned. Clump ambled over, took the feather from out of her hand and then looked inside the wagon. He could see a pile of old stones thrown in the bottom and then something moved and he saw two green eyes, the colour of emeralds, blink back at him. He knew what it was straight away. It was a mining troll and he wasn't the least bit pleased. It was common knowledge that the surrounding mountains and all the mines had numerous trolls such as this one working inside them.

"It's a blasted mining troll," Clump explained, his bottom lip dropping into a frown. "I'd stay well clear if I was you, they're renowned for being unfriendly." The mining troll clearly took offence at Clump's words because in a flash he was climbing out of the wagon and shouting profanities.

"Hey, that's enough, you're in the presence of a princess," Clump roared, turning fierce. "That's no way to talk in front of a lady." The little fellow, dressed in a dirty shirt with short, cropped trousers held up with a pair of leather braces, stood his ground.

"You two have no right to be down here," he hissed, clearly trying to sound official. Clump stared at him, almost inclined to eat him just to get rid of the horrid little creature.

"We've every right," Clump argued, "we're here to find the Demon's Altar."

The troll laughed. "Good luck with that," he said with a sneer. "Don't tell me, you're searching for the Book of Souls."

212

"Yes, we are," Crystal cried out, sounding hopeful. "Look troll, can you help us find it?"

"My name is Elwid and I don't wish to help you," he replied, giving her a smirk and then he pushed the wagon backwards. To Clump's complete surprise the wheels rolled as though they were sitting on tracks.

"Quick, he's getting away!" Crystal shouted and before he could stop her, she was chasing after him, diving head first inside the wagon, much to both Clump's and the troll's dismay. The rope suddenly tightened around his waist and he shot forward. He ran, desperate to catch the wagon as it gained momentum.

"Hurry!" Crystal cried.

Clump panicked, almost falling when he tripped over a stone embedded in the ground. He rammed the feather into his mouth, fearful in case he dropped it and watched Crystal pull at the rope, reeling him in like a plump fish. His breathing was ragged, he couldn't run at this speed for much longer and he desperately tried to reach out, his fingers only inches away from Crystal's. Suddenly he felt a sharp tug and he saw the princess entwine her fingers with his and before he knew it, he was being dragged over the rim of the wagon and he lay there, exhausted, on the floor.

Elwid glared down at him and he looked furious.

"You shouldn't be in here," he squawked selfishly, stamping his feet.

As he tried to get his breath, Crystal pleaded with Elwid to help them. Of course her pleas fell on deaf ears. No matter how much she begged, she could not persuade the troll to show them where the Demon's Altar was hidden.

With a sudden jolt, the wagon stopped rolling and tipped over, spilling them out onto the ground.

Clump kept his beady eye on the troll whilst Crystal got back onto her feet. He watched Elwid brush the dirt off his trousers and look around as though he knew a means of escape. Clump thought of an idea, a way to grab his attention and perhaps even a solution to finding the Book of Souls. He delved inside his bag and brought out the two bottles of Buttermead Bruis had left behind. He wasn't sure but he had a sneaking suspicion that mining trolls were rather partial to a glass or two of this refreshing mead. He checked the bottles over, relieved to see they were both still intact.

Elwid spotted them and rushed over, almost doing a cartwheel in the process.

"I simply adore Buttermead," he gushed, rubbing his little hands together with glee.

Clump tried not to look as though he was the cat who ate all the cream.

"I tell you what I'll do then," he said, in a casual tone, "I'll strike a bargain with you. If you take us to the Demon's Altar I'll give you one of these bottles in exchange."

Elwid grinned, showing off a row of higgledy-piggledy teeth. "I can do better than that. If you give me both bottles I will not only show you the way in, I will also lead you out of the mine once you have found what you're looking for."

Clump held back for just a second. "Agreed," he said, giving up the two bottles. Elwid hugged them closely to his chest and grinned broadly, running off to a darkened corner where he began digging in the dirt with his hands, kind of how a rabbit digs a burrow. He soon buried his treasure and then he returned to where both Clump and Crystal waited.

"The place you're looking for is closer than you think," Elwid revealed, doing a strange little dance. He was busy kicking his heels together, and jigging about and then the walls of the tunnel simply fell away and Clump found himself standing next to Crystal in the most magnificent forest imaginable and right in the centre sat the infamous Demon's Altar.

Chapter 27

Clump had never seen such a place before. Each ancient tree was covered with bright red leaves and the altar appeared to be made of shiny gold. Crystal went over to stroke the altar with her fingertips. Clump notice the jewel in the centre of the amulet glowed golden and a haze of brilliant light blazed around her.

"Why is that happening to her? Clump asked Elwid, a little worried.

Elwid shrugged his tiny shoulders. "I don't know, I've never seen that before. However, I'd hazard a guess that the amulet is protecting her." Clump nodded. She looked like an angel standing there all aglow and his heart melted even more. He didn't mind admitting to himself that he really cared for the hot-headed princess with hair that matched her temperament. He prayed to the Gods that the amulet really would keep her safe.

His eyebrows twitched and the first pang of unease wormed down his spine. He couldn't see the moon from down here and wouldn't know when it was high in the sky. He sensed it would be soon and didn't wish to be in the princess's company when he transmuted regardless of how he felt about her. No matter what, he would never be able to trust himself as a wolf.

Clump untied the rope from around his waist and looked for something he could use to dig. There was nothing remotely adequate in his bag and so his eyes scanned between the trees in the hope of finding something suitable. To his surprise, just inside a dark hollow sat an old spade. The hairs on his neck bristled. That was just too convenient. He understood how the mountain folk were deceitful and used trickery to stay one step ahead of the game however, demons, well, they were in a league all of their own.

He turned his attention towards Elwid. "Which side should I dig to find the Book of Souls?" he asked.

The troll's eyes grew shrewd. "How should I know?" he replied, "I'm guessing the south is a good place to start."

"Then I'll dig on the north," Clump decided, heading towards the altar and stabbing the spade into the dirt.

Crystal came to his side. "But Elwid said to dig south?"

"Since when do you trust the word of a troll?" he spat, shovelling a pile of earth over his shoulder.

Crystal glared at the troll, her eyes narrowing when she caught sight of Elwid's red face. "Why the lying little ..." Elwid stuck out his tongue and pulled a mean face, stomping over to sit by a tree. He plonked himself down and then pretended to go to sleep.

Clump shook his head despondently.

"You must learn never to trust any mountain folk, they can be extremely devious, however, I must admit I did once meet three Dwarfits who were rather kind."

"Dwarfits?" asked Crystal, sounding surprised, "what are they?"

Clump let out a chuckle. "They're dwarfs with big hairy feet," he explained, glancing down at his own toes to see lots of creepy crawlies running over his ankles.

"Argh, I hate things that wriggle," he gasped, lifting his feet and squashing the little critters deeper into the earth."

Crystal let out a giggle. He looked up and caught her eye. "You're such a wuss at times," she said, knocking his shoulder playfully with the palm of her hand.

Clump smiled, lifted his shovel and ... clonk, he hit something hard.

"Hey, I think I've found what we've been looking for," he said, throwing his shovel to the ground and digging into the earth with his bare hands.

"I expected the book to be buried much deeper," said Crystal with a frown. "I hope we haven't fallen into some kind of trap."

Clump shook his head.

"No, I don't think that's it. Remember most folks who come here don't even make it this far and if they were unlucky enough to bump into Elwid, then they would have been digging on the wrong side of the altar."

He bent down and brushed the last remnants of dirt away to reveal a large, leather-bound book. He lifted it up so Crystal could finally see the Book of Souls for herself.

"Well, well, well, say hello to the sorcerer Merguld's grimoire," he said, gently stroking the cover.

"Can't you open it?" Crystal asked, her voice all a quiver.

Clump felt the first niggles of apprehension grip him and knots started to bind inside his stomach.

"Only another magician can open this book," he explained.

"But neither of us are magicians," Crystal cried, disappointed. "I haven't come all this way to find we can't open the damn thing."

"There is a way," said Clump, catching her eye, "but to open another's grimoire you need blood."

Crystal stared back at him, her face turning white. It was clear by her expression that she was suddenly afraid.

"Whose blood, exactly?" she asked, as her voice cracked.

"Err, isn't it obvious?" Clump replied, and he felt his mouth go dry. "I believe you are part magician therefore perhaps your blood will open the spell book."

Crystal took a step away from him. "If that's the case, how are you planning on getting my blood? You're not going to kill me, are you?"

Clump almost choked in surprise, he couldn't grasp that she could think, for one millisecond, that he would ever hurt her. Her accusation cut him deeply.

"Are you out of your tiny mind?" he hissed. "Do you honestly believe I brought you all this way just to kill you? No, we need a few drops of your blood, that's all."

He watched her breathe a sigh of relief.

"I'm sorry," she said, looking a tad embarrassed, "It's just that I'm feeling a little paranoid."

Clump held the large book in one of his hairy palms and then he grappled inside his bag, pulling out the ceremonial blade which the witch had given to him.

"Just a few drops are all we need," he pleaded.

Taking a deep breath, Crystal thrust out her arm, pulling up her sleeve so her bare skin was visible.

"Make it quick," she insisted, closing her eyes, and Clump was swift, slicing the blade just above her wrist.

Crystal gasped and opened her eyes. Clump turned her arm over so that the ruby red droplets dripped directly onto the grimoire. Then the blood flow started to slow and Clump noticed the princess was beginning to self-heal.

217

"I think that should do it," he said, letting out a sigh of relief. He watched the blood soak into the cover, the leather turning a vibrant red. He walked over to the altar and, after bending down, placed the book onto the ground.

The moment the blood-soaked cover touched the earth the pages flew open and a bright, blinding light shone from within its centre. A heavy gust of wind rose through the trees and it was so powerful that it blew Clump clean off his feet. He grappled with the wind, unable to stop himself from flying through the air. He was thrown several feet and hit one of the solid tree trunks and was severely winded. He heard Crystal scream and looked up to see her clinging onto one of the lower branches. Just as quickly the wind died away and he dropped like a stone to the floor. He felt pain in his side, realising his ribs hurt, probably bruised. He tried to ignore the dull ache; his only concern was for the princess.

Something caught Clump's eye and he turned his head, his eyes opening wide when he saw Elwid being sucked inside the grimoire. The little troll was literally scratching at the ground, desperate to find something on which to cling to. The power of the spell book was all-consuming and it was clear Elwid was losing the battle. A sound like a pipe being suctioned filled the air and then Elwid vanished.

Clump simply couldn't believe his eyes and he almost jumped out of his skin when a set of arms curled around his waist and he looked up to see Crystal trying her best to help him to his feet. He put his arm around her neck, noticing all the leaves from the trees were falling to the ground, making a sea of red. Clump watched as they moved; like a snake in the grass they slithered along the ground and he became unsettled. Merguld's magic was still very much alive, and the wizard was clearly not impressed that someone had come along and opened his spell book without his permission. The leaves swirled into the air, twisting this way and then that way, moulding themselves into what looked to be a reading lectern. The spell book rose from the ground and floated in the air, landing on the slanted top of leaves.

"I think we should get out of here," Clump urged, but no sooner were the words out of his mouth than a male voice boomed, "who dares to enter here and open my spell book?"

Before he could utter a word, Crystal took a step forward and shouted out, "I do sir. I'm really sorry magician Merguld if we have offended you, but we need to release the fourth mage."

A crackle in the atmosphere, a flash of light and Clump was thankful that there was a tree behind him to hold him up when the magician materialised right in front of him. He was levitating in the air, his long, green robes flowed like rippled silk and he noticed his pale blue wizard's hat was sitting slightly wonky on his head. He saw Crystal begin to tremble when Merguld flew a little closer, his eyes narrow and his long white beard floating all the way to his feet.

"What are you talking about," he cried, his face red with fury. "You know as well as I that the fourth mage has already been released!"

"I- I- I don't understand, that's impossible," Crystal blurted, turning towards Clump, her eyes shining with confusion. The Windigo stared back at her, his mouth twisted into a long frown. Surely Merguld had got his facts wrong?

A loud scuffle caught his attention and then he saw five complete strangers scurrying through the trees. He didn't recognise any one of them, but Crystal clearly did. She gave a loud shout, her voice high pitched with delight.

"It's my father, the wizard Bridgemear, he's found me at last!" she declared, and she ran from his side towards a blonde-headed man whose arms were already outstretched. He watched her fling herself inside his embrace, hugging him tight, and Clump felt a moment of despair. Seconds later he watched her dive towards a fair-haired young man. There was something about the way he held her, the way he nuzzled her neck, that made Clump feel a little uncomfortable. No doubt this was the young man Crystal had spoken of when they were camping outside the mine.

Merguld's evil laughter grew loud and Clump dragged his eyes back towards him. The wizard wriggled his fingers towards the altar and a stream of white light and pretty stars flew through the air. In a flash his magic connected with the altar. Merguld suddenly roared, sounding hysterical. "You will pay for your trickery and deceit," he bellowed, and an almighty rumble followed. The earth shook beneath his feet, and then the altar exploded like a time bomb.

The explosion was so powerful; everyone standing close by were blown clean off their feet.

"Get out of here whilst you still can!" Clump yelled out above the din, dodging a piece of flying shrapnel. He scurried over the rubble, trying to get to the princess. "You must leave here at once," he rasped, as soon as he reached her. "By all accounts, it appears the fourth mage has already been released. We were not to know, but now it's time for us to part ways," he said, dodging yet another flying missile.

"What are you saying?" the princess cried, confused. She gasped as the penny finally dropped and she reached out and grabbed hold of his arm. "No, I won't let you leave," she cried in dismay. An eerie creak filled the air and Clump glanced up, before he pushed her away. She fell to the ground and he dived on top of her. He felt pressure on his back and then he moved his head to stare at the fallen branch which had almost killed her. He pushed up with all his might and the branch fell away. He rose to his feet and checked the princess was unharmed.

"I'm afraid I have no choice but to leave. We were simply sent on a fool's errand," he said, reaching out to squeeze her hand. "Please, forgive me, I had no idea things would turn out this way."

His heart twisted with sorrow when tears spilled down her pale cheeks. "Crystal, please, don't cry," he begged. "The witch was wrong about the fourth mage, perhaps she didn't know any better?" He felt the tick above his eye become more intense. If he didn't leave soon he would transmute right here, in front of everyone.

Crystal openly sobbed. "Please don't go," she pleaded. "Not like this. Better still, come home with me and I promise I'll look after you."

Clump felt a lump rise in his throat which almost choked him. "I can't, princess," he gasped, trying his best not to fall apart. He would love to be with her, live with her as a true friend but he knew this could never be a reality. He bit down on his bottom lip and tasted blood, trying his best to keep it together.

"You know as well as I do that I am thought of only as a monster and should I return with you to the Kingdom of Nine

Winters, without doubt I would soon be dead." He went to add something else but a deep-throated growl escaped his lips instead. Shocked, he drew his hands to his mouth.

"Goodbye," he cried, trying to find an escape route, and as he ran off, the princess called after him, still begging him to stay.

Within seconds poker-hot pain seared down his spine and it was so excruciating that he dropped on all fours. He struggled to get away, claws scraping at the dirt. His senses heightened and he felt his bones break, only to reform seconds later, and he let out a painful howl. He was horrified, unable to move, aware he was changing right before her very eyes. No matter what, he couldn't let that happen so he forced himself to crawl away into a tunnel. He turned and looked at her one last time. Her tear-stained face stared back at him and his amber eyes filled with sorrow. He had never wanted to hurt her, only to help.

Out of the corner of his eye he saw her jump to her feet and start running towards him and knew she mustn't reach him. He opened his mind, accepted the transformation and in an instant he became a timber wolf. His powerful legs broke into a run, loud noises filling his ears and without a backward glance, he ran into the cover of darkness and out of sight.

Chapter 28

When Horith awoke his mind was groggy and he looked down to see his two front paws were tucked snugly beneath him. He couldn't remember falling asleep and only vaguely remembered entering the mine. He jumped up onto his three good legs, spinning around as best he could, trying to get his bearings. He couldn't remember how he'd gotten to this spot but he could remember the urgency of finding Brid.

He hopped off with caution, reaching a score of archways and twisted tunnels. He couldn't fathom which way to go. Although he could see well enough, everything was so dark and creepy and his tongue lolled out of the side of his mouth as he decided which way he should travel. He knew he was lost. Whichever tunnel he chose most probably wouldn't lead him to Brid yet he couldn't give up searching for her no matter what. He decided to keep going straight, heading through the tunnel until he came to a stone passageway. He sniffed the air, aware that particles of dust and dirt were filling his mouth and he sneezed. His eyes were vigilant, his feet silent as he rounded a corner and collided with something that was large and furry, causing him to yelp in surprise. He raised his hackles, his teeth bared at the intruder. He heard a low-throated growl, recognised the scent and his heart almost leapt out of his chest.

Clump, is that you? He heard a whimper, and then a wet nose touched his muzzle. He lifted one of his front paws and in return Clump jumped up onto his back, almost knocking him over. He chuckled inside, reaching out and biting Clump's mouth, his tail wagging, stirring the cold night air. He couldn't believe his luck, Clump was actually here, in the mine, and he rubbed his nose against the wolf that he saw only as a younger brother.

*

Although Clump was ecstatic to see Horith again he was actually horrified to find him inside the mine. At first all he'd seen were his two blue eyes staring at him from out of the darkness. He ran over and nudged him with his mouth.

We need to get out of here and quickly.
I can't, I need to find Brid.
What, Brid's here too?
Yes, I think so, although I'm not actually sure.
You're not making any sense. Either she is or she isn't?
It's a long story. We got separated when she chased after a goblin.
What, all the way from the Canyon?
No, look, it's complicated.
Then you need to hurry and explain.

Clump cocked his head to one side ready to hear his explanation when a powerful explosion erupted down one of the tunnels. It was so intense that divots of earth and chunks of timber fell from the ceiling and they both crouched down, debris hitting them between the ears.

Clump waited for the dust to settle and then he jumped up to shake the dirt from his fur.

It's too dangerous to stay here, let's go!

He started running, his paws silent in the dirt. Horith followed, staying close to his flank.

What can we do about Brid?
We'll try and find her but not until I know the mine's safe.

A noise, similar to a mini tornado gaining speed, reached his ears and Horith stopped, looked back and growled. *What's that?*

Clump flung round and bit his neck, *Just keep going, hurry, trust me, you don't want to know.*

Bits of debris got in their eyes and a sudden pressure of air loomed up behind them, filtering dust and particles of dirt through the air once again, only this time it filled their nostrils. They both sneezed, shaking their muzzles and through watery eyes Clump glanced up and spotted a ladder leading to an upper floor.

Look, over there!
Are you kidding me, I'll never make it with having only one back leg.

Clump nudged Horith in the gut. *We have no choice, you go first and I will help you up.*

Rather reluctantly, Horith made his way over to the ladder; his two front paws were soon fixed firmly on the second rung, his one

223

back leg struggling to hold onto the first. Through sheer determination, he managed to climb up the next crosspiece, his back leg shaking, and Clump jumped up behind him and pushed his front shoulder up under his back end. He felt Horith drag himself up the next rung of the ladder and Clump climbed up behind him. In no time at all they had made it to the upper level.

Clump bounced off the ladder and peered through the hole. A whirlwind of filth shot past in a dark cloud and bits of wood and tiny stones flew up into the air. Clump jerked, his back frozen to the outer wall, waiting for the huge billows of dust and dirt to pass.

We made it. We must keep going.

I'm not leaving without Brid.

Yes, I get it.

When it was safe to continue, Clump got Horith to follow him but Horith was struggling to keep up. Soon they came to a tunnel that veered off in two different directions.

Clump turned to Horith, his amber eyes filled with concern.

Look, Horith, I hate to say it but you're slowing me down. I think you should stay here until I've had time to check out as much of the mine as possible.

Horith was clearly not happy about this idea because he ran over and pushed Clump with his head.

No, we should stay together.

Don't you see, I'd be faster on my own. I'll check out as much of the mine as possible and then I'll come back for you.

Horith appeared agitated.

No, we shouldn't split up.

You must trust me on this. I've more chance of finding Brid alone.

Horith hung his head, his tongue lolling out the side of his mouth, and he let out a whimper.

Alright, but I'm making it known I'm not happy.

Clump stared at him, his amber eyes bright.

Don't you see it's better this way. Stay here and keep out of sight, I'll be back before you know it.

Before Horith could change his mind, Clump set off at a fast pace. His eyes scanned ahead, they were so sharp they could see pretty much everything cocooned by the darkness. He dropped his

224

head, sniffing the earth, trying to catch a whiff of Brid's scent. He pressed his nose closer to the ground but it was no use, the trail was cold. He trotted on, his ears twitched, wary of every sound. He stopped abruptly when he caught sight of an object, small and square sitting in the centre of the tunnel. It was just lying there, a few feet away from him, probably a box or a small container. He sniffed the air, his nostrils picking up the scent of water, and his long, pink tongue shot out and licked his muzzle.

He could taste dust and dirt in his mouth and he welcomed the opportunity to wash it all way. His amber eyes narrowed as he checked the shadows for possible assailants. He could see water dripping from the ceiling and guessed the container belonged to one of the mountain folk. His throat was dry and so he took the chance to quench his thirst. His paws were silent as he made his way over to the box. Sure enough there was water inside and he lifted his head, his eyes still wary, concerned it could be some kind of trap.

In the darkness, nothing stirred, and so he dipped his head inside and started to drink. He soon washed the dust and grime from the back of his throat. He closed his eyes enjoying the cold sensation on his tongue until he heard a noise, a rumble, and he lifted his head, water dripping from his mouth. His ears pinned back, his legs half bent, ready to run. He felt the floor vibrate and before he could bolt, the ground fell away, collapsing beneath his feet. The sensation of weightlessness made the moment feel unreal and his front paws grappled at nothing but air. He tried his best to stop himself from falling, his attempt futile. All he could see was a wall of earth zooming past his face and he panicked.

A flash of bright light exploded before his eyes the second he landed onto something soft and springy. He yelped, confused, and his backend throbbed from the impact. His vision cleared and he gave himself a few seconds to recover before trying to stand. He rose on all fours, relieved to find that by some sheer miracle, he hadn't suffered any broken bones. He did, however, feel giddy and light-headed and he shook his head fiercely because his eyes were playing tricks on him. He was surrounded by rolling flames which licked at the ceiling and ran along every wall. The heat from the fire should have felt like an inferno yet the air was cool. Clump wasn't afraid because it was obvious that he must have banged his head on the way down.

He screwed up his eyes in the hope of clearing his vision, only to re-open them to find nothing had changed. He heard a sound like claws clambering on wood and he looked past the flames to see something white move into view. He took a step back in alarm, letting out a frightened whine when an animal covered in sparkling gold came and stood right in front of him. The canine was magnificent and he recognised it to be the wolf he had seen in Forusian's castle.

He started to shake, intimidated by the sheer size of the beast, not to mention that golden flames which rose from its fur.

Do not fear me. I am only here to guide you.

Who ... who ... are you?

My name is Manadeth and I have come to help you save your sister.

Manadeth, why that means you're my ...

That's right, I'm your grandmother and I have been watching over you since the very day you were born.

But my father said you warned him of grave times ahead.

The wolf took a step closer, hackles rising.

Yes, yet your father didn't listen. I'm afraid his heart has turned black but do not fret for you are the one chosen by the Gods. I must protect you because one day, everything will rest upon the decisions you make. You hold the key to the tribe's future survival in your hands. Clump looked back at her in bewilderment. Clearly she didn't realise what had happened to him and that he had been cast out of the village.

As the wolf spoke, she turned slightly to reveal a stone staircase.

Your sister is safe for the time being but only you can save her. Take the stairs and when you find her, follow the golden glow of fire which will run along the corridors to help you find your way out of the mine.

Clump simply stared at the wolf in disbelief. Manadeth was spectacular and at least three times larger than himself. Her fur was creamy-white, mixed with speckles of orangey-gold. She was a truly magnificent sight to behold and he just couldn't keep his eyes off her.

Clump continued to use telepathy to talk to his grandmother.

There is another of our kind whom I left behind in one of the tunnels.

Manadeth began panting, her manner a little calmer.

Don't worry about him, he'll soon find his own way out. Once he realises you fell down that gaping hole and that you're not coming back, he will have no choice but to head off in the opposition direction.

Clump glanced down at all the fallen debris scattered around him, aware he was lucky to be alive. Manadeth gave a deep-throated growl.

What are you waiting for? she urged, her body facing the direction of the stairs. Y*ou must hurry and reach Brid before the sun rises, otherwise you will both be trapped inside these lower tunnels forever.*

Clump didn't need telling twice. He raced past his grandmother and dashed up the stone steps, taking two at a time. He soon found himself in a narrow passageway which was only just wide enough for his large bulk to squeeze through. He ran on, his head low until he was stopped by a rounded door. There was no handle on it, just an iron ring in the centre. He growled with frustration, gripping hold of the circle of metal with his front teeth. He tugged hard, praying he would not snap his fangs in the process. The door creaked open just enough to let him get through and he let go of the knocker and pushed his way inside. He found he was in a large burrow and in the distance he could hear voices cursing. With slow, meticulous steps, he crept closer.

He past an open door and saw the shadows of three small figures. Without making a sound he made his way inside. He saw three Thumpers with their backs to him and they appeared to be defending themselves against something he couldn't see because their bodies were blocking his view. He saw that one of the Thumpers was protecting himself with a small, wooden stool.

"Get back, I tell ya, if you get any closer we'll have no choice but to lock you in here," said one of the Dwarfits, dressed in green. Clump stopped dead in his tracks. He was confused, for a second

227

there he thought the little dwarf was talking to him but now he could hear a threatening growl and the snapping of jaws.

"A fine mess we've got ourselves into," said another Dwarfit dressed in blue. "Tell me, how on earth are we going to hold her off 'til morning?"

Clump recognised Bodwin's voice and he sidled up behind him, giving a light whine of acknowledgement. Bodwin spun round and stared straight into his amber eyes. Clump noticed he was also holding a small wooden stool. Clump watched as his face paled and then Bodwin reached out to shake his brother by the shoulder.

"Err, Rodwin, we appear to have a slight problem," he whimpered, refusing to take his eyes off Clump.

"You're right there." his brother replied. "She's going to attack us the moment we put down our stools."

"No, I think you'll find she's the least of our worries," said Bodwin, pulling at Rodwin's tunic until he turned around. He then pointed a chubby finger towards Clump.

Rodwin's eyes rounded and his lower lip trembled.

"Todwin I think you need to see this," he said, his voice a little high pitched.

Todwin stopped what he was doing, glanced over and then he did a double take. He grasped and broke out into a wail. "Oh, no, that's it; we're definitely going to be dinner now because they're coming at us from all angles!"

Clump didn't have a clue what they were talking about and so he sat on his haunches, trying to figure it all out.

"Hang on, isn't that Clump?" asked Rodwin, daring to peer a little closer. "Yes, I'm pretty sure I'd recognise that wolf anywhere."

Clump still didn't understand what was going on but he could see relief in their faces.

Bodwin gave him a tight smile. "Hello Clump, I don't know how you've managed to get in here, but I was wondering if you might be able to help us with a slight problem."

Clump got up and came and stood beside him. He remembered the Dwarfits and how they had been kind to him. He stuck his nose between Rodwin and Todwin and to his surprise, he saw Brid cornered with one of her back legs shackled to the wall. Her teeth were bared and she was pulling at the chain which was coming loose from the wall.

"We had no choice but to chain her up," Rodwin explained, sounding apologetic. "I'm afraid to say she became vicious the moment she shifted."

Clump hung his head feeling slightly ashamed of his sister's outburst, aware she would not be in control.

"Look out! She's going to break free at any moment," shouted Todwin, clearly petrified.

Clump's attention focused purely on his sister and he called out to her by using his thoughts.

Brid, it's me, Clump, just take a moment and calm yourself.

For a few seconds Brid continued to snap and snarl, jumping up into the air, her fangs flashing white as she tried to bite the Dwarfits. Clump called to her again, only this time, recognition flashed inside her eyes.

Clump, it's you, you're alive!

Yes, and I've come to help you escape. These wee folk are friendly so you mustn't try and hurt them.

Brid became still and she cocked her head to one side.

I just remember waking up and being shackled. They're not my friends, they want to hurt me.

She jumped up onto her back legs and snarled once again and the three Dwarfits backed away.

Clump trotted over to his sister.

Listen to me, you've got it all wrong.

Brid sniffed his coat and then her demeanour changed and she was biting his muzzle in greeting.

Clump, I'm so pleased you found me.

They were both delighted to see one another again but then Bodwin coughed and Clump spun round to face him, his ears straight, his eyes bright.

"I'm guessing you two know each other, but who is she?" he asked, shaking his head, confused. Clump whined and dropped his head, realising they had only ever seen him with Bruis.

"Look, does it really matter?" asked Todwin, plonking himself down on his stool. "The fact remains that they need to get out of here before something terrible happens to one of us."

Clump came over and nuzzled his hand.

"You know what I'm trying to say," Todwin added, stroking his fur.

Clump understood only too well. Although he had no appetite for Dwarfits, Brid was a completely different story.

Bodwin broke through his thoughts.

"They need to leave now if we are to have any chance at all," he interjected, pointing back towards the door. "The tunnels are small, I'm sure Clump was barely able to make it through. However, if they wait much longer, she will snap that chain and kill us all. Not to mention if they don't go now they'll never make it to the surface in time."

Clump was listening intently to what he was saying and he quickly hurried to Brid's side.

Brid, you must listen to me carefully. I am going to get the Dwarfits to unlock the chain but you must promise me you will do them no harm. If we let them live we can leave and find Horith.

The mere mention of Horith's name was enough of a clinch.

What, Horith's here?

Yes, he's been looking for you and he's at the top of the mine. We must leave here to go and find him.

He bent down and lifted the links of chain into his mouth, turning back to stare at the Dwarfits.

Todwin pushed his fingers through his white hair. "He wants us to unlock the chain," he said nervously, jumping up from his stool and almost tripping over his gigantic feet.

"But we can't do that," Bodwin gasped, "she'll eat us!"

Todwin turned to his two brothers and his face was deathly pale.

"It appears that we don't have much choice," he said, directing his gaze from one brother to the other. "I fear if we don't set her free she'll break the chain and then we will be at her mercy. However, I believe Clump knows what he's doing so we must trust him and let her go."

Bodwin shook his head. "It's too much of a risk," he cried.

Todwin stood his ground. "No, I believe this is the right thing to do," he acknowledged, delving inside his trouser pocket and bringing out a small key. Rodwin came over to his side and patted him on the shoulder. "Yes, I must admit for once, I think you're right."

Bodwin screwed up his face and gave a huge sigh. "Bah, alright," he said, not convinced. "But if we get killed, I'm not coming to your funeral."

Chapter 29

When Brid was finally released, the Dwarfits rushed from her side and hid behind the door. To their relief, Brid ignored them; she was too busy clambering down the narrow passageway, chasing after her brother. Clump was in the lead, his ribs pressed against the narrow walls. Brid was right behind him and within minutes they hit a junction, but it didn't give any indication as to the way out.

Your guess is as good as mine! Brid panted in his ear.

For a moment Clump was unsure which way they should go but then a fine, golden line of fire ignited along the edge of the tunnel.

It's this way, he declared, shooting off in the direction of the flames and Brid was quick to follow. They dived around corners, jumped up ladders, and climbed over mountains of debris. It took them what appeared to be hours but suddenly the tunnels were wider and the roof appeared much higher.

Brid slowed and Clump tried to keep her motivated.

We're nearly there, not long now.

I can't, I'm exhausted.

Clump urged her on.

Do you really wish for Horith to be disappointed when I walk out of the mine without you? His comment was enough to spur her on and within no time at all they were in the upper chambers. Clump started to feel his body temperature soar and under his fur he began to sweat.

He turned to stop Brid in her tracks.

It must be almost dawn?

Yes, I can feel it too.

They both lay down in the dirt and waited for the inevitable to happen.

The transformation was quick and Clump was actually quite pleased to be back on two feet. He looked up and saw a bright light in the distance and a ray of hope burst inside his chest.

"We've made it," he gasped, grabbing hold of Brid's hand and setting off at a fast pace. He half turned when he heard Brid give a light-hearted chuckle and he smiled back at her. They burst into the sunlight and he lifted his arms to the heavens, thankful they had made it out alive.

"It's a good job we had those flames to show us the way out or we would have never made it," said Clump with a grin.

Brid looked back at him and he saw her brow furrow.

"What flames?" she asked.

"Why, the golden glow we've been following ever since we left the Thumpers," he replied.

Brid shook her head.

"I didn't see anything like that," she replied, screwing up her face. "I was merely following you."

Before Clump could explain, a whoop of noise filled his ears as he heard an excited yell.

"Brid! Thank the Gods you're safe."

Clump saw Brid turn to see Horith run out from within the trees.

"Horith!" Brid yelled, and she ran to him and almost leapt into his arms. They both nuzzled one another and nibbled each other's top lip.

Clump's eyes widened in alarm. What was going on here?

They let go of each other and Clump plucked up the courage to ask them why they were both so far from home. Horith was holding Brid's hand, caressing the backs of her fingers.

"We ran away," he admitted. "Your father was waiting for Brid to get well enough so he could take her to live with the Polak tribe. I knew if that happened I would never see her again."

Clump couldn't believe his ears. "But you know what Serpen will do if he catches you together."

"Yes, but it was worth the risk," Horith replied.

Clump felt his stomach knot. "I hate to be the one to tell you, but Serpen's here."

"Yes, I know," said Horith, looking crestfallen.

"What? Here at the mine?" Brid interrupted, "how can that be possible?"

Clump's lips turned down into a frown.

"I don't know how he got here, exactly, but what I do know is that he's somewhere close by. He attacked me last night, pretty much where you're standing."

"Attacked you? Why?"

"There are plenty of reasons, do you want only one?"

"Okay, so, what were you doing all the way out here anyway?"

"Just trying to help someone."

Brid shot a confused look at Horith before her eyes turned back to him.

"Help someone? Like who?"

"Does it really matter? All you need know is that Serpen was spoiling for a fight."

Horith lifted his hand to make them both fall quiet.

"Hang on, are you trying to tell me you actually had a fight with Serpen last night and survived?"

For the first time ever, Clump could hear admiration in Horith's voice and it made his chest swell with pride.

"Yes, I won, but then I let him go," he announced, but his moment of glory was quickly snatched away because Brid was shaking uncontrollably.

"We ... we ... we need to leave here," she stuttered. "Before he finds us and kills us." Horith tried to take her hand once again but this time she pushed him away. "No, he mustn't see us together," she cried, taking a step away from him.

Horith hung his head, "I think it's a little late for that," he said, clearly stung.

Clump could see their dilemma and, more importantly, he knew Brid was right. If Serpen was to come across them he would kill them both where they stood. He cleared his throat.

"Look, I know a place where we can hide." he stated, pointing towards the ice-peaked mountains.

"Where? Is it far?" Brid asked, her eyes lighting with hope.

Clump's own eyes flicked towards the trees. "First, we need to get out of sight, find a place where we can make camp, get something to eat and perhaps grab a few hours' sleep."

"No, I want to know about this place now," Brid demanded, stamping her foot on the ground.

Clump grabbed her arm. "This isn't the time to throw a tantrum," he warned. "Serpen could be watching us right now, as we speak."

Horith pushed his hand away and he took hold of Brid's forearm.

"Your brother's right," he admonished, pulling her close. "Our safety must always take first priority."

With a sigh, Brid agreed and Clump set off in the lead, heading straight for the cover of trees. He wandered through the undergrowth, following the ridges and slopes. He wasn't sure where he was going but he soon found a very fertile patch where the bushes were extraordinarily thick and the grasses extra tall. They lay down to rest, each taking their turn, keeping watch whilst the others slept. Both Clump and Horith had lost their bags so they had no food to share. Clump roamed around looking for anything he could find for them to eat. He was an experienced forager and soon came back with his hands filled with wild pears, edible green pods and even hawthorn berries. Both Brid and Horith were grateful for the feast and ate hungrily.

"Tell us more about this place you talked about earlier," Brid urged, once she'd eaten her fill.

Clump was sitting beside her, lounging on a bright green carpet of moss.

"It's just a place I know close to the Kingdom of Nine Winters," he explained, staring up at the sky.

"But that's the realm of the elves, we can't go anywhere near there, they'd kill us the moment we were seen."

Clump shook his head and rested his gaze upon her.

"No they won't. I'm talking about an area of land which is situated just outside their realm. It's in no man's land and it's called Gobb Loch."

"I've heard of such a place," said Horith, spitting a chewed up blade of grass from his mouth. "But it's at least four, possibly five, days' journey from here on foot."

"Yes, that's the problem, it's a bit far but if we make it, we'll be free forever."

"Forever," Horith scoffed, "that sounds far too good to be true."

"I promise you it is true. None of us will ever be able to return to our families therefore it's our only chance of finding happiness."

At his words a dark mood swept between them. Clump felt a little guilty for stating the obvious so he tried to lift their dampened spirits.

"If we make it to Gobb Loch we will be safe because I have a warm, dry cave there," he explained.

Brid lifted her eyes and all he saw was sadness mirrored inside them.

"That's nice," she sniffed, "but what about us?"

"It's not like I'm going to leave you behind," said Clump, rolling his eyes. "There's enough room for everyone and there's plenty of food and water too. The cave is well hidden so we will never have to worry about Serpen again."

"But how can it be so safe?" Brid replied, clearly unable to believe her ears, "after all, you found it."

Clump chuckled.

"Ah, but I didn't, it was a gift. I met a Plainwalker and he gave me a piece of wood which is enchanted. If you draw a picture of a dwelling into the sand the actual image becomes real."

For the first time Brid looked excited and a smile spread across her thick lips.

"A Plainwalker," she gasped, pulling herself up onto her haunches, "that's incredible."

Clump nodded and returned her smile.

"Yep, and I have hidden the piece of wood by a blackened tree at the side of the loch. It will be safe there until I return."

Now that Brid appeared a little happier, they soon travelled on, secretly afraid to linger in the forest for too long. Clump picked up the track which had been used by Kyte and they headed back along the trail.

By noon they reached the infamous caves of the Ice Dragons. Clump explained how they must hurry and not dawdle. He was worried about the time of day and the fact the dragons would not be asleep. They hurried on past the dark holes which housed a whole colony of dragons.

Clump kept his eyes focused on the road ahead. Suddenly a roar filled the air and he closed his eyes and prayed to the Gods that they would stay safe. He glanced back to see a huge claw, followed by a gigantic head; drag itself out from one of the caves.

236

"Run for your lives! One of the guardians has smelt us," he yelled, aware that trying to get past a dragon twice without incident was never likely to happen. They broke into a run, and Clump glanced over his shoulder once again to see an Ice Dragon emerge, flapping its huge wings. A snort of blue fire rolled from its nostrils, its cunning eyes burned with murderous intent.

Brid reached out and grabbed his arm.

"We're never going to make it," she cried, "those creatures can fly faster than we can run."

*

The dragon, with its virtually transparent body and wings, rose up into the air. The enormous beast soon gained momentum, circling in the sky high above them and the Windigos saw there was no escape. Horith looked up when a piercing wail shattered the silence, and he saw a creature only just slightly smaller than the dragon fly into view. He narrowed his eyes to get a better look, instantly recognising the long grey and purple body of a Wyvern. He gasped in disbelief, could the flying serpent possibly be Serephine? He was elated at the thought, yet frightened for her safety. It appeared to him that the Wyvern was enticing the dragon away from them and he soon realised if it truly was Serephine, she was doing her best to save them.

They kept on running, the rough path disappearing, and they found themselves on a steep slope. They each carried on, rolling flames of fire from the Ice Dragon exploding onto the ground and the yellow rockroses and rabbit-cropped turf were soon set alight.

Horith looked up to see who he thought was Serephine, flick her mighty tail like a whip through the sky. It hit the Ice Dragon straight in the chest, embedding itself between the scales, the tip cut through its protective layers of skin before dropping away. A mighty scream filled the air the second the lethal poison entered the dragon's bloodstream. The Ice Dragon's huge wings crumpled like paper and the beast fell out of the sky.

Another roar filled the air and Horith turned to see yet another Ice Dragon clamber out of the caves. Horith panicked, if it was Serephine flying up there, he needed to warn her. He cupped his hands around his mouth.

"Serephine, There's another beast on its way," he shouted towards the sky.

He didn't hear a reply but he caught the open-mouthed stare from Brid, which told him she thought he'd gone mad.

"What on earth are you doing?" she gasped, and in reply Horith pointed to the sky.

"Can you see the Wyvern?"

"Yes."

"Well, when I was searching for you, I came across Serephine. I saved her from an ogre and in return she brought me to the mine."

Just then Serephine broke through his thoughts.

I cannot hold this one off for much longer. Meet me at the Plateau of Dragons as soon as you can.

Horith had never heard of such a place. He stopped running and grabbed Clump by the shoulder.

"Do you know where to find the Plateau of Dragons?"

Clump nodded. "Why, yes, I think so. It's not too far from here. We will cross it after we have left the valley."

"Excellent because Serephine said she would meet us there."

"What?" Brid cried, "But why?"

Horith shrugged his shoulders just as a line of trees came in to view.

"I have no idea, but one thing's for sure, I'm rather eager to find out."

*

After coming across the boat Serpen had left behind, they crossed the river. They carried on, arriving at the plateau just as the sun was inching towards the mountains and long shadows were creeping along the ground. They were all exhausted and Horith headed to where two boulders sat with little shade. He stood with his back lent against the stone. It was still hot and his breathing, ragged. Brid was bent over double trying to catch her breath whilst Clump was resting his hands on his knees pretty much doing the same.

"What do we do now?" asked Clump, in-between deep breaths.

"We wait," said Horith, wiping the beads of sweat from his brow.

238

Clump looked across the plateau to see the sun was beginning to set. It was strange because it appeared to him that the blue sky was on the same level as the plateau, which he couldn't comprehend. So, after waiting a while and getting his breath back, he ventured off to see how this could be possible. He soon found out that the plateau rested on a cliff and he quickly turned around and hurried on back.

Although he hadn't gone far, when he returned and much to his horror he found Serpen standing there with his back towards him.

He felt the blood drain from his face.

Brid was whimpering in Horith's arms and Clump saw the flash of a knife in Serpen's hand.

As Clump approached, his father's voice blew like invisible smoke towards him.

"I can't believe you would do such a dishonourable thing and leave with Horith," he heard Serpen say.

Brid was crying yet trying to talk at the same time.

"I'm sorry father," she sobbed, "I never meant to hurt you."

"Hurt me?" Serpen scoffed, "the only one who's going to get hurt is you."

Brid turned her face away and Clump saw Serpen raise the knife.

"Just kill me and let her go!" Horith begged, pushing Brid away and when she tried to return to his embrace he moved her behind him.

Serpen gave a menacing chuckle. "Oh, don't worry, neither of you will live to see another day," he hissed, pointing the blade at his chest.

Slowly, Clump bent down and picked up a rock.

With silent steps he crept closer and closer. He could smell the fear from both Horith and Brid and he swore right at that moment that they would never suffer like this again.

In a flash, he leapt at Serpen, hitting him hard on the back of the head.

Whack! He used all his strength to beat him and he swore he heard his skull crack. Blood spurted from the wound and Serpen fell onto his knees, letting go of the knife. He brought his fingers to his head, and a roar of anger left his mouth. He was kneeling on the ground and Clump couldn't believe that he hadn't managed to knock him out. He didn't know what to do next. He couldn't kill his own father, not in cold blood.

Clump signalled to Horith and Brid to run.

"Go! Leave us, head to Gobb Loch," he cried, in despair.

At his words, Serpen slid round in the dirt to face him and it was clear that if looks could kill, Clump would already be dead.

"You!" he said, his voice a hiss. "Why, I never thought you had it in you."

To Clump's surprise, Serpen pounced, forcing him to jump back in the dirt. Serpen tried to grab him and missed, falling back onto his knees. He then tried to stand, but it was obvious he'd lost a lot of blood and he fell to the ground, gasping and shaking his head.

A piercing cry filled the air and Clump looked up to see the Wyvern diving down, heading for the plateau. He heard Horith cry out, "No, Serephine, I cannot leave him behind."

"What's wrong?" Clump cried out, although in his heart he already knew the answer.

Horith looked stricken. "Serephine says she can only carry two."

"Then you must go," said Clump, understanding his dilemma. "Get Brid away from here. Go to Gobb Loch and find the cave. I'll meet you there as soon as I can."

Brid sobbed once again.

"No, I'm not leaving without you," she wailed, and she rushed over, throwing herself at his chest.

Clump lifted her chin so that her eyes were in line with his.

"You must leave whilst you still have the chance," he said, stroking her long ears with affection. "I'll be alright, I promise."

Out of the corner of his eyes he could see Serpen was still on the ground, blood spattered all over his fur.

"Go now!" Clump commanded, pushing Brid towards Horith, "before it's too late."

Horith came over and squeezed his shoulder. "Thank you, brother," he rasped, and with that he grabbed hold of Brid and practically dragged her over to the Wyvern. Clump watched them climb onto the back of the flying beast before she rose majestically into the air, her huge bat-like wings stirring the dust and warm air.

She soared higher and higher until she was only a minute speck in the sky. He felt a lump swell in his throat. Chances were he would never see either of them again.

He was so busy watching them all disappear that he didn't see his father sneak his foot across the ground and, with his toes, collect the knife.

Suddenly Serpen jumped to his feet, the blade held tightly in his hand. He lunged at Clump and stabbed him straight in the shoulder.

Clump screamed with shock, the knife slicing through flesh then bone. An indescribable pain exploded in his chest. He found he couldn't move his left arm and he stumbled backwards.

Serpen stalked him as though he was prey.

"You don't know how happy it makes me feel to know I'm going to kill you once and for all," he grinned wickedly.

Clump tried to talk some sense into his father.

"You don't have to do this," he pleaded.

"Oh, yes, I do," Serpen hissed, "you should have died that day on the ridge. Since that fateful day the tribe has done nothing but doubt my word and, worst still, you have made your mother hate me."

Clump watched his face twist in torment.

"I'm sure Isis still loves you," he said, trying to think of ways to pacify him, "please, father, don't do this."

"I'm not a fool," Serpen replied in a soft, yet deadly tone.

Clump was slowly backing away from him and once again Serpen lunged, but this time Clump was ready and kicked out, his foot connecting with his groin. Serpen gasped from the force of such a blow and his legs buckled. Clump seized the moment, turned and ran, fear pumping adrenalin into his veins. He heard something whizz through the air and a burning pain exploded in the back of his lower leg. He stumbled, staring down, his eyes widened at the knife embedded in the back of his calf. Without a second thought he bent down and yanked out the blade.

The bolt of searing heat which shot through his calf was that of a red-hot poker being plunged inside his lower leg. The veins in his neck protruded as he fought the agonising scream that rose from deep within his throat. A cry of agony escaped when it all became too much to bear, his eyes almost blind with pain. He shook his vision clear and swung around to see Serpen was hunting him, his stance every bit the predator. Clump dragged his foot as he tried once again to run, blood pouring from the wound. It was obvious Serpen was over his beating; instead he was getting ready for the kill. Clump saw there was no escape. He had run in the wrong direction and was heading straight for the cliff.

He closed his eyes and prayed to the Gods for a swift death. Suddenly he felt pressure on both his feet and he looked down to see Serpen's hands were around his ankles. Before he could react, his father yanked him to the ground and he dropped like a stone. He managed to roll over in the dirt, like a snake with its prey, forcing Serpen to let go. Serpen struggled to his feet and then lunged, grappling with him once again, using his powerful arms to crawl up his upper body and in seconds Serpen's twisted features were in line with Clump's own.

"Enough's, enough," Serpen spat, and his right hand shot out and pinned Clump's good arm down to the floor. He raised his free hand and a blade flickered silver against the sun. Clump blanched, and in a flash lifted his good leg and kneed Serpen straight in the gut. He used the last of his strength to raise his lower leg and with all his might pushed up with his foot. Serpen gasped from such a blow, veins pulsating within his neck but he wouldn't let go of Clump's arm and instead somersaulted over his shoulder. There was a sudden cry and Clump's arm flew above his head and he could feel his father's fingers digging into his flesh. Clump tried to shake him free, turning over onto his belly, and gasped in horror. His father was hanging over the cliff, only Clump was saving him from falling to his death.

"Help me up," Serpen shouted. "It's alright, I promise, I won't hurt you."

Clump knew he was lying, however, this was his father and no matter what, he couldn't be responsible for him dying in this way. He felt his hand slip and he dug his fingers into his father's wrist, refusing to let him go.

"Hold tight and I'll get you up here in a jiffy," Clump declared, trying his best to heave his father back over the ledge. Serpen appeared to be using his upper body strength to pull himself up.

"That's it, you're doing great," Clump urged, and this time Serpen was able to grab hold of the ledge with his free hand. Clump was relieved to see he was going to be safe. Serpen's face peered over the edge, and just as Clump was about to help him up, Serpen grabbed hold of Clump's neck and tried to pull him over the cliff. Clump panicked and pushed back, forcing Serpen to let go and hold onto the ledge once more.

A deep-throated growl came out of nowhere and, startled, Clump looked round to see a flash of gold. He saw the wolf the second it dropped on all fours, its teeth bared. Shocked at seeing Manadeth again, Clump just lay there. He thought she was there to help and so he allowed the wolf to creep closer to the edge. Serpen's head appeared once again but this time, to Clump's utter dismay, the wolf attacked his father. Serpen tried to swing a punch at the wolf as it bit him, letting go of the ledge to do so. In a flash the wolf turned and its teeth nipped Clump's wrist. It wasn't a hard bite, but it was enough for him to flinch and he automatically snatched his hand away. At the same time Manadeth's jaws closed around Serpen's arm. There was a scream as she let go and Clump dived forward, but it was too late, Serpen had already landed on the rocks below, a broken body, surrounded by a pool of his own blood.

He turned to the wolf, his eyes all glassy with tears. "How could you do such a despicable thing?" he cried, and he placed his arm across his face and sobbed like a baby.

Manadeth came and sat by his side.

I'm afraid I had no choice. It was either your life or his.

"No, you could have saved him," Clump blubbered, still sobbing.

I'm sorry, Clump, but I'm afraid to say your father was way beyond saving.

Chapter 30

Clump didn't go straight to Gobb Loch as intended. Instead, he headed back to the Red Canyon after Manadeth told him that he must return and speak to the Elders, explaining the demise of Serpen. At first he didn't want to go. The mere thought of telling his mother that his father was dead filled him with utter dread. He also didn't want to be the one to make her cry. Then there was the fact that the village had sentenced him to death and he was still hurt at their cruel decision to kill him. He had been forced to flee, to run for his life, and they would have been well aware of the consequences once Serpen caught up with him. He felt betrayed by those whom he would have thought to protect him and this made it even harder to return. However, Manadeth insisted on him going back and wouldn't let the matter drop until he agreed.

To speed up his return journey, she allowed him to ride on her back. He was very grateful for this. The stab wound in his leg was deep and the one in his shoulder was very painful. Having lost a lot of blood he felt weak and wanted to wait a day or two before travelling. Manadeth wouldn't listen to his tales of woe and took him to a patch of wilderness where special, medicinal herbs grew. She explained which plants would help to cleanse his wounds and then she encouraged him to eat alpine pennycress, which she said would fight off any infection.

Once Clump appeared in better shape and his wounds were wrapped in large green leaves, Manadeth began the mammoth task of returning Clump to his tribe. She ran and ran, never stopping until Clump begged her to. The journey was swift, Clump unable to sleep as the gigantic wolf sprang over huge rocks and rugged terrain and late at night, when he became a wolf, she ran by his side.

*

The next day when the dark rocks protecting the village finally loomed before them it was mid-afternoon. Manadeth slowed her pace, eventually standing still long enough to allow him to climb down from her back.

"Is this goodbye then?" Clump asked, when she nudged him with her wet nose.

Perhaps, who knows? However, now is the time to focus on looking after your family and ensuring the rest of the tribe stays safe. The elves are coming and you are the only one who can save our kind from extinction.

Clump felt afraid.

"Why me?"

Because times are changing and things cannot stay as they once were.

"Things, what things?"

You will see, everything will become clear soon enough.

Clump stared into her huge golden eyes and felt nothing but admiration for his grandmother. Her only thoughts were always for the tribe and their survival. Even after death she was both loyal and powerful enough to return to the land of the living. He thought about the fourth mage and decided there was no doubt she could give him a run for his money.

Go now, she whispered inside his head when he loitered, *your mother needs you.*

Reluctantly he came to her side and pressed his face into her soft fur. He wrapped his arms around her neck and gave it a tight squeeze. She smelt good. Her scent reminded him of the snow on the mountains, fresh and clean, and this thought calmed his taut nerves.

"There are a lot of things I would like to say but most importantly I must thank you for saving my life," he said, and his voice cracked. He took a step back when he heard her whine and before she could reply, he turned away and began to walk towards the village. He didn't look back. He didn't wish to see the sadness in her eyes. There were tears stinging his own yet he wanted to enter the village as an adult and not as the young pup he had been when he had been forced to leave. He heard the scouts cry out, their signal that someone approached.

He entered the camp and was immediately challenged. A number of scouts carrying heavy clubs ran towards him just as a group of Elders were leaving one of the communal caves. It was early afternoon and the sun was still high in the sky. Zebulon was at the forefront, his white mane blowing gently in the breeze.

The scouts were quick to circle Clump, lifting their clubs and jeering at the one they saw to be an outcast. A dissonance of high-pitched wails surrounded him and Zebulon raised his hand in the air and called for quiet the moment his eyes made contact with Serpen's son.

With slow, meticulous steps the Elder approached.

"My, my, to think you're still alive," he said, his eyes wide.

Clump bristled.

"Well, it's no thanks to you," he replied, his shoulders back, tense.

Zebulon's face peered closer.

"I have to say, you've some nerve showing up around here," he said, and Clump watched his dark eyes narrow. He took a bold step towards him. No matter how he felt inside, he would not be intimidated by this ancient Windigo a moment longer.

"Why shouldn't I come back to my own village? I've done nothing wrong," Clump responded, lifting his chin. "In fact, it is you who saw fit to force me to flee from here, my own home."

"It was your actions in Forusian's castle which sealed your fate," the Elder replied.

Clump immediately saw red.

"Oh, well, of course it was. I bring Horith back alive and I'm seen as a traitor."

"It wasn't that, you betrayed your own father," Zebulon snapped, his mouth twisted. "Being put to death is nothing less than what you deserved."

Clump felt his cheeks burn.

"Deserved? How dare you! None of you had any proof of any wrongdoing and even Serpen only had his suspicions. My crime was that he never saw me leave the castle. I can now tell you that I made a deal with a witch inside those castle walls, a promise which saw both Serpen and Horith return home. I never betrayed my father; my only offence was that I saved him."

Zebulon shook his head. "Do you really expect me to believe that?" he scoffed. "If this is true then why didn't you say something at the time? No, I believe this to be another lie which you've conjured to save your own skin."

Clump's heckles rose and he caught sight of a number of Elders standing to the rear of Zebulon who sniggered behind their hands. He felt anger boil up inside him. How dare they treat him this way!

"Believe what you like, but I know the truth!" he roared, his chest heaving with fury.

Zebulon's eyes turned to slits. "You're a born liar with a very vivid imagination," he stated. He turned towards the scouts. "Seize him and take him to the Emerald Cave until I decide what to do with him."

The scouts rushed forward but before anyone could lay a finger on him, a deafening noise, an evocative howl, pierced through the air. Everyone who heard it, froze.

Zebulon took a sharp intake of breath, his eyes scanning the rocks in search of what had just given the warning sound. Then the call came again, the undeniable cry of a lone wolf.

"No, it cannot be!" Zebulon exclaimed, pushing Clump out of the way. He quickly left the security of the rocks with at least half of the village following behind.

Clump, with two scouts at his side, hurried on after him.

He watched Zebulon head out into the Canyon and then out of the shimmering haze of the sun, Manadeth appeared. A gasp left everyone's mouth, Clump was just as surprised to see his grandmother as everyone else. Orange and gold flames were rolling from her coat as she made her way towards the Elder. When she stopped and dropped her head, Zebulon came to her, his own head bowed. Clump tried to strain his ears but he couldn't hear the conversation between them. Several times he noticed Zebulon turn around to stare at him but he couldn't catch the drift of what was being said. A sixth sense made him stand and wait for his return and after what seemed like an age, Zebulon bowed once again only this time Manadeth melted away into a haze of golden fire.

The Elder made his way to where Clump and most of the villagers were waiting. His features appeared to have softened and Clump thought he looked a tad embarrassed.

"Please, forgive me," he said, lowering his gaze. "Your grandmother has explained everything and I have since learned that a Plainwalker saved you from the clutches of your father. The mere fact you are protected by the Gods means that you are welcomed back into the tribe with open arms. I hope you will forgive us for our foolishness at allowing Serpen to treat you in such a way."

Clump was astonished by this turn of events and he was actually enjoying the fact that Zebulon appeared to be squirming under his gaze. He heard a commotion, someone shouting, and the crowd parted like the sea and he spun around to spot Isis and Felan running towards him.

"Clump!" his mother yelled, dashing towards him and flinging her arms around his thick waist. Felan almost jumped on top of him, making a barking noise in the back of her throat, a sign of her happiness at his return. He grinned broadly and looked down to see his mother laughing and wiping away stray tears.

"Oh, your leg's hurt and you have a gash to your shoulder," she suddenly rasped, the light in her eyes fading.

"They're just scratches," Clump insisted, and he nudged his mother aside so he could embrace his sister. Those standing around moved away to give them a little privacy and after much hugging and playful biting Clump's smile faded. His thoughts flew to the reason why he had been asked to return. He was just about to get it all off his chest when Zebulon came over and slapped him hard on the back, causing him to wince.

"I think this is cause for celebration," he stated, waving his hand to those who would be given the honour of organising the unexpected event. Clump didn't know what to say so he said nothing at all. All he could see was his mother beaming up at him.

"You can have him once I find out where he's been hiding," she declared, grabbing his hand and Zebulon nodded in agreement.

"Very well," he acknowledged with a flick of his wrist, you can have time to catch up with him until the celebrations are ready to get underway." Felan let out a high-pitched noise of delight and then Clump was hurried away by his dear mother and sister.

On approaching a cave, Isis pushed the hides aside and he entered Lyra's home. The second his feet were over the threshold he felt an intense wave of emotion wash over him. Since that fateful day when he'd been forced to flee, he'd never dreamt for one second that he would ever be allowed to step one foot in the village again. He felt hot tears swell and he tried not to let them fall. It was so wonderful to be back in the bosom of his family and his emotions were running high. Lyra was nowhere to be seen and Felan caught hold of Clump's hand and dragged him into the centre where there was lots of space to hug one another and they all made happy whooping noises in the back of their throats.

"Why can't we go straight home?" Clump asked, thinking it was nice to be in Lyra's den but there was no place like your own cave.

Isis flicked her gaze towards Felan before she replied.

"We no longer live there," she said, dropping her hands. "After you were forced to flee, your father threw me and your sisters out. He went out one day and brought back a new partner." She took a deep breath. "Her name is Greer and she now lives in what was once our cave."

Clump couldn't believe his ears. Why would his father hurt his mother in such a way? He believed Serpen cared for Isis very much and his words at the plateau came flooding back. *You made your mother hate me ...*

There was a sudden hollowness inside him that he would never have thought possible. Felan dropped her arms from around him.

"There's something else we need to tell you," she said, glancing down at her feet. When Clump didn't reply she lifted her head and took a deep breath. "Father has left to hunt down Brid and Horith. We think they ran away together, but we don't know for sure." Clump stared from one to the other and he could see tears welled in his mother's eyes.

"If he finds them, he'll kill them," she whispered, clearly unable to hold onto her emotions any longer.

Clump licked his lips. "I can understand your concern but there's no need to fret. I've seen Horith and Brid only recently and they're both fine," he said, trying to smile. Felan and Isis both gasped with relief and his mother reached out to steady herself.

"I've been worrying myself stupid for days," she admitted, grabbing hold of his hand and giving it a squeeze. "You know as well as I that Serpen is such an experienced tracker and I therefore thought they would be dead by now."

Clump let out a deep sigh. He realised now was as good a time as any to come clean about his father's fate.

"Mother, Felan," he began, "that said, I'm afraid I come as the bearer of bad news."

His mother immediately pointed to the floor and sat down. Felan made herself comfortable beside her, her face quizzical. When Clump hesitated, she gestured for him to join them.

"What is it, what's wrong?" she asked, her eyes fearful, and his mind flew to Manadeth and how she told him that he must be brave.

He sat down, crossed-legged, his eyes sweeping to his mother then back over to his sister.

"I need to tell you something about father," he began and he saw Felan flinch. His mother let out a moan which made him switch his attention back to her.

"Please, just tell us what it is," she pleaded, her once shining eyes now dull.

Clump pursed his lips and took a deep breath.

"I'm afraid Serpen's dead," he announced.

The moment the words were out of his mouth, Isis gasped, clutching her throat.

"What! How?" she cried. Clump's nostrils flared, this was the hardest thing he'd ever have to do. Manadeth's words pushed their way to the forefront of his mind.

Just tell them the truth ...

"I saw him fall over a cliff," he choked, refusing to tell them that Manadeth had taken his life to save his.

"But that doesn't mean he's dead," Felan declared, her fingers covering her mouth.

Clump shook his head, inside he was weeping.

"I'm afraid it does. I saw his broken body lying on the rocks below. He fell from at least a hundred feet and there was no way he could survive such a fall."

It appeared it was Felan's turn to struggle with her emotions and she reached out and grabbed hold of her mother, a roar of grief finally erupting from her body.

"I can't believe he's gone," she wailed, sounding devastated. "I know he wasn't always a good father, but he was the only one I had." Isis stroked her ears and then her back, all the while her eyes never left Clump's face.

"We'll manage the best we can without him," she said, softly. "The Gods always say that everything happens for a reason so we must wait and find out why his life was taken."

Clump gulped. He hoped more than anything that his mother never found out the real circumstances as to how Serpen had died.

*

Once Isis and Felan managed to pull themselves together, they joined Zebulon for the celebrations. It was clear that they were both upset, but they each managed to put on a brave face.

Inside the Emerald Cave, an ancient table made of stone had been filled with an abundance of treats in anticipation of his arrival.

Clump scanned the table and his smile soon slipped from his lips. In preparation of the feast, femur bones had been split to reveal the delicate interior flesh and sun-dried livers, kidneys and hearts sat in dishes ready to be eaten. In the very centre sat crow's gut, a delicacy of the Windigo, this was stuffed with meat after being roasted over the coals. Clump tried not to heave. He then spotted brown and white tripe, cut into strips, lying in brine. His forced himself to look away and his eyes rested on a cooking pot filled to the brim with blood soup.

"Come, join us," Zebulon encouraged. "I bet you didn't know that the internal organs of a griffon could be used in so many different ways."

Clump averted his gaze and tried not to retch, thus catching his mother's stare. He could see from her expression that she knew he was feeling nauseous. Thankfully, Zebulon didn't notice, he was too busy feasting his own eyes on what he thought to be an impressive spread.

"Sit, and enjoy," he insisted, and forced him into a chair. "After what you've been through, it's less than you deserve." Clump glanced down and spotted a display of pink and white flesh in a bowl. He tried not to gag, unable to look at the portion of raw brains without feeling his stomach lurch.

251

"Eat up," Zebulon commanded, plonking himself beside him. "It's not every day you get to enjoy the pleasures of a banquet in your honour."

Clump nodded and winced, watching his Elder tuck into the brains, slurping each piece into his mouth and making disgusting noises as he chewed.

Inside Clump was mortified, he just wanted to get out of here as fast as he could. Isis was sat on his right and Felan was by her side. The huge table held the other important members of the tribe whilst lower-ranking Windigos and their young were sitting on the floor, enjoying whatever titbits were thrown to them.

"Try and hold out," Isis whispered, catching his attention. "I've been practising making bread from dry corn and I think you will find it's quite to your liking." Clump's eyebrows arched in surprise. As far he was aware this was the first time his mother had ever tried to make anything that was not made from an animal or an immortal. He stared back at her with wide eyes.

"Why would you do that?" he asked, ensuring his voice was low enough for Zebulon not to hear.

Isis shrugged her shoulders and reached for the tripe. "Because whatever eating disorder you may have, it's probably my fault." Clump's brows furrowed yet a smile twitched at one corner of his mouth. How could she think his eating habits were anything to do with her? Inside he smiled. It was so typical of her to blame herself for something she had no control over.

He reached out and patted her hand. "It's not your fault I'm the way I am. I was simply born this way." Before she could argue, he glanced away to scan the many faces and spotting some of his father's loyal friends. He caught sight of a pretty female who sat alone, at the far end of the table. He didn't recognise her and when he caught her eye, she smiled shyly at him.

His attention shot back to his mother. "Who's that over there?" he asked, glancing back at the young female, trying not to appear too obvious. He heard Isis groan and he turned to see her mouth pulled into a deep frown.

"That's Greer," she moaned, "your father's new partner."

Clump was shocked; she was so ... young ... and ... beautiful.

252

"What will happen to her when everyone realises Serpen is dead?" he asked, leaning to one side so he could whisper in her ear. Isis paused and her voice sounded a little softer, almost forgiving. "She will be cast out into the wilderness because the cave belongs to you now."

*

Although the feast appeared to take forever, Zebulon finally declared that he wanted to meet with Clump alone. Clump was led from the Emerald Cave and taken to Zebulon's own quarters. His home wasn't much to shout about, just a dark hole, littered with worn-down, ancient-looking stones but at least it was cool and dry.

"What is it you want to see me about?" Clump asked, feeling rather nervous.

Zebulon turned to him and offered him a stone seat and Clump sat down.

"I have to say, seeing your grandmother in her spirit form today was quite astonishing," Zebulon admitted. He filled two hollowed-out tumblers with root wine and placed one in front of him. Clump nodded and accepted the drink. He took a quick gulp, wiping his wet lips with the back of his hand.

"Yes, I guess it must have been a bit of a shock for everyone," he agreed, his eyes never leaving his Elder's face. Zebulon went to take a sip of his own drink but then appeared to change his mind, resting the cup on top of a small shelf instead.

"The thing is, I was more surprised by what she told me," he admitted, stroking his mane thoughtfully.

Clump lifted a furry eyebrow, his curiosity having got the better of him and he leaned forward. "Really, why, what did she say?"

"Well, for starters, she told me Serpen's dead."

Clump sat back and took another mouthful of wine. "Oh!" was all he could think to say and he averted his eyes. He still felt guilty, as though Serpen's death was somehow his fault.

Zebulon cleared his throat.

"Yes, it's all such a sorry state of affairs," he breathed, his voice turning soft, almost holding a note of sadness. "Manadeth explained to me how we all need to protect you and that you will be

253

our key to the future. I'm sorry to say that I scoffed when she first told me, but she soon put me in my place."

Clump felt himself gulp. He didn't have a clue how he was going to be the salvation of his tribe. His heart began to beat a little faster.

"Did she tell you *how* I'm going to save everyone, exactly?"

"No, she just said you have the ability to lead the way and find peace within the realms."

I do? Clump thought to himself, well, that was certainly news to him.

"Apparently, when the time comes, if we listen to what you have to say, you will show us the right path that we must take."

Clump almost laughed out loud. To ever think Zebulon would listen to anything he had to say almost made him want to chuckle.

"Clump, I think you should know that I have spoken to the Protector. He told me he was with your father the day he was given the gift of premonition. He also said that after his initiation your father's mind was very rarely open to the Gods, suggesting that he refused guidance which he would have needed to become a great chief."

Clump felt a cold shiver run down his spine; he sensed Zebulon was about to tell him something important.

Zebulon let out a deep sigh.

"According to the Protector, because your father was so stubborn, most of what the Gods predicted was never accepted by Serpen. You see, a good leader listens to the Gods, they are powerful and wise and are there to guide us all. On the day your father was made chief he was given a warning, a sign of things to come. One of the Gods forewarned him that one day, if he didn't change his ways, he would most likely kill his only son."

Clump felt the blood drain from his face. He couldn't believe what he was hearing, Serpen had been forewarned. He could feel pain at the back of his eyes but there was no way he was going to allow Zebulon to see how his words affected him.

"So, are you telling me he tried to kill me of his own accord?" Clump asked, his throat dry.

Zebulon nodded his head. "Yes, I'm afraid so and if it wasn't for your grandmother's intervention he probably would have succeeded too. But what you don't realise is that the Gods became angry with him. You see, although Serpen understood the premonition this also meant he was given the chance to rectify such events. It was a test by the Gods and he failed. Had he done his best to save you, to change your destiny as one would have expected, then we would not be sitting here having this conversation."

Clump felt the need for some air and got to his feet. He didn't want to hear any more. He felt overwhelmed by what the Elder had just told him. To think that if Serpen had reacted in a way a real father should, he wouldn't be dead now.

"Thank you for sharing these facts with me, but I have to go," he said, placing the cup onto his seat. Zebulon nodded and Clump left the cave. His mind was like thick mud, his thoughts bogged down with despair. What Zebulon said hurt him deeply. To now know that his father did not care enough for him to try and save him, cut him to the quick. No matter what happened between them he in turn had loved Serpen very much. His mind was sluggish with despondency. Confused, he made his way to Lyra's cave.

"Are you alright?" asked a voice he didn't recognise.

Surprised, he turned around to find Greer standing there.

"Oh what? Yes, I'm fine," he lied, trying to give her a weak smile.

"I'm sorry for your loss," she said, and he watched her bow her head.

"What, you know about that already?"

"Yes, your mother just told me."

"Then I am sorry for your loss too."

It was Greer's turn to try and smile, but he saw her lower lip tremble instead.

"Yes, it did come as a bit of a shock, but he never loved me anyway," she said, and he saw she was holding back tears.

Clump didn't know what to say. He felt sorry for Greer and the predicament Serpen's death now left her in. He took a step towards her, trying to think of something comforting to say but Greer turned on her heels and quickly hurried away.

He threw back the hide to Lyra's cave and a gush of air snagged at the flames, the fire under the cooking pot roared into life. Felan called for him to drop the hide.

"Are you trying to set the place on fire?" she asked, giving him a light-hearted grin. Her humour caught him off guard, her playful expression helped him fight the darkness which threatened to consume him. He tried to push his troubles from his mind. He loved how Felan could change his mood, whether good or bad, with just a few simple words. He walked towards her doing his best to return her grin. He was home now and that was all that mattered.

"How did it go with the old grump?" she asked.

"He told me a few things that I really didn't want to hear."

"Hmm ... what kind of things?"

Clump came over and stroked her arm affectionately, enjoying the softness of her fur under his fingertips.

"It really doesn't matter, so, let's not talk about it."

"Alright," she muttered, her blue eyes searching his, "whatever makes you happy."

A noise made them both look up to see Isis standing there. Clump smiled at her but she did not smile back.

"Clump I need to speak with you, alone," she said. Felan caught Clump's eye and she stopped what she was doing to head towards the exit. Clump watched her leave and he felt the hairs on the back of his neck rise.

"What's wrong?" he asked his mother, as she walked towards the fire. He saw a look of sadness sweep across her face.

Isis turned towards him and he felt a shiver of unease. "There's something I need to tell you," she said, filling a bowl with hot soup from the pot. "On the night of your birth I stupidly took a magic potion. It was only meant to stop me from feeling hungry and eating you all alive, but it appears there was a serious side effect, one which I could not have foreseen."

She hurried towards him and offered him the bowl. Clump couldn't move, he was terrified by what she was about to tell him and so he let Isis stand there with the bowl cupped in her hands, like a stone wedged between them. He watched her struggle with her emotions before she continued.

"Although it's hard to comprehend, I took a black pearl which not only stopped me from eating your flesh but it also turned you into a vegetarian. I didn't realise this at first. I was simply grateful that I had managed to get through the birth without losing one of my cubs, but as you grew older and wanted to only drink my milk it was then that I understood something was wrong. I couldn't fathom it out at first, not until the day I saw you throw your food into the fire. I saw how the taste of flesh made you screw up your face and it was at that very moment when I realised you were cursed. I have gone over this fact a thousand times as to why it only affected you and not your sisters, but I will never know the answer and have since learned to live with the guilt of what I did to you."

Clump simply stared at her as though she had gone quite mad.

"Are you trying to tell me that I don't eat meat because of some strange concoction you once drank?"

Isis nodded, her eyes downcast. "Yes, I'm afraid so. If I'd known what it would do to you, I swear I would never have taken it."

"But why are you telling me this now?"

"Because after your behaviour at the banquet today some of the villagers are suspicious. You never eat in company and always refuse every meal you're ever offered. It's only a matter of time before your weakness is discovered."

Clump simply couldn't believe his ears. To think, he now understood the reason why he was so different from all the rest. However, it would never have occurred to him in a million years that it was all down to his mother drinking a magic potion. His brain fitted all those odd clues together. He felt relieved to see the whole picture and yet, he was starting to feel angry too. Could this be the reason why his father hated him so? He had to admit he was furious and found himself flaying his hand and the bowl of soup flew up into the air.

"How could you do this to me?" he roared, his grief erupting.

Isis let out a wail. "Please forgive me," she cried, her hands automatically covered her mouth. "I never meant to hurt you."

Chapter 31

Clump was still upset about his mother's unexpected revelation, but outwardly he put on a brave face and refused to speak about the matter again. He loved Isis very much and although he was angry, at the same time he could not punish her for something which was unforeseen. At least he now understood what made him so very different from the rest of his kind, he was cursed, and he believed this understanding would one day make him a better leader.

After a few days he was more like his old self, thanks to Greer whom he was secretly becoming rather fond of. Since they met, they appeared to have rather a lot in common. Unlike Serpen, Clump took the time to get to know her. He found her easy to talk to and rather fun to be around. She was kind and considerate and he liked that about her. She may not have been able to cook or clean when she first met Serpen but she was proving to be a fast learner.

He soon plucked up the courage to tell his mother about her. Isis had been furious when he first told her he was seeing her, claiming it was madness. However, after noticing how much weight the young Windigo had lost and how her long hair no longer shone, she soon became a little more sympathetic. After many sleepless nights, she found it in her heart to forgive Greer for taking Serpen away from his family. After this, Isis became a little kinder to Greer, showing her how to run a home and how to make clothing from what sparse supplies she had.

Early one morning, the Elders called a meeting and invited Clump along. They talked over several matters, one of which was about Clump being chief. They all decided that because Clump was still very young, he must wait until he reached maturity before he became their leader. Clump was secretly relieved. He wasn't ready for such a huge commitment, however, he was now a very important member of the community and therefore allowed to sit with the Elders and discuss all future plans.

Later, on a cool October morning just as a golden sun rose, Clump was asked to join the Elders for their weekly gathering. They all sat in a rather misshapen circle, some were dressed in their tunics whilst others wore nothing at all. Clump was placed next to

258

Zebulon and after a few noisy barks of greeting to one another, talks began.

"Today we are here to decide the fate of Greer," said one of the Elders who Clump knew only as Orib. He was old and wizened, pretty much like the rest of the group only he bore the distinct markings of a black patch under both eyes. Clump's ears pricked up as soon as Greer's name was mentioned.

Zebulon turned to face him.

"Have you any thoughts on the matter?" the Elder asked, "because you are well within your rights to send her into the wilderness if you so desire."

Clump rose to his feet. "I would never do such a thing," he exclaimed, aghast.

"That maybe so," interrupted Orib, "but for you to have your cave back she must first leave it."

Clump paused, and then took a step closer to his Elder.

"Yes, that is very true, however, I have spoken to Isis and although she wasn't happy about it at first, she is now willing to allow Greer to stay with us. My mother said she will continue teaching her to cook and sew so that in time she may become a valued member of our community."

Orib along with several of the Elders knocked on the floor with their knuckles, a sign they were displeased with this decision.

"Why are you not in agreement with me?" Clump asked, in surprise. "Surely it's better for her to be taught valuable skills than to be cast out into the Canyon?"

Zebulon gave a heavy sigh and then he too rose from the ground, his eyes dark with concern.

"That sounds all well and good but the problem is that with Serpen's demise she is no longer welcome here. The fact remains she is no longer any use to us. With her partner dead she cannot bear any cubs so she has no worth."

Clump stared at him in disbelief. He couldn't believe what he'd just heard.

"You cannot cast her out just because she is unable to bear any offspring!" he cried, his voice rising. "Her partner is dead and all you want to do is punish her by forcing her into a life of solitude.

Why, it's no wonder those who live beyond the mountains think of us as monsters."

Zebulon stared back at him open-mouthed, clearly shocked by his outburst. He then turned his attention to the other council members. He put the question to them. Under the circumstances, should Greer be allowed to stay? Some of the Elders shrugged their shoulders in reply whilst others simply nodded their heads. Zebulon's gaze rested once again on Clump.

"I can see you have a valid point and I have listened to what you have to say. I personally feel that if your mother really is willing to teach Greer to cook and fend for herself so that she doesn't become a burden, we can show leniency this time. However, be aware this is highly irregular and should she leave your family for any reason, she will be cast out from the village and will never be allowed to return."

Clump let out a sigh of relief, for a moment there he thought the Elders were about to refuse his proposal.

He noticed Orib did not look quite so pleased but Clump didn't care. Greer's life had been ruined due to no fault of her own and he felt it was up to the tribe to fix it.

And so the days turned into weeks and the weeks into months, and peace finally came to the Canyon. Clump was extremely happy with his life, for now he not only had his mother and Felan, there was Greer too. She appeared to have settled into their family routine so easily and Isis soon had her doing all kinds of chores. Within weeks she could make simple stews and learned how to strip the agave ready for weaving. She was always kind and helpful and was no longer seen as vain and self-centred.

Together they all lived inside what had once been Serpen's cave. Clump found that living with three females was not always easy, but there was a closeness, a bond between them which grew stronger day by day. Since his return, his mother had learned how to cook and bake without using meat of any kind. First it had been the corn bread but then she started making syrups and jams and food which oozed with so much flavour he thought his taste buds would burst. To his delight, his friends and neighbours started to steal her recipes and within a few months the whole village was making tasty vegetarian dishes. Of course they still enjoyed meat, but now they were no longer suffered from hunger and Clump noticed that a kind of harmony had swept throughout the village.

Then, out of the blue, Zebulon received word that he must go and meet with the Polak tribe about Felan. This made Clump's family very nervous because Felan no longer wished to leave the village. Zebulon would not be swayed and said it would be dishonourable for her to try and retract the sacred oath her father had taken when accepting the betrothal.

The day Zebulon left, Clump decided to try and keep Felan's mind occupied. He came up with the idea of escorting her to the well. Most of the females would congregate there and idle away the hours. The well was just outside the village and because they needed water for the cooking pot, this made a great excuse to get her out of the cave for a while. Unfortunately for them, they hadn't even reached the outer boundary when Clump heard a commotion. He quickly placed the tall, earthenware pots onto the ground and hurried back towards the caves with Felan running at his side.

When he arrived, to his despair, he saw a group of hunters close to the campfires and it looked as though they had gotten themselves something rather tasty for dinner. He felt the hairs on the back of his neck rise up. In the centre of five meaty clubs was a very frightened elf woman. She didn't look very old and she was dressed in fine clothes. Her long hair was coiled, showing her Elvin ears, and her fingers sparkled with several glittering gemstones.

"Please, don't hurt me," she begged, and she tried to push forward, but the hunters lifted their clubs closer to her face. She cried out, and recoiled. The Windigos heckled like a bunch of hyenas.

Clump let out a growl from deep within his throat.

"Felan, stay here," he ordered.

"Why, whatever's the matter?"

"I don't like what I see."

"But you mustn't get involved," his sister warned, sounding fearful.

"I have no choice. This can't go on any longer."

Felan reached out and grabbed his arm. "But this has always been our way of life."

261

Clump ignored her, shrugged her hand away and headed straight for the hunters.

"What's going on here?" he demanded, marching towards them.

One of the hunters turned and squared up to him.

"Why? What's it to you?" he hissed, his wet nose twitching. "Can't you see that we've caught ourselves some Elvin gentry."

Clump couldn't believe his ears. How on earth did they manage such a catch? His eyes scanned the ridge, then across towards the mountains.

"Where's her entourage?" he asked, shifting his gaze back to the hunters. "Surely she didn't venture out here, alone?"

The males glanced at one another before lifting their shoulders and giving them a shrug.

Clump felt a sharp stab of cold fear.

"You went beyond the boundaries, didn't you!" he accused, adding, "if you don't want trouble, you should take her back to where you found her."

At that moment Orib came out of his cave after hearing a commotion.

"My, my, what have we here?" he cried, moving closer to the prisoner.

Clump was relieved to see him.

"Tell them they must release her," he said, pointing to the elf. "Whoever she is, if we harm her and the elves find out we will have a war on our hands." Orib's black eyes appeared to darken. "One elf isn't going to be missed," he snapped, "and anyhow by the time we've finished picking her bones clean there will be nothing to prove she was ever here." Clump could feel tension building in his shoulders. He needed to make his Elder see sense, to realise she would bring nothing but trouble.

"No, you're wrong," he insisted. "It wouldn't take much for the magicians to figure out where she was last seen. There's no doubt she will be missed. Can't you see by her clothes, she is nobility and not some waif and stray." Orib shook his head, refusing to listen and lifted his hand to shoo him away like an irritating fly.

"Clearly you are not putting the needs of the village first," he declared thickly, and with a flick of his fingers signalled for two of the scouts to take her into the cave which they used for butchering meat.

As soon as they laid a hand on her, the elf let out a piercing scream, writhing and dragging her feet in the dirt in an attempt to try and break free. Clump couldn't bear to see her so distressed and something inside him snapped.

"Stop what you're doing!" he roared, his voice rising above the wail of the scouts, and everyone looked up, startled.

"You will not take her into the butchery!" he commanded, and in their confusion both scouts dithered, looking beyond him towards Orib.

Orib's face appeared to have gone a strange shade of purple.

"Who do you think you are?" he gasped. "You are not the chief yet."

Clump felt himself bristle.

"That may be so, however, I am also not a fool and if you could see past your stomach you would understand that I am trying to prevent us all getting killed," he bellowed.

Orib took a deep breath, the colour in his face not quite so acute.

"It is not your place to make such decisions," he hissed, rather sourly. "With Zebulon away, I'm in charge."

"Then for all our sakes, do what's right," Clump declared, his eyes pleading.

Orib hesitated and for the first time doubt shone in his eyes.

"I have made my decision. Seeing as you are so hell bent on releasing the prisoner we will wait until tomorrow when Zebulon returns and he can decide her fate."

Clump heaved a sigh of relief.

"Yes, what a good idea," he acknowledged, wiping the beads of sweat from his brow.

Orib scowled, shouting to the scouts, "Put her in a cage until Zebulon returns." Both the scouts and the hunters roared their displeasure but Clump raised his hand and called for quiet. "You only have a day to wait," he declared, his voice never wavering, "surely even you can wait that long?"

Chapter 32

That night Clump couldn't rest. His thoughts were mashed inside his brain and he worried over the Elvin woman they had trapped in the cage. When darkness fell and the moon shone down, the rest of the village transmuted, and the sound of jaws snapping and spurts of furious growls escaped from the disgruntled wolves. Although Clump couldn't remember everything that had been said that day, his instincts wouldn't let him leave the woman's side. He understood enough to know that he must keep her alive at all costs.

The cage was situated in an alcove between the butchery and several smaller caves. These caves were used for storing tools. Some housed such things as the mealing stones used to grind bones into flour, whilst others held an array of war clubs, huge bones used to bludgeon their victims to death.

Clump stood guard, his lips curled and his white fangs glistened in the moonlight. Many of the pack trotted past, their ears pinned, their bodies taut. A few circled around him, snarling and snapping their jaws, but Clump stood his ground. No matter what, he would not let them near the elf.

That night, Clump tried to sleep with one eye open. A few tried to challenge him, push their luck, but he would jump up, lunge forward and bite their flanks. It was enough to make them yelp and run away, but by the time dawn arrived he was both physically and mentally exhausted.

Clump lay on the ground when it was his time to turn and closed his eyes in readiness. It had been a long night and he hoped Zebulon would be home soon. He believed the Elder would do what was right for the village and so he lay in the dirt and waited for his transformation.

He felt a sudden excruciating pain in his thigh which made his eyes spring open and he turned to see an arrow embedded in his hip. He roared more in disbelief than pain and at the same time heard the scouts wail a warning cry. He tried to sit up, his eyes trying to spot where the arrow had come from; already realising they were under attack.

The next few minutes happened so fast everything became a blur. The wailing intensified as an array of elves, riding on horseback, charged through the village. Clump tried to get to his feet just as the ground beneath him thundered with hooves. He glanced towards the caves and spotted Elvin warriors jumping from rock to rock. Some wielded swords, others bow and arrows. They were swift, like lightning, and to his despair Clump could already see several Windigos with arrows in their backs, lying either dead or seriously injured on the ground.

"No, wait! Please," he begged, trying to catch their attention but the angry cries of the riders simply drowned out his words. He panicked, not sure what to do when he spotted Isis running towards him, her eyes wide with fear.

"They're killing us all!" she yelled, sounding petrified, "Clump, you must run for your life!"

"Mother go back! Find Felan and head for the cave," he shouted, but the noise around them was deafening and Isis carried on running. Then, to his horror, he saw her falter and she looked up to the sky, her eyes rolling and then her knees buckled and she fell like a stone onto the ground. Unable to believe his eyes, Clump simply stared in disbelief as she lay sprawled out in the dirt, an arrow embedded in her back. He roared in utter dismay, trying to run over to her, dragging his injured leg behind him in the dirt. He glanced around looking for help and saw everywhere was chaos.

Elves were shooting arrows indiscriminately and many of the Windigos were dashing between the rocks screaming, trying to terrorise them enough to make them stop. The elves continued to fire their arrows, the wailing having no effect on them whatsoever.

Clump made it to his mother and he dropped onto his knees. Lifting her upper body, he turned her over so he could see her face. Her eyes were closed and he heard the arrow in her back snap.

"No!" he cried, when he saw she was limp and he let out a wail that came from his very soul. He pressed his face into her chest, rocking her to and fro, refusing to come to terms with the fact that his mother was dead. He heard a horse whinny and the sound of hooves vibrated along the ground and he looked up with tears in his eyes to see someone wearing a deep scarlet cloak, pull their horse to a standstill. Although his vision was blurred, he could see that the male rider was not an elf because his ears weren't pointed. He blinked, tears rolling down his cheeks, and he saw a man sat on the horse, his robes fit for a king. His blonde hair was plaited down both sides of his face and Clump guessed he was most likely a magician. Still clutching hold of his mother, he watched the mage raise his silver sword and he closed his eyes, waiting for the fatal blow that would slice his head from his shoulders. He didn't care to live any more, not now he had lost his sweet mother and his grief was so intense that all he wanted to do was to join her in the afterlife. He heard the swish of the blade as it swept through the air and he squeezed his eyes tight.

"S-t-o-o-o-o-o-p!" someone yelled, "Don't kill him!"

Stunned, Clump opened his eyes to see the blade frozen in the air. A horse charged towards him, dirt flying through the air, but there was no mistaking that head of red hair.

"Crystal?" he gasped, "what are you doing here?"

The princess dropped down from the saddle and ran over to him. She squeezed his shoulder and then scurried past. He half turned to see she was heading straight for the Elvin woman.

"Mother!" she cried, and a zap from her fingers saw the door to the cage fly open.

Clump watched them hug one another and then Crystal helped the woman get on a horse.

Clump closed his eyes and thanked the Gods that he'd been given the foresight to keep the elf safe from harm. He would never have imagined in a million years that he had actually been trying to protect the Queen of the Elves.

Crystal hurried back to his side and Clump looked up into her sapphire-blue eyes.

He felt himself gulp. "I didn't know she was your mother," he said, shaking his head in dismay. "I forewarned them this would happen if they didn't return her to her people."

There was a scuffle of hooves as the horses danced in distress, clearly freaked out by being in such close proximity of a Windigo. The Queen pulled at the reins and then she pushed her mount forward.

266

"I believe what he says to be true," she declared, looking down at him from her horse and Clump saw the magician reach over and take her small hand in his.

"Amella, are you alright?" he asked, his voice clearly filled with concern.

"Yes, I'm fine and it's all thanks to the bravery of one Windigo. I didn't dare break free because I knew if I tried, the rest of the tribe would tear me to pieces and yet he helped to keep me alive," she replied. She let go of the magician and took hold of the reins once again.

"We should all be safe now," said Crystal, pulling something from her ears.

Clump gave a look of bewilderment when he saw what looked to be two small rounded grubs in the palm of her hand. His thoughts went straight to the barrels of glow worms he'd seen in the mountain but these little creatures didn't appear to be moving.

"Homemade earplugs," she explained, when he lifted a quizzical brow. "Something I learned to make in the ordinary world which doesn't require magic and which are extremely effective against wailing," she explained. He looked back at her, his face still clouded in confusion. Crystal smiled, crouching down beside him on her knees.

"I'm guessing this is someone you care about?" she said, pointing to the body lying in his arms.

"Yes, this is Isis, my mother," he cried, and his voice broke with emotion.

Crystal bent forward, pressing her ear against Isis's chest. After a few seconds she sat upright.

"I'm relieved to say she isn't dead, yet, but she will be soon, if I don't try and do something."

"Then you must," Clump pleaded, lifting his mother's body towards her, "and in return, I promise to do anything you ask."

Crystal looked deep into his eyes and he sensed she was troubled. "If I do this, if I save her, we must work together to ensure nothing like this ever happens between us again."

Clump nodded and his heart filled with hope.

"Yes, anything," he replied, "just save her— please."

"Alright, place her face down on the ground so I can remove the arrow."

Clump didn't hesitate; he simply did as he was asked. He was vaguely aware that there were more horses approaching and a continual array of distressed shouts coming from his neighbours, but his mind was only focused on saving his mother. He watched Crystal remove the arrow and he winced, blood pouring from the wound. The scarlet stain crept like a red river down the centre of his mother's spine. He saw Crystal place both her hands over what should have been a fatal wound, pressing the torn edges of skin together.

"Don't worry, her skin should knit fairly quickly," she explained, sounding encouraging. Clump remembered how her hands had healed all of the bite marks he'd endured from Serpen. He held his breath, and unconsciously glanced at his hip.

"I'll deal with your injuries as soon as I have a minute," Crystal said, following his gaze.

"Oh I don't care about myself," he spluttered. "I was just thinking about the last time you helped me when I got into a scrape."

Crystal grinned at him. "Yes, my timing does appear impeccable," she replied, "but that arrow will need to come out."

Clump's eyes saw Crystal's fingers stroke his mother's skin and already he could see the flesh beginning to heal. His eyes widened, the wound was actually shrivelling away, like when the sun evaporates rain. He found he was holding his breath and then Isis shuddered and he heard her exhale. A light groan left her lips and then she raised herself up onto her forearms.

"What am I doing face down in the dirt?" she moaned, and Clump gave a cry of relief, helping her stand on her own two feet.

She was a little unsteady but she was alive.

Clump looked back at Crystal and his face was surprisingly stern.

"I need you all to put those things back inside your ears for a minute," he said, and he waited until those around him had done what he asked. He then took a deep breath, his chest expanding and he gave the loudest, most harrowing cry, like when an animal is fatally wounded.

268

He bellowed so loud he thought his lungs would burst but when he finished, he looked around to see every Windigo had stopped fighting.

"No one else must die!" he ordered, and he nodded to the Queen who took out her earplugs and raised her arm, a signal to the Elvin warriors to put down their weapons.

Clump reached out and plucked the little grubs from out of Crystal's ears.

"Now we have all learned a valuable lesson. I think it's time we took the first steps towards making peace."

Chapter 33

It wasn't long before Clump's leg healed and he was able to help Isis back to the cave. Once inside, he was grateful to find both Felan and Greer were unharmed, having hidden themselves under a great heap of agave stacked in a corner. Outside he could hear the other Windigos howling, mourning their dead, and Clump was filled with sorrow. He had seen this coming, he had tried to warn them but no one would listen. He thought back to the princess, aware she was blessed with the power of healing, but even she could not bring back the dead.

Later that same day, a funeral pyre was built and from the safety of the rocks Clump stood with Crystal, Queen Amella and the wizard Bridgemear. They each saw flickering flames burst into life and it was a terrible sight; one which Clump knew would haunt him forever. The distinct smell of burning flesh filled his nostrils and he watched as the bodies of his neighbours twisted and melted into blackened effigies. Inside he cried for them all, aware he must never let such a tragedy happen again.

When the time was deemed appropriate, he guided Crystal and her parents to his cave and Isis took care of them. She was grateful to Crystal for saving her life and so she offered her root wine and flat cakes made with agave sugar. Satisfied they would not be harmed, Clump left the royal family to wait for Zebulon's return. The Elder arrived a few hours later and he was met by both Clump and Orib. He did not return alone. With him was a stranger, a male Windigo probably from the Polak tribe, and Clump guessed it was Felan's betrothed. Clump raised his hand to stop them both from entering the village.

"I'm afraid you may wish to brace yourself before you enter," he said, directing his gaze at Zebulon. "Earlier this morning, after the hunters brought a woman back for slaughter, we were attacked by elves."

Instantly Zebulon's temper ignited and he let out a roar. He pushed Clump's hand out of the way but he stood firm. His arms reached out and encircled his Elder's upper torso, pinning his forearms to his side to force him to stay put.

"You know full well we only have ourselves to blame!" Clump cried. "How many times will we do this to elves, knowing there will always be consequences for our actions?"

Zebulon tried to break free, breathing hard, but Clump held him fast, refusing to let go.

"Remember what my grandmother said to you, I am the key to our salvation."

Zebulon looked down into his face and Clump held his gaze. He felt his Elder relax a little.

"Are the elves still here?" Zebulon barked, lifting a furrowed brow.

Clump nodded. "Yes, and they are ready to sit down and talk with us until we can settle this once and for all."

Zebulon bit his lip and sneered. "Although I want to rip off their heads I will listen to what they have to say only because of what your grandmother said to me. Our ways have always been to kill immortals and that will never change. Tell them to wait inside the Emerald Cave until I have prayed to the Gods for our terrible loss."

"Agreed," said Clump, releasing his grip. "I'm sorry to say there are many who have perished, but we must look past today and think only of the future. There are bridges to build and perhaps a new era is approaching."

Zebulon gave a growl, clearly he did not agree. Clump watched him enter the village under a dark cloud.

Felan approached them and Zebulon gestured for her to come closer.

"This is Shay and he is your betrothed," he stated, rather matter-of-factly. Felan crossed the distance between them, an eyebrow lifted in surprise.

"Oh, why is he here?"

"Because as usual I was left to sort out your mess," Zebulon snapped. "You made it perfectly clear that you did not wish to live with the Polak tribe. Thankfully, Shay here has offered to save your skin by coming to live here with us instead."

Felan gasped at the unexpected turn of events.

"Why would he do that?" she asked, her eyes wide.

"Well, why don't you ask him yourself?" Zebulon replied. "After all, he's standing right in front of you."

271

Felan looked across at Shay and he grinned back at her. He was tall and strong and like many of the Polak tribe his body hair was a chocolaty brown.

"Is it true?" she asked.

"Well, yes, actually it is. We had a long discussion and as you may be aware my brother will one day be chief of our tribe. He likes to fight a lot and, more importantly, to win. We are at loggerheads with one another most days so when Zebulon explained how you were reluctant to leave your family, I decided that it would probably benefit us both if I moved down here with you."

Felan smirked. "I can understand your dilemma," she said. "I have a brother and a sister of my own who are a bit rough with me at times."

She glanced at Clump and his brows arched. As far as he was aware, Felan was usually the one dishing out the beatings.

"I'm afraid you've arrived at a very bad time," Felan said, and her expression turned dark.

Clump saw the smile slip from Shay's face.

"Yes, I'm saddened by the news that you have lost so many," he acknowledged, in hushed tones.

Felan nodded and pulled a frown. "Let's not talk about that now. How about I show you around instead?"

"Yes, I would really appreciate that," Shay replied, and without further ado Felan led him away.

Clump felt Zebulon's gaze rest upon him.

"Well? At least she likes him," said Clump, with a shrug.

Zebulon let out a heavy sigh.

"I'll never understand the young," he said. "Still, now that a catastrophe has been averted, perhaps it is time to make ourselves ready to gather everyone for the ceremony of the dead," he said, and headed off to what was left of the funeral pyre.

*

The ceremony of the dead took many hours and in all that time, the royal family waited patiently inside the Emerald Cave. Isis had taken them there having made it her sole purpose to look after their guests. Since Clump explained how Crystal saved her life, Isis vowed she would always watch over the girl with the hair of fire.

On Bridgemear's orders, many warriors had made camp just outside the village. The soldiers were nervous, never in their entire history had Windigos ever sat down with elves before. The camp was restless. They didn't trust the Windigos and feared their Queen could be eaten at any moment.

Back inside the village, once the grey ashes of the dead were finally scattered to the four winds, the Elders, led by Zebulon and Clump, finally entered the Emerald Cave.

The row of twelve Elders, which included Clump, must have looked quite daunting as they made their way inside. Each wore robes only used for such a ritual and Zebulon looked magnificent with his white mane threaded with colourful gemstones.

The wizard Bridgemear sat by the Queen who was seated at the centre of the table with Crystal at her side. The group of Windigos came and placed themselves opposite the royal family, a long row of intimidating monsters alongside three unexpected guests.

Clump was placed at Zebulon's right hand so he was sitting across from the princess. He looked up and grinned shyly. He couldn't help feeling strange, her being here in an official capacity made him feel rather odd. He tried to put himself at ease, managing to catch her eye and she smiled back at him.

Once settled, Zebulon cleared his throat and a hush fell over the entire assembly.

"Let me take this moment to introduce myself. My name is Zebulon and I am the oldest Elder of the tribe. We have recently lost our leader so I believe I speak for everyone here when I say that what you did to our village was nothing less than despicable."

The Queen was heard to take in a sharp intake of breath and Bridgemear jumped to his feet, his eyes wide with hostility.

"Do my ears deceive me?" he hissed angrily. "Your hunters sneak onto my land, kidnap my wife with the intention of making a meal out of her, yet you have the audacity to say we are despicable!" he roared, clearly aghast. "Actually, I think we have wasted far too much time waiting for you to arrive. We should have simply finished you all off whilst we had the chance."

An outburst of fury saw several Windigos jump to their feet, some banged their fists on the table whilst others peeled back their black lips to show a row of meat-ripping teeth. They snapped their jaws together, making a rather menacing sound.

Bridgemear drew his sword.

"I think it's time we left," he said, putting a protective arm around the Queen. Clump watched Amella grab hold of Crystal, pulling her to her feet.

"No! Please, wait!" roared Clump, over the din.

Bridgemear lifted his sword and the blade flashed.

"Clearly, there's nothing here for us except trouble," he stated, moving away from the table.

"No, don't leave like this. Just give me a moment to explain and I'm sure we can work this out."

Bridgemear didn't look convinced and Amella's face was definitely unsure, but Crystal was quick to intervene. "Clump's right, we've made it this far we may at least hear what he has to say."

Clump glanced up at Zebulon, widening his eyes, he pleaded for him to say something that might make them stay.

"I apologise for my outburst," Zebulon declared, through gritted teeth. "I think the princess is right and you should at least listen to Clump before you make any hasty decisions. Let's stay calm and sit back down. In his defence, he will one day be our chief therefore we should let him try and make peace if he so desires."

Under his long hair, Clump turned scarlet.

"It is not if I desire peace," he snapped, affronted. "It is whether we *all* desire a life without pain and suffering." Inside he was furious at Zebulon and couldn't believe he could say something so foolish.

He turned towards Bridgemear and the Queen, his eyes pleading.

"Please, take a seat. All I ask is just five minutes more of your time."

"Then make it quick," snapped the magician, still clearly ruffled, but he remained standing.

Clump gave a sigh of relief and then he took to the floor. He didn't approach the royal family as perhaps everyone expected, instead he turned to face his Elders.

A row of small, button eyes blinked back at him in expectation.

He cleared his throat and gained his composure before he spoke.

"For centuries it has been our way to intimidate and frighten the people beyond the mountains. Our way of life since time began, our survival, has always seen us take the lives of the living to feed on their flesh. In choosing this path, we created our own destiny that saw us banished into the Canyon and surrounding mountains.

As far as I'm concerned, we brought it all upon ourselves, built a life of desolation with our own bare hands and filled it with misery and hardship. We became bitter, blinded by what we were doing. Because of this, in a world which could offer us a life of plenty, we actually enjoy so very little."

Zebulon, let out a groan of discontent. "Just get on with what you're trying to say and stop beating about the bush," he stated impatiently.

Clump took a deep breath before he continued. He knew this was going to the hardest thing he would ever have to do.

"My Elders, although what I am about to say will make you disbelieve your ears, what I propose will not only bring peace to our lands but will also allow us to live together in harmony." A surprised gasp left the mouths of several Windigos, some sitting forward in their seats, listening more intently.

"The only way things will change is if a miracle happens," Orib mocked, and he laughed out loud.

Clump felt himself redden at his Elder's attempt at ridicule and beads of sweat peppered his brow.

"No, there's no need for something as drastic as a miracle, all that's required is for Windigos to show some self-discipline," Clump replied, his eyes beseeching. "You see, the answer to all our prayers is simple. If we want the life we crave so badly, then we must first stop eating the flesh of immortals."

An explosion of noise filled the cave as the Elders, astonished by his outrageous proposal, went berserk. Clump did his best to try and calm those who thought he had totally lost his mind.

"What! You're suggesting we have no meat at the table," cried Zebulon, "why, I'd rather die!"

"That could be arranged," said Bridgemear, still holding his sword, and Zebulon turned and snarled at him. Clump had to think on his feet before everything turned sour.

"That kind of attitude from both of you isn't going to get us anywhere!" he cried, and some of the Elders bent down and started throwing anything to hand. He ducked, several large stones bouncing off the walls.

"You're simply not listening," he cried in bewilderment, "don't you see we can still eat animals, just not immortals."

"And how do you suppose we live like that?" roared Orib, finally losing his cool. "We barely scratch a living and don't have enough to eat as it is."

Clump turned his attention to the Queen and Prince Regent.

"The Andark tribe can only make these changes if we have your help. If the Kingdom of Nine Winters is willing to show us how to farm, then we could raise meat stocks of our own."

"It wouldn't work," someone cried out, "we have eaten immortals since time began."

Clump switched his attention back to the Elders.

"Yes, it would, our diet is already changing. Most of the villagers are now using my mother's recipes. Your cubs are no longer hungry, your larders are full of food made with natural ingredients found in the Canyon and you have a constant supply of corn bread."

"I think what you're asking is impossible," said another of the Elders. "It's been a tradition for far too long, we cannot change who we are, not even if we wanted to."

"Yes we can," a female voice interrupted. Everyone in the cave turned to see Isis standing right in front of them. "I haven't eaten anything human since my son and Serpen first left the village. I had no hunters to help me find food so I foraged within the Canyon for an alternative to feed my daughter. At first I thought we might starve, but then I learned how the many varieties of plants and wild berries growing throughout the wilderness could be mixed with plentiful ingredients to make tasty dishes. Since I have stopped

276

eating the flesh of immortals I am far more energetic and feel years younger."

"Are you serious?" asked Orib in surprise. "Do you truly expect us to believe we can change the way we are by simply altering our diet?"

"Yes, absolutely," she replied. "Think of all the benefits if we do. We can leave the Canyon without being hunted ourselves. Travel further than we ever dreamed of, exchange our wares within the city walls and even live a life of peace. For the first time ever, we will truly have our freedom, surely that's worth the sacrifice?"

A sense of awe showed on the Elders' faces, as though a light had been switched on inside their heads, awakening thoughts to what the future might really hold for them.

Zebulon turned to face the Queen, his tone surprisingly light considering his recent outburst.

"Your Majesty, if what Clump and Isis say is true then we cannot do this without your guidance. It would be a lie if I said it sounds easy because we are all set in our ways. However, Isis is right, the benefits outweigh everything. If you could see to it that we are given livestock and shown how to grow crops, in return we will not harm a living soul and will share with you a percentage of what we reap."

Amella straightened her cloak and then she turned towards the Elders.

"I have to say I am extremely impressed with this turn of events. Already I can see for myself how Clump has a vision for the future and I'm sure he will make a great leader when that day comes. He is already very wise for one so young and clearly only wants the best for everyone. For the elves to finally have peace within the Canyon I feel that giving you the supplies you need is simply a small price to pay. If in exchange you will give me your word that you will never lay a finger on another immortal again then I am willing to sign a treaty with you that will see these dreams turned into reality."

I give you my word," said Zebulon, placing a fist to his heart and lowering his gaze.

"And mine too," said Clump, doing the same and the rest of the Elders quickly followed suit.

"Then it is settled." said the Queen. "From this day forward we will begin a new era, one that will see peace within our lands and I thank the Gods with all my heart for giving Clump the foresight which will soon enrich all our lives."

Chapter 34

After that fateful day, and true to their word, the Andarks never touched immortal flesh again. An unexpected peace fell over the entire land and then, one by one, other tribes of Windigos began following in their footsteps.

The elves kept their promise and brought Clump's village special seeds which would grow well within the dry soil. They showed them how to build large sheds and storehouses so they could look after their animals and grain. For them, life in the Canyon was changing for the better and Clump was the happiest he could be – well, almost.

One day he ventured out of the Canyon and headed for the plateau. He quite often ventured into the wilderness alone. He would go there to think without interruption and his thoughts were always about Brid and Horith. Although the plateau sometimes brought back bad memories, in some strange way he also found this place made him feel a little closer to Brid. Since his return to the village he had not made it back to Gobb Loch. His life had transformed beyond recognition for now he was a vital member of the tribe with many responsibilities. He in himself had changed in so many ways. Thanks to Greer he was far more confident and self-assured with matters concerning the village. He also had Crystal as a close friend and she often came to visit him. His life was enriched, yet it was as though a vital piece of him was missing.

At moments such as these Clump would sit for hours, staring at the horizon, hoping the Wyvern would rise before him with his sister and her partner on its back. He tried not to think about the fact that they may not have made it to Gobb Loch safely. He'd received no word from them at all since his return and so he pushed these nagging doubts to the furthest corner of his mind, choosing to believe they were still alive.

He squinted when a dark shadow flickered across the sun and his stomach did a triple somersault. His eyes focused on a speck of black which grew larger with each passing second and he felt his heart thud in his chest. After several minutes, he saw something flap about in the breeze and his thoughts of Horith and Brid were dashed, replaced by someone far more sinister.

Clump took a deep breath, his euphoria instantly replaced with dismay. He dithered, what should he do? Should he run for cover or stay and see what had made the witch seek him out once again? Then again, was it just mere coincidence that the witch was in the neighbourhood? His nerves got the better of him and he decided to dash for home. He jumped to his feet and broke into a run. His legs took long, broad steps and his arms which were powerful and strong forced him to move quickly.

A sudden breeze blew against his back, causing the hair on his body to ripple, and he automatically looked up towards the sky.

"I hope you're not running on my account," said a voice, he would never forget.

Clump gulped and slowed his pace. Above his head he could see a weather-worn pair of shoes dangling just inches from his nose. The witch gave a cackle, shot off in front of him and he watched her land her broomstick a few feet away. His heart dropped like a stone.

"Cheer up," said the witch, making her way towards him. "Anyone would think you'd seen a ghost."

Clump tried to smile, but he found his lips were sealed together. The witch laughed, clearly amused.

"Don't worry I'm not here to make you do anything you don't want to," she said, staring at two small boulders which jutted out from the ground.

"Then why are you here?" he asked, lifting a quizzical brow.

The witch pointed to the rocks. "Come, sit with me for a moment."

Clump did as she asked and they both sat down together. The witch tucked her cloak between her legs to stop it blowing in the wind and Clump turned towards her and waited for an explanation.

At last she spoke.

"I hear, things didn't go quite to plan when you were down the Stannary Mines with Crystal?"

Clump shook his head.

"No, they didn't. In fact, I think I can safely say that everything pretty much went wrong."

The witch let out a deep sigh.

"Well, yes, none of us knew that the fourth mage had already been released. As far as we were concerned, we were still in dire need of him."

"So did you ever find out who he was?"

"Yes, and all you need know is that Crystal's aware of his true identity," said the witch, tapping the side of her nose. "Although nothing actually went to plan, in the end the fact that you met Crystal was enough to change our future forever."

"It was?" replied Clump in surprise.

The witch nodded.

"Oh, yes, by meeting her and forming a valuable friendship, you not only helped to save your own kind from extinction but also created peace throughout these lands." She gave a toothless smile. "You see, had you not met the princess, most likely you would be dead right now and the Kingdom of Nine Winters and the rest of the realms would be getting ready for war. When I asked for your help, even I never believed events could turn out this way. Clump, you are a remarkable creature and I came all this way today because I wanted to wish you well."

Clump couldn't help but feel a little overwhelmed. He had never, in a million years, expected the witch to come all this way just to tell him that. He felt his cheeks burn. He didn't feel such a brave Windigo, more likely he was more gullible than anything else. However, he was wise enough to keep his thoughts to himself.

"If there is anything I can do for you," said the witch, getting to her feet, "just let me know."

Clump jumped up. "Well actually, there is one thing," he said, suddenly feeling brave. He really didn't want to ask her for anything but at the same time he understood how this might be his only chance.

The witch looked back at him, her eyes wide with curiosity.

"I'm intrigued, what is it that you want?"

Clump took a deep breath.

"Well, the thing is ... I would really like to know what has happened to Horith and Brid. You see, I was supposed to meet them at Gobb Loch, but I never made it and I've had no word from them since."

The witch stared at him for a moment.

"So you wish for me to find out whether they're alive or dead?" she asked, her face half-cocked.

Clump nodded.

"Very well, I will see what I can do and I will meet you here in three days."

Clump let out a huge sigh of relief.

"Thank you, I'm eternally grateful," he said, smiling at last.

The witch stared back but her voice held an edge he didn't expect.

"Don't thank me just yet," she warned, "I will most likely return with bad news."

Clump nodded once again. He understood, but he needed to know, one way or the other.

The witch climbed onto her broomstick, her cloak billowing in the breeze.

"Three days," she reiterated, and before he could reply she was up in the air and heading back towards the sun.

Chapter 35

The next three days turned out to be the longest of his life. In his cave, Clump became moody and restless. He didn't want to tell Isis or Felan about the chance of finding Brid, just in case their hopes of her being alive were dashed. He turned instead to Greer. They were becoming extremely close and appeared to have a lot in common, talking together in whispered tones, sometimes for hours on end. In the early evenings he would sit by the fireside, watching her strip the agave. Her fingers probed and pushed, twisted and tugged until the long strips were finally peeled away from inside the leaves. She would then lay the fibres beside her to dry before taking them to Lyra for weaving.

On this particular evening the two of them had been left alone for considerably longer than usual. Isis and Felan were out visiting some of the older members of the tribe and would be back soon to prepare the evening meal. Clump wasn't feeling too well and he rubbed his throbbing temples as pressure built behind his eyes. The witch had already been gone a day, yet the hours passed so slowly and the tension of waiting for her to return was making him rather anxious.

"Would you like me to fetch you a drink of cold water?" Greer asked, glancing up from her work.

Clump tried to smile. Shaking his head he made his own way over to where a large wooden barrel held a gallon of fresh water. His temples were hammering so hard he thought his skull was about to explode and without thinking he stuck his head straight inside the casket. He felt the cold water shock his senses clear of pain and he lifted his head and gasped, the cold sensation momentarily taking his breath away. He wiped the droplets from his eyes, feeling instantly refreshed.

"I don't think your mother will be too impressed if she finds out what you just did," said Greer, coming over. "I actually think she was planning on using some of that for cooking tonight."

"Oh, I will be in a lot of trouble if she finds out," said Clump, pulling a face, "so just to be on the safe side, I'd rather you didn't mention it."

"Don't worry, I won't," Greer chuckled, grabbing hold of an old piece of cloth to rub his wet hair dry. Clump couldn't help gaze into her eyes. She was so lovely and kind and he could feel her warm fingers touching the side of his face. He shivered, enjoying her close proximity.

Greer grinned at him, her eyes seemingly dancing with amusement. "I promise I won't tell her as long as you help me stack the agave in the corner so I can clear up ready for supper," she teased.

Clump took the cloth and wiped the last of the water from his cheeks before lifting a mountain of agave neatly in a corner, out of the way.

"Do you still miss him?" Clump suddenly asked her.

"Who, Serpen?"

Clump nodded.

"No, not really. I was on my own quite a lot and before he left me we rarely spoke to one another."

"That must have been hard on you?"

"Yes, it was at the time. At first I was excited at becoming his mate, but it soon became clear he still cared for Isis and that I was not who he really wanted."

"They were together a long time."

"I know, and I was young and naive. I was a fool to ever think that I could take her place. I realise that now."

His fingers accidentally brushed against hers yet she didn't pull away.

"Well, I'm glad you're able to stay here, with us."

Greer looked up and smiled at him, her pretty eyes crinkled at the corners.

"Yes, me too ... I just wish things could be different ... I mean, in another life I would have liked for us to have gotten to know each other better."

Her words took him by surprise and he felt his mouth go dry. He hadn't expected her to say anything which could lead him to believe she had feelings for him and his heart fluttered with delight. He felt odd, light-headed and his whole body suffered a strange tingling sensation. He couldn't help admit to himself that he wished they could be together. Ever since they had begun to share the cave

284

he had felt a connection with her as though he had known her his entire life.

A cool draught of air was followed by someone clearing their throat and Clump glanced up to see Isis and Felan standing in the doorway.

He tried to act casual even though he guessed they had seen the way they were both looking at each other.

"Oh, it's you, I wondered where you two had got to," he said, moving towards the cooking pot to try and put some distance between himself and Greer. He could see a strange expression creeping over his mother's face and Felan looked to be doing her best to hide a smirk.

"Anything I can do to help with supper?" Greer asked, rushing over to them.

"Err, yes, I guess so," said Isis, pointing to a large amount of recently decapitated flower heads. "Lyra said she would like to use the Abal flowers to sweeten a few pies."

"Oh, well, in that case I'll take them right now," said Greer with a tight smile. She reached out for an old wooden dish, placing a handful of the petals inside.

"I won't be a tick," she announced, heading out of the door.

Once she was out of earshot, Isis turned on Clump.

"What on earth do you think you're doing?" she demanded.

Clump stared back at her, aware his cheeks were burning.

"What do you mean?" he asked, feeling a niggle of apprehension worm its way down his back.

"You know very well," Isis scolded. "I saw the way you were looking at her just now."

Clump was lost for words. He couldn't deny it any longer; he was in love with Greer. He tried to think of something which could defuse the situation but thankfully Felan was quick to intervene.

"What does it matter anyway?" she interrupted. "It's obvious they care for each other, so where's the harm?"

Isis was aggrieved. "It's not that simple. Greer once belonged to Serpen and that fact cannot be undone," she replied.

"But they were never close," declared Felan, showing her stubborn streak. "Everyone knows he only brought Greer back here to spite you."

"That's simply not true," Isis retorted, flinging her head.

"Yes it is," Felan argued. "We all know he never wanted her, not really, he just wanted to punish you."

"That's enough!" roared Isis, becoming infuriated. "It's no use arguing, I don't make the rules!"

A rustle made them all spin around to find Greer standing there. She had clearly overhead what had been said because her face was stricken.

"I ... I... didn't mean ..." she blurted and her eyes filled with tears. Before anyone could reply she turned around and ran out of the cave.

"Now look what you've done," Felan hissed, and she quickly chased after her.

Clump glanced over at Isis and saw her bottom lip tremble.

"I understand you're only looking out for me," he said, reaching out and patting her shoulder. "However, sometimes rules are made to be broken."

Isis stared up at him and her face was etched with lines of worry. "Perhaps you're right," she said, her voice breaking a little, "although no matter what you might think, I wouldn't hold your breath if you're hoping the Elders will allow you to be together."

"We'll have to see about that," said Clump, turning stubborn. "If Greer wants me as much as I want her, I will do everything in my power to make that happen," he replied, finally admitting his feelings.

Isis sighed and he thought her eyes looked pained.

"I truly hope you know what you're doing," she said, and with that she pulled away and began preparing supper.

*

The next day Clump visited Zebulon.

"What can I do for you?" asked the ancient Windigo when he approached his cave. Clump tried to stand tall. He wasn't sure how the Elder was about to take this latest turn of events but he didn't care, he loved Greer and he was willing to fight for her.

"I need to ask your advice," Clump explained.

"Yes, of course, out with it," Zebulon replied and gestured for him to come inside. "Tell me, is something wrong?"

Clump didn't waste any time explaining what was stopping him from sleeping at night. Zebulon simply listened to his every word, his brow soon furrowed into the middle of his forehead.

"I can't say I'm surprised," he admitted. "I always knew that if Greer stayed with you she would cause havoc."

"No, she hasn't," Clump reassured. "I simply want her to become my lifelong partner." Zebulon looked up at him and his mane appeared to turn a little whiter, as though he had aged considerably in the few minutes Clump had been in his company.

"This is all very unusual, but if you feel you cannot live without her then your only choice is to visit the Protector and see what he has to say. Only he can shed any light as to whether the Gods will permit such a joining."

Clump nodded. This was just as he expected.

"Then I will go and see him this very second," he said, and he rose to his feet.

Zebulon remained seated.

"As you wish," he stated, "however, remember it is the Gods and not you who will decide whether you can be together."

"I understand," said Clump, with a nod, "and no matter their decision at least I'll know in my heart that I tried." Without looking back, Clump dashed away and headed towards the Emerald Cave. There were a lot of villagers standing around the open campfires but Clump didn't notice any of them, his mind already focused on talking to the servant of the Gods.

He followed the curve of the rock, unaware of a sudden breeze which filled the darkened sky, causing the flames from the outdoor reed stalks to flicker and dance. He saw a flash of colour out of the corner of his eye and he stopped in his tracks, sensing he was being followed. He turned around and caught sight of Greer hurrying after him.

"What are you doing out here?" he enquired.

Greer looked a tad sheepish.

"I saw you leave Zebulon's cave and I put two and two together. I think you're either very brave or very foolish to face the Gods alone so I've decided, if you're going to see the Protector then I'm coming with you." Clump felt his chest swell. He'd never met anyone like her before and all he wanted to do was nuzzle her face off right there and then. Instead he gave a shy smile and shook his head.

"Greer, you know no one except the males of the tribe may gaze upon the Protector's face. These rules have been in place for thousands of years and only Manadeth was the exception."

Greer nodded in reply.

"Yes, I understand all that but this affects me too," she argued.

Clump pulled his lips tight. "You do want to be with me, don't you?" he asked, sounding a little unsure.

"Of course I do," she gasped, clutching his hand, "but I feel we should face the Protector together."

Inside, Clump was about to burst with joy, but outwardly he tried his best to remain calm. He was so happy, but he understood that they must first receive a blessing from the Gods if they were ever to be joined as one.

He relaxed his shoulders and shuffled his feet closer to hers. "I hear what you're saying but we must not anger the Gods. I will go and see the Protector alone and argue the case for both of us."

Greer's shoulders appeared to sag and she propped herself up against the rock. Clump reached out and wrapped his arms around her. "I will do us justice, I promise," he said, pulling her so close he could feel her warm breath on his lips. "No matter what happens, we *will* be together."

Greer peered into his eyes and he thought he saw a look of doubt swirl within them.

"Trust me," he said, finally letting her go and then he turned and shot from her side. He headed straight for the Emerald Cave, grabbing hold of one of the reed stalks on his way inside. He dashed down the steps, his feet silent as they brushed the stone.

When he reached the bottom, he lifted the torch to try and chase away the darkness which surrounded him.

"Protector, are you there?" he called out. He heard a noise; a shuffling of robes and then a light, not much brighter than his own, appeared from out of the shadows. Clump's eyes had adjusted to the gloom, enough for him to be able to see a figure dressed in dark robes heading straight towards him.

"Who wishes to speak with me?" a gruff voice demanded. Clump felt his earlier courage start to diminish. "Out with it?" the voice commanded when he dithered, "tell me, who has sent you here?"

Clump took a deep breath.

"Protector, it is I, Clump, son of Serpen. I have come here in the hope of seeking your advice."

A spark of interest must have ignited inside the Protector because when he spoke his voice was less aggressive, in fact, it now held an edge of curiosity.

"Clump, I did not expect to see you down here for quite some time yet," he stated, edging closer and Clump had to do his best not to look repulsed when he saw the Protector's skin was peeling away from the bone.

"Yes, err, well, my circumstances have changed somewhat and so I need your council," he replied, a little wary. He had never been on his own in the cave yet alone in the presence of the Protector before and if he was honest, he was terrified. The Protector shuffled to his side, lifting the lantern.

"Ah, yes, I can see the resemblance to your father now," he acknowledged with a nod. "Tell me, have you come to learn about your role as chief?" he asked, cocking his head to one side.

"No, it's not that," said Clump, and he lifted his hand so he could block out the light. "There's something else which I feel is far more pressing for us to discuss."

"More pressing than becoming the chief?" gasped the Protector, in surprise, "is there really such a thing?" He turned away and moved closer to the water's edge, setting the lantern down on a small rock, causing shimmers of light to bounce along the gentle ripples of the water.

"I can't deny it, I'm intrigued," he announced, turning his attention back to the young Windigo. "So, what is it you wish to speak to me about?"

Clump took a deep breath, and his hand clasped the reed stalk a little tighter.

"I'm here to talk about Greer."

"Who?"

"Greer."

289

"Oh yes, wasn't she your father's partner?"

Clump felt several knots begin to ravel inside his stomach.

"Well, since he's dead, she isn't his partner anymore."

The Protector chuckled.

"Oh, really, well, some would say she is bound to him forever."

Clump watched the Protector place his full attention upon him. The reflection of the water against the stones caused sparkling pools of light to dance in his eyes. He saw his purplish lips turn into a thin line.

"What is it that you want – exactly?" he asked.

Clump couldn't help but stare into his eyes and he found he was almost mesmerised by the two black pools which stared back at him.

"I wish for Greer to become my lifelong partner," he blurted.

The Protector's eyes widened and Clump saw him stiffen.

"What! Are you serious?" he gasped, clearly astounded.

"Yes, I am," Clump replied, his shoulders rising. "As far as I'm concerned there is no reason why we should not be together, after all, Serpen and Greer were never *together* in that way."

The Protector gave an unexpected sigh.

"What a predicament you find yourself in, young Clump. My, I can see your point, but she does in fact belong to the Gods now and they don't take kindly to those who want to claim what they cannot have."

"But why does she belong to the Gods?" he retorted, confused.

"Because Serpen will most likely be sitting with the Gods and waiting for her to join him in the spirit world."

Clump felt a rush of anger course through his veins. He didn't believe for one minute that Serpen would be given such an honour. Not after all the cruel and wicked deeds he'd done in his lifetime. No, he believed if he was sitting anywhere it would be in a pit of burning coals.

"He would never want her by his side." he declared, out of sheer desperation. "If it was true and he wanted someone he once loved, he would claim Isis, not Greer."

The Elder shook his shoulders in reply.

"Perhaps you're right," he said, "however, if you wish to try and take something precious from the Gods then there must be a trade."

"What do you mean?"

"I must take something from you."

"From me?" repeated Clump in astonishment, "like what?"

"I would need something that's personal to you alone."

"But I have nothing of value to give," said Clump, shrugging his shoulders in despair.

"Who said it had to be something material?"

"I don't understand, what else could it be?"

"Well, what if I was to take something from inside of you and offer this to the Gods in return for Greer?"

Clump's eyes widened.

"Like what?" he gasped.

"Let me explain," said the Protector, coming over and placing his arm on his shoulder, drawing him close. "The Gods enjoy receiving gifts such as strength and passion, but inside you there is something far rarer."

"There is?"

"Oh yes! For you hold the ability of never having the need to eat the flesh of the living."

Clump suddenly blanched and felt the blood drain from his face.

"What, you know about that?"

"Of course I do. I know everything."

"And the Gods are not angry?"

"No, quite the opposite, in fact, they're rather curious. You see, what happened to you is quite unique and so, if you agree to my offer, the Gods will be very pleased and in return they will be willing to give you what your heart desires."

"So if I give up my curse, I will be blessed with Greer?"

"Yes, that's right."

"But does this also mean I will then suffer the constant urge to eat flesh like everyone else?"

Clump watched the Protector nod his head and his hand slipped from his shoulder.

"Yes, I'm afraid that's most likely," he replied.

Clump lowered his head, looking at the ground for a few seconds before searching out the Protector once again.

"But I can't face living like that, not now, not ever."

"Then Greer will never be yours," the Protector explained, his voice flat.

Clump found himself panicking, aware of the sacrifice he was being forced to make. He was appalled by the mere thought that if he agreed, he would crave the flesh of the living for the rest of his life. This made him feel physically sick, yet he wanted to be with Greer more than anything. He thought about the tribe who, in his opinion, were the ones who were really cursed. However, since the treaty had been signed, he was proud of his kind for their ability to stop their natural craving for flesh, therefore showing great courage and self-discipline. Deep inside he now fretted that once the curse was broken he would not be able to show the same restraint.

"Surely there's something else you can take from me instead?" he urged, hoping to find a solution to his quandary.

The Protector shook his head, looking solemn.

"No, I'm afraid you have nothing else of value to give," he stated, and pursed his lips.

Clump exhaled, but then something flickered inside his mind, like a bird fluttering its wings when trapped. He heard a whisper, as though a gentle breeze touched his thoughts. He tried to focus, recognising the voice when it rose like a wave inside his mind.

Do what he asks and take up his offer, the voice urged softly.

"Manadeth," he gasped out loud.

"What's that?" the Protector asked, turning swiftly towards him.

Clump shook his head, refusing to look him in the eye.

"Err, nothing. I was simply accepting your proposal."

The Protector almost smiled.

"Excellent, then we have a deal. Come, step this way and let us begin."

Clump hurried after him. He decided it didn't matter about the consequences any more. His only wish was to be able to hold Greer in his arms without fear of being punished, wanting only to tell her how he felt about her without constantly glancing over his shoulder.

The Protector led him into a chamber which was like nothing he had ever seen before. Everywhere he looked there was a multitude of circular pools, lapping gently over a large stone floor. The water was so luminous there was no need for the lantern and the Protector was quick to extinguish the flame. Clump placed his reed stalk in a convenient hollow before following him.

As he glanced around, the first thing that struck him was the sweet aroma of sage in the air. He breathed deeply, enjoying the unexpected pleasant smell. To him the chamber felt mysterious, causing a shiver of anticipation to run down his spine. He glanced towards the ceiling, mesmerised by how the reflection of the water flickered along the roofline like a thousand tiny mirrors.

The Protector cleared his throat and caught his attention. Clump stared back at him, noticing he was holding a piece of rope in one of his gnarled hands.

One end held a knot.

"Come closer," the Protector gestured, "there's nothing to fear here." Clump moved with caution to his side. Secretly he was terrified, but no matter what was about to happen, he was prepared to see it through to the end.

The Protector lifted the rope a little higher and it was probably no more than twelve inches long.

"Before we start, I must tell you that this is no ordinary rope," he warned, giving a sly grin.

"Well it looks ordinary enough to me," said Clump, trying to sound carefree.

The Protector's grin widened.

"I can assure you it isn't, and for me to take from you what you have offered to the Gods you must swallow the rope, leaving only the knot visible." Clump's fingers flew to his lips as though this gesture would stop anything being placed inside his mouth.

"Are you serious?" he replied, his voice at least an octave higher than he intended.

"Yes, I'm deadly serious. The rope will not be easy to swallow but once you manage to do this we can make a start."

"Then I will swallow it right now and get it over with," said Clump, taking a bold step forward.

"Very good," replied the Protector, dropping the hood of his cloak. "Then we will begin." He reached out and rested one of his large hands onto Clump's shoulder, looking him straight in the eye. Clump found he couldn't hold his gaze because the Protector's face was so hideous. His skin looked to be rotting and what hair he had left stuck out in small wiry tuffs. His features were ghastly and to make matters worse, so was his breath. Clump rested his eyes towards his shoulder instead and saw the Protector's nails were yellow with age. Repulsed, he quickly turned away and heard the Protector exhale and his eyes automatically shot back towards him. He watched the old Windigo close his lids. He then made a strange noise, a high-pitched note that whistled through his teeth. Instantly, the whole chamber began to vibrate, causing the stones to appear to tremble, and Clump looked up to see his reflection ripple above his head.

His attention returned to the Protector whose eyes shot open and Clump could see they were white, like milk in their sockets. The servant of the Gods lifted the rope up towards his face and began chanting a spell ...

"With this knot I seal your fate,
You will not sleep, nor feel, nor hate,
Like the breath from your body I take from thee,
Your special gift, for another will be.
The Gods will smile and use it well,
They will toil and fall under your spell,
The taste of flesh will soon be upon your lips,
Whilst blood pours down from your fingertips."

Clump continued to stare at him and when the Protector pressed the rope into the palm of his hand he felt ice-cold fear ripple down his spine. Unknown voices filled the air, excited whispers which Clump thought might belong to the Gods. He believed they had come to witness him give them what he now thought to be a very precious gift and for just one second he pondered over whether he was actually doing the right thing.

He quickly shook this thought from his mind, closed his eyes and took a deep breath. Very, very, slowly, Clump threaded the thin piece of rope into his mouth. He gagged the moment the twisted fibres touched the back of his throat but he conjured Greer's face to help motivate him and he was able to force the rope further down his windpipe. He automatically gagged again. The reflex was overpowering and his lungs expanded through the lack of oxygen. He persevered, the rope feeling much thicker than he'd first anticipated, and he suspected he would soon be suffering a sore throat.

He unconsciously shuddered when a strange sensation made his oesophagus tingle, something wasn't right, the fibres in his throat were ... contracting ... His eyes flew open and he glanced down, past his nose, confused when a soft texture pressed on his tongue and to his horror, he saw the body of a snake dangling from his lips.

He tried to gasp and recoiled, his automatic reaction was to drag the snake from between his teeth but he heard Manadeth call for him to stay calm from inside his head.

You mustn't remove the snake if you want Greer, she warned. *Concentrate on what the Gods want from you and think only of your sweet reward ...*

Clump couldn't believe that she was asking him to keep the snake inside his mouth. He was petrified and he had to physically force himself from ripping the reptile free.

"You're doing well," the Protector encouraged. "The snake will seek out and extract the magic from your body. Once it finds what it's looking for, it will draw the liquid which your mother passed onto you through her blood the night you were born. When the creature leaves your body, it will bring with it the vital ingredient I need to create the same unique potion to give to the Gods."

Clump thought he might faint when he felt rough scales slide closer towards his stomach. He could only breathe through his nose and panic was making this very difficult.

He felt a sharp pain in his abdomen as though the snake had sunk its fangs deep inside his belly and he almost choked from the unexpected sensation. He saw silver stars burst in front of his eyes and he became light-headed. His knees buckled and then just when he thought he couldn't bear the feeling of intrusion any longer, the snake recoiled. He saw the Protector move towards him, coaxing the bright-coloured reptile from between his lips.

"It's over," the Protector sighed, and the snake lifted its head and flicked its long black tongue towards him. Inside Clump cringed, revolted, and then he placed his hands onto his knees and tried to get his breath back. He filled his lungs with sweet air, yet he found his chest was tight. He was feeling very odd indeed which was not really surprising after his ordeal, and without warning, spewed the remnants of his last meal all over the floor. He vomited until his stomach was empty, until it felt hollow inside. Once he felt better, he wiped his mouth clean and followed his guide.

Through bleary eyes he noticed the Protector had taken the snake over to a tall piece of limestone. The enchanted creature was thrashing its orange and white tail and he saw the Protector place the snake's fangs over the lip of a cup. Clump simply stared, fascinated by the Protector's ritual, watching as the servant of the Gods threw the snake high above his head. A flash of light saw the creature vanish and a piece of rope fell from the air instead.

Clump gasped at witnessing such magic.

The Protector knelt down beside a small dark hole. Clump could see twisted roots and the cusp of a plant inside with something purple lying beside it. Clump's curiosity swelled when the Protector poured a few drops of liquid taken from the snake's fangs over the secret ingredients. He then raised his hand and everything inside burst into blue and black flame.

The ancient Windigo turned to face him.

"The Gods accept your gift and in return you shall claim Greer as your own," the Protector exclaimed, giving Clump a knowing smile. "From this day forth, you belong to one another, so treat her well and you will have a long and happy life together."

Clump was ecstatic at hearing such news. He couldn't believe he had somehow managed to endure such a grotesque task so he could gain Greer as his partner forever.

The Protector pointed towards the doorway.

"Go home and I will ensure the Elders know of what has been agreed between us today. However, be aware, you are no longer the same creature as when you entered this cave. Your senses and tastes will change over the next few days and you will soon begin to crave flesh just as you should," the Protector warned.

Clump nodded and he felt his stomach lurch.

"I understand," he said, inwardly praying he would be able to cope and keep the dreaded hunger at bay. Clump headed out of the cave and yet he could still hear the Protector's words ringing in his ears.

Clump focused on telling Greer the good news and after grabbing the reed stalk he made his way home. He ran up the stone steps, taking two at a time and then he rushed through the village as fast as his legs could carry him. All the while he was thinking about Greer and hoped she would still be there, waiting for him. He entered the cave, his breath ragged and he thought his heart would burst with joy when he saw her sitting all on her own by yet another enormous heap of agave. She jumped to her feet when she saw him and dashed over.

"Are you alright?" she cried, her eyes searching his and he wrapped his huge arms around her.

Clump hugged her tight.

"Yes, against the odds we have been given permission by the Gods to be joined."

Greer put a hand to her mouth.

"I'm simply astounded, but tell me, how did you persuade them?" she gasped, her eyes wide.

It was Clump's turn to be a tad sheepish. He didn't wish to tell that he had given away the one special thing which made him so very different from everyone else.

"It doesn't matter how," he said, with a light smile, "what does matter is that we can now be together."

Greer put her head to his chest.

"You're right," she said, snuggling closer. "I just can't believe you're going to be all mine."

Clump thought his heart would explode with love for her but just then, Felan dashed into the cave.

"I've just heard the news," she cried in delight.

Clump pulled away from Greer in surprise.

"Really?" he said, in awe, "but I've only just left the Protector."

"Good news travels fast," she giggled, "and even mother knows!"

"Wow, that is fast, what did she say?"

297

"She's coming right now so you can ask her yourself," Felan cried, pushing back the hide.

Greer pulled him close and he could feel her tremble.

"You have nothing to fear anymore," he said, tightening his grip. "We've come too far now."

Isis entered and everyone turned towards her.

"I guess you've heard our news," Clump said, staring directly at her. He noticed she carried a basket filled with Lyra's home-made pies. She didn't reply, instead she walked towards the table and set the basket down.

"So, do we have your blessing?" he asked, as she took the pies out of the basket and he felt Greer clench his arm.

Isis turned towards him, her face solemn but then, to his relief, she gave a broad smile.

"Yes, of course, I'm pleased for you both," she announced, much to his delight and Greer left his embrace to rush over and hug her new mother.

"Oh, I'm so happy to hear that," Greer burst out and Isis laughed.

"Don't leave me out!" Felan squealed, dashing over and pushing her way into the centre of the two females.

Clump gave a huge sigh and, not wishing to be left out, made his way over and wrapped his huge arms around all three females. Everyone made whooping noises in the back of their throats and the whole room was filled with their laughter.

"This is the best day of my entire life," said Clump, turning his head towards Greer. "I simply cannot believe that I am finally back in the bosom of my family with the most beautiful Windigo at my side."

Felan let out a yelp. "Hey I'm beautiful too," she cried, giving him a nudge in the ribs.

"Yes, indeed you are," said an unfamiliar voice, and everyone turned to see Shay in the doorway.

"Oh, come on in," Clump invited, "we're celebrating my joining to Greer."

"Congratulations," said Shay, making his way over to Felan and Clump noticed his sister was beaming from ear to ear.

298

Chapter 36

Ever since Clump performed the ritual within the Emerald Cave he'd been feeling very unsettled. Even though Isis and Greer tried to tempt him with delicious treats and tasty dishes the fact remained that food was the last thing on his mind. This was not just because his throat was still sore after the incident with the snake. The truth of the matter was that he worried about how he would cope when facing immortals, and it didn't help that today was the day he was to meet the witch. For a start, he was fearful he might try and eat the old hag. He told himself over and over again that he would have to be pretty desperate, not to mention she was so grotesque that he wouldn't want his lips anywhere near her flesh. He shivered at the thought and turned his attention to Horith and Brid instead. Secretly he feared what she was about to reveal to him, convinced it would be something terrible. He didn't want to think like this but he couldn't help it. It had been many months since he'd last seen them both alive and there had been no word.

He set off on his journey early that morning. Greer stood at the entrance to the cave and he hugged her tight before leaving. Their joining had finally been approved by the Elders, and if it wasn't for the meeting with the witch today he was sure he would have been floating on air. He didn't tell Isis or Felan where he was going, but Greer knew. They had spoken about it in low whispers when they were alone at night and although she had never met them, Greer was also concerned for the safety of Horith and Brid.

He set off from the village at a brisk pace, wishing to finally learn the truth, good or bad, by the time he returned. He didn't want to suffer any more uncertainty and yet he fretted that more distress was yet to come. By the time the sun was high enough to bake the already dry soil, Clump arrived at the same place where he'd last seen the witch. He glanced around, found himself a rock on which to perch and then made himself comfortable. He waited and he waited, scanning the horizon for a glimpse of that black speck which would darken the yellow ball of fire. His vision soon became bleary, but no matter how long his eyes stared towards the distant mountains, he could see no sign of the witch. By midday he was both hot and bothered, and rather frustrated, and he started to believe he may have been taken for a fool. He doubted himself for ever trusting the witch and as time passed, he inwardly cursed his own stupidity.

By early afternoon Clump decided to call it a day. His head was as hot as a poker and he was in desperate need of a drink. He began the solitary trek home. He could feel the sun beating down on the back of his neck and all he could think about was finding shade.

His strong arms hung by his side and he lifted a hand to wipe the beads of sweat from his brow. It was then he felt something stir in the air and a sudden breeze blew against his skin. At first the gust of wind was a gentle relief but then the dust rose high in the air and he felt himself being pushed forward.

He staggered, the wind whipped around his ears and when he couldn't see his hand in front of his face he stumbled to a halt. His senses warned him of danger and although it was hot, a shiver snaked down his spine. He was suddenly afraid to turn around, afraid that the witch was there, standing right behind him. He took a deep breath and tried to pull himself together. If he wanted to learn the truth about Horith and Brid, he was going to have to be brave and face his fears. At this thought, his courage rose like a wave, whilst the wind continued to whip the air around him almost blowing him off his feet. He pursed his lips, closed his eyes and took another deep breath.

With some reluctance, he turned around.

He forced his eyes open, small particles of dirt flying through the air but he could see well enough to make out that it wasn't the witch who was causing such a stir. His eyes widened when he saw two powerful wings bow towards him and his jaw dropped. He couldn't believe it, he was staring at a purple and grey Wyvern. He took a step back, momentarily stunned at seeing the huge creature, but then recognition ignited behind his fearful eyes.

He gave a loud gasp. Was this the very same creature which had carried off Horith and Brid to Gobb Loch?

He watched the Wyvern's outstretched wings dip and then they flapped much slower as the mighty beast made its descent. Clump closed his eyes when once again a thick layer of red dust rose from the ground. He put his hands up to protect his face and felt something grab at his wrists and, startled, he fought the urge to pull away. His eyes flew open and he found he couldn't believe what he saw because standing there, right in front of him, was ... Horith.

"Is it really you!" Clump gasped, and he reached out and wrapped his huge arms around his friend's shoulders and gave him a tremendous hug.

"Ease up before you break a rib!" Horith roared, and he slapped Clump hard on the back. Clump was elated at seeing him alive and well.

"Where have you been?" he demanded, "I truly thought I'd never see you again."

"You can't get rid of me that easily," Horith replied, with a chuckle. "Brid and I have been living safe and well in that wonderful cave of yours."

At the mere mention of his sister's name, Clump exhaled.

"She's well then?" he asked, with a grin. He manoeuvred his head a little to the side, wishing to catch a glimpse of her.

"Yes, of course," Horith replied, a smile tugging at the corners of his mouth, and he quickly stepped out of the way.

Clump's grin broadened.

"Brid!" he gasped in delight. Heading straight towards him was his sister but ... she carried something in her arms. Clump simply stared in disbelief because there, snuggled to her chest, were two small baby Windigos.

"Clump!" she cried, dashing to his side to throw herself into his arms, pressing the young ones to his breast.

"I can't believe you're really here," she sobbed. "For a time I thought father killed you on that fateful day."

Clump felt a lump grow in his throat.

"It was close, I can't deny it," he said, unable to swallow.

Brid looked up, her eyes crinkled at the corners.

"What's wrong with your voice," she asked, "you sound hoarse!"

Clump quickly changed the subject, pointing down at the fluffy babes instead. "Err, do these two belong to you by any chance?" he asked, giving her a wink.

Brid beamed broadly, placing the youngsters into the crook of his arms. "Yes, meet your new little nephew Clump and his slightly older sister, Keesha."

"What! You named your boy after me?" asked Clump, and his chest swelled with pride.

"Yes, of course we did. It was the biggest honour we could think to bestow upon him. If it wasn't for you, my dear brother, we would all be dead and these two little treasures wouldn't be here at all."

Clump blushed underneath all that hair.

"Well, it wasn't all down to me. I did have lots of help."

Brid shook her head fiercely. "No, we are all alive because of you and we will always be eternally in your debt," she announced, lifting her hand and gently stroking the head of one of the sleeping babes.

"Are you coming home then?" he asked, his eyes bright with hope.

"For a little while at least," she replied, "because I hear there's to be a special joining ceremony," she added, and Clump swore he saw her eyes twinkle.

"How do you know about that?" he gasped, taken by surprise, and he started to jiggle the infants when one began to cry.

"The witch told us when she visited," Horith explained, leaning over to take hold of his son.

"I have to say she was a bit scary and it took a lot of convincing but she explained what happened to Serpen and asked for us to be here today."

"I'm so pleased she was as good as her word," Clump said. "By the way, did she also tell you that Felan is going ahead and being joined with her betrothed?"

"Really?" exclaimed Brid, allowing a note of pleasure to flow from her voice. "No, she never said."

"Well, yes, and he's very nice too, even mother approves!"

"How is she?" asked Brid, her voice turning serious, "I mean, with what happened to father and everything?"

Clump gave Keesha back to her.

"It hasn't been easy for her especially with the situation concerning me and Greer, but she's been a rock and now, thankfully, everyone's happy."

"Yes, it must have been very hard for her," Brid agreed.

Clump nodded.

"Yes, mother had to come to terms with her loss and accept Greer. Now she has become part of our family and I'm sure you'll like her when you're properly introduced."

"I'm sure I will," said Brid, placing her hand on his shoulder to give it a squeeze. "I never actually met her when she was with father but I'm pleased to hear she's become a big part of your life. As far as I'm concerned, you both deserve a little happiness and I'm glad things have worked out for you both."

Clump nearly yelped with delight. He was overjoyed at seeing his sister again. The fact she approved of Greer made their reunion all the more sweet.

"I need to go back to the village and tell everyone of your imminent return," Clump stated, thinking of the excitement that will soon spread throughout the entire village, especially when Isis found out she was a grandmother. "Things are very different now. I'm positive you will be made welcome and mother will try and convince you to stay."

Horith stepped towards Brid to place his arm gently around her shoulder. Clump watched him pull her close and he felt a moment of pure contentment. To see Brid so happy with her new family after everything she had gone through meant more to him than he ever realised.

He cleared his throat.

"I think it's time I got going, Greer will start to worry," he explained.

Both Horith and Brid grinned and then his sister was shooing him away like a fly. "Yes, hurry up, we are dying to see everyone again," she said. "The Wyvern will have us there within minutes so we will have to wait a while before we follow you back to the village."

"I won't take long, I promise," said Clump with a rueful chuckle, "because when you arrive home I will have the whole of my family safely inside the fold again."

He stepped forward and gave Keesha a light kiss on the top of her head before rubbing little Clump's hair affectionately. The baby Windigo immediately stopped crying.

"It looks as though you have the magic touch," said Brid, clearly unable to resist teasing him.

"Me?" Clump responded with a grin. "No, not a chance, but you just wait until Isis and Felan get their hands on these two, you'll not get them back for at least a week!"

Chapter 37

Considering they were once seen as traitors, the news that Horith and Brid were still alive sent everything topsy-turvy. As Clump expected, once he explained they were due to return of their own free will, the Elders welcomed them with open arms. Of course it helped that Serpen was dead and Brid's betrothal to the heir of the Polak tribe had been vanquished, but Clump felt it was more likely because they brought with them the start of a new generation.

Things had certainly changed for the better and it appeared to those who looked beneath the surface that the Elders had chosen to have rather short memories. The rest of the village accepted Horith and Brid's return with little fuss. Life was a lot simpler these days and ever since they had stopped eating flesh they were all much friendlier to one another. Isis and Felan were soon up to speed with what had happened to them over the past months and Isis was ecstatic to learn she was to have Brid and her new family all to herself.

That first evening, Horith and Brid sat quietly and talked about their ordeal since leaving the village. Isis offered them oatcakes and strips of beef and neither appeared perturbed when she explained how the whole village no longer ate immortal flesh.

However, poor Clump could still only eat pureed vegetables and watery soup. His windpipe had taken quite a beating during the ritual and was taking its time to heal. His voice was still gruff and his stomach even now was rather delicate. He was secretly dreading the moment when he would desire something a little more substantial. He understood that he needed to keep his strength up, but inside he was fearful, frightened by the mere thought that very soon he would feel the urge to eat the flesh of the living. He wasn't sure, but he thought his senses were starting to change. He was grateful that this feeling hadn't been immediate and that the impulse had not been sudden, like death.

Inside he was filled with turmoil, worrying when the fateful day would arrive so he decided to focus his mind on his joining to Greer instead. This was his one salvation, a dream come true, and he vowed that nothing would spoil his one moment of happiness. Clump stayed in Lyra's cave with Horith until the ceremony. Since the treaty was made with the elves, the pack no longer hunted in the Canyon at night, they stayed close to their caves and Clump found he was unable to sleep the night before his joining.

When dawn broke he rose from his makeshift bed and watched a golden sunrise. He would have never believed he could ever find someone to love him and now the blessed day had arrived, he was convinced Greer would change her mind.

Horith did his best to reassure him.

"Of course she'll be there," he said. "I've seen for myself how she only has eyes for you."

Clump looked back at him with a doleful expression.

"Do you really think so?" he asked. "I mean, she's so kind and generous so why would she want to live the rest of her life with the likes of me?"

Horith let out a chuckle. "I think you're suffering with a serious case of pre-joining nerves," he said. "Stop worrying. Now get dressed and I promise you she will be there."

Shortly before midday, Clump made his way to the Emerald Cave.

This would be the place where they would have their official linking of hands. Many guests attended, some were from other tribes but Clump was ecstatic when he spotted Princess Crystal and the Queen of Nine Winters in the crowd.

He caught Crystal's eye and she gave him a somewhat timid wave. She had been the first person he had ever cared about who was not one of his own kind. In return, she had not only shown him affection but also compassion. It had almost killed him to leave her behind in the Stannary Mines but yet he'd been given no choice. Her reaction to him leaving had been heartbreaking to see and a part of him would always love her. He smiled at the Queen. He was grateful she had come to share his special day and this was also history in the making because never before had immortals been invited to such a gathering.

At the mouth of the cave, Zebulon was waiting, dressed in his ceremonial robes. Clump met him with a bow and they waited patiently for Greer to arrive whilst the rest of their honoured guests stood behind him.

Clump heard a gasp, a delighted noise from the crowd and he half turned to see Greer heading towards him. He unconsciously sucked in his breath because he had never seen a female Windigo look so ravishing or so beautiful. Greer's tunic was a pale cream with pearls around the neck and silver gemstones sewn around the sleeves. Wild flowers were woven through her hair and Clump thought his heart would burst when he saw her smile shyly at him. She looked incredible, a vision of beauty standing right before him and he felt his emotions rise. She came to his side and he held out his hand. She entwined her fingers in his and at that moment he knew he would love her forever.

Zebulon gestured for them both to step forward. They moved in unison and then the Elder reached out and took their hands in his.

"Today we are here to witness the joining of Clump and Greer. They have chosen one another and against the odds have acquired the blessing of the Gods." A sudden rumble of acknowledgement rippled throughout the crowd; this was indeed a great honour.

Clump looked steadily at his true love, wishing to tell the whole world how he felt about her. Inside he was dancing on air. A fast, pulsing thrill pumped throughout his body. He could sense her love as she gazed into his eyes and a sudden glinting smile, he knew, was for no one else but him. How he ached to be alone with her at that very moment. He didn't want to waste a precious second of their time together and now Greer was his to love and cherish he felt invincible.

He continued to stare at her and he could see her eyes widen with devotion.

Zebulon broke the spell.

"And now they have become one," he said, and Clump smiled broadly, laying a hand on her shoulder and brushing a kiss along her brow which was the custom. He rubbed his hands up and down the side of her body. He was so happy he shuddered, not quite able to bite back the moan of pleasure which escaped from his lips. An explosion of noise broke out behind him as Crystal, the Queen and her entourage clapped their hands and all the Windigos who were present, roared with delight.

"Let the festivities begin," Zebulon shouted, and everyone drifted towards the banqueting table which had been set up close to the cave. Greer hurried over to where both Isis and Felan were waiting. Clump held back, to watch his mother welcome his new love into the family. He was just about to join them when he caught a flash of movement from within the cave. He took a step forward, peered inside, and a gnarled finger came out of the darkness and beckoned for him to come closer.

Clump swallowed. It was the Protector.

He looked to see if anyone was watching and then he quickly darted inside.

"Protector, have you come to wish me well?" he asked, nervously. Without saying a word, the Protector pulled him closer to the shadows. Clump couldn't see his face. As usual the servant of the Gods was wearing a hooded robe.

"What's the matter?" he gasped, "is something wrong?"

"The potion didn't work," the Protector hissed close to his ear.

Clump pulled away and out of his grasp.

"What are you talking about?" he asked, confused.

"I mean that the Gods have told me that the potion I made didn't give them the power they desired."

"So what does that mean?" asked Clump, pressing his fingers to his temples.

The Protector chuckled. Clump thought it sounded like he was choking.

"It means that it was not the black pearl that made you intolerant to flesh after all. You were simply born that way."

"I ... I ... don't understand!" Clump cried. "Surely that's impossible?"

The Protector's shoulders relaxed.

"Obviously not. The Gods are as baffled as you are, however, we are not the first creatures to adapt to our ever-changing environment and we won't be the last. When Greer bears your cubs, they will have hereditary knowledge and will be born just like you."

"Are the Gods willing to allow this to happen?" asked Clump, astounded.

"Yes, they can see what your offspring will bring to the village. They hope you will have many litters enabling the future of the Windigos to be preserved, enabling a life that will be much richer for generations to come."

Clump was overjoyed by the revelation, but then he heard Greer calling for him and her voice sounded anxious.

"I must go," said Clump, taking a step back into the light.

"Indeed you must," said the Protector. "Enjoy your new life and I will see you when you are ready to become our chief."

Clump nodded and stepped away, just as Greer ran into the cave. Her eyes were only on Clump as she entered and she didn't see the Protector skulking in the shadows.

"What are you doing in here? Everyone's waiting!" she scolded, threading her arm through his to tug him towards the light.

Clump sought out her hand and squeezed it tight. "I just needed a moment to compose myself," he said, trying to sound convincing.

Greer stopped in her tracks to lift her face towards him, resting her forehead on his cheek. Clump cupped her face and then tilted her chin so they were looking into one another's eyes. There was no denying he was totally smitten with her and he decided, right then, that he wouldn't spoil the moment and burden her with the Protector's revelation. Instead, he gazed at her and thought only of the many sons and daughters they would one day share together, and his heart almost burst with joy. He leaned forward until their lips met and he gently nuzzled her mouth. He heard a soft purr rise from deep within her throat and he found it hard to pull away. When he did, he saw her smile, and he reached out and stroked her face. With a spring in his step he guided her towards their guests and to a life which would be filled forever with peace and harmony.

Biography of Lynette Creswell

Lynette was born in London, but moved to Burnley, Lancashire when she was a small child. From the tender age of five she was raised by her grandmother and given books to help keep her quiet. Lynette found she had a passion for reading and subsequently started writing once she began school.

Years later, Lynette's husband was so impressed with her ability to capture children's imaginations with her stories that he encouraged her love of writing by buying her a laptop in the hope she would write something more substantial. So, with a little push in the right direction, Lynette decided to write a fantasy trilogy and the subject would be something that all children love to read about (and most adults too) – ***magic!***

Her inspiration came from childhood books written by Enid Blyton *The Enchanted Wood* and *The Faraway Tree* were her first real taste of fantasy and the reason why she writes today.

Her first novel, *Sinners of Magic,* was published in 2012 and is now receiving attention from both London and American film producers. *Betrayers of Magic* became the second book of the series followed by *Defenders of Magic*.

Lynette has since had one of her short stories published in America hitting No 4 in the US bestsellers charts. *The Witching Hour* is only available via Amazon Kindle.

Lynette now lives in North Lincolnshire with her husband and King Charles spaniel, Ruby. All of her grandchildren are the apple of her eye.

You can contact Lynette via her website and blog:
www.Lynetteecreswell.wordpress.com

Follow her on Twitter: @Creswelllyn

Lightning Source UK Ltd.
Milton Keynes UK
UKOW04f1136031215

263957UK00001B/4/P